Maureen Child writes for the Mills & Boon Desire line and can't imagine a better job. A seven-time finalist for the prestigious Romance Writers of America RITA® Award, Maureen is the author of more than one hundred romance novels. Her books regularly appear on bestseller lists and have won several awards, including a Prism Award, a National Readers' Choice Award, a Colorado Romance Writers Award of Excellence and a Golden Quill Award. She is a native Californian but has recently moved to the mountains of Utah.

Karen Booth is .... the South, raised on .... of *Forever* by Judy B......................reak from the art of romance, she ....usic with her college-aged kids or sweet-ta......ng her husband into making her a cocktail. Learn more about Karen at karenbooth.net

THE PRICE OF PASSION

MAUREEN CHILD

FORBIDDEN LUST

KAREN BOOTH

MILLS & BOON

First Published in Great Britain 2020
by Mills & Boon, an imprint of HarperCollinsPublishers,
1 London Bridge Street, London, SE1 9GF

The Price of Passion © 2020 Harlequin Books S.A.
Forbidden Lust © 2020 Harlequin Books S.A.

Special thanks and acknowledgement are given to Maureen Child for her contribution to the *Texas Cattleman's Club: Rags to Riches* series.

Special thanks and acknowledgement are given to Karen Booth for her contribution to the *Dynasties: Seven Sins* series.

ISBN: 978-0-263-27925-2

0620

MIX
Paper from
responsible sources
FSC™ C007454

This book is produced from independently certified FSC™ paper to ensure responsible forest management.

For more information visit: www.harpercollins.co.uk/green

Printed and bound in Spain
by CPI, Barcelona

THE PRICE OF PASSION

MAUREEN CHILD

For my mom, Sallye Carberry,
because she introduced me to the
magical world of reading...which eventually
led me here! Thanks, Mom.

One

Nothing much had changed in Royal, Texas.

And Camden Guthrie was glad to see it. Sure, the town was a little bigger than he remembered and there were some new shops, but it was still the place where he'd grown up. Cam was only just beginning to realize how much he'd missed it. He'd been in self-imposed exile in Southern California for fifteen years, and now every breath of warm Texas air felt like a homecoming.

Damned if he'd ever leave again.

"Cam?"

He turned and smiled at the sheriff. Nathan Battles was older, so they hadn't hung out much as kids, but no one was a stranger in a small town.

"Good to see you, Nate." Cam held out a hand and Nate took it in a firm shake.

"I heard you bought the old Circle K ranch."

"Of course you did." Cam shook his head. Gossip was the lifeblood of small towns, and Royal was no different. And, given that Nate's wife Amanda owned and ran the Royal Diner—basically ground zero for information exchanges—she probably kept him up-to-date on whatever she heard.

Nate grinned. "You want secrets? Don't use Natalie Barnes as your real estate agent. She's been telling everyone who will listen that you bought the ranch where you and your folks used to work."

Cam nodded at the reminder. The Circle K had been a huge part of his life. His parents had both worked as horse trainers for the owner, and Cam, as a kid, had done whatever needed doing—from feeding the animals to mucking out stalls and carpentry work.

He had a lot of good memories of that place—along with some he'd worked hard to forget. Like the loss of his parents in a stable fire when he was seventeen. Bad wiring had started it, and his mother and father had been so determined to free the stalled horses that they'd been trapped inside when the roof finally collapsed.

But the ranch had remained his home. He'd continued to live and work there while he finished school. Two years ago, when he'd decided to come back to Royal, Cam had made an offer on the property, and when it was accepted he'd figured it was fate. Sort of coming full circle.

Now that he was back, he had a lot of ideas for improvements on the ranch and plenty of plans for its future. *His* future. A future he'd once believed would include Beth Wingate.

Damn. Even thinking her name had his blood racing. Fifteen years since he'd seen her. Fifteen years since he'd touched her. Yet, Beth was there. Always. In his mind. In a dark, locked-up corner of his heart.

"Yeah," he finally said in response to Nate. "It's good to be back."

He wondered, though, if he'd feel the same once he'd seen Beth again.

Just thinking about her now could bring up so many mixed emotions. He buried them all because how the hell could he sort through them? He hadn't come back to Royal for her. He'd come because this was his place. His home. Texas was in his blood, and Royal was his heartbeat. Over the years he'd silenced the urge to come home. He and his late wife, Julie, had built a life and a fortune in California, but always there had been the ache for Texas. Now he was back, and nothing would make him leave.

Not even the one woman who still haunted him.

Nate pulled the brim of his gray hat down lower over his eyes. "I hear you're stocking some Longhorns on your ranch, along with the Black Angus."

Cam laughed. "You hear plenty."

"I do." The sheriff gave him a shameless grin. "And I'm glad if it's true. The Longhorn is pure Texas. It's good you're doing what you can to help the breed survive."

He had bigger plans than just the Longhorns, but Cam wasn't ready to let anyone else in on what he had in mind. Still, the thought of what was in the works made him smile.

"Well, it is true. I've got a small herd of a few hundred arriving end of the week." Cam was finally living the dream he'd had since he was a kid. His own ranch.

Run his way. "We'll be keeping them separate from the Angus. Don't want any crossbreeding."

Nate laughed. "Better you than me. Riding herd on the town is enough excitement for me."

Cam nodded and glanced around Main Street again. It was a quiet town and, he thought, a little bigger than he remembered it. The closest large city was Dallas, but here in Royal was everything anyone could need. County buildings crouched around a park with tidy flower beds, live oaks and manicured grass. Along the street were restaurants, a bank and dozens of shops— everything from hardware to hair salons.

The sidewalks were bustling but not crowded, and that was a relief. In Southern California, you practically had to lock yourself in a closet if you wanted some space for yourself.

Now, in the first week of June, summer was just a promise and the humidity hadn't quite reached air-conditioning-or-die level yet.

"I wanted to tell you," Nate was saying, "I was real sorry to hear about Julie."

Pain, sharp and swift, stabbed at Cam, stole his breath and then slowly slipped away again. He'd come to grips with the death of his wife two years ago. It was losing Julie that had finally convinced him to come back to Royal. But when he was reminded of it out of the blue, it could still hit him hard.

"Thanks, Nate. I appreciate it." Polite but cool, letting his old friend know without saying that Cam didn't want to talk about it.

Nate got the message. Nodding, he said, "Well, I'm guessing you've got a lot to do here in town. I'll let you get to it."

"Yeah, I'm headed to the bank." Had to open a new account and arrange for his money to be wired here from LA.

"I'm headed back to the office, but let's get together soon. Tell some lies."

Cam grinned. Relieved to be back on solid ground, he said, "Sounds good."

He watched the sheriff walk away and envied him for a moment. Nathan Battles had always known his place. He had found it years ago, and now he walked through Royal, a man at peace with himself and the life he'd carved out.

Cam was back in Royal to do the same.

It took him nearly a half hour to walk to the bank because he was stopped every few feet by old friends. Back in California, he was a successful businessman. A self-made millionaire. But in Royal, Texas, he was a home-grown success story. People being people, they were all curious about what he'd been doing the last fifteen years. And these people, being Texans, would want their questions answered.

Funny, because back in the day, he'd been the half–Native American son of ranch workers, and his only claim to fame was starring on the Royal High School baseball team. Back then, he'd had major-league dreams that fueled his imagination. Cam had gotten scholarship offers based on his pitching abilities, but he hadn't taken any of them because his world had been abruptly upended after graduation.

Yet here he was, returning to his hometown a millionaire many times over and the owner of the very ranch where his late parents had worked. Life could be strange—even when it was satisfying.

He walked into the bank and paused, taking it in. A big building with the stamp of Texas all over it, there were wide red tiles on the floor, paintings of Texas on the walls and dark wooden beams on the ceiling. The counters were of gleaming dark wood to match those beams, and the tellers worked behind a wall of thick plexiglass. There were several manned desks opposite the tellers and a staircase leading to the second floor in the corner. Cam's gaze swept the desks, looking for the bank manager. But when he spotted him, it wasn't the man Cam focused on, but the woman sitting opposite him.

Beth Wingate.

Every ounce of breath rushed from his lungs, and his vision narrowed until she was all he could see. It was as if the world had disappeared, leaving her in a bright spotlight.

Cam couldn't have looked away if it had meant his life. Because at one time she had *been* his life. And, apparently, his body remembered. He was hard as stone, his breath laboring, his heart racing. His palms itched to touch her again, and even as he silently admitted that simple fact, guilt rushed into his mind to tear him a new one.

Hell, his wife had only been dead two years, and here he was lusting after the woman who had ripped out his heart and pushed him into Julie's arms.

As if she could *feel* him looking at her, Beth slowly turned her head and fixed her gaze on his.

Her eyes were filled with memory as his own must have been. Once upon a time, he'd thought the world began and ended in those green eyes. Now he felt the power of her gaze slamming into his chest like a punch to the solar plexus. Why did she still have to be so damn beautiful? Her hair fell long and straight to the middle of her back, still blond but with highlights now that made it shimmer like gold when she shook her head. She was tall and thin, but not so skinny she didn't have curves that he remembered all too well. As he watched, she stood up and held herself like a damn queen.

He should be irritated by that, because of course she did. She was a Wingate, and in Royal they were at the top of the ladder. Hell, Beth's mother, Ava, had been the interior designer of the Texas Cattleman's Club, and there was no club that better described Royal. The TCC was renowned for its membership. Every wealthy, influential person in this corner of Texas was a member, and those who weren't were trying to get in. As Camden would be.

Beth stood there staring at him, and he let his gaze drag up and down her body lazily. She wore a summer dress, sleeveless, in a dusty blue with pale yellow stripes. Her tanned legs were bare, and she wore three-inch heeled sandals on her narrow feet.

She looked…too damn good. And he probably looked like just what he was—a man struck dumb by lust and need. Why the hell had he run into her in a public place? Knowing Royal, everyone in the bank was watching this meeting. Waiting to see if there would be a fight, or fireworks of a different kind.

There would be neither, Cam vowed. Damned if he'd let Beth see that she could still turn him inside out.

She sauntered toward him and he admired that slow, perfect walk. She'd always had a way of moving that made a man think of silk sheets and moonlight.

"Hello, Cam," she said, and that deep, throaty voice of hers fell over him like warm water.

"Beth." He kept his gaze on hers and saw the flash of…*something* there.

"I heard you were moving back."

"Hard to keep secrets in Royal," he said. Just as it was hard to read her expression. Her eyes were shimmering—but with what? Memory? Desire? Irritation? Hell, if he knew.

"Were you trying to keep it a secret?"

"No," he replied. "Why would I?"

"No reason, but for the fact you've been back a week and this is the first time you've been in town."

His mouth quirked. "Keeping tabs on me?"

"Hardly." She shook her head, sending that golden hair of hers into a brief, soft swing. Then she lifted one bare shoulder in a shrug that had the bodice of her dress strain against her perfect breasts. "You said it yourself. Hard to keep a secret here. So have you been hiding out at the ranch?"

"Hiding from what?"

She tipped her head to one side and studied him. "Interesting question."

He knew damn well she thought he'd been avoiding her. And, honestly, he wasn't so sure she was wrong. But the point was that she should be on the defensive here, Cam reminded himself. Yet somehow, she'd turned things around until he felt as if he should be explaining himself to her. Well, the hell with that.

"Yeah, I don't hide. Never did. I don't care what other people have to say," he pointed out. "Unlike some."

Anger zipped across her eyes, and he silently con-

gratulated himself on scoring a point. Weirdly, he realized that not only had his attraction to her remained
sure and strong, but a streak of bitterness filled him,
as well. Fifteen years hadn't been enough to take the
sting out of her betrayal.

"That was a long time ago," she said quietly, obviously aware of their rapt audience.

"Doesn't feel so long." Hell, she still wore the
same scent. Flowers and mist and the scent of a rain-
drenched day that reached out to grab him by the throat
and hold on. He really hated that.

Her gaze narrowed. "It does to me."

For a heartbeat or two, their gazes locked and the
tension arcing between them was almost a living
thing. Cam felt it. He knew she did, too, though she'd
never admit it. Memories rushed into his mind. Nights
wrapped together in the back of his truck. Plans for a
future that would never happen. And, finally, the last
conversation they'd had all those years ago.

That memory dropped ice chips into his heart that
were almost enough to quench the blistering heat he
felt at simply being near her.

Beth broke first. She tore her gaze from his, glanced
at a slim gold watch on her left wrist, and then looked
at him again. This time her green eyes were blank, re-
flecting nothing of what she was feeling. Cam wondered idly when she'd learned to do that.

"I'm sorry," she said. "I have an appointment. But
of course, welcome home, Cam."

Her welcome was as cool as her tone. He turned to
watch her go, his gaze dropping to the curve of her butt
and the nearly hypnotic way it swayed with every step.

His body stirred, and silently Cam cursed the fact that Beth Wingate could still turn him into a drooling fool.

But he was older now. Wiser, too, by a long shot. There was no way in hell he would allow Beth to tear his future apart as she had his past.

Beth couldn't stop shaking.

For the last week, since she'd heard he was back in Royal, she'd been preparing herself to see Cam Guthrie again. And all of that preparation had gone right out the window the minute his eyes had met hers. Sitting there at the bank president's desk, she would have sworn she'd felt the temperature in the room rise a few degrees, just from Cam's presence. She'd felt his gaze on her as strongly as she would have a touch, and the instant she'd seen him her heartbeat had jumped into a wild gallop.

His dark brown eyes were filled with shadows. His black hair was cut shorter than she remembered, and he wore a well-tailored suit as easily as he had worn jeans and scuffed boots back when he was the center of her world.

Beth took a deep breath and tried to steady herself. It should have been easy. More than a decade since she'd laid eyes on Cam should have meant that seeing him would be like running into an old friend.

But she'd been fooling herself. Cam hadn't been her friend. He'd been *everything*. Until that last night. When she'd discovered that what a man said and what he did were sometimes two different things.

Now he was home and she'd be dealing with him all the time. How was this fair? Why hadn't he stayed in California? Then she thought that maybe his wife's death had been enough to drive him from the state that was no doubt filled with memories of the two of them together. Had he missed Julie so much? Had he loved her more than he'd ever loved Beth? Because he'd come back to Texas, where he had to face *her* every day and that apparently didn't bother him.

God, she had a headache. Rubbing at the spot between her eyes, Beth reminded herself that nothing had to change because he was here in Royal. There was nothing between them but for the bittersweet memories they shared of being too young and reckless to realize that love wasn't always enough.

"Fifteen years, Beth. Neither of you are the same people you used to be." Wise words. Now all she had to do was listen to her own good advice.

The early summer sun blasted down on her until she felt as though she was about to combust. Internally, fires were burning while, externally, the Texas heat was only making things worse. She stopped under a bright blue-and-green awning stretched over the florist shop window and hoped the shade would help lower her body temperature.

"It would take more than that," she muttered, and shot a quick glance around to make sure no one had overheard her.

On the busy Main Street, she was alone and she wondered how everyone in town could be going on about their business as if the world hadn't just shifted. Cam was back. He was gorgeous. And treacherous. Sexy. And faithless.

Looking into his eyes had cost her every ounce of self-control she'd worked so hard to develop.

"Hi, Beth!"

She jolted, looked up and nodded at Vonnie Taylor as she pushed her twins past in a double stroller. Beth ignored a twinge of envy as she watched the woman hurry down the sidewalk and reminded herself that she had a rich, full life and she didn't need a man or children to fulfill her. It was true of course, but a part of her still yearned.

Not for Cam, though. That was over and done a long time ago. A few stray thermonuclear hormone reactions notwithstanding, she was fine on her own. Hadn't she just a month ago told Justin McCoy that she wasn't interested in a relationship? Not that the man listened at all. They'd been dating for months and Justin was pushing for more of a commitment. Which was exactly why she'd told him they should take a break from each other.

Having zero men in her life had to be less complicated than what she was dealing with now. With that thought firmly in mind, she started walking again and didn't stop until she came to the Royal Diner. She stepped inside and a wave of air-conditioned air slid across her skin. Grateful, she sighed a little, looked around the room and spotted her friend and assistant, Gracie Diaz. Thankful to get her life back to normal, Beth smiled and headed toward the booth in the back.

The Royal Diner hadn't changed in decades. Well, that wasn't quite true. There had been updates of course, but when the work was done, the color scheme and feel of the place remained the same. Black-and-white checkerboard-tiled floor, red faux-leather booths and even a working juke box on one wall.

Sooner or later, everyone in Royal stopped in at the diner, and so naturally it was the gossip hub. Anything you wanted to know, you could discover here. She couldn't help wondering how long it would be before she and Cam were the latest hot topic of conversation.

She waved to Amanda Battles, who owned the diner along with her sister, Pam.

When Beth was halfway to her booth, Pam called out, "Hi, Beth! The usual?"

"Yes, thanks. You're a lifesaver." She slid into the seat opposite Gracie and set her cream-colored bag beside her on the bench seat.

"Rough morning?" Gracie quipped and smiled.

"You have no idea." A wry smile curved her mouth briefly. She really needed this time with a friend. To cool down. To regain some sort of stability after that quick, devastating encounter with Cam.

Looking across the table at Gracie, Beth saw warm brown eyes, long, straight dark hair that fell, as Beth's did, straight down her back. She wore a pale yellow sleeveless summer blouse and khaki slacks with a pair of sandals that Beth had coveted since the first time she had seen them.

Gracie had grown up on the Wingate ranch, since her parents had worked for Beth's parents. As kids, they'd played and run wild on the ranch. In school, they hadn't really hung out because Beth was three years older than Gracie. But at the ranch, they'd been close and supported each other through the inevitable crushes on boys. And when Gracie had graduated from college, Beth had hired her as an administrative assistant. Best move she'd ever made, since Gracie was as organized as Beth, and together they kept the many different charities Beth managed straight and growing.

Gracie studied her for a long minute, then said, "Okay, something is really going on. Tell me."

Beth waited as Pam served her the usual. A club sandwich and a tall glass of unsweetened black ice tea. "Thanks, Pam."

"You bet." She turned to Gracie. "Can I get you another soda?"

"No, thanks. I'm good." To prove it, she took a sip, then idly picked up one of the french fries that accompanied her burger.

"Okay then," Pam said. She looked at both women and added, "Need anything, just ask."

There was comfort, Beth thought, in the ordinary. In the routine of life in Royal. Of knowing the people in town and realizing that they knew and cared for her, too. So she'd just cling to that mental comfort while she thought about the *discomfort* of seeing Cam.

She took a sip of tea and blurted, "I just ran into Camden at the bank."

Gracie, being the excellent friend she was, didn't need more. "Oh, my God! That had to be awful. Everyone watching…"

"Exactly." That had actually been the hardest part of the whole thing. Beth had felt the curious gazes locked on the pair of them, as if everyone at the bank had been waiting for a big scene. Heck, she'd half expected one herself. The last time she and Cam had *talked*, it hadn't gone well.

"How's he look?" Gracie asked.

"Delicious," Beth muttered.

"Uh-oh."

Beth's gaze shot to her friend's. "Oh, no. No worries there. He's gorgeous and tall and sexy and—" She stopped and took a breath. If she really wanted her hormones to die down, she had to stop thinking about just how good Cam had looked. "It doesn't matter. I made my choice fifteen years ago."

"Uh-huh."

It was Gracie's sarcastic tone more than her words that caught Beth's attention. "I'm sorry? Whose side are you on again?"

"Yours, but," her friend added, "I know bull when I hear it, too."

Like a balloon meeting a sharp pin, Beth simply deflated. Shoulders slumped, she took another sip of her tea and admitted, "Fine. I'm still susceptible to the Guthrie magic."

"There you go. The first step is admitting you have a problem."

Beth laughed shortly. "Is there a Getting Over Cam Guthrie meeting I could attend?"

"You're there already," Gracie said. "I'm here to help you be strong. To avoid all thoughts of sexy Cam and remember just how badly it all went back in the day."

"Not like I could forget it," Beth mumbled, and picked up a triangle of her sandwich. Taking a bite she didn't really want, she methodically chewed, and as she did, she remembered the last time she'd seen Cam. Back when he was *all* she could see. Back when she believed he loved her. Back before he left town with Julie Wheeler, never to be seen again.

Her heart thudded in her chest, and what felt like an ice-cold stone dropped into the pit of her stomach.

"There you go." Gracie gave her a smile. "Cam was the past, and now you have Justin."

Oh, she didn't want to get into Justin McCoy right

now. That was over, too, though he hadn't accepted the fact yet.

Deliberately she took another bite of her sandwich, chewed and said, "Enough about my pitiful love life. Did you track down the caterer for the Fire Department Open House?"

"I did." Accepting the change of subject, Gracie dug into her black oversize leather bag and pulled out a manila folder. "Turns out she's been in Galveston for a family thing."

"That's nice," Beth murmured. "But she's on track and we're covered for the event this Saturday?"

"Oh, absolutely. She's emailed me the finished menu for your final approval. I've got it right here." Gracie handed over a single sheet of paper, and while Beth looked it over, she continued. "She says they'll be there by ten a.m. to start the setup."

"Okay, that should work." She handed back the paper. "The menu looks great. Finger food, easy to carry around so people can talk and walk or sit down if they want to."

"I'll let her know."

Beth nodded. "The open house at the fire station starts at one, and I want to hold the raffle by three. Give us time to get as many people there as possible."

"It's a brilliant idea, Beth." Gracie shook her head in admiration. "Getting Connolly motors to donate a new truck for the raffle? A nice write-off for them, and raffling it off to raise money for the firehouse is really going well."

Beth thought about that for a minute and acknowledged that her assistant was right. By the time the raffle was done, the Royal Fire Department would have enough money to renovate the old station and buy new equipment without dinging the town for it.

With the catering, the live country music band she'd hired and the guided tours of the firehouse, Beth knew that most of the town would turn out for the event. All of them would be hoping to win that shiny red truck.

"Well, now that we've got that one figured out, let's talk about the food drive for the local shelter."

"Great." Gracie dipped her head, and her long, dark brown hair fell across her shoulders. "We've put up signs at the schools, asking kids to bring in canned or boxed food. Granted, it's the end of the school year, so that won't last long. Still, it's going great, so far. Plus, the grocery store is pitching in, running a special on canned foods. They've set up donation boxes at both entrances, trying to make it easy for people to pitch in."

"Perfect. It's only June," Beth said, opening up her phone and checking through the lists on her notepad. "I want to make sure everyone's fully stocked long before winter."

"You bet. I've got Tucker Davis hauling the donations to our storage units." She glanced up. "The drive ends next Friday, and Tucker said he and his brothers can deliver all of it to the shelter, so we don't have to hire a separate company."

"Awesome." She made a quick note, reminding herself to call Tucker herself and thank him for his help.

While Gracie went through the inventory, Beth's mind wandered. Naturally, it took a sharp turn back to Cam Guthrie. He'd been such a huge part of her life, and then he was gone.

He'd unexpectedly married Julie Wheeler, a girl

from their class, and the "happy" couple had left Royal—all within a month of Beth refusing to marry him.

He'd turned to Julie so heartbreakingly fast it had forced Beth to admit that Cam had never really loved her. It had all been a lie, and she was lucky that she'd had the sense to end it before she'd married the man.

Lucky, she reminded herself.

She was alone.

And lucky.

Two

Beth was beginning to feel depressed and wasn't going to put up with it. "You know what, Gracie?" she said suddenly, "Let's eat our lunch and let the rest go for today."

Surprise flashed in the other woman's eyes. "What about the masquerade charity ball at the TCC?"

Beth frowned a little and nibbled at a french fry. That was a big one. They'd be raising money for the children's wing of the local hospital. So that ball had to come off perfectly. She smiled to herself. There was nothing to worry about. It was months away and they were both on top of the situation.

"It'll be perfect, Gracie, because you and I will make sure of it. But we don't have to do it today. The ball's not until October, so we've got a little wiggle room. Enough, at least, for us to enjoy the rest of the day anyway."

"You convinced me," Gracie said, smiling. She picked up her hamburger and took a bite.

"That was easy." Beth laughed, too, and bit into her own sandwich. When she'd swallowed, she asked, "So, did you get your Powerball ticket?"

Gracie grinned. "You bet. My mom always said if you don't play, you can't win. So I buy my ticket once a month, just like she always did—until she decided to save her money instead." Laughing a little, she added, "If I win, I'm going to buy Mom a big house in Florida near her sister, and then I'm going to start up that event planning business I've always wanted."

Beth sipped at her tea. "You know, I'm still willing to back you in that. If you won't take money as a gift, we could call it a loan. Just enough to get you started."

Gracie shook her head firmly. "Nope. Thank you though, Beth. I appreciate it. But I'm saving my money, and when I have enough, I'll apply for a small business loan. I need to do it on my own. But once I'm open I may be ready for investors…" She grinned at that. "And maybe I'll win the lottery!"

"God, you're stubborn." Beth laughed and picked up her sandwich again.

"That's why we get along so well," Gracie told her. "We have so much in common."

Wryly she said, "Good point."

For the next half hour, Beth didn't think about Cam and what him being back in town might cost her.

Cam was still reeling from bumping into Beth at the bank. Hell, it had been ages since he'd seen her. He for damn sure hadn't expected his body's instant response to her, and there was no denying it, either. One look into her eyes, and he was back in the past, on hot summer nights, in the bed of his truck, lying on a blanket, tangled up with a naked Beth.

For years, he'd pushed those memories into a deep, dark hole in his mind. He had been married to Julie after all, and she was the one who had deserved his loyalty. They'd had a good marriage, he told himself. Together, they'd built a house-flipping business that had made them more money than either of them had dreamed possible. They'd been happy. Until Julie got sick. Then it had been doctors and hospitals and a fast slide to the end. In a matter of months, Cam had lost her and any interest he might have had to keep their business going.

But with her gone, there was nothing to hold him in California, and the pull of his roots was too strong to fight.

Now he was back and he'd bought the ranch he and his parents had once worked on. The Circle K… "Have to change that," he muttered, stepping out of his truck to stand and take a good look around.

The sun was hotter now, beating down on him until he thought that maybe Texas was planning on giving him a baptism of fire as a welcome home. The air was still, not a hint of wind to rustle the live oaks surrounding the ranch house.

He turned to look at the place and felt a stir of pride. Buying this ranch was satisfying in a way Cam hadn't really expected. It was as if coming back to Royal was returning to Texas, but owning this place was coming *home*.

He'd only been back in town for a week, but this house… It was as if it had been waiting for him all these years. It needed fixing up, definitely some up-dates. The kitchen alone made him cringe and ready to grab a sledgehammer. And he had plans for expansion, too. Some of it he'd do himself, because fifteen years of being both entrepreneur and carpenter was hard to shake. But for most of what he wanted done, he'd already hired Olivia Turner and her construction company.

He leaned back against his brand-new gleaming black truck and took it all in. Two stories, the house was built of river stone, boasted a red tile roof, and its design successfully mixed Spanish and craftsman styles. There was a wide balcony around the second floor of the house and a wraparound porch on the ground floor.

The view from the front was a wide sweep of ranch-land, the corral and, off to the side, a barn that was painted the rich, dark green of young meadow grass. There were outbuildings for the ranch hands, a bunk-house and a separate house for the foreman, Henry Jordan and his family.

Cam's plans to turn this place into a sort of working dude ranch meant that he'd need Olivia's company to build a dozen cottages for guests and another stable for the extra horses he was going to have to buy. Which meant, he told himself, they'd also require more ranch hands, but he'd leave the hiring to Henry. He'd be working with them and knew practically every cowboy in Texas, so there was no point in Cam sticking his nose in. He was a big believer in delegating. Find the best person for the job and then get out of their way.

One day, Cam would think about making the house

bigger because he wanted a family, eventually. He and Julie had tried, but things hadn't worked out.

When his cell phone rang, Cam reached for it gratefully. He was willing to thank whoever it was taking him out of his own head for a while. He glanced at the screen, smiled and answered.

"Hi, Darren."

"Hey, do you miss us yet?"

Cam laughed a little. Darren Casey was his partner in a home improvement line of products they'd started up four years ago. Darren had the manufacturing experience and Cam had his name and the fame he'd built as a house flipper.

He hadn't been looking to be famous, just to make a good living. But, as word had spread about Cam and Julie's gift for rehabbing houses, they'd earned sponsors, clients and, finally, their own show for two years on a home and garden network. Then Julie had gotten sick and…

Shrugging out of his suit jacket, he loosened his tie, undid the collar button on his shirt and wished desperately for the gray Stetson he'd left in the house that morning. He undid the cuffs on his shirt and rolled the sleeves up to his elbows.

"That depends," he answered, only half joking, "what's the weather in Huntington Beach like?"

Darren laughed. "Same as every year at this time. About sixty-five and cloudy."

Right now, Cam thought with a glance at the cloudless, brassy sky, the June Gloom of Southern California sounded great.

"Are you frying in Texas already?"

Damned if he'd admit to that with it only being

June, so Cam changed the subject. "You call to talk about the weather?"

"Not really. We got an offer to expand our line of tools into the biggest home improvement hardware outlet in the country."

"Yeah?" He grinned and leaned back against the truck. They were already in a nationwide department store, but this offer would seriously put their tools into the hands of do-it-yourselfers across the country.

"Tell me the details." While the other man talked, Cam let his gaze wander across the house, the land and the future he planned to build there.

Beth used to love this house, he remembered. They had talked about buying it one day, raising a family here. But that was when they were kids and the future looked big and bright and the only problem he had was keeping his hands off her whenever they were together.

Back then, Cam had had no money but lots of dreams. Now he had enough money for ten men, but no dreams.

He'd come home to change that.

So much for taking the day off.

Beth hadn't been able to stand it. If she was going to be seeing Cam on a regular basis, then she wanted to lay down some ground rules. She'd practically run from him at the bank and that really bothered her. Why should *she* run? He should have turned around the moment he'd seen her. But, no. Cam Guthrie did what he wanted, when he wanted. Always had.

Well, she promised herself, until now.

Which was why when they'd finished lunch, she'd left Gracie in town and steered her car toward Cam's new ranch. If her stomach was dipping and rolling at the prospect of being near him again, she ignored it. Eventually she'd get used to having him in town, right? All she had to do was get past the first rush of whatever was driving her crazy.

The road stretched out in front of her, and Beth realized she could have driven to him in her sleep. She knew every dip, every curve and every damn oak lining the road. Just as she'd once known Cam—or thought she had, anyway.

"Doesn't matter," she muttered. "The past is gone, this is now."

Even as she thought about it, that past roared into life in her mind. The images tumbling through her brain were so vivid, so real, she had to shake her head to dislodge them or risk driving her car right into a tree. It didn't matter that she could remember how Cam had smiled at her. How he would swoop in to kiss her and lift her off her feet as he turned her in a slow circle while their mouths fused. Didn't matter that he'd left her because of one fight.

That he'd turned to Julie overnight and married her as if Beth hadn't meant a thing to him after all. How much time had she wasted wondering if there'd been signs all along that he didn't really love her? Had he been cheating on her with Julie behind her back? She wanted to know—and she didn't. Just like she didn't want to revisit her old relationship with everyone she bumped into just because Cam was back in town.

He'd been gone a long time and she'd been here. Building her life. Her reputation. She wasn't going to risk any of it just because Camden Guthrie had decided to return to Royal.

She punched the accelerator and was suddenly glad she'd left the top down on her bright scarlet BMW. Yes, her hair would look like hell when she got to Cam's place, but hopefully, the rushing wind would push all memories out of her mind.

No such luck.

Because as she made a left into the wide drive, those memories flooded into her consciousness whether she wanted them or not.

Oaks still lined the drive, though of course they were bigger now. Flowers grew wild and tangled in the once tidy beds, and the drive itself needed to be regraveled. But the house at the end of the drive was as she remembered it, if in need of some fresh paint on the storm shutters and the front porch. Beth had always loved this place, but now she wondered if it was only because Cam had lived here.

"Doesn't matter," she assured herself.

His truck was parked out front. As she tore up the drive, Cam opened the front door and moved to the edge of the porch to watch her approach. Her heart did that frantic, racing beat again, and as much as she fought it, Beth was half-afraid this would always be her reaction to him. But that didn't mean she had to act on it.

"For God's sake, *remember* that," she muttered as she threw her car into Park and turned off the engine. Quickly Beth ran both hands through her hair, then opened the door and stepped out. The air was breathless—or maybe that was just her.

She looked up at him. "Hello, Cam."

He nodded. "Beth. Didn't expect to see you here," he said.

"Yes, well," she answered honestly, "I didn't expect me here, either."

He laughed shortly and took the six wide steps down to the drive. She'd always loved watching him walk. It was definitely a cowboy amble, a slow, deliberate stride that made a woman think that he did *everything* that slowly. And Beth was here to testify that he certainly did. At least some of the time. He could also be fast and explosive. Either way, she admitted silently, was memorable.

Cam had traded his expensive suit for a black T-shirt that clung to his broad chest and a pair of jeans that hugged his long legs and stacked on the toes of his black boots.

Danger! Danger! She heard the warning shriek in her mind, but she was here now and it was too late to walk away without looking exactly like the coward she would be if she left.

"What can I do for you, Beth?"

Oh, there was a loaded question. She could think of so many things he could do for her. And that was not what she should be thinking.

She inhaled sharply, gave herself a silent, stern warning and said, "Cam, I thought we should talk, now that you're back home."

He came closer, stopped a foot from her, leaned against his truck and folded his arms over his chest. "Talk about what?"

"Seriously?" Beth stared at him for a long second or two. "You can ask me that?"

"What's got you so worried, Beth? Me? Or *you*?"

A little of both, but he didn't need to know that.

"Please. I'm not a love-blinded teenager anymore, Cam. I'm not here to throw myself at your feet."

"Good to know." He pushed one hand through his hair. "Fine. You want to talk? Let's talk about why we have to dredge up the past."

"Oh, we don't," she assured him. "I'm here to talk about what happens now that you're back."

"Uh-huh."

"Look," she continued, since he was just staring at her. Damn it. "I just think we need to have some ground rules. So we both know where we stand."

"Is that right?" He straightened up, and one corner of his mouth quirked. "And I suppose you get to decide what the rules are?"

"You bet I do," she countered quickly. "I'm the one who's been here. You left."

All semblance of a smile left his face. "And you know why."

She blinked at him, stunned. Did he honestly believe that? "No, Camden. Actually, I don't know. And fifteen years later, I don't want to know. What I want is to not be gossiped about. Again."

"Bull." One word. Clipped. Angry. "You know what the hell happened as well as I do. As for not wanting to be gossiped about? Can't avoid that, Beth. Gossip is the blood of Royal."

"Don't tell me about the town you haven't set foot in over a decade."

"I grew up here, too. Far as I can tell, nothing much has changed."

He had a point, but that didn't mean she had to admit it. She spun around, took two steps, then turned back to face him. "This is my home, Camden."

"Mine, too," he said tightly. "I'm here and I'm not leaving. You're going to have to get used to it. I know you prefer having everything run the way you arrange it, but some things are just out of your control."

Again. Stunned. "Maybe I do have a little bit of a control issue, but let's remember who it was who had our whole *lives* planned out. That was you, Cam."

"Yeah. Worked out great, didn't it?"

Beth felt as if the top of her head might just blow off. She deliberately took several deep breaths and reminded herself how far she'd come from the girl she'd been so long ago. She didn't owe Cam anything, but she owed herself plenty.

"I didn't come out here to fight," she said calmly.

"And yet…"

She gritted her teeth. "We have to come to an arrangement." Cam was insisting he was home to stay, but she wasn't sure she believed him. He'd been in California for so long, why wouldn't he get tired of ranching life and run right back to the beaches?

Off in the distance, Beth heard the whinny of horses and a couple of the working cowboys shouting to each other. The wind was still, the sun was blasting down on them, and Camden's brown eyes were filled with shifting shadows.

"What do you have in mind?" he asked.

She lifted her chin, met his gaze and stiffly said, "We keep our distance from each other for one."

"Not a problem."

That was easy. A little insulting, but easy. She remembered a time when spending one day away from each other had been like a short visit to hell.

As if he could read her thoughts, his mouth curved

again. "What's the matter, Beth? Afraid you can't keep your hands off me?"

She gritted her teeth again. Why had she once found him so irresistible? "I think I can manage."

"We'll see, won't we?"

"Then you agree?" she asked.

"Not yet."

"What?" She hadn't expected that. They'd been apart forever. She hadn't seen him in years. He'd been *married* to someone else, for God's sake. Why would he have a problem with the two of them avoiding each other? "Why not?"

He looked down into her eyes and drawled, "Did you really think I'd just roll over and do whatever you told me to do?"

Yes, damn it. "Of course not. I'm just trying to make this easier on both of us."

"Ah." He nodded. "So thoughtful. Well, thanks for your concern, but I can take care of myself."

"So you won't agree?"

"I didn't say that."

Irritation fired up inside Beth until she wanted to tear at her hair. "What *are* you saying then?"

"Simple. You have a plan. I'll go along, but I want something in return."

Outraged, she sucked in a gulp of air. "You're really going to ask *me* for a favor? You're going to *bargain* with me? After what you did?"

He held up one hand. "Nope, not talking about the past, remember?"

Beth fought the urge to climb back into her car and drive away, leaving him in a cloud of dust. The only thing keeping her there was the knowledge that she had to get him to agree to a truce or Royal wasn't going to be big enough for both of them.

"And it's not a favor," Cam said. "Let's call it quid pro quo."

Folding her arms across her middle, Beth tipped her head to one side and met his gaze steadily. She should have known Camden wouldn't go along with her plan. He'd always been stubborn. Always wanted things his own way. Of course, so had she. Which was just one of the reasons that their relationship had been filled with fire, excitement, passion... She shook her head. "Fine. What do you want?"

Squinting, he said, "Getting hotter out here. You want to come in and get out of the sun?"

She shot a quick glance at the house, then looked back at him. Alone in the house with him? Hoo, boy. That was too much of a temptation. "No. Just tell me, Cam."

"Fine. I want to join the TCC."

That's what he wanted? Seriously? She'd thought that maybe he wanted to call a truce between them. Or donate a kidney to some deserving soul. Or hell, paint his house neon yellow. But the TCC?

Throwing up her hands, she demanded, "Well, who's stopping you?"

He scrubbed one hand across the back of his neck. "No one that I know of," he admitted. "Yet. Burt Wheeler's the treasurer though and he's not one of my biggest fans. He won't do me any good when my application comes before the membership committee."

Burt Wheeler. Camden's father-in-law, who still blamed Camden for taking Julie away from Royal. He'd never really gotten over his daughter moving away to

California, and when she died, it had nearly killed Burt. Beth could understand why there might be bad blood between Cam and the older man.

"Fine. What do you expect me to do about it?"

"Use your influence." He shoved both hands into his back pockets. "Hell, Beth, you're a Wingate. Your family has always ruled this town. You speak up for me to the president— Who is president of the TCC now?"

"James Harris." Two years older than Camden, the two men hadn't been friends growing up, but it was impossible to grow up in Royal and not know everyone.

"Good. He's a fair man." Cam nodded. "If a Wingate speaks to James for me, it'll go a long way."

He wasn't wrong, Beth acknowledged. The Wingate name carried a lot of weight in Royal and in many other places, as well. She used that name to foster the charities she supported and ran. So supporting Cam at the club would be an easy enough thing to do. But, first, she had to know what was driving him.

"Why is this so important to you? You never used to care about the Texas Cattleman's Club." Had he really changed so much? "Heck, you used to make fun of the old guard gathering at their own private 'watering hole.' Now you want in?"

"I'm opening a business and I want that support behind me when I do." He pulled his hands free, slapped one palm on the hood of his truck and instantly lifted it off again with a hiss of pain. "Damn thing's hot. Anyway, everyone knows you need the TCC stamp of approval if you want a business in Royal to succeed."

A business. She wondered why he would bother. Beth knew darn well that he was already sitting on a fortune. Why not just be a rich cowboy and enjoy what he'd already built. What did he have to prove? He'd been on *television* for heaven's sake. Huh. Was that what he was up to?

"You fixing to flip houses here like you did in California? Want to film a new handyman show? Because you won't find that many run-down neighborhoods in Royal."

"No." He shook his head. "I'm done with all of that."

She waited, but he didn't offer any more information and Beth didn't ask. She wanted to, but damned if she'd give him the satisfaction of knowing she was curious. Was he finished with the flipping business because Julie was gone now and he couldn't bear to do it without her? Had he loved his wife that much? Were memories of Julie haunting him? A twinge of pain ached in her heart. Beth pushed it aside, though she couldn't stop the questions rushing through her mind. Still, she kept quiet.

"Fine," she said finally. "I'll do what I can for you at the TCC on one condition."

His brown eyes narrowed on her. "You already laid down your condition. We don't talk. We avoid each other. Remember?"

"Yeah, but now that's not enough." She had him and they both knew it. He needed her and she wasn't going to waste this opportunity.

Wary now, he asked, "What do you want?"

"A very hefty donation to my favorite charity."

Both eyebrows rose. She'd surprised him. Well, good. Maybe that would convince him that he didn't know her as well as he thought he did. They'd both changed a lot over the years.

"We're going to build a new children's wing at Royal hospital and I'm in charge of raising the money." She smoothed the skirt of her dress. "I'm fund-raising now, and I think a donation from you will go a long way toward convincing the TCC membership that you're the kind of man they want as a member."

His eyes narrowed on her suspiciously. "Sounds like blackmail to me."

"That's an ugly word." She examined her fingernails and made a mental note to get a manicure tomorrow. "I prefer the term *extortion*."

He snorted.

"There's going to be a big charity ball at the TCC in October to raise money for the new wing," she said, catching his eye. "And if you make a *substantial* donation, I'll make sure you're a member before then."

He took a deep breath and let it out again. "Hell, you've got more of your father in you than I ever noticed."

Beth knew he meant that as an insult. Her father hadn't liked Cam at all back in the day. Cam, of course, had decided it was because his mother had been a Tigua Indian.

Trent hadn't cared about that, though Beth had never been able to convince Cam of it. Her father's resistance had come from the fact that he hadn't wanted his daughter falling in love with a simple ranch hand. She was a Wingate. That meant she had a duty to marry someone as rich as they were. To continue the dynasty.

Beth had ignored her father's plans for her because, back then, all she'd been able to see was Cam. And, she told herself, look where that had gotten her. Thankfully now, her eyes were wide open.

"If you mean that, like my father, I know how to get things done, then yes. You're absolutely right."

He snorted again.

"That's so rude."

Cam grinned. "I know. Okay, we have a deal."

"The whole thing," she qualified. "The donation, the staying away from each other…"

"And the membership in the TCC," he put in.

"Agreed." She held out one hand and his right hand enveloped hers.

Three

Instantly, Beth knew she'd made a mistake in touching him. Heat erupted, shooting up her arm to her chest, where it settled and burned with an intensity she hadn't known in fifteen years. Shaking hands with Cam had obviously been a bad idea—yet she couldn't regret feeling that burn again.

She'd been with other men since they had broken up, of course. Most recently, Justin McCoy. But it was only Cam who could make her feel like this. Only Cam who could make her blood sizzle with a look. Make her yearn with a mere touch.

When she tried to pull away, he tightened his grip, holding on to her hand as he locked his gaze with hers. Electricity seemed to dart back and forth between them, forging a link that blistered and burned.

"Stay away from each other?" he asked, and his voice was so deep it rumbled in the still air.

She swallowed hard. "Yes. Definitely, yes."

He let her go and she curled her fingers into her palm in a futile attempt to somehow keep that heat close.

"All right." He nodded. "We'll do it your way. Again."

Well, *that* had her head snapping up and her eyes firing into his. The fresh memory of heat and hunger disappeared in the rush of fury. "Again? What are you saying? Somehow this is all *my* fault?"

"You're the one who broke up with me, remember? Who the hell else's fault could it be?"

Beth laughed as she stared at him, dumbfounded. "I didn't break up with you. That's only what you heard. All I said was we had to slow down."

"Right." Cam snorted. "Slow down. Female code for 'see ya.'"

Stunned, she gaped at him. "Wow. That is so sexist."

"I'm not a sexist."

"So you just say stupid things."

"Not stupid, either," Cam retorted, his gaze drilling into hers.

"And I don't speak in code."

He laughed shortly again and she thought the sound was so damn annoying it grated on her every nerve.

"All women speak in code."

"Just because men don't understand anything that doesn't begin with their zippers…"

"Ah, sure"

"And lumping me in with my entire gender is insulting."

"Too bad. You just lumped me in with mine." Shaking his head slowly, he kept his gaze fixed on hers. "You might not like the memory, Beth, but that doesn't change a damn thing. You were the one who set this all in motion. Just you."

"No, you don't." She took a step closer and kept her gaze fixed on his so he wouldn't miss the outrage glimmering in her eyes. "If you want to rewrite history, do it with someone who didn't live it with you. I'm not the one who turned away and married the first person they saw and then left the damn state."

"If that's the way you're looking at it, you're wrong. *You* walked away, Beth," he said tightly. "I just walked *farther* than you did."

Her head snapped back as if she'd been slapped. Did he really look back and see that he was the good guy? The innocent? How long had it taken for him to absolve himself? Until his wedding night with Julie? Is that when Beth had been shoved neatly into a drawer and forgotten about?

Or had it been sooner?

"I can't believe this." Her voice was low, carrying the ring of astonishment. "You're *defending* what you did? Do you know how humiliating it was for me around here? For months after you and Julie left town, people stared at me. Wondering what had happened. Spreading rumors."

She'd never forget it. The sympathetic stares from people or, worse, the amused glances of girls she'd thought were her friends. "My own mother thought I was pregnant and that's why you left. Everywhere I went, whispered conversations stopped when I got close. There were guys who thought they could move right into your place. And my so-called friends turned on me like rabid snakes, gossiping, laughing.

"There was no way to avoid any of it. I was alone

because you were *gone.* I finally left for college and it felt like an escape."

He laughed a little under his breath. "Wow. You escaped. Good for you. Do you want a prize? Do you know the crap I heard when my friends found out you'd dumped me?"

"I didn't dump you. *You* dumped *me.* Pretty damn publicly, too. And you didn't have to listen to them for months, did you?" She glared up at him, feeling the fury that had been buried inside her for fifteen years rising up to the surface. "Just how long had you been cheating on me with Julie?"

Clearly shocked, he blurted, *"What?"*

"You married Julie like a week after we broke up—"

"So you agree, you broke up with me."

"No, I didn't say that. And don't change the subject. You and Julie got married and skipped town in like ten seconds. And I was left here, trying to explain how my boyfriend of three years had married someone else!"

His brown eyes turned thunderous and a part of Beth was happy to see it. Why should she be the only one upset?

"I don't owe you an explanation, Beth," he ground out.

"Yeah, you do. But I'll never get one." She whirled away, took a step and looked back. "You go ahead and tell yourself whatever lie you have to, to make yourself feel better. I know the truth. And whether you admit it or not, so do you."

He was after her in a heartbeat. She shouldn't have been surprised, but she was. She'd forgotten how fast he could move. Beth gasped as he took her arm, spun her around and then held on to her shoulders. He was looming over her and he did it well. He was so tall she had to tip her head back to meet brown eyes that were flashing with indignation.

"You think it was easy for me?" he demanded.

"Yes," she snapped. "You're damn right I do. You and Julie got out. Just the two of you. It's more than I had."

"You're wrong," he said. "Nothing about leaving here was easy."

She hoped not. "I don't care."

"Yeah, you made that clear the last night we were together."

He kept trying to make her feel guilty about that night. But she'd done nothing wrong. She couldn't regret it even now. She'd been right to go with her gut. With her heart. It hadn't meant she didn't love Cam. It felt as if she'd *always* loved him. And a part of her still did. Naturally, she kept *that* part locked away in a corner of her mind she never explored.

"I was only eighteen, Cam."

"And I was nineteen," he reminded her. "What's your point?"

"My point is, I did what I had to. You didn't see how young I was—how young we were—back then, and you still don't."

"I saw it," he argued. "I didn't care. Didn't think it mattered. We had a plan, Beth. And you scrapped it without a thought. Well, I did what I had to do, too. I found a way to survive what *you* did to me."

She laughed again and the sound was painful, even to her. "Marrying Julie was a survival technique? Well, hell, Cam. You should teach a course on that at the city college. *How to Get Over Heartbreak by Marrying Someone Else.* I'm sure tons of men would sign up for that one."

"That's not what I meant."

"It's what you said."

"Damn it, Beth." He shook his head, stared up at the sky for a slow count of five, then looked back at her. "You always had the hardest head."

She inhaled sharply and held up one hand. "Don't. You don't get to pretend you still know me. I'm not that young girl anymore. We're not together now and we're never going to be."

"Who said I wanted us back together?"

His words stung in spite of what she was feeling. She wouldn't let him see the hurt, though. "Good, then we're on the same page."

"Almost."

She huffed out a breath. "What's that supposed to mean?"

"Well, hell, if we're going to avoid each other and we're never going to be together again, then we need to do something we *didn't* do fifteen years ago."

Actually, Beth couldn't think of a single thing they hadn't done back then. And remembering everything they *had* done made her heartbeat skip and her blood hum through her veins. It seemed fury wasn't enough to squash the kind of desire that pumped through her whenever Cam was near. "What's that?"

His gaze fixed on hers, one corner of his mouth lifted into a tiny, secretive smile that used to drive her crazy with need. "Well," he said softly, "we never did kiss goodbye."

And he swooped in on her just like he used to.

* * *

She'd pushed him, just as she used to. Made him feel too much, just as she used to. And just like when they were kids, Cam swept Beth off her feet and pressed her tightly to his chest. Then he fused his mouth to hers as if she held his next breath. And while he fed a need that had haunted him for years, one corner of his mind was alert to her reaction.

Would she push him away? Would she tear her mouth free and shout "no"? It would kill him to stop, but damned if he'd hold her if she didn't want him to.

But she hooked her arms around his neck almost instantly and everything in him roared into life.

The taste of her filled him. Her scent seemed to surround him, drawing him in, drawing him back to a time when she was everything to him.

But memories paled when compared to having her back in his arms again. She parted her lips and at the first slide of his tongue against hers, Cam was electrified. His body turned to stone, and all he could think was *more*. He held her tighter, pressing her body to his so that she had no doubt of what she was doing to him. His hands swept up and down her spine, and every time she shivered, he felt the fires inside erupt.

Years fell away. Old aches, hurts and regrets faded into the rush of heat that swamped him. All he wanted was to carry her inside to his bedroom, stretch her out across the mattress and bury himself inside her. He craved that connection as he did his next breath.

And that was enough to have Cam breaking the kiss, setting her on her feet and taking a single step back from her. Damned if he'd seduce her on his driveway when a dozen cowboys could glance over at them and get a show.

He looked at Beth as she stared at him while she struggled to catch her breath. He knew how she felt. His own heartbeat was raging, and the ache in his balls made him want to brace his hands on his knees and do some deep breathing until the pain eased.

He hadn't asked for this to happen, though he'd known that coming back to Royal would mean being around Beth again. And maybe pretending it wouldn't happen again really would be lying to himself. What he had to do was remember that she'd betrayed him. Yeah, they were different people now, but how could he trust her, remembering?

Maybe Beth's idea to keep their distance was a good one, but damned if he could see that bargain lasting for long. Royal wasn't big enough for them to avoid each other. But one more episode like this one just might kill him.

"Okay then," she said finally, sounding a little breathless. "You've had your goodbye kiss…"

"Yeah. About that." He locked his gaze with hers. "Didn't really feel like goodbye. It tasted more like *welcome back*."

"No, it didn't." She shook her head as if that action would help.

He grinned in spite of everything. Hell, he remembered Beth arguing even when she was wrong and knew it. In fact, she'd fight back even harder if she was wrong. Like she was now.

"Well, then let's try it again," he challenged, even though another kiss at the moment would bring him to his knees. "See which one of us is right."

She skipped backward a couple steps. "I don't think so. I already know who's right and it's not you."

"Guess we'll see, won't we?" Oh, this wasn't the end of whatever was still simmering between them. Cam knew they were just starting and she knew it, too. Which was why she was inching ever closer to her car.

"Whatever you might be thinking, Camden?" she said, fumbling behind her for the car door handle, "I haven't been standing still waiting for you to come back. You got married. Moved on. Well, so have I."

Surprised, he asked, "Seriously?"

"Is that so hard to believe?" She looked insulted.

"No. But I didn't hear anything about you being married..." And he didn't like thinking about it. Whether it made sense or not didn't matter.

"I'm not," she said. "But I didn't join a convent, either. In fact, there's a man right now who wants to marry me."

"Who?" His guts twisted.

"None of your business. I'm not here for you, Cam. We're not going to hook up again just because we're in the same town now."

His gaze dropped to her left hand. Empty. He hated that he was relieved to see it. "Well, you're not wearing a ring. So I guess we'll just see what happens, won't we?"

"Nothing's going to happen, Camden."

"Something already did, Beth. Hell, you felt it, too, when we kissed."

She shrugged that off. "It was just a kiss."

"Uh-huh. And a Texas summer is just warm."

She opened the car door and pulled it wide. "I'm not playing this game with you, Cam."

He dropped one hand on the car door and leaned in. "Not a game, Beth."

"Whatever it is, I'm out."

"For now," he said.

"Forever."

He didn't believe that. Not for a damn second. Cam still held on to what she'd said to him their last night together. How she'd walked away from him and everything they'd planned. She'd cut his heart out with a few well-chosen words. But he could also feel the sizzling threads still connecting them. One kiss and he wanted more. And when he had more, he knew it still wouldn't be enough.

Hell, if *he* was willing to set aside the past, she would be, too. She just had to argue about it for a while.

He could wait.

"I'll get you that donation," he said abruptly.

"Right." She nodded, swallowed hard and then slid into her car, the hem of her dress riding high enough on her thigh to make his mouth go dry. "Once you do that, I'll talk to membership at the TCC and get that ball rolling."

"You're going to wait until you get the money? Don't trust me?"

She looked over her shoulder at him. "Nope."

He laughed. "Fair enough. I don't trust you, either."

Beth put her sunglasses on so he couldn't read her eyes anymore. "Then we know where we stand."

Then she gunned the engine and peeled out of the drive, sending up a wake of dirt and gravel behind her.

The woman always had known how to make an exit.

* * *

She wasn't a mile from Cam's ranch when her cell phone rang. Beth glanced at the screen on her dash and sighed. When she answered, she didn't bother to hide the sigh. "What is it, Sutton?"

One of her twin older brothers. Sutton was three minutes younger than Sebastian and way more relaxed and fun than his stoic, dutiful twin. As he constantly reminded everyone, including Sebastian.

"Well, hello to you, too," he said, then asked, "are you driving with the top down? I can hardly hear you."

"Yes, I am and I can hear you fine." Not really. "What is it, Sutton?"

"Why do you bother to answer the phone when you're driving?"

"Why do you *call* me when I'm driving?"

"Because you're always on the move. When else am I going to reach you?"

"Good point." She was always busy. Running the numerous charities that the Wingate Corporation supported was pretty much a 24/7 job. She spent most of her time driving to businesses to wrangle donations or meeting with supporters. "Okay, what's up?"

"Family meeting at the house."

"What?" She steered around a curve in the road, straightened out and demanded, "Why? We just had a meeting two weeks ago. I've got appointments to keep."

"Believe it or not, little sister, we *all* do."

Fine, he had a point. The Wingate family didn't simply sit around and count their money. Their biggest company, WinJet, was huge, having outgrown Texas many years ago. Her brothers, and cousins Luke and Zeke, did most of the heavy lifting there.

"Right. So what's going on?" She barely noticed the scenery flying past as she whipped her beloved BMW convertible down the road. And though she was managing to hold a conversation with Sutton, her mind was still on Camden. Unconsciously, she lifted one hand to her mouth, as if she could still feel his lips on hers. And, really, she could. It was as if he'd branded her.

"Mom called the meeting."

"Mom?" Ever since the death of Beth's father, Ava Wingate had stepped back from the company. She'd gone to Europe for an extended stay, along with one of her oldest "friends," Keith Cooper. How Mom was oblivious to the fact that Keith was clearly in love with her, Beth couldn't figure out. Then again, maybe Ava didn't want to know the truth.

"Did she say what the meeting's about?" Beth asked, concentrating on the road again.

"No. All she said was, attendance is mandatory. Hell, she's even got Piper coming in from Dallas for it."

"Okay, that makes no sense." Her mother's younger sister, Piper Holloway, wasn't even a part of the company.

"Yeah. Look, all I know is Baz called to tell me about the meeting and ordered me to spread the word."

"Ordered?"

He laughed. "You know Baz. He's always ordering everybody around. Part of his charm."

True. Their oldest brother had stepped into the void left behind when their father, Trent, died two years before. Sebastian had a tight grip on the company and under his leadership, Wingate Enterprises, with Win-Jet in the lead, was growing like it never had before.

"Fine," she said, just managing to bury the sigh. "When?"

"Now."

"Damn it!" She pressed harder on the accelerator. "I'm about twenty minutes out. Baz will have to be patient."

"Sure," Sutton said with a laugh. "That'll happen." After a pause, he asked, "Where exactly are you?"

Her mouth worked because she didn't want to say the words, but then told herself she had nothing to be ashamed of. "I'm on Old River Road."

"Huh."

"What?"

"Nothing." Sutton's voice was amused as he added, "Isn't that where Camden Guthrie's ranch is?"

"How do you know that?"

"Everybody knows that. What I don't know is why you went there."

"It's not what you're thinking." Beth winced. She'd known people would start talking about the two of them again.

"How do you know what I'm thinking?"

"Please."

"Fine. I'll leave it alone."

"Thanks." Beth sighed a little.

"For now."

Way too many men were telling her that today.

Family meetings were an unavoidable fact in the Wingate family.

Usually those meetings were at the company headquarters, but for whatever reason, Ava Wingate had insisted this meeting be held at the family ranch. Boasting forty acres of prime Texas ranch land that had never actually been worked, the Wingates kept horses for personal riding and plenty of chickens for their kitchen needs. The barn and stable were on one side of the property and the guesthouse on the other. The main house sat on the highest point on the property, affording views of untouched rolling hills, a private lake and stands of oaks.

The house itself was sort of a mix of Southwestern and California ranch, made of cream-colored stone and stucco. There was a red clay tile roof, a wide front porch and a wraparound balcony on the second floor.

Beth loved it. She lived at the main house, along with her mom, Sebastian and Sutton. The house was palatial in size, so everyone had privacy and plenty of space. The Wingate cousins, Luke and his twin, Zeke, lived in the guesthouse, so they were close enough to be a part of everything and far enough away that they could get space when they needed it.

Sitting in the formal dining room at a table that could easily seat twenty, Beth glanced around. There were paintings of the ranch dotting the cream-colored walls and the heavy, dark wood beams added interest and a sense of timelessness.

Beth's brothers were on one side of the table while Luke and Zeke sat beside her. Everyone was waiting on Ava and wondering why they were there in the first place.

"The gang's all here," Piper Holloway said brightly as she hurried into the room. She took a seat next to Sebastian and looked around at all of them in turn. Piper was forty, looked thirty and was Ava's younger sister. She was more of a sister to all of them, too, than an aunt. Tall and slim, she kept her dark brown hair in a short, edgy style that looked perfect on her. She owned an art gallery in Dallas, but came home to Royal often. Her dark green eyes were filled with questions as she grinned at Beth.

"Anyone know why we're here yet?"

"No," Beth said. "Mom's running late."

"Was there an apocalypse?" Piper's eyebrows went up. "Ava's never late."

That was true, too. Starting to get worried, Beth leaned into Zeke. "What time is it?"

"Ten minutes past when she said she'd be here."

Beth sighed. She still had to meet with the owners of the local wine store about their donation to the TCC charity masquerade.

"So fill me in," Piper said, looking at all of them. "What's new at the company?"

Sebastian looked at Luke. "You're the VP of New Product Development…"

Luke grinned and leaned both forearms on the shining walnut table. "We've got some interesting drones coming out of R & D."

"Drones?" Beth asked. "They're not new, right?"

"These are." Luke held up one hand, palm out. "They fit in the palm of your hand, and they're so easy to use kids will love them."

Zeke jumped in. "I've got our top guys working on ideas for digital ads as well as commercials already. Luke's drones are awesome."

Zeke and Luke were the sons of Ava's older brother, Robert, the product of his marriage to Nina, an African American woman. When Robert and Nina died in an accident, Ava had insisted that Luke and Zeke come to Royal to be with family. Now it felt as if they'd always been there.

The twins were both tall and gorgeous, with caramel-colored skin, closely cropped black hair and bright green eyes. Zeke was the VP of Marketing while Luke was in charge of New Product Development. The genius of Luke's creative mind was its flexibility, and Zeke's inner adventurer kept everyone on their toes. Beth was nuts about both of them.

Thankfully, they weren't identical, because Sebastian and Sutton were sometimes hard to tell apart. Beth shifted a look at her brothers.

They were tall and handsome, with dark blond hair and the Wingate green eyes. Sebastian was the CEO of Wingate Enterprises, Sutton was the CFO, and Beth was grateful the four guys did the majority of the worrying and working on the family business.

Piper was nudging Sebastian, trying to coax a smile out of him. Meanwhile, Sutton was kicked back in his chair, grinning at something Zeke had said. Zeke elbowed Luke to bring him in on the joke, and Beth smiled to herself, just watching them.

Sutton and Sebastian were as different as they were identical. Baz was always serious, all business, while Sutton had a ready smile and a relaxed attitude that put everyone at ease.

The only ones missing now, she thought sadly, were her brother Miles and their sister Harley. But Miles had left Royal for Chicago and his own security company years ago and Harley and her son, Daniel, were living in Thailand while she ran her nonprofit, Zest. Beth missed them both. Especially at times like this.

"Anyone know what this is about?" Sutton's question hung in the air.

"You guys would know more about it than I would," Beth said, and looked at Luke.

"Nope. Not a clue," he replied, shaking his head. Then he looked at Sebastian. "Aunt Ava hasn't said anything to you?"

"No." He didn't look happy about that, either. "Ever since Mom came home to work at the company again six months ago, she's been moving around from section to section. Like she's familiarizing herself with everything again."

"It's a good idea," Zeke said.

"The question is," Piper put in, "why did she call us all here?"

"The answer is a simple…yet complex one." Everyone turned to look at Ava as she entered the room.

Everyone came to attention in their seats and Beth had to marvel at it. Ava Holloway Wingate commanded a room once she stepped inside it. Almost sixty, she was the picture of refined elegance. A slight touch of gray at her temples shone in dark blond hair that was pulled up into her standard chignon, and her gray-green eyes swept the room with a glance. She wore a pale blue business suit and black heels.

She and Beth's father had been incredibly close, to the point where sometimes it seemed as if they forgot they'd had five children together. But because of how they'd been raised—including Piper—the Wingate siblings had stuck together, and that closeness remained today.

Ava took a seat at the head of the table and folded

her hands together in front of her. "I won't waste time on pleasantries…"

Beth threw a glance at Sutton, who shrugged in answer. Ava *never* wasted time on pleasantries—like *How are you? I've missed you.* Or even *I love you.*

"You all know I've been spending time at the company these last six months," their mom was saying in her clipped tones. "I wanted to get to know each department in turn, get a handle on how things were running."

"Mother," Sebastian interrupted quietly. "Why don't you just tell us what it was that required this meeting?"

"Fine." She looked at all of them, her cool eyes appraising. "I've found a discrepancy in accounting."

"What?" Sutton sat forward, all pretense of casual disinterest gone.

Sebastian, in charge of his siblings and cousins, as always, held up one hand to quiet everyone. His gaze fixed on his mother, he said, "What exactly did you find, Mother?"

"In the simplest terms," Ava told him. "I've discovered money missing. Being quietly, carefully, skimmed from several different accounts."

"How much?" Zeke's question broke the stunned silence.

Ava looked at him directly. "At this point, it's difficult to be sure. But, at a minimum, several hundred thousand dollars."

"What?" Sebastian slapped one hand on the table and Piper jumped. "Sorry," he muttered.

"How long has this been going on?" Beth watched her mother's face and noticed the tightening at the corners of Ava's mouth.

"From what I can tell at this early stage," Ava said, "it's been going on several years."

"Who the hell would do that?" Sutton demanded of no one in particular.

"And how?" Luke asked.

"It couldn't have been easy," Piper murmured.

"Easier than it should have been," Ava said with a quick look at her sister. "Every department is compartmentalized. Every section has their own bookkeeping division. No one knows what's happening anywhere else."

"That was done deliberately," Sebastian reminded her. "Breaking it up seemed the best way to keep everything from being centralized."

"I know. But that plan obviously has its flaws." Ava looked at her oldest son, then included everyone else when she said, "I've decided to hire an outside auditor to go over the books. Once we know how long it's been happening and how much has been stolen, we can look for the thief."

"I'm on board with an auditor," Sebastian murmured, "but we need to keep this quiet. Wingate Enterprises is big business. WinJet alone is a billion-dollar firm. We don't want outsiders worried about the health of Wingate. Until we get to the bottom of this," he added, looking at his siblings and cousins, "we keep this in the family."

"Agreed," Ava said, then looked around the table.

Everyone else concurred and apparently that was enough for Ava. She stood up and added, "Once we know more, we'll meet about this again."

She walked out of the room, and the rest of them were left sitting at the table, staring at each other. Beth looked at Piper. "Did you know about this? Did Mom talk to you first?"

Piper held up both hands and shook her head. "Not a word."

"Auditors," Sutton muttered. "If this is as big as Mom thinks it is, we could be in serious trouble."

"Let's wait for the reports before we panic," Piper told him.

"No one is panicking," Sebastian put in, dropping into his chair again. "But we damn well should start some planning."

Four

Later that day, Cam followed Olivia Turner around the yard and watched her making notes, taking measurements and so many pictures that he wondered why she didn't just take a video and leave it at that.

But he appreciated her thoroughness, too. Olivia's construction company had a great reputation for coming in on time, on budget or under, and her work was always top grade. So whatever estimate she gave him, he'd accept it. Of course, she didn't know that.

"Okay," she said, and turned to face him. She tapped her tablet a few more times, then lifted her gaze to his. "I've got a good idea of what you're going for here, and it's a good plan."

"Thanks. How long to get your estimate on the job?"

She tipped her head to one side, and her bright red braid swung out and across her shoulder. "For the whole job? I mean, for the remodel on the house as well as the guest cottages and everything else?"

"Yeah. All of it."

Her eyebrows shot up and her green eyes narrowed thoughtfully. "That's a big job. You'd basically be hiring my crew for the next six months or more."

He nodded. "I would be. Can you handle that?"

She took a breath, sighed and looked around the land. He knew what she was seeing. Live oaks, open space filled only with the potential of what it could be, and his house, about two hundred yards from where they were standing. He knew she was seeing it as it would be when the job was completed. He liked that. In his experience, a contractor needed to have imagination and vision as well as talent. Hell, he could see it, too, and wanted it done sooner rather than later. Finally she turned to look at him.

"I'd have to hire on more help—and there are two or three jobs I've already lined up," she warned. "I can't leave those people hanging."

"I respect that. The question is," he continued, "can you juggle those jobs and mine, and still give a hundred percent to all of us?"

At that, she straightened up, lifted her chin and assured him, "I always give a hundred percent. If we take on a job, it gets our best."

"Good to know." He nodded, taking the sting out of his question. He had already known about her reputation, but it was good to have it confirmed. "So. The estimate?"

She laughed. "In a hurry?"

"Yeah," he said, and looked down the path toward the barn and the stables and the fields beyond. He wanted to get going on the next chapter in his life and wasn't one to just stand around waiting. "I am. Can you handle that?"

She laughed. "I grew up with brothers. I can handle pretty much everything." Glancing at her tablet again, she added, "I'll go over these figures and get back to you by day after tomorrow with a firm number."

"A number," he reminded her, "that also includes another stable capable of stalling twelve horses."

She laughed again, shaking her head. "If I stay here much longer, are you going to keep throwing more jobs at me?"

"You never know." Cam turned to glance at his house. "You can leave the remodel of the house to the end. I'd rather have the rest up and running as soon as possible."

"Okay, that works." She paused, then said, "Seems to me, you're rushing to get back into the swing of being in Royal."

"Yeah, you could say that." He'd missed this place while he was in California. And the sooner he was in business and a member of the TCC, the sooner it would feel like he'd never really left.

"Well, if you want to see half of Royal, you should come to the Fire Department Open House this Saturday."

"Is that right?"

Olivia shrugged. "They're raffling off a new truck to raise money to fix up the station and maybe get some new equipment. But there'll be a band and free food and, like I said, no place better for you to mingle with all the people you want to see."

"It's a good idea," he agreed. And it sounded like

something Beth would be attending. He wanted to cross paths with her again, and doing it while surrounded by half the town seemed like the safest way to go.

"Great. I'll see you there. You can probably meet most of my crew, too." Then she turned to look at his stable. "Are you wanting basically a copy of the building you already have?"

He grinned. "Basically, but on the interior, I've got a few ideas."

Olivia tossed her braid back over her shoulder, took a breath and said, "Of course you do. Okay, let's hear 'em."

The following day, Beth stood at her office window, staring out at Royal. Her mind was whirling with the implications of her mother's discovery. In fact, the whole family was in an uproar. Who could be stealing from them? She didn't believe for a minute it was anyone in the family. But that meant one of their employees was a thief, and that was hard to fathom, as well.

Her brothers, cousins and mother had been talking about nothing but this situation, and while Beth couldn't blame them, she'd happily come into work and put the worry aside for a while.

Leaving the house today had felt like she was escaping a pressure cooker. Taking care of business on her charities was practically a vacation when compared to the nonstop speculation happening at the ranch.

Since her office was at the end of Main Street, directly opposite City Hall, her view included the landscaped grounds around the 150-year-old building. Summer flowers dazzled in brilliant colors at the bases of the oaks sprinkled across the lawn. There were benches in the shade, allowing places to sit and relax, and at the moment several people were taking advantage of them.

Beth's mind jumped from one subject to the next, as if it couldn't find one specific thought to settle on. It was hard to admit that thinking about a thief at the family company was soothing compared to thinking about Camden Guthrie.

Ridiculous to still be focusing on that *kiss*. But here she was. Her dreams last night had starred Cam, that bone-melting kiss and then so much more that she'd finally awakened, her body aching with need. Being awake didn't stop the mental torture that her mind gleefully inflicted, though.

Funny that she could remember the fire, the all-consuming heat between them and, at the same time, cruise over the pain she'd experienced when he left town with another woman. That pain had remained for a long time and had colored every relationship since. How could she open her heart to anyone when the one man she'd trusted with *everything* had betrayed her?

"And if I don't stop thinking about Cam, I'm never going to finish working on the Fire Department Open House." Saying it didn't make her leave the window and go back to her desk. Instead, she watched people streaming down the sidewalks.

Then she spotted *him*. Camden Guthrie. As if her hunger had conjured him. Her stomach did a spin and dip, and a curl of heat settled low in her belly. He was wearing jeans, a white button-down shirt, black boots and a gray Stetson. What was it about a man in jeans? And what was it about this one man that could turn her inside out so easily?

Her gaze was fixed on him to the exclusion of everything else in Royal, so when he stopped and looked across the street to her office, she swore their eyes locked. Silly though. He couldn't see her with the glare of the sun, and still she felt a rush of desire that only bristled and grew when he crossed the street, headed her way.

Why did she care? She shouldn't. She'd promised herself she wouldn't. Yet here she was—mouth watering, nerves rattling and her heartbeat thudding heavily in her chest. Desire mingled with regret and the last vestiges of a romance she'd once lost herself in.

He crossed the street in long strides, pushed her door open, stepped inside and swept his hat off. "Beth."

Well, their agreement to stay clear of each other hadn't even lasted twenty-four hours. But then she'd known at the time it was a futile bargain. Like metal shavings to a magnet, Beth had always been drawn to Cam and it looked as though the years that had separated them hadn't done a thing to lessen that draw.

She looked into his dark brown eyes and felt the heat of his body reach across the few feet of space between them. How had she gone fifteen years without seeing him? How would she stay away from him now?

Trying to salvage the situation, not to mention her pride, she said, "Didn't we agree to not be around each other?"

"We did."

"And yet?"

He grinned and her heart tumbled. This was so much harder than it should have been. Couldn't she just remind herself that he'd married someone else?

Someone that Beth had once called a friend? That he'd betrayed her, left Texas for California and had never looked back? Why was her body so eager to forgive him while her mind held on to the painful memories?

"I was at City Hall checking out some building regulations—"

"Okay," she said, interrupting him. "But why are you *here*?"

He reached into his shirt pocket, pulled out a cashier's check and handed it to her. "I stopped at the bank earlier so I could make good on my part of our deal."

Right. Their other deal. Not about staying apart, but about getting him into the TCC. Fine. That was good. She was pleased. Really. He wasn't here to kiss her again—he was simply here to wrap up a business deal. She unfolded the check, glanced at the amount and gasped.

Astonished, she looked up at him. "A hundred thousand dollars?"

One eyebrow arched. "Not enough?"

"No. I mean yes." She shook her head, took a breath, and when she could speak again without babbling, she said, "It is enough. It's more than generous. I wasn't expecting so much."

And didn't know what to make of it. Was he doing this just to help? Or was he trying to impress her? Because he had.

He grinned briefly and reached for the check. "I'm happy to take it back and give you less."

Beth whipped the check into the pocket of her cream-colored capris and shook her head. She might be confused about a lot of things at the moment, but on this, she was perfectly clear. "Oh, no, you don't. This is great. It's going to make a huge difference for the children's wing. Seriously, thanks."

"Not a problem."

She kept her gaze locked on his and tried to read what she saw there. But he was stoic, hiding whatever was running through his mind. Was the donation his only reason for stopping in? And why did she hope it wasn't? Had she learned *nothing* in the last fifteen years? He'd left and she'd stayed, building a life. And she was damn good at it.

It had taken a lot of work, but she had thrived without Cam. Was she really willing to put all of that aside in favor of the kind of passion she remembered so vividly?

Yes, she knew he was no longer the simple ranch hand she'd once loved. Knew he had money. But, really, she'd never thought about how rich he actually was now. What else had changed? She wondered what her father would make of the man he was so sure would amount to nothing more than a "ranch hand."

"So now you'll talk to the TCC membership board?"

She came up out of her thoughts and told herself to pay attention. "I will. That was our deal." She'd stop by today to see Burt Wheeler, Cam's father-in-law. Just thinking that gave her a twinge of…what? Regret? Envy? Cam had married Julie Wheeler and lived a life with her that Beth had once thought would be hers. It felt small and petty to be jealous of a dead woman, but that didn't change what she was feeling.

At the same time, though, she had to wonder if Beth and Cam had run off together so long ago, would things have worked out the way they had? Would he be a successful entrepreneur? Would she be working for the family corporation? She'd never know. More questions with no answers.

"While I'm here, there's something else I wanted to talk to you about," he said, and she noticed him turning the brim of his hat in his hands.

Was this what the big check had been about? To soften her up for whatever else was coming? He looked nervous. But that couldn't be the case. After all, Cam had never had trouble going after exactly what he wanted. It's one of the things she'd found so exciting about him.

"What is it?"

"You don't have to sound so suspicious." He smiled and shook his head. "Are you so much like your father now that you're wary of everything?"

Another stab at her late father, but on this one she could agree. Her dad had looked at everything with a cynical eye. Including—maybe *especially*—Camden Guthrie. She had been the daughter of a very wealthy man, and Cam was the son of horse trainers. Trent had never trusted Cam, and once he left town, Beth had asked herself if she shouldn't have been more like her father. Still, she couldn't blame Cam for holding on to a grudge against the man who'd thought of him as not worthy.

But if Cam didn't understand that her cynicism where he was concerned had more to do with what *he* had done to her than anything her father had done, then he was being deliberately oblivious.

"No," she said at last. "It's not my dad who affected my trust issues. I learned fifteen years ago to be wary of people."

His eyes flashed, and she knew she'd scored a hit. Somehow, it didn't give her the sense of satisfaction she'd been expecting. What good would it do her to throw proverbial stones? Holding up one hand for peace, she said, "Sorry. Never mind all that. Just tell me what you wanted to talk to me about."

Nodding slowly, he kept his dark eyes on hers. Beth could have warmed herself with the heat in them. "All right. It's about the other deal we made yesterday."

"You mean keeping our distance from each other?" She laughed shortly. "Yeah, since you're here, that one clearly isn't working so far."

"And it won't, either." He held on to his hat with one hand and tapped it idly against his left thigh. "Avoiding each other isn't going to work. I'm home to stay, Beth, so we're going to be seeing each other plenty. What're we supposed to do, run and hide every time we spot each other on Main Street? Because I'm not doing that."

Running and hiding were the furthest things from her mind right now, too. "Me, either. Okay, what's your solution?"

"That we do the opposite," he said bluntly. "Instead of avoiding each other, we start spending time together."

Her stomach spun. She was having a hard enough time around Cam as it was. Spending more time with him would only make that more difficult—not easier. "And that solves…what?"

"It gets us used to each other again," he said. "Accustomed to being together and *not* giving in to the attraction between us. With any luck, after some time passes, that'll cool off."

Not from where she was standing. Just having him

in her office was lighting up her insides and making her blood burn and bubble. The way he was standing so stiffly, so obviously filled with tension, told her that he was feeling the burn, too. "You think so?"

"I do. We keep our hands off each other, but hang out, and we'll get past this...need."

"Seems risky."

"I can do it if you can."

A challenge. He'd always known the way to get to her. Tell Beth she *couldn't* do something and she would find a way to accomplish it. "Why couldn't I? You're not completely irresistible, Camden."

That was a lie because, yes, he was. At least he always had been to Beth. But she wouldn't be admitting to that anytime soon. She still wanted him, and she probably always would. However, she'd learned the hard way a long time ago that want and need didn't translate into forever. And she wasn't about to set herself up for more pain.

"If that's how you really feel," he said, "then this shouldn't be a problem for either of us."

Well, he'd boxed her in neatly there. If she said no, he'd realize that she didn't trust herself around him. If she said yes, then she was taking a chance she might be sorry for. Yet, what choice did either of them have? They were going to be seeing each other around town for the rest of their lives. If he actually stayed in Royal. Wasn't it a better idea to learn how to do that without opening up old wounds?

She took a deep breath to steady herself. It didn't work. "Okay then, we'll try it your way."

"Good. Now, on that, I've got a plan."

"Of course you do."

His mouth curved in a slow smile and flames licked at her core. Oh, this was *so* not a good idea.

"The word around Royal is that you had a big hand in setting up your family's offices. You know, not decorating exactly, but—"

At least they were on safe ground here. "You mean designing the interiors for function and style?"

He snorted. "Okay, I wouldn't have used those words, but yeah. Well, I'd like you to help me out with my project at the ranch."

Intrigued in spite of everything, Beth felt a tug of interest, but she had to tell him, "I'm not a licensed interior designer, you know."

"I don't care about that." He glanced around her office and then back to her. "You've got a good eye, and that would help me out a lot."

She knew what he saw when he looked at the space she'd created. Beth was proud of her work here and at her brothers' offices. In her own place, she'd simply taken the space available and made it more her own with the bookcases, tables, chairs and plants that spilled out of brass pots. She didn't own the building, so she wasn't able to do all she would have, given the chance. Still, the atmosphere was rich but homey, and put people at ease the moment they walked in.

In her brothers' offices, though, she'd been able to affect how they were remodeled. Hidden bathrooms, large work area, with window placement to expand the view and the feel of openness. Then the flooring, the paint and the accessories that made an office more personal, less industrial chic.

Beth had to ask, "What exactly did you have in mind?"

"I told you about the dude ranch project I'm going to be setting up."

"Yes…"

He walked farther into the room and looked around. Beth's gaze followed him and she saw his eyes slide over her desk, the framed family photos, then he turned his gaze back to hers. "I've hired Olivia Turner to build a dozen guest cottages to start."

"To *start*?"

He gave her an all too brief grin that lit up his eyes. "Yeah. Thought I'd start out small. See how it goes. I can always add more in a year or two if I want to."

Beth knew the Circle K well, so she was aware that there was more than enough room for what he was planning. And Olivia Turner would do a great job. "How do I fit into all this?"

He leaned one shoulder against the wall, hooked one foot over the other ankle and said, "I was thinking you could work with me. Make those cabins… special. Something out of the ordinary. I want them to stand out from any other outfit like it. Hell, from every other dude ranch in the West. Olivia will build them, but I want her to have some specific ideas to work with."

She stared up into his eyes and told herself that this would be a mistake. Working closely with him was just too much temptation. But a small voice in her mind whispered if she was going to prove to herself *and* to Cam that she was well and truly over him, wasn't this the best way to do it? To be tempted and not surrender? Couldn't she use this as a lesson for herself? And, yes, she knew she was mentally trying to find a way to do this because it sounded like fun.

"Working together could be dangerous, Cam."

"No. It's just the first test in our new bargain." He pushed away from the wall to stand up straight right in front of her. He looked down at her and said, "Really? You think we can't control ourselves? Are we still eighteen and full of hormones?"

"No." *Yes.*

"We're both adults," he continued. "I think we can restrain ourselves. Are you worried?"

That was a direct challenge and she knew it. "Not about me…" He was so close she could have laid her palm on his chest and felt his heart pounding. She could have gone up on her toes and laid her mouth over his. She did neither.

He nodded. "Fine. An amendment to the new bargain. I won't make a move until you do."

It was her turn to laugh, though it sounded a little strained, even to Beth. "That's not going to happen."

"Then there's nothing to worry about, is there?"

Oh, there was so much here to worry about. "I guess not."

"So you'll do it."

"Yes."

One corner of his mouth tipped up. "Great. Come out to the ranch tomorrow and I'll show you what I'm thinking."

"I can't be there until afternoon," she said, mentally flipping through her appointments and obligations.

"That'll work. I've got that Longhorn herd arriving early in the day. I'll be able to get away by afternoon."

In spite of her bravado, Beth knew that being around Cam was going to be torture. The memories of his touch, his kiss, were too fresh now. Before he'd returned, those images from fifteen years ago had been watery, misty pictures in her mind. Like a Monet, beautiful but indistinct.

Now everything was crystal clear again. She knew how he felt pressed up against her. The taste of him clung to her lips, and she could nearly feel his strong hands sweeping up and down her spine. Heat coiled inside her, a spring ever tightening, ready to snap. And it wouldn't take much to push her past the point of no return. So, was this foolish? No doubt. Was she going to do it anyway? Absolutely.

When the door opened behind Cam, Beth jolted, tore her gaze from his and nearly let her internal groan slip out.

Justin McCoy stood there, his gaze fixed on Cam. In a split second, she compared the two men and Justin definitely came up short. He was tall but soft, his belly already a little paunchy. His skin was pale, his eyes a watery blue and he kept his white-blond hair cut short to obscure the fact that he was already losing it. He was a wealthy rancher who never went out on his own land. He had "people" for that.

Looking at the two men now, Beth couldn't imagine why she'd ever gone out with Justin in the first place. She guessed she'd been lonely enough to take a chance. And she'd known almost from the first that it wasn't going to be what Justin was hoping for. Once they'd had sex, she was sure of it. There'd been no fire. No flash of desire so overwhelming you couldn't breathe. No desperation to touch and be touched. Just a mildly interesting half hour that was quickly forgotten.

She'd dated Justin on and off for a while, but called an end to it a few months ago because he wanted a commitment from her that Beth couldn't give. She didn't love him and wouldn't even consider marrying him. Still, Justin wasn't one to take no for an answer.

"Justin. Hi, this is a surprise." Not an altogether happy one, either.

"I was over at City Hall," he said, walking to her side. "Thought I'd stop in and see if I could take you to lunch."

Beth realized that, although he was talking to her, he was looking at Cam. The two men were practically bristling as they gave each other challenging stares. Best to end this now.

"Oh, I'm sorry. I'm too busy to take lunch today," she said.

"Is that right?" He was still staring at Cam.

She sighed. "Justin, you remember Camden Guthrie, don't you? He's just moved back home recently."

"Oh," he said quietly, "I remember him."

"I was going to say the same thing." Cam's features were grim, his voice a low rumble.

"Aren't you the one who ran off with Burt Wheeler's daughter, Julie?"

Cam's jaw tightened and Beth breathed deeply. She had always been able to tell when Cam's temper was beginning to spike. His eyes were narrowed and flashing out a danger sign.

"I am," he said. "Aren't you the one who was kicked off the football team for cheating on your biology exam?"

"I didn't cheat."

Cam glared at the other man. "You did. In more ways than one."

Justin's pale cheeks flushed with barely contained

rage, and Beth wondered what Cam was talking about. Now wasn't the time to find out, though.

"Okay." She spoke into the tense silence that followed. "I think that's enough testosterone poisoning for today. Cam, maybe you should go."

Both eyebrows rose when he looked at her. "You want me to leave?"

"Please."

Justin looked smug that she'd chosen to have him stay, but that wasn't the reason she'd asked Cam to go instead of him. It was simply that she'd known Cam would do as she asked and had been positive that Justin wouldn't have.

Cam nodded, with one last, hard look at Justin. "All right. I'll go." He shifted a glance to Beth. "I'll see you tomorrow?"

"Yes," she said, though she knew that wouldn't make Justin happy. Not her problem.

Once Cam was gone, Beth looked up at Justin and saw his eyes flash with irritation,

"Justin, thanks for the lunch offer, but I really am too busy today."

He ignored that and groused, "I don't think it's appropriate for a nearly engaged woman to be alone with Guthrie's kind of man."

That she hadn't expected. Even leaving aside the *nearly engaged woman* thing for a moment. "Excuse me?" Beth blinked at him. "Guthrie's 'kind of man'?"

"Money doesn't buy class. He's still the same as he was in school."

"All of us are, apparently," she muttered. She clearly remembered Justin and his friends trying to bully Cam because he was half Native American, but they hadn't succeeded because Cam had never cared what anyone had had to say about him. He just went on with his life and fought back only when he was forced into it.

"Justin, I'll be alone with anyone I choose. You're not in charge of who I speak to. And, more importantly—" she paused for emphasis "—I really want you to hear me on this… We are *not* engaged."

"As good as," he argued.

"Not even close," Beth said firmly. Honestly, she hadn't wanted to hurt Justin's feelings, so she'd dated him for far too long. She hadn't wanted to be mean when she turned down his proposal, and he'd interpreted that as uncertainty. Now she was done. "We're never going to be engaged, Justin. In spite of the fact that you simply won't listen to me."

"Beth, I've been more than tolerant of your indecision, but I believe I'm running out of patience."

Talking to Justin was exhausting. Like beating your head against a steel wall trying to make a hole. All that happened was a headache.

"As am I," she said, suddenly so tired of this whole thing that all she could think of was to get rid of Justin so she could have some peace. If the man wouldn't respond to her polite refusals, maybe it was time to be less polite. "And I haven't been indecisive. I've told you repeatedly that I wasn't interested in a relationship and nothing has changed. We're not engaged. We're not going to be. No one tells me who I can speak to. And I don't want to go to lunch."

He gave her a sadly indulgent look. "Beth, honey, ladies don't show their tempers."

"Oh, for heaven's sake, Justin!"

He frowned, more disappointed. He tucked both

thumbs behind his oversize silver belt buckle and said gently, "Now Beth, honey, calm down."

"Telling someone to calm down does not calm them down, just so you know."

He only stared at her. "What was Guthrie doing here?"

Beth sighed and said, "Cam's an old…friend."

"Yeah, I know all about that. I live here, remember?"

"Okay, Justin, the truth is Cam dropped off a donation to the children's wing at the hospital."

His mouth worked and she could see the muscle in his jaw twitch as he ground his teeth. "Fine. But I don't think it's appropriate for you to be alone with your ex, Beth. People know we're a couple and—"

"Justin, we're *not* a couple." She shook her head as she bit back on her annoyance. "I've explained this to you already. Multiple times. Including just two minutes ago. We are not together and we're not going to be."

Sunlight sliding through the front window slanted across that hideous belt buckle and nearly blinded her. She took a step back just to keep her vision clear.

"I'm sorry, Justin, but I think you should go now."

She didn't even watch him leave.

Five

"You sure you want me to wait in the car?"

Beth sighed, glanced at Gracie and looked back at Burt Wheeler's ranch house. Truthfully, she'd rather have Gracie's company. Heck, she'd rather not be here at all. But a deal was a deal, And since she'd be seeing Cam later today, she was here to hold up her end of their bargain.

"Yeah, if you're out here, I can use you as my excuse to leave quickly if I have to." Beth smiled at her. "Keep the AC running if you want, but parking under this old oak should help with the heat."

"I'll be fine," Gracie said, reaching into her bag for her tablet. "I'll go over the donations list while I wait."

"God, you're good." Another sigh. She really wished she could trade places with Gracie, But she climbed out

of the car and walked across the yard to the Wheelers'
white Victorian ranch house.

It was in beautiful shape, with a freshly painted,
swept porch with bright blue tables and chairs sprinkled along its length. The window glass shone in the
sun, and there was a summer wreath hanging on the
front door. She knocked and waited and, when Burt
opened the door, steeled herself for the conversation
to come.

"Beth Wingate," he said, his voice a gravel road.
"What're you doing out here?"

"I've got a favor to ask, Burt," she answered brightly.
"Can I come in?"

"Sure." He stepped back, a big man with a rounded
belly, a full gray beard and a gleaming bald head. His
brown eyes were curious as he steered her into the
living room.

Burt's wife's stamp was all over the house. Over-
stuffed pastel furniture was gathered in conversational
knots. Polished tables, family photos on the walls—
Beth's gaze went directly to a shot of Julie Wheeler
with her brothers. Her fun-filled smile was frozen in
time, and it must tear at the Wheelers whenever they
looked at it. She shifted her gaze back to Julie's father
when he started talking.

"My Dottie's in town at the market…"

"I didn't come to see your wife, Burt," Beth said,
though she had to admit this conversation would have
been easier if Dottie Wheeler had been there. "It's you
I need to talk to."

"Sounds serious." He crossed his arms over his
broad chest, tucked his chin in and watched her warily.
"What's this about?"

"It's about Cam Guthrie," she blurted.

His features turned instantly to stone. "I've got nothing to say about him."

"I understand, Burt, but—" She'd known it would be hard, but Beth could see both anger and pain in the older man's eyes, and she regretted causing it.

"You don't understand," he interrupted. "You can't. Only me, Dottie and Julie's brothers do. That man ran off with my baby girl. Took her away from her family. From her home. And then let her die out in that godless city in California."

Julie had died of cancer. It must have been horrible for her family—and for Cam. But it was hardly Cam's fault. "Burt…"

"No." He shook his head, and if he'd had hair, it would have whipped around like a lion's mane. "Whatever he wants from me, he doesn't get."

His voice, already rough and deep, got louder, and flags of red appeared on his cheeks. Beth wasn't afraid of him, but she was a little worried that he might have a heart attack. Burt was well-known for his temper and for his ability to cut people down to size with a sharp tongue that took no prisoners. But she wasn't going to be intimidated, no matter how much she might be sympathizing with him.

"Whether we like it or not, Cam's back in Royal now," she said in spite of his anger. "He wants to join the TCC and you're the membership chair."

"I am and I'll vote no on letting him in," he assured her. "He got my little girl pregnant! High school kids is all they were and she was pregnant!"

Beth swayed under that blow. Julie was *pregnant*? How had she never heard a whisper of that rumor?

And how could Cam insist he hadn't cheated on Beth, if he had married Julie because she was pregnant? And if she had been pregnant, where was the child? How many lies were flying around Royal these days? Oh, she really was almost as furious as Burt, yet the hurt she felt dwarfed the rage.

"Didn't know about that, did you?" His voice dropped as if he was sympathizing with her now. "Well, we didn't spread it around. Only her mother and me and Camden Guthrie knew the truth. We didn't even tell her brothers."

Beth swallowed past the knot of humiliation lodged in her throat and wondered how many more times Cam was going to slice at her heart. Why hadn't he at least told her the truth before asking her to speak to his father-in-law? Why hadn't he given her all the information she needed so she wouldn't be caught like this? She breathed deeply and said the only thing she could. "It was fifteen years ago, Burt."

"You think our pain *ends*?"

"Of course not." Hers hadn't. Why would Burt and Dottie's? "But Julie and Cam made their decision a long time ago."

"So it was my girl's fault?" His eyes were wide with astonishment.

"I didn't say that. But Cam didn't force her to run. She went with him, as hard as that is to accept. She was with Cam. She ran away with him and stayed with him willingly." Beth wanted to blame Cam alone and so did Burt. But the truth was Julie had been a part of it all from the beginning. It took *two* to make a baby. And that thought twisted her heart until it was nothing more than a painful lump in her chest. He'd made a baby with Julie while making plans with Beth. How had she missed it?

Now is not the time, she told herself. "Burt, all Cam wants is a fair shot at joining the TCC."

"He'll have that," Burt said hotly, and ran his palm across the top of his head. "He has the right to apply for membership. Like I said, he won't have my vote, but it's not my place to block him from the club."

Cam would have to accept that, Beth told herself, because it was the best he was going to get from Burt Wheeler. Burt was well-known about town as a bully... loud and aggressive, but he was also a father still in pain at the tragic loss of his daughter. Beth reached out and laid one hand on his forearm.

"Thank you, Burt."

He jerked a nod.

"And I'm really sorry about everything. About dredging this up."

"You're a nice girl, Beth." He blew out a pent-up breath and gave her hand an awkward pat. Gruffly he said, "Your daddy was a pain in the ass, but you're a nice girl. And you didn't dredge up anything. Julie is always with me."

She couldn't blame him for not liking her father. Many people hadn't, including his own kids most of the time. As for the rest, she understood what he meant in saying that Julie was always with him. Cam had always been with her, too. Did that make her a fool?

As she left the Wheeler house, she was already planning just what she would have to say to Camden Guthrie.

Camden worked through the morning, hoping to ease his mind by concentrating on a single task—making sure the Longhorn cattle arrived safely to take their place on the Circle K rangeland. A couple of days ago, his ranch hands had temporarily fenced in a two-acre plot where the Longhorns could rest up for a day or two. Cam wanted to make sure they were all healthy and strong enough to be turned out to graze.

In spite of his mind twisting with thoughts of Beth—and the shock of seeing her with Justin McCoy of all damn people—he smiled as he watched the most quintessential Texas breed of cattle stepping down the ramps of the cattle truck. The Longhorns were wildly diverse in color: no two were alike, and the spread of their horns ranged from four feet to nearly nine.

The rattle of their hooves on metal and the clack of their horns slapping together filled the air. He caught more than a couple of the cowboys grinning like children just watching the legendary cattle slowly claim their new home.

"They're really something, aren't they, boss?" Henry Jordan sat his horse right beside Cam, and both men stared out at the cattle.

"They really are." It was a damn miracle the breed had been saved back in the 1920s. People had been smart enough to realize that crossbreeding with imported cattle was going to destroy the one breed that had evolved on their own to survive and thrive on the range without any help from humans.

"My boys are loving this. They've never seen a Longhorn up close," Henry said, pointing to where his three teenage sons were working the herd with the other cowboys.

"A lot of people haven't, Henry," Cam replied, leaning both hands on the pommel of his saddle. "But we're going to fix that with the dude ranch. Our tourists are going to get a glimpse of the real Texas."

His starting herd was small—two hundred head, with a lot of females and yearlings. It wouldn't take long for the herd to expand, and Cam welcomed it. He had plenty of open land for them to graze. All the ranch hands had to do was make sure they didn't drift onto the land reserved for the Black Angus cattle. Damned if he'd allow crossbreeding on his own ranch.

"The vet suggested we leave the herd penned in for at least a couple of days. Quarantine to make sure they're all healthy and give them time to eat and get their strength back after the travel." Even a two-day trip was hard on cattle. "You guys keep an eye on the herd, and by early next week, we'll move them down to the south pasture."

"You got it." Henry tipped the brim of his hat, then rode off to join the others.

Cam watched it all for a few more minutes, then headed back to the house to get his truck. He had one more appointment before meeting Beth that afternoon.

Seeing her at her office had cost him nearly every damn ounce of his self-control. It had taken all he had to keep from reaching for her. And what the hell was she doing with Justin McCoy hanging around? Scowling to himself, he kicked his horse into a gallop, hoping to drive that image out of his head.

McCoy was a snake and Cam had more reason than most to know it. Was Beth really foolish enough to hook herself up with that bastard? Because if she was, he'd be happy to step in and tell her the cold, hard truth about Justin McCoy.

Beth. It all came down to Beth. She was the same

and yet so different. She wasn't the open, laughing girl he'd once known. She'd grown, as he had. They'd changed and maybe that was best. It forced them both to get to know the people they were now—not just to depend on what had once been.

Beth had built herself a good life here and he admired that. He'd done well, too, so in that regard, they were on equal footing. Not like back in the day when she'd been a Wingate princess and he was a working cowboy.

Today she was so much more. Hell, he hadn't been able to think about anything but her for days. Her smile. Her scent. The taste of her. The way her eyes snapped with indignation when her temper was up. He'd missed her. In spite of his marriage to Julie, he'd never forgotten Beth.

The guilt of that had nibbled on him for years. And now thinking about Beth the way he was had that same guilt growing and snapping at him with razor-sharp teeth.

He'd known coming home to Royal wouldn't be a walk in the park, but damned if he'd figured that Beth would once again tangle him up in knots.

Naturally, the Royal Diner was crowded, and that was fine with Cam. He noticed people watching him, heard the whispers as he passed, and he paid them all no attention. Cam could put up with the staring and whispering. For a while.

Tony Alvarez was sitting at a booth overlooking Main Street, and Cam slid onto the bench seat opposite him. Tony's black hair was cut short, his brown eyes were sharp and his quick grin was the best welcome home Cam had had so far.

Sticking his right hand out, Tony said, "Damn, it's good to see you."

"You, too." Cam shook hands with his old friend, then eased back into the booth. "Been too long."

"Well, that's what happens when you move to California and get rich and famous."

"Look who's talking," Cam said, laughing. His old friend had played Major League Baseball and had made a hell of a name for himself before retiring.

Tony waved that off. "I played a game and got paid for it. You got on TV for knowing how to build things."

"I wasn't really famous," he said. His and Julie's show had done well for two years, but it was one of a dozen remodel shows. Then Julie had gotten sick, and everything ended.

"Rich though." Tony grinned again.

Cam laughed because Tony had always been the guy who said exactly what he was thinking. Even back in high school, you always knew just where you stood with him. It was a trait Cam admired and he was glad his old friend hadn't changed.

And, yes, he'd gotten richer than he'd ever thought possible. When he was a kid, he'd figured that making his own fortune would solve all of his problems. Yet now that he had more money than he could spend in two lifetimes, he knew money didn't solve anything. Made things easier, for damn sure, but the problems you had, you would still have. You'd just drive a better car and live in a bigger house.

Amanda Battles stepped up to the booth just then.

"Hi, Tony." Her gaze shifted. "Cam. It's good to see you home."

"Thanks." He smiled and meant it. "I appreciate it."

"Nate tells me you're doing a lot of work on the old Circle K."

"I am," Cam said, sliding a glance at his friend.

"Good." She nodded. "That tells me you're here to stay." Pulling an old-fashioned order pad out of her pocket, she poised her pen over it and asked, "What can we get you two?"

Once they'd both ordered, Amanda left them alone and Tony asked, "So what did you want to talk about?"

Cam sat back and laid his right arm along the top of the red vinyl booth bench. In high school, Tony and Cam had been best friends. They'd played on the championship baseball team and both had dreamed of making the bigs. The only difference between them was that Tony had actually made it. He'd played eight seasons for Houston before blowing out a knee, which had ended his career.

But Tony being Tony, that hadn't stopped him from finding success somewhere else.

"Are you still running that baseball camp of yours?"

"Oh, hell yes," Tony said with a smile. "Thanks, Pam," he murmured when Amanda's sister brought them both cups of coffee. Then back to Cam, he said, "It's bigger than ever. We've got forty kids lined up for this coming winter. Twenty in the first camp and twenty more in the second. I'm still renting the land we operate on. Soon though, I'm going to have to look for more land. Build a permanent site. Maybe hold camps all winter and up to spring training."

He held the coffee mug cupped in his palms. "I'm

thinking about doing a dream team thing for adults, too. Get the older guys who used to fantasize about playing big-league ball out to meet some players and have some fun."

Cam nodded, thinking. Tony's baseball camp had started out small about five years ago. Cam might not have been living in Royal, but that didn't mean he hadn't kept up with what his friends were doing. And in the last five years, Tony's business had really grown. Not only did he have the reputation on his own, but every year his old teammates showed up to impress the kids and to help them work on their games.

"That sounds great," Cam said. "Maybe I'll sign up, too."

Tony looked surprised. "Shoulder good enough?"

He rolled his right shoulder and smiled. "I can't throw the hundred-mile-an-hour fastball anymore, but I can hold my own."

"Good to know. So why are you asking about the camp?"

Cam shrugged, then grinned. "You said you're looking for a more permanent camp?"

"Yeah."

"As it happens, I've got twenty acres at my place that's available."

Tony paused with the coffee cup halfway to his mouth. "Are you serious?"

"Why not?" Cam leaned forward, bracing his elbows on the laminate table. "I'm looking at building a sort of 'dude ranch' at my place."

Tony stared at him for a second or two, then laughed. "No way. Why the hell would you want to do that? Cater to tourists and wannabe cowboys?"

In spite of his friend's words, Camden laughed. "Why not? I'll be running herds on the ranch—had some Longhorns arrive just yesterday…"

"Now that's cool."

"It is," he agreed. "But the thing is, when I was living in California, that place was so crowded, so jammed with people, some days it felt like you couldn't draw a breath.

"And every time someone found out I was from Texas, inevitably, their reaction was, *Oh, I've always dreamed of living on a ranch. Being under the stars.* And every other cliché you can think of."

"Yeah." Tony smiled up at Pam as she delivered his slice of apple pie. "They never think about all the work that goes into ranching."

"Exactly!" Cam glanced at their server and thanked her for his blackberry cobbler. When Pam was gone, he started talking again. "So the idea is to give city people the chance to live like country people, a week at a time. We can do riding lessons. Have bonfires at night, chuck wagon food…"

Tony took a bite of pie, chewed and swallowed. "And how does my baseball camp for kids fit into that?"

"Easy." Cam waved his fork at his buddy as he warmed to his subject. "We could be a big help to each other. Your baseball players might see the ranch and decide to come back. My tourists might like baseball."

Tony snorted a laugh. "Well, who doesn't like baseball?"

"Exactly." Cam grinned again and took a forkful of the cobbler. Meanwhile, he could see Tony thinking this through, and he was pretty sure his old friend was going to go for it.

Wouldn't hurt to sweeten the pie, though. "You know, with twenty acres, you could build a regulation diamond, a couple batting cages, pitching areas...and some bunkhouses for your campers to stay in."

"Hmm. That would be good."

"Think about it," Cam urged. "Where do the campers stay now?"

"At the inn outside of Royal," Tony admitted. "It would make it easier to have them all on-site..."

"Damn right it would." Cam had him and he knew it. Hell, he didn't need Tony's camp to be on the ranchland, but it'd be fun. And that in itself was a good enough reason.

"Hell, you could build yourself a house on the land and provide housing for all of your employees, too."

His friend's eyebrows arched at the suggestion and Cam could practically see the wheels in his mind turning.

Tony cut off another bite of pie and said, "You knew I'd say yes, didn't you?"

Cam shrugged. "You haven't said yes yet."

Laughing, Tony said, "Hell, of course it's yes."

"Great." They shook hands on it, then Cam said, "Why don't you come out to the ranch right now? We can plot out your twenty acres, then call Olivia Turner to tell her she's got another job to do."

Beth and Gracie had their list of potential donors to the silent auction to be held at the TCC masquerade ball in October. They'd already gotten promises from several of the business owners in town, but there were many more to contact.

After her visit with Burt, Beth didn't really feel up

to the task of talking to a lot of people. But this was her job and she was going to do it well. She wouldn't let Cam affect the life she'd built. Besides, once this task was finished, she'd be talking to him about all of this and she'd have her answers then.

"Do you want to split the list right down the middle?" Gracie asked. "I'll take the bottom half, you take the top?"

"That would probably be the best way to do it," Beth admitted. Then she looked at Gracie and smiled. "But it's more fun when we go together."

"True." Gracie laughed and reached for her cell phone when it rang. She glanced at the screen, then slid the phone back into her purse.

Beth sent her a questioning look. "You don't have to take it?"

"No, it's just my mom," Gracie said. "She's probably calling to tell me she and my brother have made it to Galveston safely."

Beth sighed. "A week at the beach. Sounds like heaven right now." Especially because it would get her out of Royal and away from Cam so she could do some serious thinking.

"I know. Mom loves the ocean so much I hate that she can't be there more often." Then Gracie gave a sharp nod. "When I win the PowerBall lottery, the first thing I'm going to do is buy Mom a huge house on the beach in Florida. She'd be near her sister, and that would make her happy, too."

Smiling, Beth said, "Big plans."

"Dreams," Gracie corrected wryly. "But dreams are wonderful, aren't they?"

Hers used to be, Beth admitted silently. When she

was a girl, she'd dreamed of a life with Cam. Of owning their own ranch and raising kids and horses. Eventually she had woken up and her dreams had dissolved under a good coating of reality. Still, this wasn't about her own shattered illusions.

"You bet. So, when you buy your mom that big house in Florida, are you going to move with her?"

Gracie flipped her long dark hair over her shoulder and shook her head. "No. Royal is home. I'd miss the people. My job. And—" She broke off as if worried she'd said too much. Then she added, "I wouldn't want to leave…"

There was something she wasn't saying and Beth studied her friend for a long moment or two before it dawned on her. "You've got a man and you haven't told me anything about him!"

"What?" Gracie looked at her, wide-eyed, shaking her head. "Who said anything about a man? I'm talking about my job. You. Royal."

"And a man." Beth laughed a little and drew the younger woman to a stop on the sidewalk. "Don't even try to deny it. Your eyes went all gooey for a second."

"I do not get gooey."

"Sadly, we all do at some point," Beth argued. "So spill. Who is this mystery man?"

Gracie sighed and looked around before fixing her gaze on Beth's again. "Nobody. At least, not for me. He doesn't know I'm alive."

Insulted on Gracie's behalf, Beth started talking. "Impossible. You're gorgeous. And smart. And amazing."

"Said my friend, being completely objective."

"Fine." Beth smiled at her. "So if you like this guy so much, why don't you tell him?"

Gracie shook her head firmly. "No, I can't do that."

"Oh, Gracie…"

"Beth, I know you mean well." Gracie winced and looked uncomfortable. "But can we not? I don't want to talk about him. Much less *think* about him."

"Sure. Case closed," Beth said. "Mostly because I know exactly how you feel."

She knew what it was like to be drawn to someone in spite of knowing it was futile. After all, she hadn't been able to smother her feelings for Cam even though she knew she should. So she really wasn't in any position to give relationship advice.

"So for the rest of the day," she said, hooking her arm through Gracie's, "*men* are off the conversational table."

"But just today, right?" Gracie smiled at her.

"Absolutely," Beth replied. "Come tomorrow, I make no promises."

"Good to know. Hey." Gracie pointed. "There's one of Lauren Roberts's food trucks. Didn't you say you wanted to talk to her about a donation?"

"Yes, I did." Beth looked at the side of the truck and grinned. Gracie Diaz was really good to spend time with. Even though Beth's heart was aching and her mind spinning with way too many thoughts and unanswered questions, she was able to enjoy herself. "Besides, tacos for lunch sounds good, doesn't it?"

Lauren was a fabulous chef and her food trucks were making a real impact on Royal. Luckily, Lauren herself was working the taco truck. When Beth got to the front of the line to order, she grinned up at the woman.

Lauren's shoulder-length dark brown hair was pulled back into a ponytail. She wore a pale blue T-shirt and jeans, and the two women working with her looked pretty much the same.

"Hi, Lauren. Can we get two taco plates and a couple bottles of water?"

She smiled. "Sure. How's it going, Beth? Gracie."

"Fine," Gracie answered. "We're out gathering donations for the TCC masquerade ball in October."

Lauren slid a suspicious glance at Beth as she made change from the twenty Beth had handed her. "And?"

"And..." Beth went on to say. "I was thinking you might want to donate one of your food trucks for a night. Say someone has a party and you could cater it..."

Lauren worked while she thought about that, and the scents wafting from the truck were making Beth even hungrier. The fact that there were two other women working the stove and the prep area was something else Beth liked about Lauren's business. She hired women to work for her, paid a great wage and gave them experience they could take anywhere.

"It would be great advertising for you," Gracie put in. "Plus it's for a good cause. The children's wing of the hospital."

"Oh, I know..." Lauren looked over Beth's head at the line gathering up behind her. "But to be honest, giving away catering for a party could get out of hand quickly. I don't know if I can afford to donate enough food for a party of sixty or something."

"She's got a good point," Gracie said, and lifted one shoulder in a shrug, as she looked to Beth.

"Okay, what if we put a limit on what people can

get?" Beth could see this being a really sought after prize, so she would just have to make Lauren see how brilliant it was. "What if we say you will donate catering for a party of ten? Can you do that?"

Lauren took the two taco plates from the woman working beside her and handed them down to Beth and Gracie. Then she got the water and passed it over, as well. "Ten?" She thought about it for a second, then nodded. "I can do that. They can even have their choice of food for the party."

"Excellent! Thank you so much, Lauren."

"You're welcome. Enjoy your lunch."

"We will." Beth nodded at Gracie and they moved aside to let the line surge forward. Finding an empty bench on the shady side of the bank building, they sat and toasted each other with icy water, tacos and Spanish rice.

Deliberately Beth kept her thoughts from straying to Camden Guthrie. Her confrontation with him would come soon enough.

Six

At Cam's ranch, he and Tony were checking out the land he was going to lease his old friend. He could have just given him the land or even sold it to him outright. But this way was better—taxwise, for Tony's growing business.

"It's been a long time since I was on a horse," Tony admitted ruefully. "I'll be lucky to walk tomorrow."

Cam laughed. Tugging his Stetson down lower over his eyes, he braced his hands on the pommel of his saddle and stared out at the property. "Horseback is the best way to see the land," he said with satisfaction. Then he shot a quick grin at his pal. "Besides, you're a Texan man, have some pride."

"Oh, I've got plenty of pride," Tony assured him. "just not on the back of a horse." He winced as he shifted position in the saddle. "Not anymore, at least."

He tipped his head to one side. "Looks like you kept riding even when you were in California."

"Oh, yeah." He and Julie had lived in Orange County, not exactly a horse-friendly place. Too much asphalt. Too many houses, cars and people. Since he'd missed the feel of being out in the open, just him and his mount, Cam had found a stable in Irvine Ranch that allowed him to board a horse and explore what had once been the largest privately held ranch in California.

Of course, the Irvine family had sold off huge sections of their holdings over the years, but there were still hills and valleys that were unspoiled and just right for what he'd needed.

But being back in Texas fed Cam's soul in a way he hadn't known he needed. With the afternoon sun blasting down on them from a clear blue sky, it was a picture-perfect Texas day, even if the heat would soon be murderous in the middle of summer.

Turning to look at Tony again, he asked, "What do you think of the property?"

The other man's gaze swept the meadow that was surrounded by oaks before shifting his gaze to Cam. "Honestly, it's perfect. Are you sure you want to do this?"

"Absolutely," Cam said, his voice firm enough to convince his friend. "This section is far enough from the main house that your 'campers' won't interfere with the ranch. And it's close enough that I can ride down here when I get a need for some baseball."

Tony grinned. "Still miss it, don't you?"

"I do." Nodding, he said, "In high school, I was sure you and I would go to college together, then get drafted by the same big-league team. I pictured us playing to-gether for years."

"Yeah, me too. The best fastball pitcher in Texas with the best damn catcher in the world."

Cam laughed. "I was the best in Texas, but you got the world?"

Tony laughed, too, and Cam realized how much he'd missed this. Being with people he'd known his whole life. Being in the place where he'd grown up. Had roots. Connections.

"Long-term lease?" his friend asked.

"A hundred dollars a year for fifty years. How's that sound?"

"Perfect," Tony said. "Still don't know why you want to do this, but I'm grateful." He looked out at the land again and so did Cam. It was as if the two old friends were staring at what would soon be. The dug-outs, the fields, the batting cages. The kids, shrieking, laughing, discovering a love for baseball.

With another sigh of satisfaction, Cam said, "I'll call my lawyers. Get things moving." He turned his horse's head toward home, then looked back at Tony, who hadn't moved.

"You coming?"

"That depends. Any chance you could send a jeep back to get me?"

"Not a single one," Cam told him with a grin.

"I figured," Tony said with a half groan. "The things I do for baseball."

Beth was waiting on the porch when Cam and Tony rode into the yard. A jolt of electricity seemed to hit him dead center of the chest and left him wondering if he would always react to her like that.

Taking the front steps down to the graveled drive, she waited for them, and in the sunlight her hair looked like gold. Her eyes were hidden behind a pair of oversize sunglasses, and her mouth was firmed into a straight line. She wore cream-colored slacks, an emerald green shirt with short sleeves and a high stand-up collar, and a pair of heeled sandals that displayed toes painted a bright purple. A slight wind lifted her hair off her shoulders and it shone like an aura around her head.

"Beth!" Tony said as he slid gracelessly from his horse. "What're you doing here?" He shot a look at Cam. "Are you two on again?"

"No," Beth said before Cam could do it. "Definitely not."

There was a bite in her voice that hadn't been there before, and Cam gave her a curious glance. She ignored it.

"I'm just here to help him with some plans for his guest ranch."

"Uh-huh." Tony looked from one to the other of them, and the expression on his face said plainly that he didn't believe that for a second. Cam had always said Tony was a smart man.

Beth shook her head, walked a few steps and hugged Tony. "It's good to see you, though. What're you doing here?"

"Getting the land I need for my baseball camp," he said with a grateful nod at Cam.

"Really?" She looked at Cam, too, and he wished she'd take off the sunglasses so he could get an idea of what she was thinking, feeling. Instead, she kept those feelings hidden from him.

Cam shrugged. "It's a good deal for both of us."

"Better for me, not that I'm complaining." Tony hugged Beth again before letting her go.

It was a bitch to be jealous of your old friend embracing the woman you yourself wanted to be holding.

"But right now," Tony said, "I'm going to hobble home and get into the hot tub."

"Pitiful, man…"

Tony laughed. "Yeah, we'll see how you feel when I get you out on the pitcher's mound for the first time in years."

"Deal."

Once his friend was gone, Beth plucked her sunglasses off and looked up at Cam. He read the banked anger in those green depths made darker and greener by the shirt she wore.

"Let's get out of the sun," he said, and waved one arm toward the house. She hesitated briefly as if trying to decide if she should go in or not; finally she took the porch steps up to the front door and stepped inside.

Cam led her into the great room and watched her take it in. He hadn't been back long, but getting your house furnished quickly wasn't a problem if you were willing to pay for express delivery.

Chocolate leather couches and chairs were spread around the room. Heavy oak tables held brass lamps with cream shades, and the rugs on the wide-plank dark floor were in deep tones of red and gold. The stone fireplace took up most of one wall, and a big-screen TV held a place of honor on another. It was a man's room and he knew it. Most people would say it needed a woman's touch, but as far as Cam could tell, it was perfect just as it was.

"The house still needs some work. And I'm going to do some remodeling, but the structure's sound enough."

"Well, it is about one hundred years old, so a little work isn't out of line," she murmured.

"That's what I thought."

Beth turned to look at him. He noticed the anger was still there, glittering like shards of ice in the forest of her eyes.

"Remember how we used to make plans for this place?"

"I remember," she answered. "I remember we made a lot of plans back then."

"Yeah." He pulled off his hat, set it crown down on the closest table and ran his hands through his hair again. "We did."

"And now that you're back, you're making a heck of a statement. The donation to the hospital. Now Tony's baseball camp."

She didn't sound pleased by any of it. "Is it so hard to believe that I'm back to stay? That I want to be a part of Royal?"

"You left before, Cam," she said. "Why wouldn't you go again?"

"Because that's done. Because I *chose* to come home. Because it's where I want to be."

"Right." She nodded stiffly. Her shoulders were rigid, her chin lifted and her eyes were still bristling with emotions. "And I should take your word for that."

"What's going on, Beth?" His gaze locked with hers, and mentally he braced himself for whatever was coming. Clearly, it wasn't good.

"I went to see Burt Wheeler today."

That would explain the mood she was in. Burt was a hard man to talk to under the best of circumstances. And since she'd been there on Cam's behalf, it couldn't have been easy.

"Yeah? How'd it go?"

She dropped her purse on a table and looked at him. "As you expected it to." She tucked her hair behind her ears, and her gold earrings glittered in the sunlight sliding in through the front windows. "He's not happy, but he'll put your name up for membership because it's his job. He just won't vote for you."

"More than I thought he'd do." Cam ran one hand across the back of his neck and then shoved both hands into his pockets. He didn't much like the idea of sending Beth to his father-in-law as a go-between. He usually handled his own business. His own problems. But he hadn't had much choice, either. Joining the TCC was elemental to any plans he was going to set into motion now that he was home. "Thanks. I know it wasn't easy."

"No, it wasn't," Beth admitted, then shrugged. "But it was our bargain, right?"

"Yeah." Nodding, Cam kept his gaze fixed on her because he had a feeling another shoe was about to drop. "But something tells me there's more chewing you up inside. So why don't you just say it, Beth?"

Beth felt his steady stare as she would have his hands on her body. He'd always had the ability to look at her as if he was seeing something deep inside of her. She'd felt at times that she couldn't keep a secret from him because somehow Cam would know. Apparently, though, he had no problem at all hiding truths he wanted locked away.

She'd been holding herself together ever since leaving Burt Wheeler's place. She'd smiled through lunch with Gracie, then made a few more donation stops before dropping her friend off at her home. It was only then she'd given her emotions full rein. Only then that she allowed herself to really think about what Burt had said.

Julie. Pregnant.

She looked up at the man standing in front of her and accepted that she'd been wrong about Cam fifteen years ago. She'd believed he'd never leave. And he had. She had believed he loved her—but he'd apparently been sleeping with Julie, too.

"Beth?" His voice was low, almost intimate, and that was what pushed her into blurting out the truth.

"Burt told me Julie was pregnant when the two of you ran away."

God. Fresh pain welled up and stung her eyes with tears she absolutely refused to shed. He'd betrayed her even more completely than she'd once believed. Just thinking about it now made her want to block everything from her mind so the pain would stop.

But she couldn't do that. She had to know. Staring up at Cam, she waited for him to say something. *Anything.* But his features were cold and hard. His dark brown eyes were shadowy places where the truth lay hidden.

Yet he didn't deny it. How could he?

Beth's heart ached more with every silent second that ticked past. As she watched him, she saw his eyes fill with sympathy. Regret. That told her everything she needed to know.

Shaking her head, she turned away from him until he finally spoke.

"I'm sorry, Beth. I should have thought that Burt would say something."

"Oh, God." She turned to him again and slapped one hand to her chest to try to ease the pain of her heart being squeezed by a giant cold fist. "Julie *was* pregnant."

"Yes."

One word. Clipped. No explanation. Then again, she ranted internally, how could there be? How could he possibly explain getting another girl pregnant while he was Beth's boyfriend?

"Thank you for that, anyway," she muttered.

"What?"

"For not denying it. For not lying to me. Again. My God, what an idiot I was." She choked out a laugh. "No wonder my father wanted to break us up. He knew I wasn't able to see you for who you really were."

"You did see me."

"Not then. But I do now."

"Damn it, Beth…" Cam stood there, hands at his sides, looking into her eyes as if willing her to give him a chance to explain. But what could he say? And why should she listen?

"No. There's nothing you can say that makes this all right," she murmured.

"I'm not going to try to explain. You wouldn't believe me anyway," he said, and irritation was clear in his tone. "Your mind is set on one thing, and you don't want to see the other side."

"What possible other side is there?" she demanded.

He scrubbed one hand across his jaw and shook his head grimly. "You're too emotional about this to hear me out."

Beth's eyes went wide and she actually felt her jaw drop. "Seriously?" she asked, stunned. "I'm too emotional? So I'm the bad guy here?"

"Who said there has to be a bad guy?" His demand rang out in the otherwise still room and seemed to hang in the air.

Beth stared at him as if she'd never seen him before. And maybe she hadn't. Not really. As a kid, she'd seen him through rainbows and flowers. Since he'd come back home, she'd seen him through the fog of memory and maybe it was only now that she was seeing Camden for who he actually was. It broke her heart.

"One of us cheated on the other one," Beth said, and gave herself points for keeping a check on the rage inside. "One of us got someone pregnant." She whirled around, took three quick steps toward the stone fireplace on the far wall, then spun back again to face him. "There is no other side to this, Cam. I was your girlfriend and the girl you *married* was pregnant."

A single tear escaped and Beth swiped it away hurriedly, hoping to hell he hadn't seen it. She wasn't going to give him her tears again. God knew she'd cried oceans of them all those years ago.

Cam pushed both hands through his hair, then let them fall. It was more than regret in his eyes now. There was surprise, as well. And anger. "How can you think I cheated on you?"

Wide eyed, she stared at him. "How can I not? You

married Julie. She was pregnant. What else am I supposed to think?"

His features were grim as he watched her, and Beth would have given anything to know what he was thinking. Were his thoughts racing, trying to find a way out of this? Trying to somehow make having a child with another woman a happy thing? That thought prompted her next question.

"And while we're on the subject," she added, lifting her chin and locking her gaze with his. "Where is your child? Should be almost fifteen, right? Boy or girl?"

The muscle in Cam's jaw twitched as if he were chewing over what he wanted to say. Finally he simply said, "Julie lost the baby when she was five months pregnant."

That stopped her for a moment. He'd cheated on her. Beth remembered the never ending wave of pain at being so completely discarded that the echoes of it could make her chest hurt. But she wouldn't have wished his child gone. "I'm sorry, Cam."

His gaze flicked to hers, and his eyes went cool and distant in a second.

"I'm not talking about this with you," he muttered. "Not now."

She laughed and the sound scraped across her throat. "Not then and not now. Perfect. That's great. You didn't tell me you were leaving and now that you're back, you won't tell me why any of it happened. Fantastic."

Beth grabbed her purse and slung the slender gold chain strap over her shoulder. "Enjoy the TCC membership, Camden."

When she stalked past him, he reached for her, but she pulled her arm away before he could grab hold.

"No. You don't get to do that. Touch me as if we still have something between us."

"There will *always* be something between us, Beth." His voice was so low she could hardly hear it. And maybe that was just as well. She was trembling, hurting and so furious at her own gullibility that she could hardly see.

"No, Camden. That ended a long time ago. When you betrayed me."

"Oh, no," he countered. "I'm willing to stand here and take everything else you said to me because I figure you've got a right. But you don't get to say I betrayed you."

Beth nodded jerkily. "Right. I forgot. *You're* the injured party here."

He didn't rise to that bait. Instead, he said simply, "You tore my heart out."

She pushed her hair back. "And you stomped on mine. Do we call it a tie?"

"We call it over." His eyes never left hers. His features were tight and his voice a deep whisper when he said, "It's done, Beth. Fifteen years done."

Her breaths were short and fast. Her heart was beating ferociously, and she told herself to get a grip. How could he stand there so calmly? She felt as if she were going to explode, but she couldn't as long as he was being so damn reasonable.

She wouldn't give him the satisfaction of seeing just how he could still affect her. Stiffly she nodded, though it cost her. How could she look into his eyes and want him so much it made her ache—in spite of their past?

Was he right about calling the past done and over?

Could she leave it where it belonged and move forward? How could she if she couldn't trust him?

"And what are you suggesting?" she asked, suddenly tired and sure that her wildly swinging emotions were to blame for that. "We start over?"

He sighed, tipped his head back and stared at the ceiling for a slow count of three. Then he looked at her again. "We're not starting anything up, right? We're just going to learn to deal with living near each other again. That was the deal."

"Yeah, we're full of deals," Beth murmured darkly. She hated it, but he was right. They weren't starting anything. They weren't a couple any more than she and Justin were. And a part of her ached with that knowledge. "Fine. We go from here. Not friends. Not lovers. Just…what, exactly?"

"Hell if I know."

She laughed again and this time it was a little less painful. "That, at least, is honest."

"I didn't lie to you."

Beth held up one hand. "I don't want to talk about it." Taking a breath, she reached for something—anything to get them off the subject of their past. "You wanted to show me what you had in mind for your guest cottages, right?"

"Yeah," he said, keeping a wary eye on her as if half-waiting for her to explode again. "The plans are in the dining room."

"Great." Better than great. This gave her something to do. Something to think about besides a pregnant Julie and a cheating Cam. She followed him across the foyer to the formal dining room.

There was some truly hideous red-and-black-flocked

wallpaper, but the space was huge and boasted windows on both walls. At the moment, the drapes were drawn as if Cam didn't want anyone else to have to see that wallpaper.

A huge reclaimed pine table sat in the center of the room and had ten chairs pulled up to it. The light fixture over the table was brass, with long arms and clear glass light globes attached to the ends.

Architect renderings and blueprints were scattered across the table, and Beth had to wonder why he needed her. At a glance she saw he had the layout of the cabins well planned.

"It looks like you've already got things set," she said, and took a closer look at the first sketch of a would-be cabin.

"They're bare-bones and—no offense to the LA architect—pretty cookie-cutter." He sighed. "I had these drawn up a year ago."

Surprise flickered through her. She shifted her gaze to him. "You've been planning to come back for a while, then."

He nodded. "It's been on my mind for a few years now. Having these done made it seem more real. Immediate. Most of the new developments out in California look like they've been stamped out on an assembly line, so that's what they design."

She half-laughed. "You really didn't like California."

He looked at her thoughtfully. "It's really not that bad. Its main problem for me was that it wasn't Texas. I wanted to be here. Now that I am, I want something different. I want the cabins to look like they *belong* there. A part of the ranch itself."

"Yeah, you said that." Idly Beth picked up a pencil and sketched a porch on one of the cabin drawings, then added window boxes and rockers on the porch. She had never been much of an artist, but it didn't look too bad to her eye. "Better?"

"Yes." He smiled at her, and her breath caught.

She didn't want to feel for him. Didn't want to be drawn to him. But it seemed what she wanted and what was happening were two separate things.

"You can make each cabin different by adding little finishes or even by differing the structures themselves. Arched doorways, painted different colors." She lifted one shoulder in a shrug. "Log cabins, Victorians, bungalows, hobbit houses. Give them each a personality."

"You're good at this," he mused.

His voice was too soft. He was standing too close. He smelled too good. Beth had come here riding on fury, but that had passed, leaving her feeling hollowed out. She still didn't have answers, but what she did have, as always, was this driving need for Camden Guthrie.

"I should go," she said.

"Don't."

Looking up into his eyes, she fought with herself internally. Beth knew she should leave, but her feet wouldn't move. She knew that if she stayed, nothing would be resolved. It was more likely the problems and mistrust between them would only grow. Sex wasn't in itself an answer and often just led to muddying things up even more.

"You're looking at me like you're trying to solve a mystery."

"Maybe I am," she admitted.

"It's just not that complicated, Beth."

"Please." She shook her head and nearly smiled. "You've always been complicated, Camden."

"There you're wrong," he said, moving in a little closer so that she couldn't breathe without taking his scent inside her. "When it came to you, I wasn't complicated at all."

She sighed, still trying to stop what was inevitably crashing toward her. "Until you left with another woman."

"You don't understand, Beth," he said. "Any of it."

"Then explain it to me. After all these years, *tell* me."

He frowned. "We open this door—there's no going back."

"Maybe there shouldn't be," Beth said, even knowing that what she might hear could tear her heart to pieces. "We keep twisting the doorknob, but we never open it. Never look. Isn't it better to *know* the truth?"

He studied her, and emotions darted across the surface of his eyes so quickly she couldn't have named them all.

Maybe she was crazy to open this all up now. Maybe it would be better if she never knew what had happened so long ago. But if she didn't take this step, her dreams would always be tortured. She would always wonder how he could have chosen Julie over her.

Keeping her gaze locked with his, she asked, "Julie was pregnant. Were you cheating on me the whole time? Were you and Julie laughing at me?"

"What? *No.*" He turned and kicked the wall, then

whipped back around to face her. "How could you think that?"

"How could I not?" she countered. "We were together for three years and then suddenly you and Julie run away to get married? What the hell, Camden?"

"We're just going to jump right in, huh? Fine." He took a step closer. "Like you said, we were together three years. We had plans, too, Beth. Or did you forget all about them that last night we were together when you shot it all down and tossed us aside? Tossed *me* aside?"

"I didn't do that."

"The hell you didn't." His voice was tight and low and thrumming with the same anger she felt. "Instead of getting married and going off to college together, you said you needed 'time.' That you were too young all of a damn sudden. *We* were too young."

She remembered it all as clearly as he did. "We were, Cam. I was only eighteen."

"Didn't bother you before that night. What the hell changed?" The challenge was clear in his tone. "Was it your father? He hated you being with an 'Indian.'"

"You're wrong." Beth shook her head firmly. "He didn't care about that. What he cared about was that you had no money. No prospects. He wanted us to wait. Was that really so wrong?"

"No, what was wrong was you parroting everything your old man said and then acting like it was your version of the truth."

Beth took a deep breath and blinked frantically to hold back tears of frustration. "All I said was I wanted to wait. To take some time apart to make sure."

"Translation—" he bit off. "We're done."

"No. You're wrong." She stormed closer, too, and poked his chest with her index finger. "That may be what you heard, but I never said I didn't want you. God help me," she admitted, her voice dropping. "Even after everything that's happened I *still* want you."

Seven

Cam grabbed her as they'd both known he would.

He pulled her in close, kissed her senseless, then lifted his head and stared down into her eyes. Beth got lost there, as she always had. It didn't matter what else was going on. This amazing, nearly magical feeling of being held by him would always drive her. She'd missed him so much. Missed *them* so much that now that he was holding her again, she could think of nothing else.

Her mouth was buzzing from that kiss, her blood bubbling in her veins, and all she could see was him. Maybe this had been unavoidable after all. This slow slide into Camden's arms.

Staring into his eyes, she whispered, "This solves nothing."

"Maybe it doesn't have to," he said softly, his gaze

moving over her face as if he'd hungered for no more than simply seeing her again.

"Maybe not," she agreed as her heart began to race. "No more talking."

"None," he muttered, and kissed her again. His mouth ravaged hers, taking, giving, demanding. She was breathless as his lips, teeth and tongue claimed every inch of her mouth and silently demanded more.

He scraped his hands up and down her back, and all she could think was that she had too many clothes on. She needed to feel his hands on her skin.

As if he'd heard that stray thought, Cam tore his mouth from hers and looked down into her eyes as he tugged the hem of her shirt free of her slacks. Sliding one hand beneath the cool green fabric, he skimmed his fingertips across her abdomen and then up to cup her breast, and even through the fragile lace, she felt the heat of him.

His thumb and forefinger tweaked at her nipple and a shiver swept over her. Need erupted and she moaned softly, arching into him, pushing her breast into his hand, wishing her bra off and away. Then he took care of that, too. He flicked open the closure between her breasts and then he was touching her. Skin to skin, the heat overwhelming.

Beth stared up at him and saw her past, her present, her future, staring back at her. For her it had always been Camden. And maybe it always would be.

"Gotta get this off," he murmured, shifting his hold on her so he could work on the tiny buttons lining the front of her shirt. "Have to touch you. Feel you."

"Yes." She watched his strong hands and nimble fingers make short work of the buttons, then shrugged out of the shirt and tossed it onto the table as soon as he was finished. He slid her bra straps down her shoulders and let the pale blue lace drop to the floor.

"You're even more beautiful than I remembered," he whispered, and bent his head to take first one hardened nipple then the other into his mouth.

A groan erupted from her throat. She tipped her head back and stared unseeing at the ceiling. Her knees were weak, but Cam had one arm hooked around her waist holding her up as his mouth did incredible things to her body. His lips and tongue pulled at her nipples. The edges of his teeth scraped the tender flesh, and when he suckled her she felt the pull all the way down to her toes. She held on to his shoulders, digging her fingers into the fabric of his white shirt and the whipcord muscles beneath it.

When he dropped his free hand to the clasp of her slacks, then dipped his fingers beneath the elastic band of her panties to drive deeply into her heat, Beth exploded with an orgasm so shattering it stole her breath. She hadn't meant to come so quickly. Hadn't expected to. But her body had been starved for him for so long that his barest touch had driven her over the edge.

He held her while she trembled and rode the wave of the sensations claiming her. When she finally drew a breath again, she looked up into his eyes and found hunger stamped there so blatantly she almost came again.

"Upstairs," he said tightly.

"Yes," Beth answered. "Quickly."

"You read my mind," he admitted. Grabbing her shirt off the table, he swung her into his arms and headed for the stairs.

"I can walk," she told him, looking up into the harsh, taut planes of his face as he took the stairs two at a time.

"Not fast enough." He kept his gaze fixed ahead and she watched him, feeling her stomach swirl with the overwhelming reactions he caused in her. Seeing the blatant need on his features only inflamed her own.

Beth tore at the buttons on his shirt, and when two of them popped free she slid one hand across his chest as he made a left turn at the landing. He hissed in a breath at her touch and she smiled, knowing that she affected him as strongly as he did her.

Her fingers defined his hard, muscled chest, and all she could think was she wanted to be lying on top of him. To feel their bodies pressed together. Then he stalked into a room at the end of the hall and Beth took a quick look around.

The huge square room was as deliberately masculine as the great room downstairs. A massive four poster bed covered in a bloodred duvet took dominance and, frankly, was the only piece of furniture she was interested in at the moment. And still, she noticed the two chairs pulled up in front of a brick fireplace. The dressers, the bookcases, and the flat screen television on the wall facing the bed.

Then her mental tour was over as Cam dropped her onto the mattress and stood looking down at her. He wasted no time tearing his shirt off and tossing it aside. Beth kicked off her heeled sandals and squirmed out of her slacks and panties, all the while watching Camden remove his boots and jeans. And when he was standing beside the bed naked, she took a moment to just enjoy the view.

His body was hard and muscled, speaking more of years of hard work than a gym. As he stared down at her, she saw his eyes flash with the same raw desire peaking inside her. Gazes locked, he reached into the bedside table drawer, pulled out a condom and, ripping it open, sheathed himself in seconds. Then he moved so quickly she hardly saw the action. He caught her legs in his hands and pulled her to the edge of the mattress.

"Camden…"

"We agreed," he reminded her. "No more talking."

"Yes, but—"

He knelt before her and lowered his mouth to her center. Instantly, talking was the last thing on Beth's mind. She gasped at the sensation of his mouth and tongue working her most sensitive flesh. Again and again, he licked at her, suckling at the center bud until Beth thought she would lose her mind. She tried to twist and writhe on the bed to ease the ache, the tingles of expectation building inexorably inside, but Cam held her fast to the bed. She was caught in his grasp, and there was nowhere else she wanted to be.

The only sound was the soft purr of the air conditioner. The duvet beneath her felt cool and silky on her skin. Her breath wheezed in and out of her lungs as Camden drove her quietly insane.

His hot breath brushed against her as his tongue stroked her into a frenzy of need so wild it made that first shattering orgasm feel insignificant in comparison. He took her to the very brink of explosion time and again and, each time, pulled her back before allowing her to fall.

She reached down, threaded her fingers through his

hair and tugged, making him look at her, making him see what he was doing to her. "Don't stop, Camden."

"Need to be inside you," he muttered, and this time when he pushed her to the very edge of oblivion, he pulled away, shifted her on the bed and then covered her body with his.

This was what she'd craved, Beth thought wildly. This melding of bodies, this press of his flesh to hers. The feel of his heart pounding against hers. And when he drove his body into hers, Beth lifted both of her legs, wrapping them around his hips as she tried to take him more deeply.

His body pounded into hers and she rocked with him, riding the rhythm he set, breathless as she scored his back with her fingernails. She tucked her face into the curve of his neck and bit him as the first explosion roared through her.

He groaned and pumped faster, harder, driving them both in their frenzy to finally at long last feel the crash of release they both needed so badly. Her insides coiled, tighter, tighter, building toward something earth-shattering. Cam raised his head and she shifted to take his mouth, to tangle her tongue with his, to draw his breath into her lungs and give him hers.

But when her climax hit her with the force of a hundred orgasms at once, Beth pulled her mouth free and screamed out his name. Head back, eyes wide, she felt herself splinter into a million pieces and didn't care. Tremors rattled her body as he drove her on and on, never stopping.

Beth wrapped her arms around his neck and held on to him as the only stable point in her suddenly spinning universe. She was still clinging to him when Cam's body exploded into hers, and together they took that fall.

A few minutes later, Cam was still trying to catch his breath. With Beth tucked into his side, he stared up at the beamed ceiling and fought his own internal struggle. Being with Beth again had soothed corners of his soul that he hadn't even realized had been ragged and worn.

And he didn't feel even slightly guilty about that. Which made him feel a pang of guilt. Hell, he'd been *married* to a woman he'd come to love, and he'd never once experienced anything like what he'd just survived with Beth. His heart was still racing and his dick was ready to go again—in spite of what his mind was currently torturing him with.

"Camden?"

He blew out a breath and turned his head to look at her. Beth's hair was a tangle of gold, and her green eyes shone in the afternoon light. Her mouth was bruised and puffy, and she had one leg hooked across him.

All he wanted was to gather her up and have her again. To feel that magical moment when his body became a part of hers. But as they'd already discovered, that wouldn't solve anything.

"That was…"

"Yeah, it was," he said, and shifted, going up on one elbow to look down at her.

She pushed a hand through her hair, swiping it back from her face. Afternoon sunlight drifted through the windows, slanting across the bed, throwing her eyes into shadow. He used to be fascinated by her eyes, Cam thought. Everything she felt was reflected there.

He always knew what she was thinking because her eyes kept no secrets.

But now she guarded her mysteries. There was a wall between them now—and a part of him was grateful for it.

Their connection was fragile and it should probably stay that way. He wasn't looking for the kind of relationship with Beth that he'd once dreamed of. Today they were different people. The fact that the heat between them had only intensified didn't change a damn thing. In fact, it complicated things further.

"You don't have to get that look on your face," Beth warned.

"What look?"

"The one that clearly reads, *How close is the nearest exit?*"

He scowled at her. "Think you know me so well, do you?"

"Absolutely," she said, then tipped her head to one side. "Tell me I'm wrong."

"You're wrong. That's not what I was thinking at all."

"Great," she said. "Then what?"

"Just that this doesn't—"

"Matter? I know. We both knew that going in, didn't we?"

All he could do was stare at her. Why was she being so damn reasonable? Where was her fury from earlier? Was she really so able to compartmentalize this and tuck it away into the back of her mind? He had been prepared to pull back, to explain that they couldn't go forward from here. Now that she'd done it for him, Cam wasn't sure what to say.

"Relax, Camden." Beth scooted up higher on the pillows banked behind them. "I don't want anything from you."

That was a little insulting. "Why the hell not?"

"Because when I needed you, you left." She shrugged. "Why would I make the same mistake all over again?"

A punch to the gut would have been easier to take. "Are we back to that, then?"

"We never left it. There are too many unanswered questions hanging in the air between us, Cam."

"You want answers?" He'd kept his mouth shut about what had happened fifteen years ago. He'd never talked about it and had rarely thought about it once his decision to marry Julie had been made. Seemed like the time had come.

"You want answers?" he repeated. "Fine. Here's one. Up to you if you believe it or not."

She watched him through suspicious eyes. "Go ahead."

"Burt was right. Julie was pregnant when we got married."

"Yeah, thanks. I know that part." She pulled the edge of the duvet up and over her as if it were a shield.

"What you don't know is the baby wasn't mine." He'd never said those words out loud before. Cam rubbed the center of his chest, aware that it felt as though a heavy weight had suddenly been lifted off of him.

Her brow furrowed, and she looked at him as if he were speaking a foreign language. "What? Why? Who? Why did you marry her if it wasn't your baby? Who was the father?"

"That I won't tell you," he said firmly with a shake of his head. "It was Julie's secret to share or not."

She huffed out an exasperated breath. "You just expect me to take your word for it?"

"I told you. Believe it or not, that's up to you." He locked his gaze with hers. "But ask yourself. Why the hell would I lie?"

Beth glared at him. "I've got better questions. Why would you leave me and marry her, knowing she was carrying someone else's baby?"

He felt the scowl on his face and worked to ease it. Hadn't he just told her that this was all fifteen years gone? Wasn't it time to get it out there?

"After you and I split up—" When she opened her mouth to argue the point, he held up one hand. "Just let me tell it."

"Fine." She folded her arms over her chest, and he saw the defensive gleam in her eyes.

"I found Julie crying the next day." He closed his eyes briefly, remembering. "Sobbing like her heart was broken, and I guess it was. Anyway, I knew how she felt."

Beth's mouth worked as if she were biting back words clamoring to get out.

"She was pregnant and terrified to tell her father. Hell," he said grimly. "You know Burt. Can you imagine how he'd have taken that news?"

She nodded. "About as well as my father would have."

"Exactly. She said the baby's father was pushing her to marry him. He had plans for his own future, and that included getting a rich girl pregnant so he could worm his way into her family and bank accounts. Julie wouldn't marry him once she found that out. And she couldn't bear the thought of an abortion. Giving the baby up wasn't an option, either, because she had nowhere to go until she had the baby. She didn't know what to do. Asked me to help her. So I did."

"And getting married was your big solution?"

"Got me out of Royal," he said bluntly. "Away from you."

Beth choked out a laugh, slid off the bed and grabbed his white shirt off the floor. Pulling it on, the hem of the thing hit her midthigh, and rather than making her look more covered, Cam thought it only made her sexier.

"You had to get away from me."

"Yeah." He got up, too, and didn't bother to grab clothes. What was the point? "We were over and I couldn't stay here to watch you hook up with someone new."

"We weren't *done*."

"As far as I was concerned we were."

She shook her hair back from her face, and that long, blond tangle made him want to thread his fingers through it. He wanted her again. Always. And that was damned lowering.

"Then Julie lost the baby."

"Yeah."

"Why didn't you divorce, then? The reason for the marriage was over. You could have come back. Come home."

To me was left unsaid, but it felt like those two words were hanging in the air like a neon sign.

"Because we were married. I promised to stay with her." He rubbed one hand against the back of his neck.

"And I did. But there were…complications with the miscarriage and Julie needed an emergency hysterectomy."

"Oh, God…"

Nodding, he just looked at her as he finished, "I couldn't leave her then. And by that time, I knew I couldn't come back here. You weren't mine anymore, and I knew you'd never understand what I did anyway…"

"You were right about that," she said. "I still don't."

He nodded. "Yeah, I get that. But you wanted the truth and now you have it. What're we going to do with it?"

"I don't know," Beth admitted hoarsely. She held the edges of his shirt together with a fist in the center of her chest.

Another defensive move?

Everything in him urged him to tumble her back onto the bed, where they could work out whatever problems they had in the one way that had always worked for them. But he didn't. Because sex—even spectacular sex—couldn't build the bridge they needed between them.

For years he'd been a husband. He hadn't cheated. He'd been loyal and had eventually come to love his wife.

It was different than what he had had with Beth, but no less important. Still, now that he'd been with Beth again, he could admit that he was finally letting Julie go. And that bothered him enough that his voice sounded colder than he might have intended.

"I can't tell you what's coming. Who the hell could?" Irritation clawed at his throat and fought with the desire already pulsing inside him again. "All I know is I want you. Always have. Always will. What we do with that…"

"Right." Beth took a deep breath and lifted her chin when she looked at him. "I might never be okay with what you did."

"I didn't ask you to be," he reminded her.

"I can't trust you," she said.

That slammed into him, and he didn't like the feel of it at all. "I didn't betray you."

"From your perspective."

"That's the only one I've got."

She smiled briefly, and even that slight curve of her mouth sent a charge through Cam's system that almost stole his breath. How had he forgotten what it was like to touch her? To be inside her? Had he deliberately forgotten so that he could survive the years without her? Whatever the reason, it didn't matter now. She was here. With him. The long time without her had only made the hunger that much more overpowering.

"Anyway," Beth continued as if he hadn't spoken. She walked around the end of the bed and stopped just a foot or so in front of him. A slash of sunlight bathed her in a soft golden glow that made her shine even more than she usually did.

"You said it yourself. That was fifteen years ago." Her gaze locked with his, and in the shadows of her eyes he read a fire that they'd rekindled only minutes ago. "We're not kids now, Camden," she whispered. "And I don't believe in hearts and flowers and happily-ever-afters anymore."

She said it so simply that he believed her, and he hated it. Cam had always loved Beth's ability to believe in good things. To see the best in everything and rush to meet it. Until that last night.

"What I do believe in is what happens when I'm with you," she said. "And I want to feel it again. Now."

Cam didn't see a future for them, either. Hell, maybe a part of him had never believed in it. He was the son of a couple of horse trainers. He was the poor son of ranch hands and she was a damn princess—or as close to it as Royal could get. When that night had happened, he'd been crushed, but a silent, observant voice in his head had whispered, *There it is*. The end. Just like you thought it would be.

And really? What had changed? She was still out of his reach. But they did have the present and maybe they'd spent enough of it talking. Without another word between them, he hauled her in close, kissed her until he thought he'd die from it and then whipped up the hem of the shirt covering her.

Her hands moved over his bare back, nails scraping, leaving marks as if branding him, and he was okay with it. As long as she was in his arms, he'd figure out the rest. He lifted her off her feet, and she wrapped her legs around his hips as he spun to brace her back against the nearest wall.

They crashed into it, both of them losing their breath but not their will to join. To be locked together. He looked into her eyes as he pushed himself into her heat, and he saw the flare of wild need electrify her eyes.

She kissed him then and tangled her tongue with his. Her breath slid into his lungs, and he let her fill him as he filled her. His hands at her hips, he held her as he rocked in and out of her body, giving himself up to the fire within. Again and again he claimed her, took her, giving as much as he got. Needing her more with every passing second.

He felt her body tighten. Felt the first stir of completion when it took her and he gave her more, pushed her higher, faster than he had before, and when she tore her mouth from his to shout his name at the ceiling, he felt her body convulse around his.

Cam watched her face as she came and realized he'd never seen anything more beautiful. She was what had been missing from his life. And for this moment at least, she was back. She was his. He was hers. For this one stolen piece of time, there was no past, no future. Only the now.

And when his own body shattered, he felt his soul go with it.

Eight

By the following afternoon, Beth was in the middle of the Fire Department Open House and watching the money add up in the giant glass barrel she'd set on the catering table.

They'd already collected enough money through donations and the sale of raffle tickets to fulfill the fire station's wish list for new equipment. But these last-minute donations, given by the people stopping to pick up sandwiches, ice-cream bars and soda or water, were creating a nice bonus. And it was fun, watching the bills and change in the barrel mount up.

This half of Main Street had been blocked off by Nathan Battles and his deputies, allowing people to stream back and forth across the street without keeping an eye out for cars. The crowd was huge, but then Beth had counted on that. People in Royal could be depended on to show up for a good cause—and keeping their own fire station well equipped served all of them.

Her whole family was there, and she grinned to see Piper out on the dance floor with old Mr. Martin as he led her in a slow, dignified Texas-style waltz. Piper caught her eye and smiled back, just before the country and western band switched it up from slow to fast and new dancers took the stage.

"This is amazing," Gracie said, and had to lean in close to Beth's ear just to be heard over the band.

"Turned out great, didn't it?" Beth looked around at the size of the crowd and then noticed Justin heading toward her.

She didn't need to deal with this today. Especially after yesterday and those amazing, soul shattering hours with Camden. God. She should be regretting the decision she'd made to sleep with Cam, but how could she? She'd never known anything like what she experienced with him. But how could she trust him? How could she ever hope for them to be more than simply lovers?

In spite of what she'd told him the day before, she *did* believe in love and marriage and the happily-ever-after that had eluded her so far. Once she'd thought that future would include Cam; now she didn't see how it could.

Still, that didn't mean her future would include Justin.

Beth turned and told Gracie, "Gotta get lost in the crowd. Justin's coming and I just can't do this today."

Gracie looked past her and said, "Go. I'll stall him."

"Remind me to give you a raise."

"I will." Gracie smiled and went to head Justin off.

Beth, meanwhile, slipped into the crowd, ducking behind people, hoping to lose herself. She caught snatches of conversation, eruptions of laughter and squeals from little kids. It was all so normal. Except for what she was up to. Imagine being a grown woman and hiding from a man rather than just telling him to go away.

But, in her defense, Justin didn't *listen*.

"What are you doing?"

She looked up and grimaced at her cousin Zeke. "Hiding. Don't give me away."

Zeke turned to look in the direction she'd come from and sighed. "Can't he take a hint?"

"Apparently not." She looked up at him and pleaded, "Help."

"Right." He grabbed her hand, pulled her onto the dance floor behind him and barely slowed down when she squawked.

"This is *not* hiding, Zeke."

"No, this is dancing." He slipped his arm around her, took her right hand in his and smoothly moved them in with the other dancers. "Don't worry, I won't let him cut in."

"You'd better not." After a second or two, she looked up at him and asked, "Don't you have someone here you'd rather be dancing with than your cousin?"

"Not at the moment," he confessed, then grinned at her. "Besides, I dance with my cousin, and I look like a great guy to all the interesting women around here."

She laughed. "So you're using me."

"Absolutely." He winked and spun her into a turn.

The crowd was a mash of color and movement. The

music was loud but catchy, and the local band knew exactly the kind of songs to play to keep their audience dancing. This was Texas, so the music was country, but the beat was so good that even those who preferred rock and roll were kept happy enough.

"You did a great job on this, Beth."

"Thanks." She looked to her right. On the other side of the fire station, the gleaming red-and-white trucks sat in the sun while children climbed all over them. "I think we pulled it off."

"I'll say. Did you see Bob Hackett when he won that truck?" Zeke laughed. "I thought his eyes were going to bug out of his head."

"Well, he's twenty-two and just got a brand-new top-of-the-line truck. That's enough to make anybody a little bug-eyed."

"Yeah, he's posing for pictures with it. I think his girlfriend, Cherry, is getting jealous. He keeps touching that truck like he's afraid it's going to disappear."

Beth knew that feeling. She'd had it yesterday when she couldn't stop touching Camden—a stroke on his arm, a caress across his chest, smoothing his hair back from his forehead. It was as if she had to keep feeling him to reassure herself that he was really there. With her. After so long without him, having him close again had been almost dreamlike.

"Oh, God."

"What?" Zeke looked at her, startled. "What's wrong?"

"Nothing. Just…nothing." She kept dancing and told herself that she was wrong. She couldn't possibly still be in love with Camden Guthrie. Not after everything that had happened. Not after he'd betrayed her, left town, married Julie Wheeler.

And she realized that, no, she wasn't *still* in love with him. This love was new. It was based on who he was now.

Yes, he was basically the same man he'd been back in the day. But now he was self-assured. Comfortable in his own skin and making no apologies for what he wanted. Then there was helping Tony out with the baseball camp. Him hiring Olivia Turner and her crew of mostly female construction experts. He had made a huge donation to the children's wing.

Hell, even the loyalty he'd shown the woman he'd left Beth for had made an impact on her. He was touching her heart again, and he was making plans for a future here. In Royal.

Of course she was in love with him again. She'd been predisposed for the fall. They shared a past that was taut with both pain and joy, and now that he was home the future dangled out in front of her like a shiny prize she just couldn't reach.

"Seriously, Beth," Zeke said. "You okay? You look a little pale."

"I'm just hot." Big lie since the wide Texas sky was studded with massive white clouds that kept playing tag across the sun, keeping the heat to a minimum. But her cousin accepted it because he was a good guy.

"Beth—" Gracie rushed across the dance floor. "I tried, but Justin's on his way over here, so—"

"Thanks for the heads-up." She looked up at Zeke. "Sorry."

"No problem." He gave her a grin that made his green eyes shine. "I'll just sweep Gracie off her feet."

"Oh, you don't have—"

Beth laughed as Gracie's refusal was lost in the dance. Zeke swung her into a country swing dance, and Beth left as Gracie was spinning and laughing up at her partner.

It wasn't as if Beth could leave the party—she was in charge of it. But she didn't want to talk to Justin. She stopped to chat with her neighbors, waved to friends as she passed and checked in with the firefighters. Some were giving tours of the station house, and others were riding herd on a dozen kids crawling all over the gleaming red fire truck as well as the EMS truck.

Smiling, Beth told herself to just concentrate on the day. To push all thoughts of Cam and whatever they were to each other to the back of her mind. It wasn't as if she could solve anything right now anyway. And as if the Fates were laughing, Cam stepped up behind her.

"You look beautiful."

She turned at the sound of that deep voice and looked up into chocolate eyes that were burning with the same kind of intensity she'd seen the day before. Her entire body snapped with the sizzle suddenly bubbling in her blood.

"Thank you." She wore a sky blue dress with shoulder straps, a squared neckline and a full skirt. Her favorite heeled sandals completed the outfit and brought her much closer to eye level with the man currently staring at her as if he could gulp her up.

She gave Cam a quick once-over and nearly sighed. His gray Stetson was pulled low over his eyes. He wore a white dress shirt, a black blazer and black jeans with a pair of polished black boots that completed the image of "dangerous cowboy." And that's just what he was.

"What're you doing here?" she asked.

He shrugged and looked out over the crowd. "I live here, Beth. I ought to be part of the town." He shifted his gaze back to hers. "And I figured it was a good place to run into you."

When her heart did a ridiculous flip, she told herself to just stop it. Unfortunately, her body wasn't listening to her head.

"Beth?" Another deep voice, easier to hear this far from the band's speakers.

She turned and smiled as James Harris stepped up to give her a quick hug. James was tall and gorgeous, with closely cropped black hair, dark brown eyes and skin the color of melted caramel.

"James, hi."

"You did a great job with this event," he said. "Makes me really look forward to the party at the TCC this October. Can't wait to see what you'll come up with for that."

"Oh," she said, smiling, "you're going to love it. I've got lots of plans."

He laughed. "I'll bet." Then he shifted a glance at Cam. "Hey, Camden. Good to have you back in Royal." He held out one hand and Cam shook it, smiling.

"Good to be back. I've been thinking about coming to see you. The word is you breed the best horses in East Texas."

"I'll agree with that," James said with a grin.

"Well, I'm going to be needing a couple dozen horses out at my place. I figure you're the man to see."

"Great. I can set you up." James was the top horse breeder in the county, and people came from all over the West to buy his horses. "Come out anytime, look them over and we'll do a deal." He paused then said, "Meanwhile, I talked to Burt Wheeler the other day."

Beth winced and Cam's features tightened. Neither of them were certain what he'd heard from Burt.

"Yeah, he's not my biggest fan."

"He did make that pretty clear," James confirmed, and let it lie, thank goodness. "But he did say you're interested in joining the TCC."

"I am," Cam said. "And I hear you're the president now."

"Guilty as charged," James replied with another grin. "Anyway, wanted to let you know that I don't see a problem with your membership at all. Burt might not be happy about it, but I'm looking forward to welcoming you all the way home."

Cam's features cleared, and Beth could almost see tension drain out of his body. "Thanks, James. I appreciate it."

"Not a problem. It'll be good to have you as a member." He hugged Beth again and said, "Now, I'm off to find a beer. You guys have fun."

"Well," Cam murmured, "that's one worry off the table."

"I'm glad for you," she said, and found she meant it. It was another tie to Royal. Another thing to keep him here, and that was more important to Beth than she would have thought.

The music changed again and this time it was perfect for a two-step. Beth tapped her foot in time and Cam must have noticed.

"The band's good. You want to see if we've still got it?"

She looked up at him and, damn it, *smiled*. The two-step had always been *their* dance. They'd even won a couple of contests as kids. "It's been a long time."

"Like riding a horse, darlin'," he assured her, and took her hand, leading her to the wooden dance floor erected for the party.

They took a spot in the crowd. Cam's right hand was positioned behind her left shoulder, and Beth rested her left arm atop his. His Stetson shaded his eyes, but she saw the shine there anyway and bubbles of pleasure raced through her. A couple of years ago, she never would have guessed that she and Cam would be dancing together again.

And then they were moving, sliding into the steps as if they'd never been apart. He was smooth and easy to follow. Their steps were quick, then slow, and they seemed to glide together effortlessly. When he spun her around she swayed with the movement, then right back again. They moved around the dance floor, part of the crowd yet separate. Their eyes locked and the years fell away.

In a blink, Beth remembered all the nights by the lake with the car radio blasting so they could practice their steps. And she remembered how those practice sessions had always ended in the back seat of her car—or his. Passion-fogged windows had encapsulated them in their own private world as they lost themselves in each other.

She moved with him so seamlessly it was as if she'd been born to be with him. And when the music ended, they danced on, oblivious, until laughter from the crowd woke them from the trance they were in. Cam smiled down at her, and Beth felt her heart take another tumble.

How could she love him so much? How could she risk her heart again? And how could she not?

"Hey, Cam!" They both looked to where Tony was standing at the edge of the dance floor. "If you're finished, I want you to meet someone."

"Go," Beth said, stepping out of his grasp and waving one hand. Grateful for the reprieve, she stepped off the dance floor. She could only take so much magic in one outing. She needed a little space to clear her head, or to hope for clarity, anyway. "I'll see you later."

"I'll hold you to that," Cam told her, lifting one hand to cup her cheek briefly.

That slight touch sent heat skittering through her, and Beth knew she was in real trouble. She watched him stalk off to meet Tony, then she slipped into the crowd again. When a woman's hand took hold of her arm as she passed, Beth nearly groaned. She just wanted some time to herself. Maybe under the shade of a tree to help ease the heat crouching inside.

Her aunt Piper gave her a rueful smile. "I saw that performance. You guys still dance together like you were born to it."

Beth turned to look back at the dance floor, where other couples were moving in tandem to another song.

"Piper," she said, looking back to the other woman, "I don't know what I'm doing."

Her aunt winked. "Looked to me like you did."

"Dancing? Sure." Beth laughed a little and hated that it sounded so pitiful even to her own ears. "But everything else? It's a mystery to me."

Piper laid one arm around Beth's shoulders and steered her through the crowd until they found a semi-deserted spot. "Honey, you still love him, don't you?"

She could have denied it, but what would have been the point? "Ridiculous, isn't it?"

"No." Piper shook her head, her short, dark brown hair swinging into an arc and then settling back into its perfect cut. "It's not."

Beth wanted to believe her. Piper had always been more of an older sister to Beth than an aunt, and they'd shared a lot of secrets over the years. Piper knew all about Beth and Cam. Knew what had happened. Knew what it had done to Beth. How Cam's leaving had sent her into a sort of spiral that she'd had to dig her way out of on her own.

"Am I just supposed to get over it?" she asked, not really expecting an answer. "To move on and not remember what happened before?"

"Of course not," Piper said quickly. "How could you? It was horrible, and at the time I wanted to find Cam Guthrie myself and slap him silly for what he did."

Beth's lips curved at the thought and at the loving loyalty.

"But, honey, you already got past it." Piper tucked Beth's hair behind her ear. "You built a good life. You stand on your own two feet and don't owe anyone an explanation for what you do with that life."

"Thanks. I do know that. Really." Beth sighed and said, "It's just I don't know if I can let myself love him this time. What if he leaves again? What if we break up and I drop into that black hole I was in before?"

"And what if the world stops turning and we all fly into space?" Piper laughed, hugged Beth hard, then stood back and gripped her shoulders. "You don't get a guarantee, Beth. You get chances. Whether you take them or not is up to you."

"And I don't know if I should."

"I do." Piper waited for Beth's gaze to meet hers. "Go for it, sweetie. Always take the chance when you get it. Living a life with regrets isn't the way to go."

Beth heard something in her aunt's voice that worried her. "Hey. Are you okay?"

A bright smile lit Piper's face. "Of course. Aren't I always?" Her gaze slid past Beth then and she said, "Oh, damn."

Beth looked and her shoulders slumped. Her mom, Ava, was here, arm in arm with Keith Cooper. All of Beth's life, she'd known that "Uncle Keith" was in love with her mother. The weird thing was that Ava never seemed to notice. Since Beth's father died, Keith had been around Ava at all times. And it looked like that wasn't going to stop.

"I really thought after they got home from Europe that Keith would give up and move on," Beth muttered. "Does Mom have zero clue that the man is crazy about her?"

Piper said only, "Don't worry about your mother, Beth. Ava's a smart woman. She's not as oblivious as you think she is."

It didn't look like it to her. "I hope you're right."

In an instant, everything changed.

Suddenly the firefighters were hustling kids off the trucks, jumping into their uniforms and driving off, sirens screaming. Most in the crowd cupped their hands over their ears, and Beth winced at the noise. "What do you suppose is happening?"

She glanced at Piper, but before she could answer, Sebastian and Sutton rushed up to them.

"There's a fire at one of our WinJet plants," Sebastian said. "I just got a call from the security company."

"The plant outside Royal," Sutton put in to clarify, since there were a few manufacturing plants to take care of the private plane orders they received every year.

The twins were identical in every way, and right now even their grim expressions were mirrors of each other.

"At least it's Saturday," Piper said quickly. "So no one's there to get injured."

"No," Sutton muttered darkly. "We're pushing a deadline, so we're running two shifts. They're working today."

"Oh, my God…" Beth's whisper was lost in the nervous, excited chatter springing up all around them.

"We're headed over there now," Sebastian said, and grabbed Sutton's upper arm.

"I'll be right behind you. I'm getting my car," Piper informed them.

"What's going on?" Cam came up behind Beth, and she was grateful to feel his steady calm.

"There's a fire," she said. "At one of our manufacturing plants." Turning to look at him, she added, "I'm riding over with Piper, but first I have to find Gracie. Let her know I'm leaving."

Cam looked to Piper and said, "You go ahead. I'll bring Beth."

Piper looked at the two of them and nodded. "See you there. I have to find Ava."

"I'll tell Zeke. He can find Luke," Beth said as Piper hurried away.

"Come on." Cam grabbed her hand and led her

through the crowd. In one corner of her mind, Beth was amazed at how the crowd seemed to part right in front of him. People made way. Whether it was Cam himself or the fact that they could tell there was an emergency, she didn't know. But she wouldn't have been surprised to find it was simply Cam's commanding personality that had people stepping out of his way.

She paused when she saw Zeke, still on the dance floor. This time, he was doing a complicated ten-step with his friend, Reagan Sinclair. Reagan's long, dark brown hair flew out behind her like a velvet cape as she laughed up into Zeke's face.

"Sorry to break this up," Beth said, tugging at Zeke's arm. "Reagan, I really need Zeke."

"No problem." Reagan looked concerned but didn't slow them down with questions.

Quickly Beth explained everything and watched the fun in Zeke's eyes drain away and be replaced by solemn resolve.

"Reagan, gotta go," he said. Then he turned to Beth. "I'll find Luke and we'll meet you at the plant."

Beth and Cam set off again and found Gracie near the donation table talking to James Harris. It only took a minute to explain what was happening and that she needed Gracie to take charge of the rest of the party.

Cam's truck was parked close by, and before long they were on the highway leading out of Royal. "So talk to me," he said. "This is a WinJet plant?"

"Yes," she replied, willing them to go faster. "Sebastian said there's a whole shift working there today to make up time on back orders. If the fire…"

She didn't even want to think about it, really. A fire sweeping through the plant could spread quickly.

Anyone caught inside was in real danger. There were so many potentially flammable things stored there. Chemicals used in working on the planes, paints, fiberglass… Fire was the absolute worst thing that could happen. She could only pray that everyone had gotten out safely.

Cam didn't ask any more questions and didn't offer meaningless platitudes, for which she was grateful. He only grabbed her hand and held on. Beth curled her fingers around his, thankful for the support. As they neared the turnoff, she could see thick black smoke snaking up into the sky and twisting in the breeze. "Oh, God."

Cam took the turnoff and drove straight to the front of the parking lot, where Beth's family was already gathered, watching the firefighters attack the blaze. Beth was out of the car before he'd put it in Park, and Cam wasn't far behind her.

Beth grabbed Sutton's arm. "Did everyone get out?"

He looked down at her and his features were tight. "Everyone's out, but three of the men on the line were hurt."

"How bad?"

"Bad enough," Sebastian said darkly, and nodded a greeting as Cam came up behind Beth. "There's smoke inhalation, a couple of second-degree burns, and one of the guys broke his leg when he jumped off a ladder to get out."

"But they *are* out and they're going to be fine," Zeke put in.

Absently, Beth noted Cam draping one arm around her shoulder. She liked it. It spoke of solidarity and silent comfort, both of which she needed at the moment.

Sebastian turned to look at all of them, and his gaze flickered briefly when he noticed Cam's arm around Beth. But he stayed on subject when he said, "The men have already been transported to Royal hospital. They're being taken care of, and everyone else is being checked out by the EMTs, just in case. The real question is how did the fire start in the first place?"

Good point. Beth watched Nathan Battles, his face set in grim lines, walk up to join them. "Sorry to see this, but the fire captain says they'll have it out in another hour."

"Can we go in then?"

Nathan took off his hat and ran his forearm across his forehead. "Probably not. The fire marshal has to inspect the property, then the arson inspector will be out to do the same."

"Arson?" Beth repeated, shocked at the idea.

"You can't be serious," Piper said. "Nate, you know us."

"I'm not saying the fire was deliberately set," Nathan clarified a second later. "That's standard procedure for a fire. We have to find out how the blaze started."

"He's right," Sebastian said, never taking his gaze off the firefighters now shooting foam at the flames licking at the roof. "We take care of business. First priority is making sure our people are safe. The rest we'll handle as it comes."

Sutton moved off to talk to the fire captain, and a moment later, Sebastian, Luke and Zeke joined him. Piper and Ava stood to one side with Keith. The expressions on their faces told Beth they were feeling as stunned and worried as she was.

Looking up at Cam, she asked, "Can you drive me to the hospital? I want to check on the injured men."

"Sure," he said. He caught her hand and Beth threaded her fingers through his. His warm, steady grip on her hand made her feel complete in a way she hadn't in years. In spite of everything that had happened between them, she realized in a flash that Cam was still the only man she wanted. The only man she would ever love.

She just didn't know what that meant. For either of them.

Nine

Over the next week, the Wingates concentrated on the aftereffects of the fire. The family gathered at the main house for more meetings than Beth could count. Piper was staying with them rather than making the drive from Dallas every day, and Ava and Keith were practically inseparable. Beth wanted to worry about that, but frankly she already had too much going on in her mind.

Not the least of which was why she hadn't heard from Camden since the day of the fire. He had to know what she was going through. So why was he avoiding her? Was he regretting becoming involved with her again? Was he trying to subtly let her know that she couldn't depend on him? If so, he was doing a hell of a job.

And besides Camden and the fire concerns, Beth still had her foundations to take care of. She had a lot of things going on and she couldn't exactly say *Sorry, I'm mentally fried and have no time to garner your donations.* So, in between worrying about Cam and attending the family meetings, she was running around town trying to make sure she didn't let anyone down.

Which was why taking a break for lunch with Piper and Gracie felt like a vacation.

Especially at the Courtyard shops. Only four miles outside Royal, it felt like a different world. Oak trees shaded the area in front of the small coffee stand that sold cakes, cookies and espresso-based drinks both iced and hot. There were a dozen delicate round tables that boasted bright pink umbrellas and iron scrollwork chairs. The café was kept busy by all of the shoppers thronging to the eclectic gathering of stores at the Courtyard.

The property used to be a ranch and the big red barn was still standing. Now, though, it housed Priceless, an antiques store and crafting studio. There were shops for local craftsmen making everything from artisanal soaps to stained glass, and every Saturday, booths sprang up like mushrooms for a farmers market. All in all, the place almost demanded that you relax. Sit for a while. Do some retail therapy and take a mental break. Just what Beth needed.

"There was a report on the radio this morning. The men who were injured are saying the sprinkler system at the plant malfunctioned." Gracie winced as she said it, obviously not wanting to heap more trouble on the situation.

And there went the break.

"I know," Beth said, and glanced at Piper before turning back to Gracie. She and the family had agreed to keep what they'd found between them, but Beth considered Gracie family. They'd been friends forever, they worked closely together, and Gracie had proved herself time and again to be extremely trustworthy.

So Beth didn't feel the slightest twinge of guilt telling her old friend exactly what was happening. "The injured men have all hired lawyers. They contacted us yesterday."

"Lawyers?" Gracie repeated, looking from one to the other of the women. "That doesn't sound good."

"No, it isn't." Piper picked up her coffee and took a sip. "They're talking about suing the company. Their lawyers made us aware that a formal suit will be filed within the month." She set her cup down and leaned back in her chair. "It's not exactly unexpected, but it is one more thing landing on top of an already miserable situation."

"Sebastian's furious," Beth said. "Not with the employees so much as he is with the whole mess. He's determined to get to the bottom of how this happened in the first place. It doesn't help that we still haven't been allowed back into the plant."

Leaning forward, she kept her voice down so no one else would overhear. "He and Sutton have done an internal investigation already. They've been checking over safety inspection reports, and, apparently, the company wasn't up-to-date on the inspections."

"You're kidding," Gracie murmured. "That doesn't sound right."

"No, it doesn't." Piper frowned thoughtfully. "We've never had safety issues at any of our companies, so there's obviously something wrong. We just don't know what it is."

Gracie took a breath and blew it out. "What does this mean for you guys?"

"It means," Piper said quietly, "there's going to be a big payoff to the injured men, obviously. Beyond that, no one knows yet."

"The company's healthy," Beth added, "so no one's worried about having to pay out a settlement. The real problem is finding out that someone in the company's been cutting corners with safety. We can't survive that. No company could."

That fact had made for some very uncomfortable conversations at the house this last week. Trying to wrap their heads around the idea that someone within the company, someone they knew and trusted, had sabotaged them. Though it was a horrible thought, it was the only thing that made sense.

It had to be an insider who was behind the safety inspections, the malfunctioning sprinklers and maybe even the fire itself. But who? And why?

"So what's next?" Gracie kept her voice low and glanced at the table beside them as an older couple got up to leave. When they were gone, she added, "Is there a plan for handling all of this?"

"Not much of one yet," Piper admitted. "Between Sebastian, Sutton, Luke and Zeke, there are too many ideas and not one they've settled on yet."

"It's not just the guys, either," Beth said. "Mom's putting her two cents in and driving Sebastian a little nuts with it. And Piper and I spend most of our time telling them all to calm down." Which was funny, considering what she herself had said to Justin not too long ago. *Telling someone to calm down never makes them calm down.*

"And we're bringing Miles into this." Beth's younger brother, Miles Wingate, had his own company, Steel Security, based out of Chicago. It was already one of the most acclaimed security companies in the world, and since Miles was family, he would know better than anyone how important it was to solve the mystery of the fire and the safety inspections.

"That's a really good idea."

Piper nodded at Gracie. "Sebastian's idea."

"Well," Gracie acknowledged, "he's brilliant, so I'm not surprised."

"Don't ever tell Baz he's brilliant, it'll go to his head." Beth picked up her iced tea and took a sip. She watched Gracie stand, get the newspaper the older couple had left on their table and then sit down again. "Oh, please don't show me any Wingates Are Evil headlines."

Gracie laughed and shook her head. "Promise. I'm just checking my lottery numbers."

"Well, if ever there was a day for some good news," Beth said, "today is it. So win enough to pay for lunch, okay?"

"I'll try." Gracie opened the paper and pulled her ticket from her black leather bag.

Beth was watching her compare her ticket to the numbers in the paper, and she actually saw Gracie go pale. "What is it?" she demanded, reaching for her friend's arm. "Gracie, what happened?"

Gracie lifted her gaze to Beth's and opened and closed her mouth for a couple of seconds, but no sound escaped. Finally she took a deep, shuddering breath and managed to say, "I…uh. Here." She handed over the paper and her ticket. Swallowing hard, she said, "You look. Double-check me."

"Double-check?" Beth repeated. "You either won something or you didn't."

But she dutifully compared the numbers on Gracie's ticket to the winning combination in the paper. Then she checked it again. And a third time. Excitement exploded inside her. Stunned, she stared at Gracie.

"What is it?" Piper's voice broke into the taut silence. "Will somebody please tell me what's going on?"

Beth laughed, shocked and happy and starting to really worry about Gracie. "Oh, I can tell you, but you might not believe me." Laughter rang in her voice as she said, "Gracie's buying lunch. She just won sixty million dollars."

"What?" Piper grabbed the ticket and the paper.

Delighted, Beth, still laughing, grabbed her best friend's hand and squeezed.

Gracie doubled over and said, "I think I'm going to be sick."

Cam thought it was for the best that he and Beth hadn't seen each other in a week. It forced them both to evaluate what was happening between them and decide where to go with it. The day of the fire she'd been shocked and worried, and she'd needed him. But since then, he hadn't heard from her, and Cam figured there was a reason for that.

Bottom line, no matter what he felt when he was around her, he wasn't going to set himself up for another princess betrayal.

Beth was still royalty here in Royal, Texas. And in

spite of his wealth, Camden was still a half–Native American cowboy. Things hadn't changed, not really. Society in Royal would always be two separate tiers, and climbing that particular ladder never went well— not that he was interested in their damn ladder anyway.

New money would never be looked at with the same reverence and respect as old money, and he didn't care to try to change things. Actually he didn't give a shit what anyone thought of him. He was exactly who he had always been. He just had more cash on hand now. And rich was definitely better than poor, he could admit.

But building his own life here—on his own—made more sense than revisiting the past with Beth and trying to remodel it. Loving her and yes, he had to admit that he loved her even more now than he once had, didn't change anything. Hard to acknowledge, but dangerous to ignore.

"What are you thinking about that's putting that scowl on your face?"

He looked at Tony and scowled deeper. "I'm not scowling."

"Right." Tony chuckled. He picked up the drawings of his ideas for the baseball camp that he'd spread out on Cam's dining room table and said, "It's Beth."

"It's none of your business."

"Sure." He chuckled again. "I saw you two dancing at the party last week. Just like old times."

If he scowled any harder, Cam was pretty sure his face would just crack. "Beth isn't on my mind." Lies.

"Sure she's not. So you're just nervous about the TCC meeting?"

"I'm not nervous," Cam argued, and this time he

meant it. Did he want to be a member of the TCC? Yes. If he didn't get in, would it be the end of his plans for the future? Hell, no. "Am I twelve? I'll get in or I won't. Period."

It wasn't nerves. It was…concern. That was different, he assured himself. The vote on new members was tomorrow night, and Cam would be there. Maybe he shouldn't, but damned if he'd hide and let all the other members know that he was worried how the vote would go.

Tony would be there, too, since he was already a member. Big-league baseball catcher, local businessman, of course he was in. Now it was Cam's turn, and he'd find out soon if Burt Wheeler had poisoned the well against him. Sure, he'd put Cam's name up for a vote, but he'd also had a week to talk to his friends and convince them to vote no. Hell, a part of Cam couldn't even blame Burt for it.

He'd lost his daughter and needed someone to blame. Cam was the lucky winner.

And all of this thinking wasn't doing a damn sight of good, either.

"You ready to go?" Cam's new lawyer was expecting them to come by and sign the paperwork to get Tony's camp up and running.

"Sure." Tony rolled up the drawings he'd had made and slipped a rubber band around them. "I'll take my own car, though. I've got a date after the meeting with the lawyers."

"Fine." Cam didn't have a damn date. He'd be coming back to his house. Alone. Just like he'd been all week. Hell. He couldn't even get a good night's sleep anymore because his bedroom held the ghost of Beth.

Her scent. Her laugh. Her touch. Wouldn't it just figure that the only woman he wanted was the woman he was steering clear of. Coming home to Texas had been a dance of misery and joy, and he wasn't sure from day to day which one would take precedence.

Changing the subject abruptly, he said, "Those are good drawings for your camp."

Tony grinned. "It's going to be great. Still can't thank you enough for the land."

"You don't have to. It's going to be good for both of us." He smiled just thinking about it, and that was a good thing.

"You're still pitching, I'm still catching," Tony said with a shrug. "We still make a good team."

And that was a bit of the joy in coming back to Royal. Reconnecting with old friends. Charting a future that held exactly what he wanted. And if he didn't get *everything* he wanted? Well, he'd just have to deal with it.

Beth took Gracie to her mother's house and left her in good hands. The whole Diaz family was in tears— well, except for Gracie's little brother, who immediately went online to shop.

The shock of winning the lottery really hadn't worn off for Gracie yet. And when it did, the reality of it would put her into another wild emotional spin. Beth was thrilled for her. Suddenly all those dreams Gracie had built in her mind over the years were going to come true.

Of course, her life was going to become crazy once news of her win became public. She'd be hounded for interviews and have people she'd never known coming to her looking for a handout.

"And I might need a new assistant," Beth muttered. After all, why would Gracie keep a job she no longer needed? "Oh, that's a horrible thought. Who's going to help me keep all of this straight? Oh, Gracie... I already miss you."

When her phone rang, Beth saw her sister's name pop up on the screen and smiled. Harley had been gone from Texas for years and Beth really missed her. Right now, though, she was jealous of her little sister because Harley, living in Thailand, was well out of the controversy over WinJet.

"Hey, Harley!"

"Hey, yourself." Her sister's voice came across the Bluetooth perfectly. Beth didn't know why Sutton complained about the connection from Beth's car.

She stopped at a red light and said, "How are you and my adorable nephew?"

"We're both good," Harley said. She added wryly, "Probably better than all of you guys are. How's the investigation going?"

"Slowly," Beth admitted. They'd had a conference call with Harley and Miles the night of the fire so all of the siblings were on the same page. "It's only been a week, but Sebastian and Sutton are like twin pit bulls with bones. They're hovering over every report, talking to the experts, huddling with Nathan Battles and the fire chief at every opportunity..."

"Sounds bad."

The light changed and Beth stepped on the gas, heading down Main Street and keeping an eagle eye out for people backing out of parking spots. "It is bad,

Harley. Being at the house these days is just a nightmare. I'm actually jealous of Luke and Zeke living in the guesthouse. At least they get to escape it once in a while.

"And it doesn't look like it's going to get better. Sebastian's calling Miles in to investigate."

"Well, if there's anything there, Miles will find it."

"True." And that worried her, too. What would Miles find? Was WinJet guilty of sloppy safety procedures? It was hard to believe, but right now that's what it was looking like. Unless their mysterious insider had somehow changed things so it appeared that the Wingate family wasn't concerned about safety.

So who exactly was behind that? They had to know, even if the answer would be more painful than the question.

"How's Mom?"

"She's…" Beth paused to find the right word. Ava had been right in the thick of all of this since the moment it started. For a woman who really hadn't spent much time with the family business, their mother was like a force of nature. "Tougher than I thought. She's in the middle of it all, and Uncle Keith is volunteering his time to help Mom and the twins find the truth."

"He's still panting after Mom?"

"Thank you." Beth shook her head, made a right turn at the next block and pulled into the first parking spot she found. She couldn't concentrate on driving while she was dealing with all of this, too. "I thought I was the only one who was convinced Keith was desperately in love with her."

"You're not. The last time I was in Royal, it seemed

so obvious to me. Even when Dad was alive, Keith was smitten."

"Smitten?" Beth smiled to herself.

"It's a perfectly good word. And I wonder why Mom doesn't see it."

"Piper says she does and we shouldn't worry about it."

"I guess Piper would know," Harley mused, but didn't sound confident. Then she half covered the phone and said, "Daniel, we'll go for a walk as soon as I'm finished talking to Aunt Beth, okay?"

"Give him my love." Beth sighed. "I really miss you guys. Daniel's going to be six feet tall the next time I see him."

"He's only four," Harley replied, laughing. "And you could come to Thailand for a visit."

"Trust me," Beth said on a sigh, "I wish I was there right now."

"I bet." Harley paused. "Look, Beth, I'm actually calling for a more personal reason."

"Everything okay?" Sister alarm bells went off in her mind and Beth sat up straighter.

"Yes, sure. I told you, we're fine. The problem is Zest," she admitted.

"Your nonprofit?" Beth waved at Marva Wilson, walking her ancient beagle down the sidewalk. "What's wrong?"

"We're not making enough money to stay alive," Harley confessed. "I've been dipping into my trust to make ends meet because I can't bear the thought of letting down the women who depend on me. And, frankly, I could really use your fund-raising skills."

Worry rippled through Beth. She hated to think

of her little sister losing the foundation that meant so much to her. She also dreaded the thought of Harley dipping into a trust fund meant to take care of her and her son.

Harley had helped countless women to stand on their own two feet. To help them make enough money to support their families. To build better lives. Naturally Beth's little sister wouldn't give up finding ways to keep that kind of commitment going.

"Of course I'll help."

Harley sighed in relief. "Thank you. I knew I could count on you. Honestly, Beth, you have no idea how much this means to me."

"Yeah, I do." Her sister had the biggest heart of them all, and Beth would do whatever she could to make sure that heart didn't get broken. "And you can absolutely count on me to help any way I can." Her mind was already spinning with ideas on how to pull this off.

Before she lost Gracie as her assistant, Beth was going to drag her into helping work this out. "I'm sitting in a parking space off Main Street right now, so I can't really get into anything specific."

"Ohh. I miss Main Street. Where are you parked?"

Beth looked up. "I'm across the street from the ice-cream parlor."

Harley sighed. "That's so mean to tell me that."

"Sorry," Beth said on a laugh. "I meant I'm by the tire store."

"A lie, but easier to take. Thanks."

Beth laughed again. "Let me come up with some ideas, and I'll call you next week and we can decide which way to go."

"I already feel better, Beth. You are the best sister ever."

"Also your only sister…"

"Quality over quantity," Harley said, and made Beth laugh.

"Go take my nephew for a walk and don't worry. We'll fix this."

"Thanks again. Talk to you next week."

Beth fired up her car, backed out of her space and lifted one hand in a wave to whoever it was who honked at her in protest. Back on the road toward home, Beth thought about Harley's problem, already working out ideas on how to help.

She was beyond grateful for the task. Not only could she help her sister, but this gave her something else to think about besides the WinJet situation. Her entire family was on task with that anyway.

And though she had plenty of foundations to watch over and worry about, Harley's was personal and enough of a distraction to keep her thoughts from straying to Cam.

A week since she'd seen him. Talked to him. Touched him. She'd lived fifteen years without him, and now it felt as if she couldn't draw a breath without missing him.

The day of the fire, Cam had been…essential. From the start, he'd held her hand, comforted her and offered support. He hadn't tried to take over or tell her what to do or how to feel, but he *had* been a rock when it most mattered to her.

"But since then…" She shook her windblown hair out of her eyes and gritted her teeth. Since that horrible day, she hadn't seen or heard from Camden Guthrie.

Not a word. Not even a phone call. He'd disappeared, much as he had fifteen years ago. For one day, he'd been there for her and then…poof. Gone. Did he think that the crisis had disappeared? Was he deliberately staying away to let her know that she couldn't count on him? That nothing had really changed between them? Or was this the universe telling her to forget about him and move on? That nothing between them was ever going to last?

She didn't know anymore.

Sebastian was on the phone when Beth got home. She heard him all the way down the hall from their father's study. He was furious, and though he wasn't shouting, he was talking so loud the otherwise quiet house echoed with his voice.

Wondering what new crisis had struck while she was out, Beth hurried down the hall, her heels tapping against the red tiled floor. She didn't pass anyone else in the house and when she turned into the study, she knew why. Everyone was gathered there, watching Sebastian as if they were the audience studying an actor's every move.

Ava and Piper had the two guest chairs, and the guys were all standing in a semicircle behind them. The study was both familiar and foreign. When Beth's father was alive, no one had been allowed in. He had liked his "alone" time and ran the many Wingate businesses from this well-appointed massive room.

There were floor-to-ceiling bookcases on three of the walls and an elegantly tiled fireplace, big enough for a tall man to stand up in, on the fourth. The walls were dotted with framed photos of Trent Wingate alongside presidents and moguls, and two of Piper's oil paintings of the house and grounds.

Sebastian and Sutton shared this space now, though it had always seemed to Beth that Sebastian was the most comfortable in it. At the moment, Sebastian was practically growling into the phone as he paced furiously from one side of the room to the other.

Beth sidled up to Zeke. "What's going on?"

"We got a report that the arson inspector can't rule out the possibility that the fire might have been deliberately set."

"What?" Shock had made her voice a lot louder than she'd planned.

Sebastian fired a hard look at her, silently telling her to be quiet. She waved one hand at him, unmoved by his impatience, then moved close to Piper and leaned down. "Is Zeke serious? There was an arsonist?"

Piper shrugged and said, "No one's sure yet. Apparently, the inspector said it was 'unclear.' They're going to continue the investigation."

Sebastian shot her a glowering look now as he paced back and forth behind his desk.

Piper made a face at him and kept talking, though she did lower her voice a little in deference to Sebastian's blood pressure. "And that means we can't get into the building yet. That's driving Baz crazy of course, and Sutton's right behind him."

"It's making us all a little crazy," Beth said. "Is Miles coming out soon?"

"No word on that yet," Piper told her. "Apparently he's got plenty going on right now and can't get away."

"Hey, he's a Wingate, too." A little pissy, Beth said, "Why does Miles get to choose to stay out of this?"

"Believe me when I tell you Sebastian is with you on that."

"I bet." Beth sighed and dropped to one knee while she watched Sebastian arguing with whichever poor soul was on the other end of the phone.

"How's Gracie doing?" Piper asked.

"I think she's in shock." Beth smiled. "When I dropped her off, her mother was making margaritas to celebrate and her little brother was looking up Porsches online."

"That's fantastic!" Piper laughed. "I'm so glad for her. But this is going to be hard on her, too."

"Oh, I know." Beth was still worried about her friend and the bundle of cash that had dropped into her lap. "I don't think she's figured that part out yet. She's going to be a big celebrity when word gets out and Gracie's not going to like that."

"She's got friends—like you. That's going to help."

"I hope so."

Sebastian hung up and the sudden silence in the room was deafening. His features were tight and grim, and there was a dark gleam in his green eyes. He looked at the family, set both hands on his hips and said, "You heard most of that. The investigation's ongoing. They're not saying it was arson, but they're not saying it wasn't, either."

He rubbed one hand through his hair. "If it was arson, that could make the insurance coverage problematic unless we can prove who did it and that we didn't have a hand in it."

"No one would think we would burn down our own plant," Luke argued.

"No sane person," Sebastian agreed. "But it would

put us in the bizarre position of having to prove we *didn't* do it. Hard to prove a negative."

"What happened to innocent until proven guilty?" Zeke wondered aloud.

"Good question," Sebastian snapped.

"What does Nathan say?" Ava spoke up suddenly. Not surprisingly, Keith was standing behind her.

"Nate can't do anything about this," Sebastian said. "This is all the fire marshal and the arson inspector."

"Which means we're screwed…for now," Sutton put in. "Is Miles coming out?"

Sebastian frowned. "He's busy, he said. But I'll get him out here."

"I can do that," Ava offered.

Beth thought that was probably the best way to go. No way could Miles stand against their mother.

Sebastian nodded at her. "Good, Mom. That might work. If it doesn't, I'll call him again." His gaze swept the people in the room, one by one. "Anyone have something to add?"

"Well…" Everyone turned to look at Zeke. He smiled, swiped one hand across his jaw and shrugged. "I do have something. Not about the fire, though."

"Good," Sutton said. "I can use other news."

"This qualifies then." Zeke looked over at his twin, then announced, "I'm engaged to Reagan Sinclair."

Ten

Zeke was *engaged*?

"Since when?" Beth had just seen them dancing together at the fund-raiser. She knew the two of them had been good friends for a long time, but this was the first she'd heard about a romance.

"Since today," Zeke said, and held up one hand when the questions started flying from every corner of the room. "It's sort of an engagement of convenience," he explained with another casual shrug. "To claim her inheritance from her grandmother, Reagan has to be married. So…we're hoping the engagement announcement will do the trick for the lawyers."

"Seriously? A fake engagement?" Luke shook his head at his twin.

"Hey, we're the only ones who will know it's a fake,"

Zeke said. "To everyone else, it's the real deal. I even bought her a ring."

"Uh-huh," Sutton interrupted. "And if being engaged isn't enough to fulfill the demands of the will?"

Zeke grinned. "Then we'll get married."

"You're crazy," his twin muttered, loud enough for everyone to hear.

"We're twins," he pointed out. "So if I am, you are, too. Anyway, Reagan's a good friend, and I want to help her out. If she can't get the inheritance without a wedding, we're going to have one."

Okay. Beth stood up. There had just been way too many big announcements in the last week or so. The fire. The lawsuit. Gracie. Zeke. *And don't forget Cam*, her mind whispered.

If only she could.

While the family talked about Zeke's engagement and the fire inspector, Beth slipped out of the study. She'd had more than enough for the day, and all she really wanted now was a hot bath and bed.

But she wasn't going to get it right away.

"Beth…"

She stopped at the foot of the sweeping staircase leading to the second floor. With one hand on the glossy walnut banister, Beth turned to watch Piper approach.

"What's going on with you and Cam?"

"Nothing." Short conversation, but what else could she say? As far as she knew, there was nothing *real* between her and Cam. Beth loved him, she could acknowledge that to herself. But given the fact that she hadn't heard from him in a week, she suspected that his feelings for her stopped at the bedroom.

"Come on, sweetie." Piper tipped her head to one side. "We both know that's not true."

"Fine. Do I love him? Yes," Beth admitted. "Does that change anything? No."

"Oh, Beth," Piper said, sighing. "It changes everything."

"Not always." She had thought that they were finding their way back to each other, but in the last week Beth had realized she was wrong. A relationship couldn't survive if only one of the people involved was in love.

"He hasn't even called me, Piper." Her fingers tightened on the balustrade. "In a week. Nothing. And he knows what's going on with us right now. With me. If he gave a flying damn, wouldn't he have come by or phoned, just to check in? See how I'm doing? Say hello?"

"You're right," Piper said. "He does know what's going on. But he could think that calling would be intruding on a family situation."

"No." Beth laughed at the idea and shook her head. "Cam's never had trouble 'intruding' if he was going after something he wanted."

"Fine. Then maybe he's waiting for you to call him."

Surprised, Beth looked at her aunt. "You think I should be calling Cam? I should be the one to go to him?"

"Would it kill you?"

"It might," Beth argued. "He's the one who left me, remember?"

"Of course I do. I also remember that it was fifteen years ago."

"Oh, is there a time limit on betrayal that I wasn't

aware of?" Beth's eyes went wide with faux shock. "Someone should have told me."

"That's not what I meant and I think you know it."

"Okay, do you remember how well I handled it when Cam left?" Beth hated the memory of how losing him had practically destroyed her. Hated even thinking about it.

With her heart shattered, Beth had gone off to college and become someone she didn't even know. She drank too much. Slept around. Drove too fast, laughed too loud and damn near flunked out of college. And then her father had arrived out of the blue. She'd fought him of course because she hadn't wanted advice. Hadn't wanted to think of anything but the next adventure she could use to bury her pain.

But Trent Wingate wasn't a man you could easily ignore. He'd given her one of his famous *sit down, shut up and listen* talks and, thankfully, it had gotten through to her. Especially the part where he'd told her that he was disappointed in her, letting a man dictate how she acted.

He was right. And oh, how she'd hated to admit it. Because of what Cam had done, she'd completely lost herself. That was the day she had realized that her future was up to her to design. She'd turned it all around, graduated at the top of her class with a business degree and had come home to Royal to join Wingate Enterprises.

"I let my own life go to hell because Cam left me," she admitted, though it cost her a ding to her pride. "It was pitiful, Piper. I needed him so much that without him, I was completely lost. I never want to be that way again."

Piper grabbed her hand and held on. "I know how hard it was, sweetie. But do you really think you could ever let that happen to you again?"

"Not a chance." She wasn't that naive young girl pinning all of her dreams on the boy she loved. Now she stood on her own. She was strong enough to sway with the wind, not break. Beth had learned that she could make it on her own and that sharing her life with someone was a choice—not a necessity. She'd never really thought about it before, but without the pain of losing Cam, would she have discovered who she really was?

"Then what's the problem?" Piper shook her head. "Beth, everyone wants to be needed. Even the strongest man needs to be loved as much as anyone else. And so do you. You're right. You did fall apart when Cam left. But you also pulled yourself back together.

"You're the one who made the choices for your life. You built a career you can be proud of. You became a terrific woman with friends and family who love you. All of *that* happened because Cam left, too."

That was probably all true, she thought, knowing that if Cam had stayed, she would have made different choices because she'd have had different opportunities. Would that life have been better? She'd never know.

What she did know was that she liked who she was. Liked her life.

"Beth, what if Cam's waiting to see if you need him?"

She hadn't considered that, but she wasn't convinced. If he was waiting for her to call him, why hadn't he told her that? And that thought didn't even make sense to her.

Rubbing the spot between her eyebrows in a futile attempt to ease a budding headache, Beth heard Piper say, "If you don't make a move, you'll never know what you could have had. Are you willing to live with that kind of regret?"

She looked at her aunt. "Shouldn't you be telling Cam the same thing? Shouldn't he be the one to come to me?"

"Is this about winning?" Piper asked. "Or about love?"

"Maybe it's both."

"No, it can't be. If you're both trying to win, then you both lose."

Beth frowned at her aunt because she just might have a point. But wasn't it supposed to be the guy who did the chasing? The groveling, if necessary?

"Mmm-hmm." Looking completely pleased with herself, Piper added, "I'm glad you're willing to think about it, anyway. All I'm saying is, if you want something badly enough, you find a way to make it work."

Really hard to argue with something that made sense, and Beth was just too tired to try.

"Okay, that's enough of the well-meant lecture portion of our evening." Beth turned and headed up the stairs. "I want a bath."

"A bath is a good time to do some serious thinking…" Piper called after her.

Beth should have brought a bottle of wine with her.

The following night, the Texas Cattleman's Club was crowded with members coming in for the monthly meeting. The outside of the place hadn't changed too much while Cam had been gone. The building had been there forever, a piece of Royal history.

The TCC was a large, rambling single-story building made of dark stone and weathered wood, and boasted a steep slate roof. Once women had been welcomed into the club, the interior had undergone some major changes, according to Tony. The walls were painted a cream color that softened all the heavy dark beams lining the walls and the high ceilings.

Polished dark wood floors carried the marks of generations, with more than a few scars made by indiscriminate spur-wearing by the members. Hunting trophies and historical photos and artifacts hung on the walls, and heavy brown leather furniture invited people to sit and talk for a while.

Here in one of the big meeting rooms, though, banquet style, straight-backed chairs were set out for the members attending the meeting. Cam decided to stand against the wall and Tony was right beside him.

"How's Beth?" Tony asked.

"No idea," Cam answered through gritted teeth. She hadn't called him once all week. She'd been glad enough to have him with her the day of the fire. But since that day, nothing. It was as if she was deliberately shutting him out because she'd been vulnerable the last time they were together.

"Why the hell not?" Tony asked.

Cam looked at his old friend. "She hasn't called."

Tonight was the vote on new members and Cam had wanted to be there. Maybe a stupid decision, but if he was voted out he didn't want someone having to make a sympathetic phone call to let him know. Besides, he wanted to see who supported him and who didn't. Might be a masochistic move, but he'd always believed that *knowing* was better than *guessing*.

Sliding his gaze across the room, he spotted Burt Wheeler in a black blazer thrown on over his jeans and a blue-and-white-striped shirt. His cowboy hat was balanced on his upraised knee, and the frown on his face told Cam exactly how Burt was feeling about the upcoming vote.

"And you haven't bothered to call her," Tony said, "even though you know what crap she and her family are going through right now."

Yeah, he did know. Everyone in Royal was talking about the Wingates. There were stories online, reporters streaming in and out of town and theories about the fire—lots of theories. Some made sense, and others were as outlandish as saying space aliens started the blaze.

Through it all, Beth had not once reached out to him. Clearly she believed she didn't need him around, so Cam had kept his distance. But he was about done with that. Tomorrow, he and Beth were going to talk. Whether she liked it or not. He'd find a way to convince her that he was here now and he wasn't going anywhere. "No, I didn't. Because if she wanted me there, she'd have told me."

"How the hell did you two ever get together in the first place?" Tony asked, astonished. "Two harder heads I've never seen."

"Thanks for the support, pal." He looked away and watched James Harris move slowly to the front of the room, stopping to shake hands and chat along the route. He envied James's easy, comfortable manner. The man was where he belonged and he knew it. Cam was still feeling like an imposter. The son of a couple of horse trainers becoming a member of the TCC? How his father would have laughed at the notion.

The rumble of conversation rose and fell like the tides, and, as an outsider, Cam could see friendships and wary enemies greeting each other.

"You're going to get in," Tony said easily.

"We'll find out soon." In his black suit, white shirt and black hat, Camden glanced around the room and felt as if he were wearing the uniform of the TCC. Every man there was dressed pretty much as he was. Good omen?

Then he spotted Justin McCoy, and everything in him coiled into a tight knot. The man walked through the room like he owned the place, which was just another irritation added to the rest. He carried his hat in his hand, and in the overhead light the man's receding blond hair looked almost white.

Cam stiffened as he followed Justin's progress through the room. He had to wonder if McCoy would still be welcome in the prestigious club if the members knew the truth about him.

Tony followed his gaze and sneered. "The only reason Justin's a member is because his great-great-whatever-grandfather was a founding member."

"Doesn't say much for the membership committee." Just looking at the man made Cam's hands curl into fists.

"No, really doesn't," Tony agreed.

When Justin spotted Cam, he headed right for him, a self-satisfied smirk on his face. It took everything he had for Cam to stay rooted to the spot. All he really wanted to do was meet him halfway and plant his fist in the other man's face.

Justin stopped right in front of him and gave Tony a brief nod of acknowledgment.

"You're not going to get in, you know."

Cam chuckled and his gaze never left Justin's. "You're the one reason that might be okay with me."

Justin flushed, and on his pale face, the red splotches were unmistakable.

"But me being a member isn't up to you, Justin. You just think you're important."

"You're not getting into this club," Justin repeated, then leaned in closer. "And you're not getting Beth. You don't deserve her."

A part of him might have always secretly believed that, but damned if he'd let Justin say it. "You don't want a war with me, Justin…"

"Guys, dial it down, okay?"

Cam ignored Tony's warning. "Because I'm going to tell you right now, I've got plenty of ammo to use against you if that's the way you want to go."

Justin flinched. Cam saw it in his eyes, but he still used bravado to talk his way out. "I'm not worried. Do what you want. Who here would ever believe Camden Guthrie against a McCoy?"

When Justin moved on, Tony leaned in and said. "Don't get yourself in a twist. The man's a dick. No one likes him. No one listens to him."

Justin McCoy was all that and more, Cam thought. He forced himself to put McCoy out of his mind and concentrate instead on his own future.

Beth saw it all.

Her gaze had fixed on Cam the moment she slipped into the meeting room. As if there was no one else in the place, she could see only him. He wore an elegantly cut suit and tie and held his black hat in his right hand. He and Tony were talking together when Justin came up and said something that had Cam's features turning to stone.

The confrontation didn't last long, and Beth really wanted to know what they'd been talking about. But a moment later, James Harris was calling the meeting to order.

Beth slunk down in her chair at the back of the room. She was there for the membership vote because she could at least cast her vote for Cam. But she didn't want him to see her until she was ready.

The Wingates had been members of the TCC for decades though it was only recently that women had been accepted. Even now though, there were still several of the old guard at the club who resented any female strolling through the hallowed halls of the Texas Cattleman's Club.

But, as more than one woman had said, *Too bad for them.*

Beth smiled at a couple of friends, then turned her attention to James. No matter how many times someone spoke up to interrupt him, he calmly kept the meeting on track. She didn't envy him the task of trying to ride herd on such a big group.

Quietly she watched the wealthiest, most influential people in Royal calling across the room like high school kids, laughing and talking. Her brothers were all here, too, and she thought of them all as creating a Wingate Wall against suspicion and gossip.

Everyone in town had had something to say about

the fire at WinJet. They were all waiting to see what would happen next, and Beth was right there with them.

But tonight she wasn't thinking about the family or the company. Her thoughts were focused on Camden and what her aunt Piper had said to her the day before. *If they were both trying to win, they were both going to lose.*

When the vote was finally called, Beth raised her hand to vote yes on Cam's membership, and she was glad to see that her brothers did, too. And except for a small handful of Burt Wheeler's cronies—and Justin McCoy of course—the vote was overwhelmingly on Cam's side.

She looked at him in time to see him grin at Tony, and her heart did a quick leap. Cam was the one she wanted, and she'd realized earlier that day that Piper had a point. Why should she wait for him to come to her? Didn't she have the same right as a man to go after what she wanted ?

She smiled to herself at the realization. But tonight wasn't the time for her to face Camden and tell him how she felt. He was surrounded by people shaking his hand and welcoming him into the TCC. This was a night for him to concentrate on his win. She could wait until tomorrow.

Still smiling, she slipped out of her seat and headed for the door. She felt better than she had in more than a week. She'd made a decision to go for it. To risk it all for a chance at love and happiness. She whispered, "And I won't take no for an answer."

"Beth!"

She groaned and half-heartedly turned to wait for

Justin McCoy. If Cam looked over here, he'd see her. Hopefully, he had as little interest in Justin as she did.

"I didn't know you were coming tonight," he said, face flushed from rushing through the crowd to catch up with her.

She smiled up at him. "Well, my brothers and I wanted to be here to vote for Cam."

His lips thinned into such a fine line his mouth looked like a wrinkle in his chin. "I wish you hadn't done that."

"Well, I'm sorry you feel that way." Beth inched toward the door. "I really can't stay, Justin."

"Now, no need to rush off." He draped one arm around her shoulders and Beth squirmed out from under him.

"Justin…"

"Beth," he said patiently, "it's time you got past this infatuation with Camden Guthrie and realized that you and I are meant to be."

She blinked at him. Really, she couldn't even think of anything to say to that. How did you argue with someone who was so removed from reality?

"I understand you have some memories of Guthrie, but those are long dead. The future is for *us*."

"Justin, that's never going to happen."

He held on to her again, pulling her to his side, and Beth had to work harder this time to get him off her. She didn't want to make a scene—people were talking about the Wingates already. But if he didn't stop pawing at her, Beth might show him a few of the anti-male moves her brothers had taught her when she was a teenager.

Staring up into his eyes, she willed him to pay attention. "Listen to me, Justin. The answer to you is no. It will always be no."

"You heard the lady."

Beth jolted. She had been so focused on getting rid of Justin that she hadn't noticed the man she loved walking up to them. Now he and Tony were standing side by side, and Cam's gaze was fixed on Justin. No one else had really noticed anything going on because the noise level was loud enough to drown out anything.

All Beth could see was Cam. His dark eyes flashed with heat and banked fury, and she wished Justin McCoy to the other side of the planet. She laid one hand on his forearm and felt the tension in his body. "It's okay, Cam. I'm fine. And Justin's leaving."

"Yeah, he is," Cam said, staring at Justin with an angry glare before flicking a glance at Beth. "There's a lot of things I'm willing to take, but this isn't one of them."

"What're you talking about?" Beth moved closer to Cam.

He looked down at her again. "If you don't want me, that's fine. Your choice. But damned if I'll watch you hook up with this son of a bitch."

"Who're you calling an SOB?" Justin demanded.

"Excuse me?" Beth said, outraged that he would think she'd be interested in Justin. If he'd seen the man drape his arm around her, hadn't he also seen her trying to escape? "You just heard me tell him 'no' again."

"You're not saying it loud enough," Cam argued.

"The only way I could be louder is with a microphone."

"Stay out of this, Beth," Justin said.

"Agreed," Cam said, his gaze boring into Justin's.

"This is between me and you." Cam kept his voice low enough that only their tight circle could hear him. "You think I'll let you anywhere near Beth when we both know damn well what you did to Julie."

"You don't know what you're talking about."

"What did he do?" Beth asked, shooting a wary look at Justin before turning her gaze back to Cam.

Cam speared Justin with a hot glare that should have set fire to what was left of his hair.

Speaking quietly to Beth, he said, "I promised Julie I'd never say a word about this. But she's gone now and damned if I'm going to let him strut around here acting like he's got nothing to be ashamed of."

Justin's cheeks flushed red and his eyes shifted from side to side as if looking for an escape. He didn't find one.

Cam continued and Beth couldn't tear her eyes from him.

"Justin seduced Julie. Set out to get her and he did. Got her pregnant and then tried to force her to marry him. He wanted into the Wheeler family," Cam said, voice dark and low. "He wanted her money. Wanted a piece of the ranch, and he didn't mind telling her any of it once he was sure she was going to have his baby."

Justin puffed out his chest and lifted his chin. "That's a lie."

Beth didn't think so. Glancing at the man now, she could see the truth etched into his hard features. She felt immediate sympathy for Julie. To have been used like that must have crushed her.

"It's the absolute truth and you damn well know it," Cam said.

"How could you do that to her? To *anyone*?" Beth asked.

Justin looked at her, and his mouth thinned into that straight, bitter line again.

"When she told Justin she was pregnant, he told her that she had to marry him." Cam looked the man up and down dismissively. "He knew Burt would be furious so he figured he had Julie trapped." Cam shot Beth a quick look. "But she wouldn't go along with it. She was scared to tell her father the truth, so she came to me."

Beth's heart hurt. For Julie. For Cam. For all of them. Well, everyone but Justin. "God, Camden..."

Apparently, Justin saw that Beth believed every word. He knew now he didn't have a shot with her, so he faced Cam angrily. "If you repeat any of that story, Guthrie... I'll sue."

Cam moved in on him. "You stay the hell away from Beth, I'll keep quiet about all of this. But not for you," Cam ground out. "For Julie. She doesn't deserve to be gossiped about. You did enough damage to her life."

"Julie was an idiot," Justin said, dismissing the girl he'd used and ruined. "If she'd just married me like I'd planned, none of this would have happened."

Beth sucked in a deep breath as Burt Wheeler stood up from a nearby chair. None of them had noticed him. But clearly he'd heard everything. Burt was trembling with barely controlled rage as he stalked directly to Justin.

"You did all of that to my girl. You bastard."

Justin backed up a step and bumped into Tony Alvarez. He was trapped, and the expression on his face said that he knew it.

Burt wasn't finished. "If I ever hear my Julie's name coming out of your mouth again, I swear by all that's holy, I will beat you into the ground."

Justin believed him. Beth could see that truth on the man's face. He backed away again slowly and Tony let him go. When Justin saw a clear path out of the building and through the crowd, he took it, crashing into people as he made a hasty exit.

Sympathy welled up in Beth's heart for Burt. The man looked as if his own heart had just been ripped from his chest. He took a shaky breath, then stepped up to Cam and held out his right hand.

"I was wrong about you, Guthrie. And I'm sorry for it. I'm sorrier still that my girl was too afraid to come to me when she needed help." His eyes were wounded, and Beth knew that he would be haunted by that knowledge for the rest of his life.

Cam shook the older man's hand and said, "Julie loved you, Burt. She wasn't afraid you'd hurt her. She was afraid of disappointing you."

Some of the pain in his eyes eased. "That's something, I guess." Burt sighed heavily and slowly shook his head. "I'm going inside to talk to James. I want to change my vote on your membership."

Nodding, Cam said, "Thank you, Burt."

He nodded. "You did right by my Julie. You took care of her and helped her when she needed it most. I was too blind to see that sooner, but I do now, and I thank you for that."

"That was kind," Beth whispered.

Cam was watching the older man thread his way through the people in the room. "He's not a bad man. Just a hard one."

Beth was silent for a second or two before turning on Cam. "You honestly thought I was 'with' Justin?"

He frowned at her. "You looked pretty cozy to me."

"So you didn't notice me trying to get away from him?"

"That's why I came over. I didn't like him touching you."

"Okay, I'm gone." Tony Alvarez moved away, leaving Cam and Beth alone.

Beth said, "Why haven't you called me all week?"

"You could have called to tell me you wanted to talk to me."

"Seriously?" Her jaw dropped. "I have to tell you that?"

People were turning to look. Everyone had missed the upset with Justin and Burt, but now they were paying attention.

"Damn it, Beth—" He grabbed her hand and led her through the crowd and out into the parking lot.

She had to hurry to keep up and didn't mind a bit. It was past time they talked. Really *talked*. Cam didn't stop until he was in a far corner of the darkened lot, where the shadows were deep and the nearby oaks dipped low enough to provide some privacy. A soft, warm wind blew past them and brought the scent of coming rain with it.

Beth didn't care. Lightning could have split the sky and dumped gallons of water down on them and still she would stand there, looking up into the dark chocolate eyes staring down at her.

"Look," he said tightly, "I waited a week. Gave you the time and space or whatever the hell else you needed, but I'm done now."

Her heart took another high leap. "Is that right?"

"Damn straight it is." He dropped both hands to her shoulders and pulled her close. "I get that you don't trust me. I'll earn that back if I have to work at it for the rest of my life."

She did trust him and would have said so if he hadn't kept talking.

"And, if you think I'm going away again, you're wrong. I'm here for good. And if I ever *did* decide to leave, I'd go nowhere without *you*."

Her heart was pounding, her breath coming in short, hard puffs, and she felt as if she could fly. Beth read the truth of his words in his eyes, in his expression, in the hard grip on her shoulders. "I believe you."

That surprised him. "You do?"

"Of course I do." She reached up and cupped his cheek in her palm. "I was done waiting, too. I was going to come to you tomorrow to tell you that I want you to marry me. I want us to have kids. Make a family. And live on your ranch just like we used to dream about, remember?"

He wrapped his arms around her, looked down into her eyes and said, "Why do you think that's the ranch I bought when I came home? I remember everything, Beth. And just so you know, I was coming to you tomorrow, too."

"Really?" She smiled up at him, and everything inside her settled into a warm glow that filled her so completely it should have been spilling from her fingertips.

"Really." He let her go long enough to dip into his jacket pocket and come up with a blue velvet ring box. "I drove into Dallas this afternoon. I wanted to have it with me when I asked you."

She took a breath and held it while she blinked frantically to prevent tears from filling her eyes and spoiling the view of the man she loved holding a ring.

"You have it with you now," she said softly.

"I have *you* with me," he countered, "and that's the most important thing. This—" he flipped the lid open, displaying a huge, square diamond flashing up at her "—is just a celebration of that."

Beth's breath caught as she looked up into his eyes again. "It's beautiful, Cam. It's perfect."

"Not until it's on your finger it's not." He lifted her left hand and kissed her knuckles. Beth felt that kiss all the way to her bones.

"I love you, Beth," he said, his gaze locked on hers. "I loved who you were then and I love who you've become. I don't want to spend another day without you. Beth Wingate, will you marry me?"

"Yes," she said quickly, and sighed as he slid that gorgeous ring onto her hand. She wiggled her finger and admired the flash and shine for a couple of seconds, then looked up at him. "I love you, Camden. I always have. Always will."

"That's what I needed to hear." He framed her face with his hands and leaned in to kiss her softly, almost reverently. "You know, back in the day, I'd half convinced myself that I just didn't deserve you."

"That's ridiculous."

"No." He shook his head. "What's ridiculous is I almost let myself get convinced of that again."

"I never would have let you get away with that," she said, smiling as she leaned into him and laid her head on his chest, where she heard the steady thump of his heart. "We deserve each other, Camden. And we deserve the life we're going to make together."

"Darlin'." He pulled her back so he could give her a grin. "What a time we're going to have."

And then he kissed her, and Beth knew that this time they had both won.

* * * * *

FORBIDDEN LUST

KAREN BOOTH

For the members of the Backstage Antics with Karen crew on Facebook. You guys are the absolute best!

One

Zane Patterson's heart was hammering. His T-shirt was soaked with sweat, clinging to his shoulders. "I need to get out of this town. That's all there is to it." He dribbled the basketball with his right hand. *Thump. Thump. Thump.* Switching to his left, Zane waited for his opening—his chance to drive past his best friend, Scott Randall. Their weekly game of one-on-one was tied. One more point and victory was Zane's. So very close. He did not like to lose. He hated it.

"Dude. You've been saying that since high school. It's been fifteen years." Laser-focused on Zane's every move, Scott shuffled from side to side, hands high, low and anywhere Zane dared to even think about looking. Scott didn't allow himself to get distracted by the perspiration raining down from the top of his shiny bald head. He only cared about not giving up the final point. "You either need to leave or get over it."

The reason for leaving—Joshua Lowell—popped into Zane's head. Zane despised him. He had the smuggest smile, like he was perfectly comfortable with the silver spoon firmly lodged in his mouth at birth. The entirety of Falling Brook, New Jersey, put that jerk on a pedestal, even when his father had destroyed lives and families, including Zane's. Deep down, Zane loved his hometown, but being here was pushing him closer and closer to the edge. *Get over it? No way.*

Thump. He palmed the ball. *Thump.* Left. *Thump.* Right. *Thump.* Back left. He dropped his shoulder, slipped around Scott and beelined for the basket. With Scott in hot pursuit but several strides behind him, Zane finger-rolled the ball for a layup. It circled the rim. And popped back out. Scott grabbed the rebound, spun away from Zane and hoisted up a perfect jumper. Nothing but net.

Dammit.

"Yes!" Scott darted under the basket and snatched the ball. "Rematch? Best two out of three?"

Zane bent over, clutching the hem of his basketball shorts and planting the heels of his hands on his knees. "No." The competitive part of him wanted the win. Needed it. Playing basketball was one of the only activities that had ever made him happy. He'd been at it since he could walk, precisely the reason he had an indoor court installed when his company, Patterson Marketing, took off and they built their own state-of-the-art office building. But he was too exhausted to compete. Or fight. Mentally, more than anything. "I'm done."

"This Joshua Lowell thing is really getting to you,

isn't it?" Scott rested the ball on his hip, letting the weight of his forearm hold it in place.

"I can't get away from it. The anniversary article was supposed to remind everyone what crooks the Lowells are, how they destroyed lives, how they can never be trusted. Instead, Josh's engagement to Sophie Armstrong is all anyone is talking about. It's everywhere. Facebook. Twitter. The Java Hut. My own freaking staff meeting."

"It's a big deal. He's stepping away from BC. Nobody saw that coming."

BC. The initials for Black Crescent were enough to make Zane cringe. The hedge fund, founded by Joshua Lowell's father, Vernon, had been an ultraexclusive avenue of investment for the superrich. Zane's family had once breathed the rarefied air of those on the limited client list, and for a time, the world was sunshine and roses. There was no shortage of money, and Zane's life was golden—king of the school at Falling Brook Prep, captain of the basketball team, parents happily married. Then Vernon disappeared with millions, Zane's family was left penniless and his parents' marriage was destroyed.

Losing their family fortune meant that Zane had been moved from Prep to the public high school at the age of sixteen. It was another brutal adjustment, especially since the kids at Falling Brook High treated Zane like the rich kid who needed to be taken down a notch or two. They had no idea Zane was already at rock bottom. The only consolation was that he'd met Scott there, and they'd been best friends ever since.

Scott saved Zane, mostly from himself. Scott didn't give a damn about the money; he only wanted to help, and he only wanted to be friends. They were solid from day one. When Zane's mom and dad fought, which was often, Scott's parents allowed Zane to seek refuge at their house. It was an oasis of calm—the one place happiness seemed possible. One of the best parts of those stays was spending time with Scott's younger sister, Allison. She was the coolest, smartest and most creative person Zane had ever met. She was supercute, too, but Zane had always looked past that. She was Scott's sister, and Zane would never, ever go there. Never.

"Did you see Josh's press conference? Did you hear what he said? 'She brought me out of the dark with her love'? 'Because she loves me, I am worthy'? What a load of crap." Zane didn't enjoy being so bitter, but the fifteen years since Vernon Lowell disappeared had done nothing to assuage his pain over his entire life crumbling to dust. As far as Zane was concerned, all Lowells—Vernon; his wife, Eve; and his kids, Joshua, Jake and Oliver—were pure poison. He didn't want to see any of them happy.

"You know what they say. Love makes everything better."

Zane shot Scott a look. Romantic love was a farce. It rarely, if ever, lasted. Zane's parents were a classic example. Yes, they'd been tested when Vernon Lowell stole every penny they had, but wasn't love supposed to conquer all? Not from where Zane was sitting. "Said like a very married man."

"Don't get salty because I'm happy. Last time I checked, there wasn't a law against it."

Zane grumbled under his breath. He didn't want to continue this part of their conversation.

The two men wandered over to the corner of the

gym to grab the six-pack of microbrew Scott had stashed in the fully stocked beverage fridge. Zane was more of a tequila or mescal guy, but after a game, there was nothing better than knocking back a cold beer. They took it outside to the patio, where employees often enjoyed their lunch or an afternoon meeting if the weather was nice. A warm June night, the air was sweet and a bit heavy with humidity, but there was a pleasant breeze. Zane and Scott sat at a table, and Scott popped open the first two bottles. They clinked them to toast.

Zane took in a deep breath, washing down his resentment with that first sip of beer, trying to remind himself that he really did love it here. "I never should have gone to Joshua Lowell at the bar and told him I knew about the DNA report because I was the one who gave it to Sophie for the article about Black Crescent. I should have let him wonder who her sources were. I should have let him stew in his own juices. That's what he deserves." He took another long draw of his drink. That had been a difficult confrontation. Just seeing Joshua Lowell face-to-face was enough to make him physically ill. "I wanted him to know that he wasn't as high and mighty as everyone thought. That I knew who he really was."

Zane remembered the odd jolt that went through his body when he received the DNA report in the mail, saying that Josh had a daughter and was refusing to take responsibility. It hadn't occurred to Zane just how peculiar it was for someone to have sent that to him. He hadn't even thought too hard about why the anonymous sender would pick him as the recipient. He'd only known that it was ammunition to take down a Lowell, and that had been more than enough. "The whole point of talking to Sophie was to finally tell the world that Josh Lowell is not the savior everyone thinks he is. I even gave her personal photos to use, to show her I was a legit source. Somehow that all backfired. The DNA bombshell never made it into the anniversary article, because I picked a reporter with scruples. Now everyone seems to adore him even more than before. Just in time for him to fall in love with a beautiful woman, decide to get married and conveniently step away from Black Crescent, which is the main reason to hate him. He's getting off without a scratch, just like his dad."

Scott shook his head, the corner of his mouth turned up in a pitying smirk. "Maybe you do need a break. Get away."

"Or move."

Scott set his elbow on the table, pointing at Zane with his beer bottle. "You cannot move. I need you."

"You're drunk."

"Half a beer in? I don't think so. It's the truth. You're like a brother to me. And honestly, I think you need me. Who else is going to listen to you bitch about this?"

Scott wasn't wrong. He grounded Zane and helped him stay away from his inevitable downward spiral. "Okay. So where do I go? I need a beach, preferably with lots of women."

"It does not surprise me that you would say that."

Zane let a quiet laugh leave his lips. Yes, he had been with a lot of women over the years. That was his escape. No strings attached, no messy feelings getting in the way. In high school, it had been to numb the effects of his fall from grace. The poor former rich kid proved an easy target for other guys, but the girls didn't see it that way. His money and status might have been gone, but the body he'd spent hours working on in the gym and his face were still enough to turn a few heads. So he'd taken what he could get.

"If it's the beach you want," Scott said, "you should go down to the Bahamas. My aunt and uncle's resort off the coast of Eleuthera. I can hook you up."

Scott and Zane had talked many times about making that trip. Scott's mom was Bahamian, but had moved to the US permanently after attending college stateside and meeting Scott's dad. "Yes. Dudes' trip. We've talked about it a hundred times. It's perfect."

"Sorry, man. You're on your own. Brittney just got a promotion at work, and her schedule is crazy. It's June, so the kids are out of school. I can't just take off. Plus, if you're picking up women, I think we can both agree that my days of being your wingman are over."

Zane didn't let the disappointment get to him too much. Everything was a downer of one sort or another. He was used to it. "Okay. I guess I'm flying solo. Can you text me the info? I'll call first thing tomorrow morning."

Scott shook his head. "Just give me the dates and I'll take care of it. It's on me."

"I do not need your charity. This isn't high school."

"Will you just shut up and let me do something nice for you? Plus, I gotta keep you happy. I would be ridiculously bummed out if you moved out of Falling Brook."

Zane glanced over at Scott. He didn't know what he would do without him. He was the thing tethering him to earth. Keeping him from going off the deep end. "I'm not leaving. I might desperately need a few days on that beach to clear my head, but I'm not going anywhere." He knocked back the last of his beer. "I have to at least stick around long enough to avenge this loss."

"Black Crescent?" Scott asked.

"No. Tonight's game."

When Allison Randall saw her ex-boyfriend's name on the caller ID, she flipped off her phone. Juvenile, but incredibly satisfying.

"Let me guess. Neil?" Allison's best friend and business partner, Kianna Lewis, was perched in a chair opposite Allison's desk, flicking a pen back and forth between her thumb and forefinger. They'd been discussing the state of their corporate recruiting business, which frankly, wasn't that great.

"I really don't want to talk to him. Ever."

"Aren't the movers at his house right now? What if there's a problem?"

Kianna was so levelheaded. Allison needed that. She could get tunnel vision. And a little spiteful. "You're right. I'm just ready for one of these conversations to be our last." Allison plucked her phone from her desk and spun her chair around to peer out the window of her office, which overlooked nothing more scenic than a sea of expensive cars in a parking lot. Such was LA—asphalt and BMWs. "What's wrong now?" she asked Neil.

"You could have hired a normal moving company, Allison. Hunks with Trucks? Seriously?" Her ex-boyfriend was not taking her departure from his life well. That was perfectly okay with her.

Allison snickered under her breath. Neil was in ridiculously good shape, and he loved to flaunt it. He took any excuse to whip off his shirt in public. Allison had figured he might as well spend the afternoon with a bunch of guys who were even more buff and cut than him. Served him right for cheating on her. "They hire college students, Neil. These guys need the work. For tuition and books. Just forget the name, okay?"

"That's a little difficult when their ten-foot-high logo is emblazoned on the truck outside my house. The neighbors can all see it."

What a drama queen. She should have known better than to date a movie producer. "Sounds like good marketing on their part."

"There's a crowd gathering. A bunch of women from my street are outside taking selfies with these guys."

This had gone far better than Allison could have anticipated. She nearly wished she'd been there to witness it, except that would have meant seeing Neil, and she couldn't guarantee she wouldn't strangle him. "If you hadn't cheated on me, you wouldn't have to suffer this supposed embarrassment."

"I made a mistake, okay? It happens. You need to get off that high horse of yours. Not everyone can be perfect like you."

She choked back a grumble. "Not cheating does not make me perfect. It makes me a decent human being, which is more than I can say for you."

"I've told you one hundred times that she meant nothing to me. It was just a few months of hookups. I was stupid for doing it, and I'm sorry."

Allison clamped her eyes shut. She was not going to let him manipulate her anymore. "I'm done with this conversation, Neil. Unless there's a real problem you need me to address, I'm going to hang up now."

"I want my key back, Alli."

"Change the locks. And don't call me Alli." She hit the red button on the screen and tossed her phone onto a pile of papers on her desk. The desire to scream was so intense she dug her fingernails into her palms.

"You okay?" Kianna asked, arching her perfectly groomed eyebrows.

"I'm fine." Allison was a firm believer in fake it 'til you make it. She would keep saying she was fine until she was actually fine. Still, the Neil situation had her shaken. How had she not seen that Neil was an arrogant jerk? How had she managed to miss the signs? As an executive recruiter, it was Allison's job to read people, but she'd clearly been all wrong about Neil.

"It's okay to have a human moment. Your boyfriend cheated on you. No one would blame you for crying or throwing things."

No, no one would fault her, but Allison refused to let this drag her down. Neil would move on with his life in his perfect house, with his suspiciously white teeth and 3 percent body fat. Allison was not going to let him be the only one to find happiness. "I'm fine. Let's get back to work. We need to finish this up so I can head over to my new place and meet the movers."

"Okay. If that's what you want." Kianna launched into a summary of their bottom line. It didn't take long. The upshot was too many expenses, not enough income. "All of this makes the Black Crescent account that much more important. If we nail this first assignment for them, we should be able to go on retainer. That will put us safely in the black."

Having a new client in her hometown of Falling Brook, New Jersey, was a real boon. Allison had pulled in a favor to make it happen, but she was sure it could translate into big things. "We can do it. I can do it. I will knock their socks off. I promise." The best part was that it would not only bring in money, she could see her brother, Scott. Allison had been there for his birthday last month, but she always looked forward to their time together.

"How soon are you planning to go out there and meet with them?"

Allison flipped through her calendar. "I haven't booked my travel yet, but I'm thinking next week. My plan is to walk into that meeting with the three amazing candidates we've been talking to for the position."

"Can I make a suggestion?"

"You think I should go sooner?"

"I think you should *leave* sooner, as in go somewhere for a few days. Relax. Unwind. Meet a hot guy and let him rock your world. Get Neil out of your system."

"But we have so much work to do."

"And we need you on top of your game when you meet with Black Crescent. You're wound way too tight right now."

Allison had to laugh. "Have you been talking to my mom?"

"Please tell me your mom didn't tell you to hook up with some guy."

"She didn't. But she did tell my aunt Angelique about Neil, and Angelique called last night begging me to come and stay with her and my uncle for a few days at their resort in the Bahamas. Bad news travels fast among the women in my family." Allison was incredibly close to her mom, so much so that she felt suffocated sometimes. So of course, they'd had many phone conversations about the Neil situation, and it was only a matter of time before her aunt found out.

"That sounds perfect. I say you do it. As long as there are men available, of course." Kianna got up from her chair, gathered her notes in her arms and headed for the door.

"A man is the last thing I need."

Kianna turned and cast Allison a stern look. "I'm not talking marriage. I'm talking sex. A few mind-blowing orgasms and Neil will be a distant memory."

"I'm not much for random hookups. I'm not even sure I can do that."

"Have you looked at yourself? Any sane guy would be psyched to take you to bed." Kianna turned on her heel and headed down the hall.

Allison wasn't sure about that, but maybe it was time to do something nice for herself—book a bungalow on the beach and fall asleep in the sun with a good book. She fumbled for her phone and dialed the number for her aunt.

"Tell me you're on the plane," Angelique said when she answered.

Allison smiled. She couldn't help it. She loved her entire family deeply. "Not yet."

"But you're coming?"

"As long as you have room for me."

"I have one bungalow open, so we have room. It's all yours. I hope it's okay if I put you next to one of your brother's friends, though. Zane Patterson?"

That name started a long-forgotten hum in Allison's body. Zane was the guy Allison had crushed on for every waking minute of her adolescence. "He's not coming with Scott, is he?"

"Oh, no. By himself. Just for a few days. He gets here tomorrow."

Allison's heart was jackhammering in her chest. Visions of unbelievably sexy Zane rushed into her consciousness—thick dark hair with a hint of curl, piercing blue eyes that made her melt and a long, lean body she'd wanted to touch forever. She had a good dozen or so Zane fantasies she'd concocted over the years. Why had she never thought up the one where they both ended up on a secluded Bahamian island at the same time? "Oh. Funny. I was thinking I'd fly in tomorrow, too."

"Do you know him?"

"I do. He's a great guy. It's always nice to see him." Allison couldn't ignore the way her voice had suddenly pitched to a higher octave. "Nice to see him" didn't begin to cover it.

But there'd always been a massive obstacle with Zane—Scott. The only time she'd had any real physical contact with Zane was three weeks ago, when they were at her brother's house for his birthday dinner. This was right after Allison had first found out Neil was cheating. Feeling hurt, reckless and pleasantly tipsy, she'd spent most of the evening testing the waters of flirtation with Zane. She knocked her knee into his under the table, brushed his hand with her fingertips when reaching for the butter and made a point of making eye contact when she laughed at his jokes. There was a palpable connection between them, a very real spark, and she could only play with fire for so long before jumping in headfirst. So as soon as Scott and his wife left the table to put their kids to bed, Allison had grabbed her chance. She gripped Zane's muscled forearm, leaned in and kissed him. For a blissful instant, Zane was into it.

So into it.

He'd cupped her jaw with his hand like he was drinking her in. The years of wanting him day after day had been building for that moment, and she was overwhelmed by a deluge of heat and a rush of something she hadn't experienced in too long—pure hope. She arched into him, and he followed her cue, wrapping his arm around her and pressing his chest against hers. It was really happening, and her mind had leaped ahead to what came next…a quick escape, a race back to his place, clothes coming off before they were even inside, lips and hands exploring the landscape of each other's bodies until they were both exhausted. It was going to happen. Finally.

Then he froze. And everything else became a blur. He pushed her away, ashamed to look her in the eye. He blurted something about betraying Scott. He said he was sorry. He shook his head and muttered that it had been a mistake. He pushed back from the table and rushed out the door, leaving Allison shell-shocked. How could she have been so close and have it all taken away? It felt like a cruel joke life was playing on her. It hurt like hell.

For weeks, that painful scene played in her head. But once she got beyond the hurt, she realized that the real problem had been Scott. If they'd been truly alone that night, her fantasies would've come true. She and Zane would've been naked and sweaty in no time.

But hopefully, Zane wouldn't be so worried about her hyperprotective brother if he was a thousand miles away. With close proximity to Zane and some privacy, she could finally go for what she'd always wanted—a night of pure abandon with Zane. She knew better than to hope for more than that. He was the ultimate ladies' man, and she was okay with that. He was who he was, and she still wanted him more than any man she'd ever laid eyes on. If she played her cards right, she'd at least get to fulfill this fantasy, even if it was only a onetime thing.

"Do you want me to tell him you're coming?"

If Allison had been talking to Kianna, she might have made a joke about orgasms, but that was not appropriate with her aunt. "No. Don't. I'll surprise him."

"I'm so happy you're coming to stay, Alli. It's been too long."

"I'm excited to spend some time unwinding."

"Text me your flight details. I'll have someone pick you up at the marina."

"Sounds perfect. See you tomorrow."

Allison gathered her things, closed up her office, said goodbye to Kianna and hurried out to the parking lot, feeling a new purpose in every step. She hopped into her Mercedes, cranked the stereo and headed toward her new apartment, where the guys from Hunks with Trucks would soon be waiting to move her into her new place. She wasn't even going to bother to unpack. She was going to let them in to do their work while she turned around to go shopping for a hat, a sarong and the skimpiest bikini she could find. Then she was going to get a good night's beauty sleep and get her butt on a plane tomorrow morning.

Next stop, paradise. Next stop, Zane.

Two

The flight from Miami to Eleuthera Island was not for the faint of heart. Scott's aunt and uncle Angelique and Hubert had booked a charter for Zane on the tiniest of Learjets. Still, Zane loved the freedom of hanging by an invisible thread over the jaw-dropping blue of the Atlantic.

Zane's pulse skipped a beat as the aircraft floated down to the tiny landing strip and bounced its way to an abrupt stop. Another five hundred yards and they would've been in the ocean. Engines whirring, the plane taxied around to a modest outbuilding—yellow with a rust-red roof. The crew quickly opened the cabin door, and Zane whipped off his seat belt, sucking in his first sweet breath of Bahamian air. Sunglasses on, he surveyed the landscape from his vantage point at the top of the plane stairs. Palm trees rustled in the wind, and gauzy white clouds rolled across the seemingly endless stretch of azure sky. This was exactly what he'd needed. He knew it already.

A driver from Rose Cove, the boutique resort owned by Scott's aunt and uncle, met him outside the airport building, and after a quick zip through customs, Zane was on his way to the marina in a golf cart. From there, a speedboat captain named Marcus took Zane for the two-mile trip to Rose Cove Island, off the southernmost tip of Eleuthera. The water was tranquil and clear, the wind buzzing through Zane's ears as the boat sliced through the water and the sun blanketed him in warmth. He pulled his phone out of his pocket and powered it down. He had zero plans to look at it while he was in paradise. He not only needed to unwind, he wanted to disappear. Falling Brook, the Lowell family and Black Crescent weren't even a distant thought—they'd evaporated from his mind.

Pulling up to the dock at Rose Cove, Zane was struck by the beauty of the pink sand beaches from which the tiny private island got its name. Marcus directed him down a crushed-seashell path through a tropical forest so shaded by palm trees that it was a good ten degrees cooler. Colorful birds chirped and flitted from tree to tree, while the occasional lizard skittered across the sandy ground to hide behind a rock. He eventually reached a clearing with a white single-story building of colonial architecture, with a porch that wrapped around the entire structure. Inside, Zane finally got to meet Scott's aunt Angelique.

"Welcome to Rose Cove!" she exclaimed, rushing out from behind the check-in desk, wearing a beautiful turquoise sundress, flat sandals and her braided hair pulled up in a twist. Despite her enthusiasm, Angelique's peaceful voice suggested that she lived her life at a pace far different from the rest of the world's. "My nephew has told me so much about you." She gave him a hug, showing the same warmth Zane had found in Scott's entire family. He already felt at home here. He wasn't sure he ever wanted to leave.

"You can't believe everything Scott says," Zane joked.

Angelique smiled wide. "He had nothing but great things to say." She bustled back behind the counter and unfolded what appeared to be a map. "Here's all you need to know about the island. This is the main building, where my husband, Hubert, and I live." She circled a picture of the building where they were. "The ten cottages spoke out from here and are a good distance from each other for privacy. You're in cottage number eight. You have a quiet stretch of beach, a hammock and a private plunge pool. There's a beautiful king-size bed, a luxury bath and a fully stocked kitchen. Or our staff will bring you breakfast, lunch and dinner every day. Simply fill out the card waiting for you in your room. Until then, I invite you to relax and enjoy the island. Perhaps say hello to your neighbor in cottage nine. She's been waiting for you to arrive."

"A neighbor?" *A she, no less?* Perhaps this was Zane's lucky day, although there was a part of him that knew his tendency to get lost in women was not his best trait. Really, he should be focusing on fishing and swimming while detoxing from social media and the internet.

"My niece, Allison. She arrived a few hours ago."

Zane's jaw dropped so far he had to make a conscious decision to close his mouth. He was flabbergasted. What were the chances that he and Allison would end up on the island at the same time? "Allison is here. On this island. Right now."

"Is there a problem?"

He shook his head so fast he nearly lost his sunglasses, which were resting on top of his head. "Absolutely not. I love Allison. I'm just surprised. I'll have to stop over and say hi." He hadn't seen Allison much in the years since he graduated from high school. He'd gone to college in North Carolina on a basketball scholarship, and when he returned to Falling Brook after four years, she was off to school in Los Angeles, where she stayed to start a business. She returned every Christmas, but Zane always seemed to be visiting his mom in Boston at the same time. But three weeks ago Scott's wife, Brittney, invited both Allison and Zane to a surprise birthday dinner she was having for Scott. Allison flew in for the weekend. The instant Zane saw her, he knew exactly how good the years had been to Allison—almost too good. She'd taken a straight line from cute to drop-dead gorgeous. Her long and wavy black hair was pulled back in a ponytail, showing off the incredible depth and warmth of her brown eyes. The chemistry of the entire room shifted when she smiled or laughed. He'd always found her interesting and a bit otherworldly, with a style and vibe all her own, but that night he was transfixed.

She'd surprised him many times when they were younger, like the day she got her nose pierced, but she'd flat-out shocked him that night at Scott's house. She kissed him—soft and sensuous and so packed with

sexy intent that he'd felt the earth shift beneath him.
He was so conditioned to think of Allison only as his
best friend's little sister that he'd been wholly unpre-
pared for Allison, the fully formed woman. And with
Scott in the other room, a man to whom there would
be no explaining, Zane had done the unthinkable that
night. He'd pushed beautiful, beguiling Allison away.

"Well, she has the cottage next to yours, so I'm sure
you'll see her," Angelique said.

Now Zane was wondering how in the hell he was
going to navigate these difficult waters. He didn't want
to relive the awkward aftermath of that kiss. Their
conversation from that night was permanently emblazoned on his psyche.

This is wrong, Allison. Your brother.

Don't talk about Scott.

*But he's right in the other room. He will never for-
give me.*

Women had been Zane's escape many times, but not
like that. Never before had he risked one of the most
important things in his life for a kiss.

It had been such a blur, Zane had left without saying so much as goodbye to Scott, asking Allison to tell
him that he had a headache. She told him he was getting freaked out for nothing, but Zane knew his weak-
ness when it came to women, and Allison was the one
woman he absolutely could never have.

"Mr. Patterson? Are you sure everything is okay?
Scott mentioned that you've been under a lot of stress."
Angelique looked at him quizzically, knocking her
head to one side.

"Oh, yes. Sorry." He shook his head in an effort to
get it straight. He needed to get a grip. He and Allison

had shared a kiss. It was no big deal. Scott would never know about it, and it would never happen again—end of story.

"Is there anything else you need?"

"My room key, I guess."

"There are no keys on Rose Cove. You will enjoy more seclusion and privacy than you ever imagined. But I'm happy to have someone show you to your cottage."

Zane picked up the map from the registration counter. "Not necessary. I think I've got it from here."

"You can't get too lost. Just stop when you reach the ocean." Angelique winked and grinned, then waved goodbye.

Zane followed the path and the small wood signs to cottages eight and nine. As he walked under the canopy of trees, he had to remind himself that Allison was not fair game. He would be friendly and cordial. He might even spend a small bit of time with her while they were both there, but there would be no replay of that kiss. Scott was too important to him. He would not betray the bro code. Never.

Ahead, Zane could see the water and two cottages set several hundred yards away from each other, one a shade of sky blue and the other pure turquoise, each with painted white trim and a bright red roof. All around them, the powdery pink sand was a bright and summery accent, while the sun glinted off the calm crystalline sea. It could not have been a more stunning setting, and despite his worries over how he would handle the situation with Allison, Zane could feel himself unwinding, his spine loosening and his shoulders relaxing.

He opened the door to his cottage and stepped inside, his eyes immediately drawn to the stunning vista of ocean at the far end of the house. He set down the map and strolled through the open living room, which had a vaulted wood-beamed ceiling and entire wall of windows, all open and letting in the sea breezes. At center was a set of oversize French doors, which led out to Zane's patio, covered in terra-cotta tile with an arbor above it for shade. Beyond that was his private plunge pool, surrounded by lush tropical plantings.

Not wanting to wait another minute for his vacation to start, Zane found the bedroom, which, as advertised, had an intricately carved wood bed with another beautiful view of the sea. His suitcase had been delivered by staff, and he wasted no time getting into his swim trunks, grabbing a towel from the beautifully appointed bathroom and making one more stop in the kitchen to grab a beer. He poured it into a shatterproof tumbler, and, sunglasses on, he strolled out onto the terrace and jumped into the pool.

The water was cool and exhilarating, the perfect counterpoint to the strong Bahamian sun. He slicked his hair back from his face and swam over to the edge of the pool, folding his arms up on the edge and drinking in the beautiful ocean view. As difficult as the last few weeks had been—hell, the last several years— Zane could feel that all fading away. Scott had been so right. Maybe he just needed some time to clear his head and stop thinking about Josh Lowell and Black Crescent.

Zane dropped his chin down onto the back of his hand and something caught his eye. More specifically, someone—a woman sauntering down to the water in front of the other cabin. *Allison.* It had to be her. She was turned away from him, but he'd have to be dead to not admire the view—her hair down the middle of her back, tawny skin set against a colorful sarong, lithe legs and bare feet. She stopped where the pink sand met the water and turned, ambling in his direction while gently swishing her feet in beautiful blue.

He wasn't sure what to do. Call out to her? Submerge himself in icy water and try to hide for the next five days? This never, ever would have been a question if she hadn't kissed him on Scott's birthday. She was permanently off-limits, fruit so forbidden that he would be blowing up his entire life if he dared to go there.

Before he had a chance to formulate any sort of plan, Allison looked up and spotted him. His heart instantly began pulsing, jumping to double time when she raised her sunglasses up onto her forehead for a moment, smiled and waved. Good God, she was unfairly beautiful. And she was coming his way. He had no means of stopping this. He had to go with it and try to have a casual conversation with the sister of his best friend.

So he did what he would have done if they'd never kissed—he waved back and called her name. "Allison!"

As Allison walked up the beach toward Zane's cottage, she could hardly believe this was really happening. How many times had she concocted some dream scenario in her head where she and Zane were alone? Too many to count. And what was unfolding before her was exactly the kind of fantasy she loved to weave— a perfect sunny day, not another human in sight, the breeze brushing her skin and the air so sweet.

Her pulse raced. Every nerve ending in her body was firing. Her breaths were deep, and yet she still felt as though she couldn't get enough oxygen. If she wasn't careful, she was going to hyperventilate or pass out. This was Zane's effect on her. It was as if the real Allison was no longer in control and some other version of her was pulling the strings. It had been like this since she was thirteen and he was sixteen.

But Zane wasn't a teenager anymore. And she wasn't, either. She was twenty-eight years old, and she knew what she wanted. She also knew that the world didn't go around handing out opportunities. Life didn't work like that. You had to take what was yours when you had the chance. And as she got closer to Zane's cottage and watched him climb out of his plunge pool, water dripping from his magnificent, lean and athletic form, she didn't even have to ask herself what her goal was—she knew it in her heart and in her gut. She wanted Zane's naked body pressed against hers. She needed his mouth on every inch of her. She had to have him, if only for a few days in paradise. Zane was not "for keeps," but he could absolutely be "for right now."

"Hey there," she said, stepping up onto his patio. She studied him as he toweled off his chest. She'd only seen him with this shirt off a few times, but his shoulders were just as amazing as she'd remembered. Firm and contoured from thousands of hours playing basketball. His chest was even more glorious, with a tiny patch of dark hair right at the center. She wanted to tangle her fingers in that hair. She wanted to kiss him there. She hungered to skim her lips over every inch of his pecs, rake her fingernails across the warm skin of his abs and tease open the drawstring of his swim trunks.

"How weird is this?" Zane rattled her back to the present with the question. In her fantasies, he would have opened with something far more seductive. Maybe something like, *Hello, beautiful. Can I help you with your sarong?* "We live on opposite ends of the country but we both end up at your aunt and uncle's resort at the same time?"

"What are the chances, huh? Small world, I suppose." She couldn't help but notice his body language—shoulders tight and hands clutching the towel to his chest, as if he was hiding from her. This was all wrong, and she was desperate to change the dynamic. "Can I have a hug?"

"Uh, sure. Of course." He grabbed his T-shirt from one of the chaise longues by the pool and put it on. He was definitely trying to keep his distance. She might need to take things slow. She didn't want to scare him off or freak him out. The last thing her already-bruised ego needed was another interaction like the one at Scott's birthday party. She couldn't endure it if he pushed her away again. She spread out her arms and gave him the sort of embrace only friends exchange. It was quick and to the point, and not at all what she wanted. Just that one little taste of his body heat left her longing. Her chest ached for more.

"So what are you doing here?" he asked.

"I needed a break, and my aunt is always begging me to visit."

"Things stressful at work?"

She looked around for a place to sit. "Do you mind?" She gestured to one of two chaises under an umbrella.

"Yeah. Of course. Do you want a beer?"

"I'm good for now, but thanks." She did want one, but she wasn't sure it was a good idea. She needed to keep her wits about her while she was trying to suss out where his head was at. They hadn't talked once since the kiss a few weeks ago. For all she knew, he thought she was a lunatic. "I just broke up with my boyfriend. We were living together, so it was a pretty big ordeal, moving out and all of that."

Zane sat in the chair next to her and reclined, crossing his legs at the ankle. He had incredibly sexy legs, a mile long but still pure muscle, with just the right amount of dark hair. "I'm sorry to hear that. If you need a shoulder to cry on, I'm a pretty good listener. Plus, I figure I'm forever in debt to the Randall family."

"For what?"

"Where do I start? Turning around my entire life when I was at my lowest point?"

Allison waved it off. He still clung to a debt of gratitude for her family, but the truth was that Zane had given them a lot, too. He'd never been anything less than a positive presence. For Scott and Allison, who'd had a mostly stable childhood, watching Zane battle through his family's reversal of fortune had taught them a lot about humility. "Are you kidding me? My parents love you. And obviously Scott is obsessed with you." Her phone, which she had tucked into her bathing suit top, rang. Things at work were so tenuous right now that she couldn't afford to turn off her ringer, as much as she wanted uninterrupted time with Zane. "I'm sorry. I should look to see who it is." She glanced at the caller ID. It was Scott. Did he have some sort of psychic ability to interrupt her at the most inopportune time? For an instant, she considered sending the call to voice mail, but she knew that he would just keep calling her back.

"Speak of the devil," she said to Zane. "It's my brother."

"Oh. Wow."

"I know." She answered the call to speak to Scott. "Were your ears ringing? We were just talking about you."

"What the hell, Allison? You're down at Rose Cove by yourself and Zane is there, too?"

Of course he's not only calling, he's taken issue with the fact that I'm with Zane. "Yes. I'm doing this thing where you travel to a place where you don't live and you relax. It's called vacation. You should try it." She glanced over at Zane, who she hoped would at least be smiling after her wisecrack at her brother. But no. Zane's handsome face was painted with entirely too much concern. She'd seen that look before, and she didn't like it.

"Is there something funny going on between you two?" Scott asked. "Don't think I didn't notice how weird you were being at my party."

Being under Scott's thumb had grown so tiresome. In many ways, Allison felt as though she'd been born under it. "We're hanging out. He's my friend, too."

Zane cleared his throat. "Hand me the phone."

Allison shook her head and held the receiver to her chest. "No. I've got this. He's being ridiculous, and you and I are sitting by the pool, talking. He needs to get over himself." She raised the phone back to her ear. "Unless you have something nice to say to me, I'm going to say goodbye now and get back to my vacation."

"He went on this trip to hook up with women," Scott blurted. "He told me as much. And I do not want you to fall for his charms. Nothing good comes of it, and you just came off a bad breakup."

Allison grumbled under her breath. As if she needed another reminder that Zane had a zillion other women waiting in the wings. Her brother was ruining her fantasy, and she wasn't going to sit around for any more of it. "Okay. Sounds great."

"You aren't listening to me. You're just saying that so Zane won't know what I'm saying about him."

"Yep. You're right. Anything else? I need to get going."

"Are you watching the forecast? There's a system forming in the Atlantic. The weather channel says it could dip down into the Caribbean. It could be upgraded to a tropical storm by late today. It could easily become a hurricane."

Allison looked overhead. There wasn't a cloud in the sky. "You are such a weather nerd. I'm not worried about something an ocean away, okay? Plus, it's June. The hurricane season just started. I'm sure Angelique and Hubert will let us know if it's anything of concern. Now, go back to your life so I can try to unwind. Kiss the kids for me."

"I'm calling you tomorrow. And just punch Zane if he tries anything. Or remind him I will kill him if he touches you."

Allison didn't want to tell Scott that if there was any smacking going on, it would be only of the playful variety, and only if she was very lucky. "Got it. Love you." She pushed the red button on her phone and tucked it back inside her swimsuit top. "Sorry about that. I think he's paranoid that there's something going on between us."

Zane got up from his seat and ran his hand through his hair. His forehead creases were deep with worry. "Then you need to call him back and tell him that absolutely nothing is going on. Or I'll do it. Give me your phone."

Allison sat back on the chaise and didn't bother to cover up when her sarong slipped open, revealing the full stretch of her bare leg and a good bit of her stomach, as well. She loved seeing the way Zane tried not to look…and failed. Did he want her the way she wanted him? Did he crave her touch? Her kiss? The thought of unleashing all of her pent-up desire on him, especially in paradise, where they could be blissfully alone, was so tempting it made her entire body tingle. It would be so easy to undo the knot of her cover-up and let it fall away. Give Zane an eyeful. Run her fingers along the edge of her bikini top, right where the swell of her breasts could draw the most attention. She wanted to do it so badly that her hand twitched. But she had to play this slowly. "Don't be threatened by my brother. He's just watching out for me. It's a bad habit of his. He needs to cut it out."

"You know why he's so protective of you. There's a good reason for it."

Allison did know there was a good reason, but she'd been a little girl when she got sick. She hardly remembered any of it—it was practically a lifetime ago. Most important, she was perfectly healthy now and had been cancer-free for more than twenty years. Her entire family needed to stop hovering over her like she was made of porcelain. "And because my family is always around, I think we should take this chance to hang out on our own terms. Talk. Like friends. We are friends, aren't we?"

"I don't know."

"What? You don't know if we're friends?"

He shook his head, seeming frustrated, which was not what she was going for. She wanted him relaxed. At ease. "I don't know if it's a good idea for us to spend time together."

"What are you afraid of, Zane? That I'm going to kiss you again?" She had a sliver of regret at putting things on the line like this at the outset, but perhaps it was for the best. If he was going to reject her, best to get it out of the way.

"For starters, yes."

Allison pressed her lips together tightly. She decided then and there that if any moves were going to be made, the first would have to be his. If he wanted her the way she wanted him, he was going to have to show her. She wasn't putting her heart and pride on the line a second time, especially not when he was so willing to say out loud that he was worried about what she might do. "I promise I won't kiss you, okay? Just stop acting like you're afraid of me, because I know you aren't."

"Of course I'm not afraid."

"Then prove it. Let me make you dinner."

Zane ran his tongue across his lower lip tentatively. It was one of his most adorable quirks and he always did it when he couldn't make up his mind about something. Allison didn't like that her offer required any deliberation at all, but she certainly appreciated the vision of his mouth. "Dinner? Nothing else?"

Allison closed up her sarong and rose from her seat. "Fair warning. You might go home incredibly satisfied." She patted him on the shoulder. "From my cooking. It's really good."

Three

Zane's entire body was humming when Allison left, which left his brain running at a clip to catch up. If Scott knew what was going through Zane's head right now and how that all centered on his little sister, he would end him. It wouldn't be a quick death. It would be a long, painful one, during which Scott would drive home a single point—Allison was off-limits. Always had been. Always would be.

But here on a dot of an island, more than a thousand miles away from his best friend, Zane couldn't deny his churning thoughts or the insistent pulse of electricity in his body. The second Allison's sarong fell open to reveal the tops of her luscious thighs, the soft plane of her stomach and that little spot on her hip where the tie of her bikini bottoms sat, all bets were off. Or most of them, at least. He'd withstood an unholy rush of blood to the center of his body, so fierce that it nearly knocked him off his feet. Thinking about it was only providing an opportunity to put a finer point on the things he'd wanted to do to her—drop to his knees, start at her ankle and kiss every inch of her lovely leg, moving north until he reached the bow at her hip. The only thing that would make sense if he ever got that far would be to tug at the string, quite possibly with his teeth, slowly untie it and use his mouth to leave her curling her fingers into his scalp and calling out his name.

Thoughts like that were going to ruin Zane and everything he held dear.

He stalked into his cottage and opened the fridge, if nothing but for the blast of cold air against his overheated skin. It didn't help. It somehow made everything worse—another bodily conflict to endure as the shot of coolness mixed with the balmy salt air—everything on this island felt good. Too good. He popped open another beer and took a swig, but dammit, it was only a pleasing jolt of sweet and bitter, a shock of frothy cold followed by a wave of warmth that made him pleasantly dizzy. The erection he'd tried so desperately to fight off was now at a full salute, begging for attention and hungry for release.

There was only one way to get past this, and it didn't involve an icy shower. He couldn't wash away Allison's effect on him. He had to get past it. He stormed off to his bedroom, shucked his clothes and stretched out on the magnificent bed. The linens were smooth and impossibly soft against his skin, another pleasure he didn't relish, but this was the only way to keep himself from doing something foolish later tonight when he saw Allison. It was time to take matters—namely, his erection—into his own hands.

He didn't bother with seduction, reaching down and wrapping his fingers around his length. He closed his eyes and allowed himself the luxury of visions of Allison—glossy hair framing those deep, soulful eyes, plump lips and a smile that could turn ice to a puddle. Her shapely legs and curvy hips. Her luscious breasts. He took long strokes with his hand, imagining kissing her again, except there was no stopping this time. He started things, and she turned up the volume, their tongues winding, mouths hot and wet and hungry for more.

The tension in his body built, but coiled tighter, a push and pull he wouldn't be able to take for long. To edge himself closer, he conjured an illusion of Allison naked and the feeling of her body on top of him, holding him down with her warmth and softness. He imagined being inside her—the closeness, the heat—and her heady sweetness perfuming the air as he brought her to her peak. With that thought, the pressure was released and he arched his back, riding out the waves of pleasure. His breath hitched in a sharp inhale, then came out in a long rush of relief. He settled back on the pillow and slowly pried his eyes open, not to the sight of Allison but to the white painted ceiling and whirring fan overhead. He turned and glanced at the clock on the nightstand. He had four hours until dinner. Hopefully this solo rendezvous had prepared him. Now to shower, read a few chapters of a book, take a nap and hope that he could keep his libido in check.

Five minutes before six, Zane headed to Allison's

cottage, dressed in jeans and a dress shirt with the sleeves rolled up to the elbows. He carried his flip-flops and walked barefoot through the sand, which was still warm from the day's rays. Over the water, the sun was dipping lower, painting the sky in vibrant shades of pink and orange. It was so obvious and easy to say, but Rose Cove really was paradise. He didn't want to leave anytime soon. Having distance from his past and from Joshua Lowell? Amazing. If it weren't for Scott, and Zane's company, he might never go back to Falling Brook.

He found himself taking his time as he strolled across the beach, now approaching Allison's. She had every window and door flung open, allowing him to watch her in the kitchen, milling about. He really hoped she wasn't going to put the full-court press on him tonight, and that her only intention was for the two of them to spend a few hours together. It was time to leave The Kiss where it belonged—in the past. Their circumstances did not allow for him to ever go there again. One thing he'd learned when his parents lost every penny of the family's money to Black Crescent and Joshua Lowell's father was that the sooner you learned to accept your personal situation and deal with what you had in front of you, the better.

"Knock, knock," Zane said, standing at the French doors to Allison's cottage. "I brought a bottle of wine, but I can't really take credit for it. Your aunt stocked my fridge."

Allison turned and smiled, looking fresh-faced and sun kissed, wearing a swishy black skirt and a royal blue tank top. Her feet were again bare and her hair was up in a high ponytail. There wasn't a single made-up thing about her, and that made her perfect, however much he wished he hadn't noticed. *She's your best friend's little sister. Don't be an idiot.* It was his new mantra. He committed himself to repeating it over and over until it became part of his psyche.

"I'm glad you came." She took the wine from him and carried it straight to the kitchen counter. No kiss on the cheek hello. No hug.

Zane was relieved, even if there was something in his body that was registering as disappointment. "Well, you know, I had so many invitations, I wasn't sure what to do." He took a seat at the kitchen island, with a view of the cooktop, where something delicious-smelling was simmering away.

Allison laughed, then handed him the corkscrew. "Here. Make yourself useful."

"Yes, ma'am." He got up and opened the bottle, then took the liberty of finding the wineglasses, which was easily done since this kitchen had the exact layout of his own. "To friends." He offered her a glass and held up his own for the toast.

"Yes. To friends." She took a sip, hardly looking at him at all.

He wondered if he'd been too standoffish earlier. He only wanted to keep things in a place where nobody got hurt. He didn't want to lose *all* of the warmth between them. Just some of it. Keep things friendly, but not too friendly. "Have you seen any of the other guests on the island at all?" he asked.

She shook her head and lifted the lid off a pot. "I haven't. Angelique stopped by and told me that a few people canceled their reservations because there's talk of a hurricane."

"That's what you were talking about with Scott, isn't it?" This didn't sit well with Zane. It would be just his luck that the weather would go bad and ruin his idyllic vacation. Worse than that, they were sitting ducks if a bad storm came through.

"Don't worry. Both Angelique and Hubert said this happens all the time. The forecasts are often wildly inaccurate, and the models have the storm going any number of directions." Allison gestured outside with a nod. "Look at that sunset. There's no way a storm is coming."

He stole a glance, even though he'd been admiring it minutes earlier. "You're probably right."

"You need to relax, Zane. The whole point of being here is to unwind. Dinner is just about ready."

Zane had thought he was relaxed. Apparently not. "What are we having?"

"A conch ceviche with lime and fresh chilies to start, then baked crab with rice and pigeon peas. All my mom's family recipes."

"That's why it smells so amazing. It makes me think of your mom and being at your house."

"Of course. She must have made this for you one of the times you stayed with us." Allison spooned the ceviche into two small dishes and sprinkled fresh herbs on top.

"That seems like forever ago." Being with Allison while memories of time with her family surfaced had Zane wedged between nostalgia and the pain of that period of his life. It was about so much more than the financial struggle. The real misery had come from watching his parents' marriage fall apart before his very eyes. Allison was a reminder of both things he cherished and things he wished had never happened, which he knew was part of the reason every sense was heightened around her. "You were just a girl then. How old were you when we met? Thirteen?"

She cast him a disapproving look. "I'm all for memory lane, but can we not talk about me as an awkward teenager?"

"Why? You were the coolest kid I ever met. You had the best taste in music. You were always reading all of these books I'd never heard of. You totally had your own fashion sense. You'd wear those flowery dresses and black Doc Martens boots. Or T-shirts with bands I'd never heard of."

Allison blushed and tried to hide a smile. "Will you please shut up? It's embarrassing."

Zane couldn't help but love that they had this history and that he could have playfully tease her because of it. She'd always had a tough outer shell, carrying herself with an air of disaffection. She wanted the world to think that she didn't care what anyone thought of her, but Zane had long suspected that wasn't quite the case. "It's the truth. That was the first thing that struck me about you. You always had an amazing sense of self. I'm not sure I ever did."

"I think you've always known exactly who you are. The problem is that you weren't always happy about it."

For a moment, the air in the room seemed to stand still. Was that his problem? Or was it that the wounds inflicted by the Lowell family had been so slow to heal? "Well, if that's the case, it's only because I'm pretty easy to figure out. Feed me and I'm happy." He smiled, hoping to lighten the mood. He'd never intended to steer them down such a serious path.

"Then I'm your girl." She held up the two dishes of ceviche.

Zane swallowed hard, and not because the food was so mouthwatering. He was reading too much into everything Allison did and said. And it was going to be his undoing if he wasn't careful. Again, he reminded himself to relax. He was more than capable of enjoying a beautiful home-cooked meal with an old friend. "Should we eat out on the patio?"

"Whatever and wherever you want."

Allison had to hand it to herself—dinner was incredible. Her mom and Aunt Angelique would be proud.

Zane sat back in one of the lounge chairs out on the patio, rubbing his belly and gazing up at the stars. "That was unbelievable. I don't think I'm going to need to eat again anytime soon."

"You went back for seconds. I'm impressed."

He turned and smiled at her, and, even in the darkness, with only the faint light from inside the house, she was struck by just how damn handsome he was— kissable lips, stormy eyes and the smile of a heartbreaker. The sight of him made her breath catch in her throat in a painfully familiar way. It was exactly like every other time she'd tormented herself with the conscious thought of how perfect he was. "Like I said, feed me and I'm happy. You fed me so well, I'd have to say I'm euphoric."

It was reassuring to know she could do this much right, but this entire evening had too many echoes of the past—the friendship was there between them, but she wanted more. She would always want more. The itch to be with him would never go away unless she had the chance to scratch it. "Any interest in working off that meal tomorrow?" She knew that there was a little too much innuendo in the wording of her question, but it was meant to be a test.

"What'd you have in mind?" He returned his sights to the night sky, not taking the chance to flirt with her.

Any other woman might be deterred or discouraged, but Allison hadn't come this close to give up now. She would forge ahead with her suggestion and keep the ball in his court. "Snorkeling. If we hike around to the north side of the island, the water and fish are unbelievable. If we're lucky, we'll see sea turtles, too. We can swim out right from the beach."

He was doing that thing with his tongue and his lower lip again, driving her crazy in the process. "Yeah. Cool. That sounds fun. What time?"

Allison wanted to spend the entire day with him, and the sun would be too strong by midday to spend too much time in the water. "Morning is best if you can haul your butt out of bed. Nine o'clock?" Just then, her phone rang. Out of habit, she'd brought it with her out onto the patio. She glanced at the caller ID and knew she had to take it. She didn't want to interrupt her evening with Zane, but this was one of her Black Crescent candidates, someone she'd been trading phone calls with for a few days. "I'm so sorry. I need to get this. You can go if you want to. I'll see you tomorrow morning." She scrambled up out of her seat and pressed the button to answer the call. "Hello? Ryan?"

"Hi, Ms. Randall. I'm so glad I reached you," Ryan Hathaway answered.

"Me, too. I've been waiting to talk to you." Allison shuffled off into the house, but something stopped her from going too far—Zane's hand on her bare shoulder. She froze, but only because that one touch was making her head swim. The power he had over her was immense. If anything ever did happen between them, she might burst into flames.

"Hey. I thought we were having a nice night." Zane glanced at the phone. "Now I feel like you're blowing me off for someone else."

Allison raised the receiver back to her ear. "Ryan, can you hold on for one minute? I need to take care of something."

"Sure thing," Ryan replied.

"Thank you. I promise it'll only be a minute." She pressed the mute button on the screen. "We were having a nice night, but all good things must come to an end, right?" She didn't want to brush off Zane, but this call was incredibly important. Not just for her, either. Kianna was counting on her.

"Well, yeah, but you're also the one who was talking a big game to your brother about relaxing and unwinding while you're here. I turned off my phone completely. It's back at my place."

"This is work, okay?" The realization hit her hard. It wasn't merely work. This was Black Crescent, and Zane might never forgive her if he found out she was working for them. The decision to pursue business with BC had been easy enough to rationalize when Zane was living on the opposite side of the country. After all, it had been fifteen years since Vernon Lowell took off with all that money, and the current powers that be at BC were not like him. But now that she and Zane were inches away from each other, and her mind had been flooded with memories since seeing him, she understood just how betrayed he might feel if he discovered the truth.

"It's nine thirty at night."

"I know. My work calls happen at odd times sometimes. I'm sorry, but I really need to take this. So you can either stay or go, but I need a few minutes."

Zane nodded, but seemed entirely suspicious. "Cool. I'll clean the kitchen while you talk."

Dammit. Allison knew there was no way she could talk to Ryan with Zane in the same room, and she ran the risk of him joining her if she went back out to the patio. "Great. I'll take the call in my bedroom." Without further explanation, she ducked into her bedroom and closed the door. "Ryan. I'm so sorry."

"No problem, Ms. Randall."

"Please. Call me Allison."

"Okay, Allison. I've rearranged my schedule so I can be back in Falling Brook for the interview next week. I'll get in the night before."

Allison loved how prepared and thorough Ryan was. "Perfect. And you're sure you're okay with the idea of working for this company in particular?" She highly doubted that Zane might be listening at her door, but she still hoped hard that he wasn't. It hadn't been her intention to hurt Zane when she'd taken the BC gig. She was trying to save her company.

"I am. I know the history. It's pretty crazy all of the stuff that happened with the Lowell family, and of course I hate that Vernon Lowell ruined so many families. But maybe that's why they need somebody like me at the helm."

"That's a great attitude to have. They've really put that past behind them and are focused on the future. This job is the chance of a lifetime. No one ever imagined the CEO position could go to someone outside the family." Allison sucked in a deep breath, amazed she'd managed to keep herself from uttering the name Joshua Lowell.

"I agree. It's an excellent opportunity. I'm excited to interview and I'm excited to finally meet you in person, too."

"Sounds great. I'm in the Bahamas right now visiting family, but I'll see you in Falling Brook next week. Good night, Ryan."

"Have a wonderful vacation. Good night."

Allison ended the call and for a moment, stared at the back of her bedroom door. She felt as though she were teetering on the edge of a cliff. The Black Crescent account was crucial to the success of her company, and she'd promised Kianna she would nail this first assignment BC had given them. But she also knew firsthand the damage inflicted by BC, and exactly how Zane would feel if and when he found out that she was working for them. This absolutely put a wrench in her romantic hopes, but she reminded herself that Zane would never be a long-term thing. He wanted the physical parts and none of the emotional entanglements. Yes, she was risking their friendship, but, in her experience, those things could be mended. If needed, she could get Scott to talk Zane off the ledge, tell him that the Black Crescent thing was just business. Surely a friend could understand that.

She opened her door and walked back into the main

room. Zane was drying one of the hand-painted plat-
ters she'd used. "Hey. I'm so sorry."

"Don't apologize. I shouldn't have given you a hard
time. You have things you have to do. I get it."

"Thank you. I appreciate that."

Zane set down the clean dish and leaned against the
kitchen counter. "Nice guy?"

"What?"

"The guy you were talking to. You seemed pretty
chummy. I thought it was just you and your partner in
that office."

For a moment, Allison struggled to figure out what
he was asking, but then she realized there was the
slightest chance that Zane was jealous. That was so
incongruous with his personality that it didn't really
compute. He could have any woman he wanted. And
he'd pushed her away the one time they'd kissed. "Great
guy, actually. Supersmart. Handsome, too."

"Yeah? Could there be something brewing between
you two?"

He might not be jealous, but he was curious, which
made her both nervous and a bit exhilarated. "I hate to
disappoint you, but no. He's a recruit. Nothing else."

Zane nodded. "Oh. Okay."

She scanned his face, and he returned the look.
Good God, she had the most urgent desire to show
him the reason why a guy like Ryan Hathaway was
not what she wanted. If only she could press Zane
against that kitchen counter and kiss him into oblivion, thread her hands into his hair and show him just
how badly she longed for him. She wanted to tell him
everything—that she'd fantasized about him hundreds
of times, how she needed to finally get him out of

her system. Being this close to him and knowing she couldn't do any of that was testing what little resolve she had left. But she had to hold strong. She would not make the first move.

"I should probably get going," Zane said, finally breaking their eye contact. "Get out of your hair."

"You aren't in my hair, Zane. This is fun. I could talk to you all night." She did her best to hide the soft rumble in her voice, the way she secretly wanted to beckon him to her bedroom with her tone.

"I need to get a good night's sleep if we're going to go snorkeling tomorrow."

Tomorrow. Allison could wait until then. Tomorrow was another chance to show Zane that she was a woman. He'd been with so many over the years, why not her? Why couldn't she have at least one taste of him? "Right. Snorkeling."

He pushed off from the kitchen counter and walked to the door leading out to her patio. Allison followed, tormented and enticed by everything about him. "Thanks for dinner. It was amazing." He ran his hands through his thick hair, seeming at least a little conflicted. She took solace in that. She was at war with herself, too.

"You're more than welcome."

He leaned in and pecked her on the cheek. It happened so fast, she had no time to grip his arms or pull him closer or even simply wish for a real kiss. It only left her once again hungry for everything she couldn't have.

"See you tomorrow morning."

"Yep. Got it." She watched as he disappeared down the beach, into the darkness. It hurt to see him go without leaving her more, but she'd felt this way about Zane forever. The yearning might never go away. It might always be an unanswered question. Still, she really wished he would finally get up enough nerve to be the one to break their never-ending standoff. Her heart couldn't take much more.

Four

Zane woke with the sun and too many thoughts rolling around in his head. He was excited by the prospect of spending the day with Allison. Snorkeling with a friend sounded fun, and "fun" was something he so rarely had. But last night had been a close call from his side of things. He'd wanted to kiss Allison so badly that he'd volunteered to clean her kitchen—not his favorite activity.

What was keeping him from going for what he wanted? He'd never felt shy about it in the past. His greatest fear was Scott finding out, even though in all likelihood, Zane and Allison could do whatever they wanted without fear of repercussions. But guilt would crush him alive. Betrayal was at the top of Zane's to-not-do list. He needed trust in his life. He'd learned that the hard way when he was a teenager and his life fell apart. Everything he'd ever counted on—the stability of his family and, more important, his parents' marriage—was upended. He realized then just how badly he needed to be able to trust in something or someone. But that was a two-way street—if he couldn't be trustworthy in return, what was he doing with his life? Giving in to his desire for Allison would give Scott every reason in the world to feel betrayed. He'd never breached their friendship like that and he didn't want to start now.

He was assuming a lot, though. Just because Allison had once kissed him didn't mean she still wanted that from him. She'd taken that phone call last night and seemed eager to distance herself. She'd said it was about work, but Zane wasn't convinced. Why duck into the other room and close the door behind her? She was an executive recruiter, not an undercover FBI agent. She obviously had some new guy after her, which should come as absolutely no surprise. Or perhaps she was doing the pursuing. He could imagine that, too.

Get a grip, Zane. Get a damn grip. Allison was his friend. Last night, they'd had a friendly dinner. Today, they were going on an adventure. This was meant to be fun. It was meant to be platonic. Nothing more.

He slathered on sunscreen, got dressed in his swim trunks and headed over to Allison's cottage. She was hanging out on her patio, again on the phone. He waved at her and, although she returned the gesture, she quickly shot up out of her chaise, plugging a finger in her free ear and hustling back into the house. Perhaps it was work again. He hadn't realized Allison was quite so driven, but it would certainly be in line with her personality. Then again, there was the chance that it was a guy. Definitely a plausible explanation. He hung out next to her pool while she finished her call, taking deep breaths and admiring the gentle lap of the water on the sand.

"Hey. Sorry," Allison said, reappearing from inside the house. She was wearing her sarong again and through the thin fabric, it was apparent she was wearing that same maddening bikini.

He prayed for strength. So much strength. "Everything okay? It wasn't Scott giving you a hard time again, was it?"

She unleashed her electric smile, which calmed him, but sent a noticeable thrill through him, as well. "No. Although, he did call again last night. He keeps telling me to watch the forecast. And to watch out for you."

Zane directed his sights skyward. "It's another beautiful day in paradise. And I think we demonstrated last night that there's no need to worry about anything else."

She nodded. "Right? He needs to get a hobby."

"I could call him and tell him to get to work, but I promised myself I wouldn't turn on my phone once while I'm here." Zane deliberately delivered a pointed glance. "Maybe you should try the same thing."

She looked at her phone and hesitated. "You know, I think that's a great idea. I will do that. I've already talked to my partner today, and honestly, I think it'll be good for Scott to not be able to reach either of us for a few days. Let him wonder what's going on." She bounced her eyebrows playfully.

Zane felt a distinct tug from his stomach. He didn't

want Scott worrying, but there was likely no avoiding that, with or without phone contact with his sister. "We ready to head out?"

"Yes. My uncle had someone drop off the snorkel gear for us about an hour ago." She grabbed two mesh drawstring bags that were sitting on the patio tile next to the French doors. "I just need help getting sunscreen on my back before we get in the water. And I'm guessing you do, too."

Indeed, that had been the one place Zane hadn't been able to reach on his own. He considered accepting the reality of a sunburn, but skin cancer was no joke. "Yep."

He followed Allison into her cottage, where she had a bottle of SPF 50 on the kitchen counter. "I'll do you first. Turn around."

Zane swallowed hard at the notion of either of them *doing* the other, but followed Allison's directive. He heard the squishy sounds as she rubbed the lotion between her hands, and even though he knew it was coming, he winced when she touched him.

"Still cold?" she asked as she began to spread the silky liquid over his back and shoulders.

"No. No. It feels great." He closed his eyes to attempt to ward off how damn good it felt to have her touch him. This was what he'd wanted, if only for an instant, that night that she'd kissed him. They'd been fully clothed then. Not now. Instead, they not only had too much bare skin between them, they also had privacy, solitude and an entire sunny day stretching out in front of them. He tried to quiet his mind, but that only put the physical sensations at center stage. Her hands were pure magic as she worked the lotion into his shoulders, then down his spine until she reached his waist. He heard her pour more into her hands, then she swiped the velvety cream in circles at the small of his back.

"You're good to go," she said, handing him the bottle. "Now me."

He turned, only to see that she'd taken off her sarong and tossed it aside. And now he was confronted with her in that tiny black bikini. She did a one-eighty, putting her back to him, gathering her hair with both hands and holding it atop her head. He tried to think of a chaste and asexual way to go about this, but it was impossible. Every fiber of his being wanted to untie her top, kiss her neck, take her hand and lead her into the bedroom. Hopefully this would be as trying as today got, so he went ahead and got to work.

The first touch on her shoulders felt innocent enough. Sure, her skin was impossibly soft and even more shimmery with the lotion on it, but he could take it. The second touch across the center of her back prompted a definite ratcheting of tension in his body. The tie of her bathing suit was right there, millimeters from his fingertips, and everything about her was so damn inviting. The third touch, however, against her lower back, all the way down to the top of her bathing suit bottoms… Well, that felt as sexual as anything Zane had done since yesterday when he'd had to pleasure himself in search of some relief.

"Don't miss a spot," she said, looking back over her shoulder.

If only she knew that was not the danger. He wasn't about to miss even a fraction of an inch. Wanting to get on with their hike and swim, and get himself out of this situation, he finished up as quickly but as thoroughly as possible. "All set."

"Thanks. Let me just grab my sun hat." She flitted off and was back a few seconds later.

They headed outside, up the beachline away from both of their cottages. At first, their walk was nothing more than a leisurely stroll along the sand, but then the coast got rocky in patches, and they would wade through knee-to waist-high water to get past the tougher terrain. A few times, they hiked inland and made their way on footpaths that wound through the forest.

"You sure you know where you're going?" Zane trailed behind Allison as they walked down a narrow trail under dense tree cover. It was a welcome break from the sun and the heat of the day. "We haven't seen a single person or even another cottage this whole time."

"Yep. I know this trip like the back of my hand. I promise. Scott and I did this a hundred times when we were kids."

"The resort has been in your family that long?"

"Yes. It originally belonged to my grandparents, but it was a little more rustic when we were growing up. The bungalows weren't quite so fancy. They didn't have all of the amenities they do now. My aunt and uncle made it into what it is today."

Ahead, Zane saw the bright sun breaking through the trees. "Is that where we're going?"

She turned back and flashed her smile at him, the one that made it hard to think straight. "Yep."

"Awesome." Zane took stock of their surroundings as soon they were out of the wooded area and back on the beach. To his right, the coast was again rocky, with a steep and densely overgrown hillside racing up from it. He then looked out over the water, spotting a tiny island. It appeared to be about the length of four or five football fields away. It had three palm trees on it but no other signs of life. "What's that?"

"That's where we're going if you're up for the swim. Scott and I named it Mako Island."

"As in the shark? Because I was more in the mood for colorful tropical fish today. Not so much into man-eating aquatic specimens."

Allison laughed. "Scott was really into sharks when we named it, but don't worry. I've never seen anything too scary in these waters."

"Oh. Okay."

"It'll take about twenty minutes to get over there, but it's an easy swim and you'll get a beautiful view the whole way. Just follow me."

Zane nodded in agreement, declining to say that if he was following her, it wasn't the ocean that would be providing the beauty. That was all on Allison.

Zane and Allison put on their fins and snorkel masks, then she grabbed the inflatable swim buoy her uncle had left for her. With a belt that went around her waist, it would float behind her, hold a few bottles of water and could double as a flotation device if either she or Zane got into trouble during their swim.

"Your aunt and uncle think of everything, don't they?" Zane asked.

"They love to be protective." Always. But she wasn't going to let things like her family come between her and a good day with Zane. "Come on."

Allison waded into the sea, feeling so blissfully at home the instant she was floating in the water. They swam at a leisurely pace, buoyed by the saline. Below, the ocean floor was dotted with clusters of starfish, while schools of fish in bright shades of yellow and blue darted between the sea plants. One thing Allison loved more than anything about snorkeling was that the only thing she could hear was her own breath. She purposely made it deep and even, forcing every stress in her life from her body. Today was for her and Zane. She'd waited fifteen years for it to happen.

As they approached Mako Island, the water became quite shallow—only two or three feet deep. That allowed them to walk the final fifty yards to dry land, or in this case, what was really a very large sandbar with a few rocks, trees and plants.

They both collapsed when they reached a shady spot on the beach, sitting down and taking off their fins. "That was incredible," Zane said, a bit breathless. She tried not to watch the rise and fall of his enticing chest. She tried not to think about how badly she wanted to touch him there. "Thank you so much for sharing it with me."

"Of course. I'll give you the quick tour of the island. It won't take long." Indeed, it was only about the size of the combined footprint of five or six Rose Cove cottages. Mostly sand and rocks, some low brush and a half dozen palms. Unfit for human life, it wasn't completely uninhabited. Plenty of birds were busy up in the trees, and there were even a few iguanas, who could make the swim from Rose Cove or other nearby islands.

They found their way back to that shady, cool spot

on the beach and took a breather. "You know, half of the fun of this is getting to show it off to someone I care about."

Zane sat forward, resting his forearms on his knees and looking down at the sand, and nodded. "That's a nice thing to say." His voice was so burdened it made her heart heavy. Why did he have to be so deeply conflicted about every nice thing she chose to say? "I care about you, too."

She had too many words on the tip of her tongue— things about her brother or other women or why in the hell he couldn't just give in to the attraction that she had to believe he felt. There was no way that the electricity between them only went one way. But she didn't want their conversation to get too serious, so she kept these nagging, negative thoughts to herself. Instead, she fished the bottles of water out of the small pouch attached to the swim buoy and handed one to Zane. "Here. Drink. I need to keep you safe out here. Scott will never forgive me if you die of dehydration."

Zane laughed. It was deep and throaty and sexy as ever. "Same for you. I think we're equally responsible for each other at this point." He took a long drink of his water, then replaced the cap and reclined back in the sand, resting on his elbows. "It's so amazing to think about, isn't it?"

"What? How my brother has an ironclad hold on both of us?"

"Well, that, sure, but that's a long conversation. I was talking more about the here and now. When we met, did you ever think that you and I would end up together on this tiny uninhabited island in the Caribbean?"

Allison hugged her knees to her chest and ran her hands through the sand, too embarrassed to tell Zane that she'd spent more than a decade crafting fantasies about him. Of the many times she'd felt like a naive schoolgirl around him, this moment might have been the most striking. It felt as though there was an invisible force between them, keeping them apart, and she didn't know how to get rid of it. "Hard to believe, huh?"

"We're so far away from it all. From everyone. From responsibility and expectations. From family and our jobs. I had no idea it would be so freeing."

Freeing. This scenario they'd found themselves in should've felt freeing, but they didn't have true freedom, and they wouldn't unless she finally shook loose the words buzzing in her head and forced the conversation. "We could do whatever we want, you know. Nobody can say a thing."

Zane was quiet for a few heartbeats, and Allison braced for a reprimand about being suggestive. "So true. We are the extent of the society on this island." Just then, an iguana jumped up onto a rock a few dozen feet away. "Well, us and that guy."

"He won't care what we do. We could scream at the top of our lungs if we wanted to and nobody could say a thing."

"Or you could sing too loud. It might drive out the wildlife, but you could do it."

She smacked him on the arm. "Hey. I'm not that bad a singer."

"Let's just say that fifty percent of the people on this island disagree with that statement."

Allison swiped at him again, but this time, Zane

ducked away before her hand could connect with his arm. He popped up onto his feet. Allison did the same. He ran into the water up to his knees and she followed in close pursuit. Before she knew what was happening, he turned and, with both hands, delivered a tidal wave of a splash, dousing her.

"Hey!" Allison protested, but she loved the playful turn Zane was taking. "That's not fair." She ran into the surf up to her waist, furiously broadcasting water back at him. He joined in and they splashed each other like crazy for a good minute, laughing and trying to outdo each other. "Okay. Okay. Truce." Allison sucked in frantic, deep breaths.

Zane relented and straightened to his full height. He was like a god standing there in the crystal clear sea, tanned and glistening with water. "I'm officially soaked." He walked several steps into the shade of a palm tree over the water, still standing in it up to his knees.

"Me, too." Allison was determined to not make the first move, even when ideas of what do with wet bathing suits were whizzing around in her head. Still, she wasn't going to avoid him. She inched closer, stepping out of the sunlight. Their gazes connected, and she reckoned with how apparent his inner conflict was. It was all over his face. It hurt to see it—he had good and valid reasons for not wanting anything physical with her. She admired those reasons. She also wished they didn't exist, or at the very least, that they could set them aside for a while.

"You're pretty when you're wet."

Something in her chest fluttered—the physical manifestation of years of wanting to hear words like the ones he'd just uttered. "Thank you. You don't look bad yourself."

He cleared his throat, and a blush crossed his face. He looked down at the water. "Your brother would kill me for what I'm thinking right now."

Her heart galloped to a full sprint. "And he's not here."

Zane returned his sights to her and tapped his finger against his temple. "Unfortunately, he's here." He then pointed to the vicinity of his heart. "And in here."

"That's so sweet. And I get it. I do." She shuffled her feet ahead on the sandy bottom.

"Do you? Really?"

"I do. You love my brother. He loves you. I admire the hell out of your friendship." She sucked in a deep breath, hoping that she could summon the courage to say what she would always regret if she didn't let it out. "But I also know that I'm incredibly attracted to you, Zane. And judging by what you just said about the thoughts going through your head, I'm reasonably sure you're attracted to me. If I'm wrong, you could save us both a lot of time by saying it. Then we can go on with the rest of our vacation as nothing more than friends."

"I'm attracted to you. A lot."

She was thankful for the forward progress, but she wanted more. She needed to seize this moment. "I'm glad. Relieved, actually."

"You had to know that."

She shrugged. "A girl likes to hear that she's pretty. That a guy is attracted to her. It's not rocket science, Zane. I'm glad you confessed what you're thinking."

"Do you want to know what I'm really thinking?"

Words seemed impossible. All she could do was nod enthusiastically.

Zane then did the thing she'd been waiting a decade for. He gave her a sign that he wanted this, too, by taking a single step closer. "You're so beautiful. I just want to see you. All of you."

Goose bumps blanketed her arms and chest, even in the warm breeze. She swallowed hard. Without a word, she reached back and pulled the string on her bikini top. As the knot fell loose, she lifted the garment over her head and tossed it up onto the sand. "Like this?"

It was his turn to move closer again, his eyes first scanning her face, then shifting to travel all over her body, looking hungry, but he would likely never know that whatever lust he was feeling for her wasn't even a fraction of what she felt for him. "Yes. Like that."

She took another step. Mere inches separated their feet. Their legs and stomachs. Her breasts were only a whisper away from his unbelievable chest. "Do you want to know what's going through *my* head?" She loved the way his lips twitched at the question.

"It would make my life so much easier if you told me."

A tiny laugh escaped her lips, but there was no mistaking the gravity of this moment. "I want you to touch me." The words came out with little effort. She'd been practicing them in her head for eons.

He raised his hand slowly, his palm facing her breast. Her nipples gathered tight in anticipation. He breached the sliver of space between them, his warm and slightly rough hand covering her breast. This was not sex, not even close, but it caused such a rush of heat in her body that she gasped.

"Like this?" he asked, gently squeezing.

"Yes." Allison's need for Zane made her breasts full and heavy. Electricity was buzzing between her legs. Now that the floodgates had been opened, she didn't merely want him anymore.

She needed him.

Five

What in the world was he doing? Zane's hands were on both of Allison's magnificent breasts, and he knew the logical next steps—kissing, trunks off, bikini bottoms gone and what he could only imagine would be the hottest sex of his life. Up against a palm tree. Rolling around in the warm sand. As amazing as that sounded, there was part of him that was terrified to go there. The temptation of forbidden fruit was no joke—he already had an erection that was not going to go away without some effort on somebody's part. He never should've started this by touching her, but the look on Allison's face right now, eyes half-closed in absolute pleasure, was such a turn-on, he wanted to get lost in it.

"Allison, I want to kiss you."

"I want you to kiss me." Her reply was swift and resolute.

He sucked in a deep breath as the ocean breezes blew his hair from his forehead. He dipped his head lower and closed his eyes, not thinking about anything other than doing what felt good. His lips met hers, and it was like tossing a match on a pile of tinder—her mouth was so soft and sexy. So giving and perfect. It was everything he could ever want from a kiss as her tongue swept along his lower lip. She popped up onto her tiptoes and leaned into him, telling him with a simple shifting of weight how badly she wanted him. But to punctuate the gesture, she reached around and grabbed his backside with both hands, pulling his hips sharply into hers. His body responded with a tightening between his legs that left him dizzy.

Allison flattened both hands on his pecs and spread her fingers wide, curling the tips into his muscles while peering up at him. "I want you, Zane. I want every inch of you."

"Here? Now?"

She slid her hands across his chest away from each other and turned her attention to points south. His swim trunks were fully tented. "I hate to make either of us wait, but I don't want to do this in the sand. The beach is beautiful, but one of our beds would be even better."

Zane didn't want to put anything on pause now that he'd made his decision. Everything between his legs was screaming at him to argue her point. But it might be wise to hold off until they could get back. It would give Allison a chance to change her mind. Zane could endure his inner tug-of-war some more. Then, if he and Allison still ended up in bed, he'd know in his heart that it hadn't been a rash decision.

She grabbed his hand. "Come on. We can get back to my cottage in a half hour if we hurry."

Disappointingly, while Zane collected their gear, Allison put her bikini top back on. They sat together in the shallow water, donning their fins. As he stood, something in the view of Rose Cove caught his eye—a sprawling white house atop the big hill rising from the beach where they'd embarked on their snorkeling trip. "Who stays up there?" he asked as they walked through the shallower depths. "I thought Hubert and Angelique lived in the main house, where the office is."

"That's the honeymoon cottage. It's undergoing renovations. They're giving it a serious face-lift. It'll probably run five grand a night when they're done."

"Wow."

"I know. I'm hoping to see the progress before we leave."

"I'd like to see it, too."

"For now, you and I need to swim." Allison pulled down her mask, adjusted the straps, plugged the snorkel end into her mouth and, like a frogman, dived into the deeper waters.

Zane followed, and this time they swam at a far less leisurely pace. Now the fish were dots of color as they zoomed past. Zane was focused on their destination until Allison came to a stop, treading water and pointing ahead. Zane scanned the depths, only to see a sea turtle come into his frame of vision. They floated in place, masks in the water as the massive creature glided toward them, then turned when it got too close, graceful, beautiful and all alone. Zane had never spent any time at all thinking about what it might be like to be a sea turtle, but he was struck by how apt the phrase "just keep swimming" was. To survive, all one could do was keep moving forward. His breaths came slow and even as he realized that he might be better served to get out of his own head every now and then and actually enjoy his life.

He and Allison watched as the turtle skated away, waiting until he was well out of sight before resuming their trek. It took very little time before they reached the beach and scooped up the rest of their belongings, including Allison's hat. She urged him ahead with a wave. "Come on. I know a shortcut through the forest."

He hustled behind her. It wasn't long before he saw her cottage through the trees. "Why didn't we go this way before? This is so much shorter."

"I wasn't in a hurry then."

When they arrived at Allison's cottage and they stepped through the door, Allison wasted no time, rising up on her tiptoes and kissing him deeply, digging her fingers into the hair at his nape. That kiss swept aside the doubts and questions he had about whether or not this was a good idea. That erection from before? It sprang to life in seconds flat as he returned the kiss and wrapped his arms around her naked waist. It felt impetuous. And dangerous. And for once in his life, he was ready to take caution and run it into the ground. Nobody had to know. This moment was all about Allison and him.

She wrenched her mouth from his, gazing up at him, her eyes wild and scanning. She probably thought he was about to bail on her like he had at Scott's birthday, but he would not do that. Not this time. He scooped her up in his arms and carried her off to the bedroom.

"How chivalrous of you," she said.

"I try," he quipped back.

He set her on her feet, and she turned her back to him, lifting her hair and letting him do what he'd wanted to do so badly before—tug on the strings of her top. With the garment gone, he reached around and cupped her breasts, which fit so perfectly in his hands. A breathless sigh left her lips, and he knew he was on the right track. He wanted to please her so much that she had no choice but to make that sound over and over again. Allison pressed her bottom against his groin, wagging her hips back and forth, cranking up the pressure already raging in his hips and belly. She craned her neck to kiss him. Their tongues teased each other, wet lips skimming and playing.

"You're so damn sexy," he whispered, moving to her glorious neck. It wasn't merely a nice thing to say. It was the truth. Every soft curve of her body had him turned on.

She hummed her approval, dropping her head to one side. He ran his lips over every available inch, exploring the delicate skin beneath her ear and the graceful slope down to her shoulder. Her unbelievable smell, sweet jasmine and citrus, mixed with the salt of sea air, filling his nose and leaving him a little drunk, although everything about Allison was intoxicating. Her voice, her words, her touch...

He shifted his hands to her hips and with a single tug at both strings, undid her bikini bottoms. She wriggled a bit and they dropped to the floor. He pressed his hand against her silky smooth belly, inching lower until he reached her center. She was slick with heat, and Allison gasped when he touched her, reaching up and back to wrap her fingers around his neck. With his other hand he caressed her breast lightly, loving the velvety texture of her skin against his palm, teasing her pert nipple, as he returned his lips to her neck. Her breaths were labored and short and, judging by the sound, she was close to her peak, but he wanted to savor this time with her. He didn't want to rush. There had been so much buildup to this moment, and he was certain it could never happen again. He wanted to appreciate this time with sweet and sinfully sexy Allison.

As if she knew what he was thinking, she turned in his arms and grabbed both sides of his head, pulling him closer in a kiss that put every other one to shame. Mouths open and hungry, wet and hurried, it was as if she was acknowledging that they could only travel this path once, and they had to make it count. She let go of her grip on him and moved to the drawstring of his trunks, making quick work and pushing them to the floor. As soon as she wrapped her hand around his length, he knew there was a good chance he wouldn't last long. He clamped his eyes shut and walked that delicate line between relishing every firm stroke she took and trying to think about anything other than how damn hot she was. Unfortunately, his best friend popped into his mind, but he quickly banished the thought. He would not disappoint her. Not today.

Again he scooped her up in his arms, but this time, he laid her out on the bed. The vision of her soft and sumptuous naked body, his for the taking, reminded him that he was a fool for wanting anything less than hours of getting lost in her. One time didn't have to mean a short time. They could make memories in this room.

She grinned as he allowed himself the luxury of

her beauty. "Coming to bed?" She swished her hands across the crisp white sheets.

All he could think about was that this was the exact fantasy he'd had the other day. And now he got to live it. He was a ridiculously lucky man right now. "Just try to stop me."

Allison could hardly believe this was happening, except that it was. Her body was buzzing with appreciation for Zane and the glee of finally having a taste of what she'd wanted for so long. Judging by his opening act, she was in for an unbelievable afternoon… and, hopefully, evening. She wondered if she could convince him to never get out of bed, or if they did, to switch to the sofa in the living room. Or the kitchen counter. Or the plunge pool. *Ooh, yes.* She wanted Zane everywhere.

But she couldn't let her silly brain get so far ahead. *Go with it. Enjoy him.*

"Scoot back, darling." Zane gestured for her to move, then set his knee on the bed. Even now, when they still hadn't done the actual deed, she knew that this had been so worth the wait. All those years of pining were about to pay off. It made her heart swell, her lips tingle and her entire body reverberate.

She did as he asked and slid herself back until her head was on the pillow. Zane was now on both knees at her feet, dragging his fingers along the insides of her calves and down to the arches of her feet. Being totally naked and exposed to him like this was so exhilarating that the goose bumps came back. She liked being vulnerable with him. It made her realize exactly how much she trusted him. Not knowing what he would do next added another level of thrill. It would be so easy to chalk all of these feelings up to this being the first time, except that this was the first time with Zane, the one guy she'd always wanted.

He gripped her ankles with both hands and spread her legs wider. His eyelids were heavy, like he was drunk on appreciation for her body, and that was such a boost to her ego she could hardly wrap her head around it. She lapped up every nanosecond of the image. He leaned down and kissed the inside of her knee, then began to move his way up her thigh, in absolutely no rush, holding his lips against her skin for a heartbeat or two each time. She arched her back in anticipation of where he was going. She had not banked on him wanting to take on the oral exam, but she should've known all along that he would not only want to please her, but that he would know exactly how to do it.

She squirmed when his fingers grazed her center again and he urged her thighs apart with his forearms. She watched for a moment in awe as he used his mouth, but the pleasure became too much. She had to shut her eyes. Her head drifted back onto the pillow, and all she could do was express her appreciation with moans and single-syllable words like *yes* and *more*. She'd never imagined he had such an artistic side, but the man was playing her perfectly, with firm pressure from his lips and steady circles from his tongue. The tension had already been building when he drove a finger inside her and curled it against her most sensitive spot. Three or four passes and she felt the dam break, and warm contentment washed over her. She combed her fingers into his hair, massaging his scalp to show her appreciation.

"That was unbelievable," she said, knowing that the

words didn't come close to telling him how she truly felt. She would need time to process what had just happened. For now, her brain was in frothy, happy disarray.

He raised his head and smiled with smug satisfaction, then kissed her upper thigh. "I enjoyed it, too."

"Hopefully you'll enjoy the next part even more. I need you, Zane. I need you inside me."

He planted both hands on the bed and raised himself above her, dipping his head down and kissing her softly. She wrapped her legs around his hips, waiting for the moment when he would finally drive inside. He was hesitating, and she could sense it. She truly admired the thoughtful side of him that felt that hesitation, but she needed him to know that it was okay. They could do this together, and it would be nothing short of amazing.

"All these years I've known you and I had no idea what talents you were hiding," she said. "You've been holding out on me, haven't you?"

He laughed quietly, but it felt forced. He nuzzled her cheek with his nose. She lowered her legs a bit and stroked the back of his thighs with her ankles. *Come on, Zane. Don't let me down.*

"I, uh…" His voice faltered.

"What is it?" She was careful to keep her voice warm and soothing. She did not want to witness another of his panics.

"I don't know."

"Don't know what?"

"I'm so sorry. So incredibly sorry." He turned away, avoiding eye contact. "I can't do this." Seeming defeated, he climbed off the bed and plucked his swim trunks from the floor.

Meanwhile, Allison was knee-deep in confusion. "Zane. What's wrong? I thought we were good."

"I thought we were, too. But I can't do it. I can't betray my best friend."

Naked on the bed and reeling from the pleasure Zane had just given her, the rejection still landed on Allison like the proverbial ton of bricks. Zane, the man she'd dreamed of for years, had just told her no. Logic said she should be incredibly hurt. Devastated. But right now, with this beautiful man still standing in her bedroom with an obvious erection, she was nothing but flat-out mad. It didn't have to be this way. And he knew it.

"Please don't do this," she said. "Don't leave."

"I have to. I'm sorry, but I do. I shouldn't be here in the first place."

His apology didn't do much to quiet her anger. "You're doing this. You're seriously putting on the brakes." She rolled onto her stomach, head and arms dangling off the side of the bed, and grabbed her sarong from the floor, where she'd tossed it earlier. Let him have a perfect view of her backside. Let him see what he was missing.

"I don't know why you're mad. From where I'm sitting, I just gave you a pretty mind-blowing orgasm."

"It *was* amazing. And not the point. I want you, Zane. All of you."

"I can't give you that. Not now."

A deep grumble was forming at the base of her throat. "Then when? Later tonight? Tomorrow morning? Please don't tell me we're going to leave this island without having sex." She wanted to applaud herself for truly putting it all out there.

"I've thought about it, and it's not a good idea. We've already gone too far."

She knew what that really meant. "You're going to let my brother come between us here? Nobody needs to know about this, Zane. Nobody. I don't kiss and tell. And I certainly wouldn't kiss and tell about you to him."

Zane turned away from her and stalked over to the French doors. His heavy steps were born of frustration, which seemed like an awfully good argument for him getting back in bed with her. But apparently not. "*I* would know it had happened. That's all that matters. I can't violate that trust."

"I would like to know where in your friendship agreement it says that you can't sleep with your friend's sister, when she's a consenting adult and so are you."

He whipped around, his eyes full of an emotion she couldn't put a label on—it wasn't anger and it wasn't hurt. It was something in between. "It's a guy thing. Plus, you and I both know that this would be nothing more than a hookup. Is that really what you want?"

"Are you saying that because it's all you're capable of? Hookups? Why is that, Zane? Why do you seek out one-night stands with women, but never actually commit?"

"Now is not the time for us to discuss the rest of my personal life."

"Oh. Right. Because you're always beyond reproach." She was so angry, it felt as though her blood was boiling. She hated that this was her reaction, but it was the only thing that made sense right now.

"That's not what I was saying. You just came off a breakup, Allison. You told me yourself that it was bad. I'm not the cure for that. The cure for that is time."

Allison jumped off the bed and wrapped her sarong around herself, tying it at the shoulder. Her breakup had been a distant thought until then, and she didn't appreciate him bringing it up or, worse, using it against her. "I don't need to be cured. I need the chance to move on." She stormed past him into the living room. Out of habit, she picked up her phone from where she'd left it on a side table. She had a text from Kianna. Nothing of paramount importance, but she replied. She watched as the bar moved across the screen, then she got an error message. *Not delivered.* That was when she saw she had no bars. "Service is out."

"You said you were going to turn off your phone."

"Well, I didn't."

Zane's eyes went wide with disapproval, and Allison was struck with a horrible realization. This really was all a mistake. Zane still saw her as a kid. He'd always see her as Scott's little sister. He'd never think of her as an actual woman.

"I love how you just come out with it," he quipped.

"I'm being honest. I told you I'd turn it off because I knew that it would be the sensible thing to do on a vacation where you're supposed to truly relax, but the reality is that Kianna and I are just barely keeping our heads above water with our business and we have an important new client that could turn into a long-term retainer. I need to be able to work."

"Oh, give me a break. That guy you were talking to yesterday? That was not work. If it was, you wouldn't have sneaked off into your bedroom and closed the door. It's not like I know a single thing about your company or what you're doing."

Allison's heart was hammering in her chest. She'd

thought it would seem reasonable that she'd want some privacy during a work call, but she had to admit to herself that it was solely because she was working for the one person on the planet Zane would hate forever. "It actually was business. I owe it to my recruits to exercise discretion. I'm sometimes going after very high-level people who already have important positions with big companies. I'm sorry if it's my regular practice to conduct those phone calls out of earshot of anyone. It's nothing personal." Except that it was, because the conversation was about Black Crescent. She regretted tacking on that last comment. Everything before it had been nothing less than the truth.

Zane reared his head back and held up his hands in surrender. "You don't have to get so angry, Allison. I'm sorry. If it really was work, I'm sorry I said anything, okay?"

She knew then that she'd overreacted, but it was only because she was so deeply frustrated. "Do you want to know why I'm so mad?" She felt her entire body vibrate from head to toe. Could she really come out with it? Tell him about the feelings that were tucked deep down inside her? These were things she'd never told anyone. Not her mom or Kianna. The pages of the diary she'd kept in high school were the only place where she'd ever come clean about Zane. And maybe that was part of her problem. She felt as though Zane needed to let go of his feelings about his past. Maybe she needed to set loose the things that kept haunting her, too. "I'm angry because over on Mako Island, and back there in my bedroom, I was so close to what I've wanted for fifteen years, and you decided to yank it all away."

Zane stood there, frozen, blinking like he had far more than a speck of dust in his eye. "Hold on a minute. What did you say?"

She couldn't suffer any more humiliation today. She'd had more than her fill. "You heard me. And you can feel free to go now. I just want to be left alone for the rest of my trip." She stormed off into the kitchen. That was when she saw a note on the counter. Even from across the room, she could tell it was Angelique's handwriting. She beelined for it.

Dear Allison,
I'm not sure where on the island you are, and I couldn't get a text to go through, so I'm leaving a note. Hubert was having chest pains, so I've taken him to the doctor in Nassau. Don't worry. This has happened before. I think it's stress. I considered staying on Rose Cove, but I wanted to be with him, and our remaining guests have opted to leave because of the weather. I don't think the storm will hit the island, but we will feel some of its effects. I would not leave if I didn't think it was safe for you and Zane to be here. You have lived through many storms at Rose Cove and know what to do. Stay safe and hunker down if necessary. I'm sure Hubert and I will be back on the island tomorrow.
Love, Angelique

Zane hadn't left her cottage as Allison had asked. In fact, he was standing right behind her. "Have you looked outside? The sky is getting menacing. I guess we didn't notice it since we walked back inland in the shade."

"The weather can turn on a dime here." Allison handed him the note from her aunt. "And we were busy for a little while after that, too." She watched as Zane scanned the note.

"Whoa. I hope your uncle is okay."

"Yeah. Me, too." Everything about this day had gone so wrong. Right now, she just wanted to go to bed and try to sleep it off. "Not much we can do right now but wait."

"But the storm. Don't you think we should figure out what's going on?"

She'd been through dozens of false alarms with storms on this island. The weather was the least of her worries. "You do whatever you want, Zane. For me, I'm going to get some sleep and try to forget that you don't want to have sex with me."

Six

By late the next morning, the rain was coming down in torrential sheets, and Zane was deeply concerned about what might be in store for Allison and him on Rose Cove. He couldn't get a signal on his phone. The other resort guests were all gone. Zane had been to the dock several times, hoping there would be a boat there, but he'd had no luck. Either they'd missed them all or no one was coming to get them. Angelique had told Allison to hunker down, but Zane wanted to make one more attempt to look for a way off this island. And he wasn't going without Allison. He had to keep her safe. Even if she hated him, he was going to drag her along.

He trudged down the beach to her cottage, rain pelting his entire body while the wind pushed against him, forcing Zane to dig his feet deeper into the sand with each step. His thighs burned from the effort; his skin stung from the sheets of rain. He squinted through the drops but could see up on Allison's patio. Her doors and windows were closed. Once he arrived at her back door, Allison was nowhere in sight, so he had to knock. As he waited for an answer, he turned back to the ocean. The waves that had been so lovely and calm a day or two ago were now starting to rage. The water was at a full-on churn like a washing machine. Best-case scenario as far as Zane could guess would be that the storm would only skirt the Bahamas and they wouldn't sustain a direct hit. But with no access to a forecast, it was impossible to know what they were waiting for, whether this was as bad as things would get or if this was only the beginning.

He turned back to the door and pounded again. "Come on, Allison. Answer the damn door." Impatient, he turned the knob and stepped inside just as she stumbled out of her bedroom.

"Zane. What the hell? You just walk in here? I was taking a nap. There's nothing else to do with this weather."

Zane hated how beautiful she looked. He especially hated the way his entire body had gone warm and his face had flushed. He might have been struck by a sudden case of best-friend guilt yesterday, but that didn't change the fact that he wanted her badly. "It's getting worse out there, and I have no cell service, so I don't know what's going on. Are you able to get any bars?"

"Oh, this from the guy who criticized me for using my phone." She turned on her heel and retreated to her bedroom.

He had no choice but to follow her. "Don't be mad about yesterday. This is important."

She was standing in front of her dresser, staring at her phone. The bed was disheveled, and good God he wanted to scoop her up and lay her down on it. But this was no time for that. "I'm planning on being mad about yesterday for as long as I feel like it." She held her phone up over her head at a different angle, then off to the side. "And no. I'm not getting any bars, either."

Zane still wasn't sure he'd heard her correctly yesterday afternoon when she'd said that thing about him taking away the thing she'd wanted for fifteen years. Was it really possible that she'd had some sort of crush on him all that time? And if so, what in the world was he supposed to do about that?

"I think we should grab our stuff and camp out by the marina in the hopes that somebody shows up."

She cast a look at him that said she thought he was an idiot. "There's no shelter out by the dock. We'd literally be standing there in the rain. Quite possibly forever."

"Do you have a better idea? I have to think that your aunt and uncle are worried about you. That they would try to send someone to get you."

"Angelique and Hubert have a lot on their plates right now, and they know the weather here better than anyone." She closed her eyes tightly and shook her head. "Now, the rest of my family is another case. I don't even want to think about Scott right now. He's probably losing it."

There was that name again—the reason for this state of torture he was in with Allison. "They're probably all worried sick. I'm also thinking there's no way they'll let you stay here if there's a way to safely get you back.

Which is why I think we need to stay as close to the dock as possible."

"Okay. Fine. Let's go. It'll just take me a minute to pack up."

"Perfect. I'll be back in five." Zane ran over to his place as fast as the rain and wind would allow, and chucked everything into his backpack. By the time he returned, Allison was waiting for him.

"This is a terrible end to what should have been a perfect vacation," she said.

Somehow, Zane sensed that she wasn't merely talking about the weather. "I know. But I'm not going to die out here, and I'm not going to let anything happen to you, either." Not thinking, he took her hand and led them around to the path that would eventually take them to the main office. When they arrived up at the clearing, the ground was littered with palm fronds. The trees were bowing with every new gale. "The wind is only going to get worse," he called out, still pulling her along.

"I'm not worried about wind so much as I'm worried about the water. If there's a big storm surge, the sea level will rise considerably. Ten feet. Maybe more. I don't know how smart it is to wait by the dock."

She had a point. When Falling Brook was hit by Hurricane Sandy, the storm surge had been overwhelming, flooding countless homes and businesses. People had died. It had been a disaster in every sense of the word. "We have to find a way to leave a message at the dock to let someone know we're still here, but then we need to find the high point of the island."

"That's going to be the honeymoon cottage up on the hill. The one they're renovating."

"Won't we be sitting ducks up there? If there are tornadoes, it could pluck the building off the top of the cliff and toss it out into the sea." It seemed that no matter what they did, they were in deep trouble.

"It's somewhat protected, because the back side of the building is built into the rocks. And it's on the western side of the island, where the winds won't be quite as strong."

"You really know a lot about hurricanes."

"My brother is a weather nerd."

"Okay, well, let's focus on the message first. Any ideas?" Zane asked, setting his backpack on the ground for a moment.

Allison let go of her small overnight bag and started untying her sarong. She was wearing the same bikini top, but this time with shorts.

"I'm not sure what kind of message you're trying to send," he blurted. This was not the time for him to have another moral crisis prompted by Allison disrobing.

"Everyone who works on this island has seen me wearing this. I'll tear it into strips and we'll tie those onto trees to lead someone up to the honeymoon cottage. We'll start with one of the metal pilings on the dock. Hopefully that will be enough of a signal that we're still here."

"Do you really want to rip that up? You love it."

Allison pulled at the fabric until it gave way and she was able to get a strip of it free. "I don't love this thing more than I love being alive." She waved him ahead as she made off in the direction of the small marina. "Come on."

Zane's mind raced as he struggled to keep up and surveyed the island landscape—the wild rustle of the palms above them and the constant sideways pelting of the rain making it seem like they were on another planet right now. It certainly felt like a different place than it had been twenty-four hours ago. This was paradise upended. Gone was the calm serenity he had sought.

They jogged ahead, breaking out from under the canopy of shade only to learn how much the trees had been blocking the wind. Allison's hair whipped like crazy. Ahead, the ocean's churn was an endless sloshing of unfathomable amounts of water. Gone was the crystalline blue. This sea was coal gray and angry. The whitecaps and foam were of no consolation; they only served as a reminder that things were not as they should be. And against that tumultuous backdrop was Allison, looking tiny and defenseless running toward the dock, even when Zane knew very well that she was as tough as nails. If anyone was well suited to survive, it was her. Zane felt as though he was still honing the skill, but he would be damned if this storm was going to hurt her. Not on his watch. Not while he had anything to say about it.

He hustled to catch up. They arrived at the dock, which was now nothing more than a series of gray wood planks nearly submerged in the water. There was no boat, nor were there any other people. Zane now doubted that anyone would be coming for them despite Allison's family's concern for her safety. The seas were too rough. It was all too dangerous.

Allison carefully started down the dock and Zane followed right behind her, just in case she slipped. They both pitched to the side with every wave that threatened to swallow up the slick wood planks beneath their feet.

Zane again told himself that he would not let anything happen to her. He had to keep Allison safe. Still, he knew that fighting Mother Nature was a losing proposition. If she decided she was going to win, there was not much to be done.

About halfway down the dock, the water was getting even deeper and Allison smartly came to a stop. She took the strip of sarong and wrapped it around the metal pole that moored the structure to the seafloor. On a calm day, this would have been a simple task, but it was pure chaos outside right now. With her hands occupied and the wind threatening to topple her, even while she used her strong legs to brace herself, Zane had no choice but to wrap one arm around her waist, steadying her while pressing his body into hers. She felt too good against him. Too right. And maybe it was the adrenaline coursing through his veins that made him think that if ever there was a time to throw caution to the wind, it was now, when life was hanging in the balance and they had no idea if they were going to survive.

Allison couldn't take any more of Zane's hands around her waist. It was too great a reminder of everything she couldn't have. She pried herself away from him now that the fabric was tied to the dock piling. She ran along the planks, but lost her footing at the very end. With a definitive *thud*, she landed on her butt. Pain crackled through her hip and down her thigh.

"Dammit!" She scrambled to her knees, embarrassed, frustrated and several other unpleasant emotions. She attempted to stand, but the dock was like a skating rink, and the ocean wasn't playing nice, either, sloshing water in her face.

"Let me help you." Zane threaded his hands under her armpits and lifted her to her feet with what seemed like zero effort.

"I can take care of myself." She twisted her torso and leaped up onto the sand.

"I'm well aware of that. It doesn't mean I can't still help you. If anything ever happened to you, Scott would never forgive me."

Allison was so tired of this. She turned to Zane, planting a single finger in the center of his chest to put him on notice. "I don't want to hear one more word about what my brother will or will not forgive you for. If I die in this storm—which, for the record, I know I will not—I will take all of the blame. You are officially recused of your bro duties."

He grabbed her hand with both of his. "But you'll be dead, so I will definitely get blamed."

"Then my ghost will haunt you and Scott and make sure you both know it was all me. Now, come on, let's finish leaving our trail of fabric." Allison didn't wait for him to respond and trekked up to the spot where they'd dropped their bags next to the trail that led to the clearing. She tore off another piece of the sarong and handed it to Zane, pointing to a tree branch she couldn't reach.

He tied it off. "We should go get whatever food we can and bring it up the hill with us."

She didn't want to give him any credit at all right now, but that was an excellent call. She hadn't thought twice about food since yesterday, too miserable over his rejection. "Good idea."

"Thanks." He smiled, which seemed like more of an apology than anything.

Allison wasn't quite ready to accept that from Zane, spoken or otherwise. So she started walking.

They split up back at their cottages, each scavenging for supplies. Allison took a moment to use a pair of scissors she found in her kitchen to cut up the rest of her sarong, but she still managed to return to their meetup spot first with bananas, bread, a flashlight and a blanket.

Zane emerged from his place second. "I brought a bottle of champagne."

Allison just shook her head. "I'd say you were a numbskull if I didn't need a drink so badly right now."

"For what it's worth, I also brought cheese and crackers, apples and a deck of cards."

"Great. It'll be just like summer camp." Chances were that it might be just as rustic up the hill. She had no idea what they were walking into, whether the solar was connected up there and whether they'd have furniture to sit or sleep on.

They retraced the inland path they had taken yesterday, stopping periodically to tie another piece of her sarong to a tree. Having some protection from the rain and wind made the trip much easier than it would have been near the raging ocean, but it was still slow going. The ground seemed to shake with every gust of wind, rain was still coming down in sheets and they were both completely soaked. Allison didn't necessarily fear for her life, but she was scared of the unknown right now. She was reasonably certain that she and Zane could work together as a team to survive, but what toll would it take on her heart when this was all over? A huge one, she feared. She was going to need a vacation from her vacation.

When they reached the base of the hill, it looked like an almost insurmountable climb. She was already exhausted and dreading what it was going to be like, holed up inside a shell of a house while riding out the storm. Even worse, the spot on her hip where she'd fallen was throbbing. "I'm really not excited about doing this," she said.

"Seriously? You? The woman who marched me all over this island and had me snorkeling long distances?"

"Seriously. Me." Deep down, the real reason she wasn't looking forward to getting herself up the hill had nothing to do with exhaustion. Yesterday, she could stay away from Zane in her own space. How was she supposed to do that when they were about to be living in tight quarters and having to rely on each other to survive?

"It's okay. We can do it. We just need to get to shelter." He peered down at her, and all she could think was that this was such a damn shame. He was perfect. The two of them together for a night or two could have been magical. But no.

"Yeah. Okay. Let's do this." She led him down a narrow path at the foot of the hill, which eventually brought them to a wider trail that zigzagged its way up the incline. The terrain was mostly low scrub, giving them zero protection from the wind and rain. They both walked with heads down, watching the trail, slogging through what was quickly becoming a muddy mess.

"Is it just me or is the weather getting worse?" Zane asked as they made the final turn on the trail. They were close.

"It is. I wish we had access to an actual forecast. It

would be nice to know if this was going to be the worst of it or if it's only the beginning. I hope this hike won't end up being for nothing."

"Better safe than sorry, right?"

She shrugged. "You can't spend your whole life staying out of trouble."

"Why do I have the feeling we aren't talking about the storm anymore?"

She came to a stop at the end of the trail, turned and confronted him. Water was running down her nose and cheeks. She felt like a drowned rat. "We aren't."

Zane's shoulders dropped in defeat. "Allison, come on. I don't want to argue."

"I don't, either, Zane. I shouldn't have to." Allison trudged her way around to the front of the house via a crushed-shell path with manicured hedges on either side. Bright pink bougainvillea was trailing from planters situated between the windows of the house. It had been years since she'd been up here, and she had no idea what state the house would be in, but the exterior already looked much nicer than she'd ever remembered, even in the pouring rain.

When they rounded to the front of the house, they both froze, even though they were standing in a complete downpour.

"Holy crap, Allison."

She didn't have a great response. It was beyond words. "I know." There was so much to take in, it was difficult to figure out where to start. First, either she hadn't appreciated the view when she was younger or it had somehow gotten better over the years. From this vantage point, you could see for miles, even with the disastrous weather. The glassy azure ocean was gone, replaced by a tumultuous cobalt sea, but it was still a sight to behold, and somehow seemed less menacing all the way up here.

And then there was the house. From the outside, everything was definitely upgraded from the last time she'd been up here. The old tiny plunge pool had been replaced with a sprawling one, complete with an infinity edge and surrounded by a gorgeous patio. If she wasn't already as wet as she could possibly be, Allison would've jumped right in.

They ducked under the sizable porch roof. "I'm confused," Zane said. "I thought you said they were renovating. I don't know what the exterior used to look like, but it seems pretty damn perfect to me. The pool's full of water."

"They *were* renovating. Or at least that's what I thought, although I didn't actually speak to Angelique about it before I came down. It wasn't like I was going to be staying in the honeymoon villa." Nor would she be staying here again anytime soon. Her romantic future looked as bleak as could be, hot on the heels of rejection by not one, but two men. First Neil and his cheating ways, and then she attempted to distract herself with Zane, which didn't work at all. Maybe she needed to just give up on men entirely. Focus on her career. The financial and professional upside with Black Crescent was potentially huge, and now that she wasn't quite as concerned with hurting Zane's feelings, she could really put her foot on the gas when they finally got out of this mess of a storm.

Zane turned and cupped his hands at his temples, peering into one of the windows. "Uh. Allison. It looks pretty spectacular inside, too."

She strode over to one of the French doors and turned the knob, then stepped inside. "Wow. Gorgeous."

The space was light and airy, twice the size of either of their cottages, but with one noticeable difference—the bed was right in the main living space. Situated on a platform that spanned the long back wall of the building, it had a soaring canopy overhead and sumptuous white linens. Allison walked across the room and took the two steps up onto the raised area, still several feet from the bed.

Zane was right by her side. "I guess if you're on your honeymoon, there's no reason to think about being anywhere other than in the sack."

"Yeah. I guess." She had to wonder what that would be like, to be so enamored of someone that you wouldn't even bother to get out of bed. The only person she'd ever imagined that with was Zane, and she already knew that wasn't going to happen.

"That bed looks so damn good," she muttered. "I just want to take a nap."

"You can do whatever you want, you know."

"My clothes are still wet."

"We should both change. You can have the bathroom, of course."

Of course. Allison snatched up her bag and poked her head into a doorway she assumed was the bathroom. Out of habit, she flipped the light switch. To her great surprise, the fixture over the vanity came on. "The light works," she shouted out to Zane.

"Thank God for solar," Zane called back.

This room would be gorgeous eventually, but was definitely still under construction, with the tile of the two-person walk-in shower not yet complete. It had the other creature comforts, though—running water at the sink and toilet. Allison was happy for the little things.

As soon as she pushed down her shorts, the pain in her hip flared. She took a look in the mirror. Her upper thigh was turning a deep shade of purple. "No wonder it was hurting." The thought of putting on more clothes that might bind against her injury was too unpleasant, so she put on a black sundress and skipped panties.

"Better?" Zane asked, wearing a dry pair of gray shorts and no shirt. He was currently toweling his hair and making it look like a seduction move. He was clearly oblivious to his effect on her.

She decided to save them both the lecture about how he should really be wearing more clothes. "My hip is all messed up." She lifted the hem of her dress to show the edge of her deepening bruise.

"We need to get some ice on that, stat." He made off for the kitchen.

"I doubt the fridge is working," she said, gingerly sitting at the foot of the mattress.

"Got it," Zane said, rattling a white plastic bin presumably filled with ice.

"Wow. A second round of applause for the solar."

Zane dug around in a drawer, eventually finding a towel and placing a handful of ice in it. He brought it to her. "Scoot back on the bed."

She raised both eyebrows at him. This was way too much like yesterday's invitation, and she already knew this wasn't going to end well, either. "Maybe I should sit on the floor."

"Don't be ridiculous. You're hurt. You should be resting. Scoot back and lie on your side."

She didn't have the strength to argue. Zane sat next

to her on the mattress, placing the ice pack on her hip. She winced at the pain.

"Just relax," he said, grabbing a pillow for her.

She took a deep breath, extended her arm and rested her head. "Thanks."

"Looks like the rain and wind aren't letting up anytime soon."

Indeed, there were sheets of sideways drops again. They pelleted the surface of the pool, creating ripples and waves. It was oddly soothing, which was nice because not much else could make her happy right now. It felt as though life was playing a cruel trick on her, sticking her in the honeymoon cottage with Zane.

"So, I wanted to ask you something," he said.

"Go for it. It's not like I have anything better to do."

"Were you serious when you said you'd been waiting fifteen years to have sex with me?"

Seven

Zane didn't enjoy putting anyone on the spot, but he'd been wondering about this since the minute Allison said it. Between that and the storm, his mind had been occupied with nothing else. Had she really had a thing for him all these years and he'd somehow managed to be oblivious? When she'd kissed him at Scott's birthday he'd assumed it was nothing more than the impetuous move of a woman who'd had a few glasses of wine with dinner. Now he was eager to find out if he'd been wrong.

Allison stared at him, shaking her head. Her talent for making him feel like an idiot was unparalleled, but she somehow managed to make it charming. "You know, I've been thinking about it, and there's no way you're this clueless. You had to know I had a crush on you back in school. So if this is just some exercise to stroke your ego, I'm going to skip it." She snatched the ice pack from his hand, climbed off the bed and tossed the cold bundle into the freezer.

"I swear I had no idea." Of course, all those years ago, his brain had been occupied elsewhere. Women seemed to be the only thing that distracted him from the misery of his family's abrupt and complete falling apart. Plus, Allison had been totally off-limits. Scott's friendship and support had saved Zane. There was no breaking that trust, but it had been especially true at that time. "But I was pretty stuck in my own head when we were younger."

"I think you're still stuck in it." She walked back to the bedside and planted her hands on her hips.

Zane was sitting on the edge of the mattress, looking up at her, mystified. "Excuse me?"

"Your loyalty to Scott all stems from this time in your life that you aren't willing to let go of, Zane. It's not healthy. Being a good friend is one thing, but it's not like you're forever indebted to my family because we were kind to you. Because we welcomed you when things were rough. That's just what people do."

"You didn't go through what I did, Allison. You have no idea what it felt like."

She closed her eyes and pinched the bridge of her nose, as if she couldn't possibly be more frustrated with him. She chose to sit next to him on the bed, which was of some consolation. "You know what? I don't know, exactly. But I do know what it's like to struggle or to get knocked down or to have a hard time. You don't have a lock on that. You need to find a way to let go of what happened. Or at least move past it."

"That's why I came to this island. To clear my head. To try to let go of my animosity toward Black Crescent and the Lowell family. Or at least some of it. I don't know that I can ever let all of it go."

"Why not? Why can't you just forgive everyone at Black Crescent for what Vernon Lowell did? It's not their fault." Allison's eyes were wild and pleading. Meanwhile, the storm outside was starting to rage like never before. The windows rattled, and rain made a thunderous chorus on the roof.

"The Lowells destroy everything. Families most of all. They ruined my family. My parents got divorced because of the things they did. And for what? So somebody who was already making way too much money as far as I'm concerned could make *more* money? I just can't forgive them for that. It's the worst kind of greed." As if Mother Nature was on his side, a massive gust of wind whipped up, smacking a massive palm frond against the French doors. He and Allison both jumped.

"Whoa," Allison said, holding a hand to her chest, breathing hard.

"It's getting scary out there." The sky blackened. It was as if the sun had been extinguished.

"I'm tired of this, Zane. So tired."

"The weather?"

She inched closer to him on the bed. "No. This. Us. We could die up here. This is serious. And I have waited for you for years."

He was still having a hard time understanding this. Years? He really had been oblivious to her feelings, and that made him feel worse. "But I didn't know. I swear."

She pressed her finger against his lips. "No. I know that now. And it makes me feel like a loser, but I don't care. I don't want to die not knowing what it's like to make love to the one guy I have always wanted."

Zane felt as though his heart was going to beat its way out of his chest. In some ways, it still felt impossible that she was talking about him. There hadn't been enough time to riffle through the memories they shared to look for hints of this crush she'd supposedly had on him. "Don't say that. Don't hold me up on a pedestal and put yourself down at the same time. You're beautiful. You're smart and amazing. You could have any guy you want."

"Any guy?"

He didn't understand the question. Had she not looked in the mirror? Did she not realize that she was not only beautiful on the outside, but on the inside, as well? "Yes. No question."

She shook her head, not taking her sights from his face. "If you think that's really true, I want you to prove it, Zane. Show me that I can have *you*."

Damn, she was clever. "I see what you did there."

"Look, I know what you're like. You don't like to feel tied down or obligated. I know you're not a forever kind of guy, but will you be mine for right now? Nobody ever has to know. Not my brother. Not anyone. I just don't want to live with this regret. I know I'm not going to get another chance."

His breaths felt as though they were being dragged from his body as Allison's warm eyes pleaded for an answer. How could he ever be good enough for her? She was everything any guy with half a brain would want. Gorgeous. Exceptionally smart. Sweet, while still standing for what she wanted. She was quite possibly the most complex and unpredictable woman he'd ever met. He cared about her. And she cared about him. These were not the circumstances under which he normally pursued sex. It was so much easier when there was nothing but physical pleasure on the line. There was more at stake here. So much more. But how could he say no to her again?

He pressed the palm of his hand against her cheek. The house shook with another gale. He watched as her eyes drifted shut and she leaned into his touch. The world was threatening to rip the rug out from under them, and she didn't care. He could see it on her stunning face as she drew in a deep breath through her nose. Warmth radiated to his hand from her silky soft cheek, and he knew then that he could not let her down. He would give in to every carnal inclination he had when it came to Allison. And he would do it because she wanted him just as badly as he wanted her.

He cupped her face with his other hand and pressed his lips against hers. They stumbled into the kiss like it was the only way forward for either of them. Her tongue swept along his lower lip, sending need right through him, like a shot to the heart. His pulse picked up, and she dug her fingers into his hair, craving, needing, curling her nails into his scalp and raking his skin. He pulled her against him and lay back on the bed, tugging her along with him. She straddled his hips and ground against his crotch with her center.

Everything in his groin went tight. His mind went blank. Need slipped into the driver's seat when she countered his weight by lifting her hips and bucking against him. He felt her smile against his lips before she got serious again, kissing him deeply and squeezing his rib cage with her knees. Zane's hands went to the hem of her dress, slipping underneath it and skimming the sides of her thighs. He sucked in a sharp breath when he realized she wasn't wearing any panties. All that time he'd spent holding the ice to her hip…he'd been so close to touching her and hadn't realized it. No wonder she'd finally put him on notice. She'd had enough.

He gripped one of her hips, but touched the other one lightly. "Does it hurt?"

She shook her head, then began to kiss his neck. "No. I don't really care about pain right now anyway. Hurt me if you need to, Zane. It's okay."

"I really don't want to."

She pressed another kiss to his lips. "I know. And I love you for it. But it's okay. I won't break."

"Promise?"

"I do." She trailed her mouth to his ear, then down his jaw and his neck, leaving a blazing white trail of heat behind as each kiss evaporated on his skin. Down the center of his chest she continued to drive him wild, her hands spreading across his pecs. Squeezing. Caressing. Exploring. He'd never had a woman show so much appreciation for every inch of him.

One leg at a time, she shifted herself between his knees. She sat back and ran one hand over the front of his shorts. That one brush of her fingers nearly drove him insane. His legs felt like they were made of rubber while his entire crotch strained with urgency. His balls drew tight. With a single finger, still through the fabric of his clothes, she drew a line from the base of his length all the way to a tip. He managed to pry open his eyes halfway for an instant—he loved the look on her face. The one that said she had him at her mercy and she was going to enjoy the hell out of this.

And he expected nothing less.

* * *

Allison didn't bother with thoughts of what might happen tomorrow or the next day. It wasn't hyperbole to say they might not ever come. The storm would take what it wanted, and so would she. So she kept her senses, her thoughts and her heart in the present—this precious moment with Zane, the one she'd waited on for so long.

She unbuttoned his shorts and shimmied them, along with his boxers, down his hips. She wrapped her fingers around his length, in awe of the tension his skin could hold. He moaned his approval as she stroked him firmly, but she knew she could do better. So much better. She could make him immensely happy.

She lowered her head and took him into her mouth, leaving her lips a little slack and letting the gentle glide of her tongue deliver the pleasure she was so eager for him to have. A deep groan left his throat, just as another mighty gust of wind made the rafters quake above them. If this was how she died, she could be happy with that. She would have had everything she'd ever wanted.

Sealing her lips around him, she built some suction, appreciating the tightness it created in his body. It radiated off him in waves. He dug his fingers into her mess of hair, but he was more encouraging with his touch than anything. He wanted her to keep going, and she did, not thinking about time, the passes of her lips slow and methodical. As his skin grew more taut, she knew that he was close to his peak. There was a temptation to drive him over the cliff, but this degree of intimacy wasn't what she'd waited for. And she wasn't about to let him get there without her.

She gently released him from her lips and sat back on her haunches. She crossed her arms in front of her and lifted the sundress over her head. The soft fabric brushed against the skin of her belly and breasts. Her nipples went tight and hard from the rush of air. She flung the garment aside, not wanting to put it back on ever.

The slyest grin crossed Zane's face as his eyes scanned her naked body. She loved feeling like his reward. It was all she'd wanted to be for so long. "Get over here."

She climbed back on top of him, straddling his hips and resting her hands on his abs. His hard erection was right between her legs, and she rocked her body forward and back, letting his tip ride over her apex. Meanwhile, she dropped her head and kissed him. She loved this all-new level of getting to know him, of being able to correctly guess when he might nip at her lower lip or tangle his tongue with hers. Even more, she loved it when he surprised her with a squeeze or lick.

Or at the moment, by rolling her to her back. He pushed her hair away from her face and kissed her deeply, full of passion she'd never seen from him. It was as if he was putting all of the intensity of his personality into a kiss. She soaked up every minute of it while trying to match it, wrapping her legs around his waist and muscling him closer. Every inch of her body felt like it was on fire right now, burning with urgency. "I need you, Zane. I want you inside me."

"Let me get a condom." He hopped off the bed and traipsed across the room to pick up his backpack.

Allison propped herself up on her elbows, in part to watch his beautiful naked form in motion, and in part to take a peek outside. The sky was so dark it looked like midnight, but it was still afternoon. Wind rasped against the windows. The wood structure of the house creaked. But fear was nowhere in sight. She had Zane, and that was all that mattered.

He returned to the bed, tearing open the packet and rolling the condom onto his erection. He positioned himself between her legs, and she raised her hips, waiting for him. He was taking things slow. Too slow. How she disliked being treated as though she were fragile. She closed her eyes, reminding herself to stay in the moment. It was then that he came inside. Inch by inch, she felt herself mold around him. She had to look at him to keep herself locked on what was really happening, and she was gladly greeted by his incredibly handsome face.

She ran her hand over his cheek and strong jaw, loving the feel of stubble against her palm as they moved together. "You feel so good. So much better than I ever imagined."

"You actually imagined this before?"

She might die of embarrassment, but she also didn't want to lie about it. "Yes. Many times."

He grinned and kissed her softly. "Were we doing it like this?"

"Sometimes."

He lowered his head and nestled his face in the crook of her neck, resting his body weight against her center, applying the right pressure. "Tell me, Alli. Tell me more."

The tension in her body was building so fast, she was a little appalled that he expected her to answer, let alone weave together the many stories she kept in her head. "In my imagination, you're perfect. You know exactly how I like it. How deep." She bit down on her lip as he punctuated her own statement with a forceful thrust. "You know that I love feeling your mouth all over my body. My neck. My breasts."

He raised his head, kissing his way from her collarbone to her nipple, swirling his tongue around the tight and sensitive bud. "Like this?"

He switched to the other side, giving it a gentle tug with his teeth and sending a verifiable wave of electricity right between her legs.

"Yes." *Yes yes yes yes yes.* Her breaths became sharp and short. The peak was chasing her down the way a lion seeks its prey. It wasn't just physical right now. Knowing she could say something, and that Zane would follow her cues, was almost too much. She was drunk on power and craving the release.

He took her nipple between his lips and sucked harder while taking more deep strokes. That was enough to push her over the edge, and her head thrashed back on the pillow, the delicious reward spreading through her body, wave after wave. Zane drove deeper and more deliberately, and she was still knee-deep in the pleasure when he came, burying his face in her neck and arching his back. His entire body froze for a moment before he collapsed on top of her and rolled to her side.

"That was amazing," she said, her chest still heaving. She was pretty proud of herself for putting together so many words. Her brain could hardly function right now.

"It was unbelievable. Just knowing that you thought

those things about me. I had no idea it would be such a turn-on."

She immediately rolled to her side, planting her hand in the dead center of his chest. "Don't you dare make fun of me for it."

"Are you kidding? I would never do that. What guy doesn't want a sexy woman to tell him the things she's fantasized about, especially when she's imagined doing those things with him?"

She was filled with a surprising amount of pride. "Okay. Good. I was a little worried."

His adorable smile crossed his face. He reached out and tucked a tendril of her hair behind her ear. "Don't worry. I'm just in awe of you, I swear."

She knew she was grinning like a fool. She could see the tops of her own cheeks. Her face hurt. In fact, she was so giddy, she couldn't think of a thing to say.

"What are you thinking?" He smoothed his hand over her bare belly. Even in the warm afterglow, she wanted more of him.

"That I hope we don't get rescued anytime soon. Or ever." It was the truth. She could stay here forever and be happy. She didn't need another thing in the world right now. It was a scary admission to make to herself. She knew what it meant—she'd been fooling herself when she'd decided that one time with Zane would be enough.

He smiled and laid another devastating kiss on her. "I don't want to get rescued, either."

Eight

Zane woke to the sound of her name.

"Allison!"

It had to be part of a dream, he guessed, but then she curled into him, snuggling her face against his chest, and he didn't question it. He stroked her hair and pulled her closer, inhaling her sweetness. He wanted to bottle up her smell and carry it with him everywhere.

"How do you do that?" she asked.

"Do what?" He was still drifting in and out of sleep.

"Make it sound like you're shouting at me from far away when you're actually right here."

"Huh?"

"Allison Randall! If you can hear me, say something!"

That was when Zane realized it was a man's voice calling Allison's name, and it was coming from outside the house.

Allison shook his arm. "I think someone has come to rescue us."

Still half-asleep and bleary-eyed, Zane could see that the sun was peeking between the clouds. The storm had passed. They were alive. "What? Where?" Zane sat up and shook his head to rid himself of the mental cobwebs. "Hurry. They're probably wondering where in the hell we are."

Both naked, they scrambled for their clothes. As much as Zane had hoped for a sexy morning with Allison, it appeared that was not going to happen. They raced to get dressed, Zane finishing first. He stumbled for the patio door and flung it open, rushing outside. Allison was right behind him. They rounded the house on the crushed-shell path. Several hundred yards away, Marcus, the man who had piloted the boat he took onto the island, was on his way up the hill.

Allison waved. "Marcus! Up here! We're here!"

Marcus's vision fell on her. His shoulders dropped in relief. "Your family has been worried sick!" he shouted back through cupped hands before resuming his climb.

Zane could only imagine. He'd witnessed the way Allison's family fretted over her. Scott was probably beside himself. "I'm sorry you had to come all the way up here," Zane said when Marcus reached them. "We decided the highest point was the safest. We were worried about the storm surge and the water more than I was worried about the wind."

"Smart. You probably saved yourselves. The cottages you two were staying in both had significant flooding."

Allison's sights darted to Zane, and it was as if he could see her heart plummeting to her stomach. Her aunt and uncle would be devastated to learn of the fate of their resort, especially on the heels of her uncle's health issues. "Do you know how my uncle Hubert is doing?" she asked.

"He had a heart bypass, but he's doing well. They ended up transporting him to a hospital in Atlanta. It was too dangerous with the storm to try the surgery in Nassau or even in Miami. They didn't want to risk the power going out. But he's recovering well. Your aunt, on the other hand, has been so worried. She said she would never forgive herself if you got hurt while staying on the island. She wanted to send me back for you earlier, but the waters were too rough."

"I was very lucky to have Zane with me. He knew exactly what to do."

Zane emphatically shook his head. He wasn't about to take credit for their safety. In truth, he'd been hoping that they wouldn't be found. He and Allison had such an amazing night. Unforgettable. Most likely a once-in-a-lifetime event, which struck him with a sense of melancholy he hadn't thought to prepare himself for. "It was a joint effort. Allison came up with the idea to leave the scraps of her sarong to send a message about where we were."

"It was smart. That's exactly how I found you." Marcus tugged the final strip of sarong fabric off a nearby shrub. "Come on. Let's get your things and get you to Eleuthera and on the plane to Miami. Your brother is waiting there."

Oh, crap. This was not a good development. Zane wasn't even close to being ready to see his best friend. If Scott was worried enough to fly to Miami, he would be that much more likely to pick up on any romantic vibes between Allison and Zane. For that reason, Zane was going to have to shut it all down way before they went near Scott. The thought pained him, but it was for the best.

"Scott flew down to Miami? Was that really necessary?" Allison asked.

"Like I said. Your whole family has been extremely worried about you," Marcus said.

Zane patted Allison's arm as platonically as possible. They needed to get back to being friends *without* benefits. "It'll be okay. We're safe. That's all that matters."

Allison, Zane and Marcus forged their way back to the honeymoon villa and collected what few belongings they still had. Zane was the first inside and found himself rushing inside to make up the bed, which was pretty much a disaster. The things he and Allison had done to each other there felt like a dream. They'd been amazing in the moment, but Zane needed to get his head out of the clouds and hop back on the straight and narrow. He desperately hoped that Marcus did not have a relationship with Scott. Loose lips could sink ships, or in this case, a deeply important friendship.

It took about an hour to make it back down the hillside and across the island to the dock. There, flapping in the bright early-morning sun, was the first piece of Allison's sarong, still tied to the metal piling. She'd been collecting the strips of fabric along the way. Zane got to it first and rescued it for her.

"Maybe you can have it sewn back together," Zane said, thinking that if he could have anything right now, it would be one more chance to see her wearing it. But he needed to stop thinking of Allison that way. Their fling was over.

"It'd be nice to keep it as a remembrance of our time together, but we're headed back to reality and my brother right now. I'd like to know where things stand." Her face was colored with a seriousness he hated to see, but he understood why it was there. This was no joke. Zane had crossed a line, and he needed to return to the other side of it.

"I can't betray him, Allison. You know that. Nothing about that has changed." Zane could see the frustration bubbling up inside her. He knew that she was tired of this argument, but it was the truth.

"But the betrayal is done. It happened, and you can't unring that bell. So now the question is what are you going to do about it?"

"You're the one who said we would keep it all between the two of us. I think we stick to the plan. It was amazing, Allison. But it's over." If only the words didn't sound so wrong coming out of his mouth. They certainly weren't enough to convince him. If only they'd had a little more time…to talk all of this through, to share one last mind-melting kiss.

"We're ready to leave," Marcus called for them both from the boat.

Allison stepped past Zane. "Let's just get out of here."

Her tone told him all he needed to know. So that's what last night had been—he'd been an itch that Allison had needed to scratch. Nothing more. He couldn't allow his feelings to be hurt by this revelation. He'd felt that way about many women in the past, and he was certain that women had felt that way about him, as well. Still, it didn't sit entirely right with Zane. Allison had never seemed like the type to love 'em and leave 'em, but her words and her posture were saying exactly that right now.

Between the persistent roar of the wind and the engine noise, Allison and Zane were unable to talk at all on the ride to Eleuthera. As soon as they arrived, a woman who said she was a friend of her aunt Angelique's descended upon them. She was a physician's assistant and insisted on joining them on the Learjet for the flight to Miami. She checked their vital signs and made sure they both ate and drank plenty of water. It was nice to feel taken care of, but at this point, Zane was just ready to get home. Between having weathered the storm, enduring the current cold shoulder from Allison and preparing himself for seeing Scott, Zane was completely and utterly exhausted.

As soon as they landed in Miami and walked into the private terminal, Scott rushed forward and scooped Allison up in her arms. "Thank God you're okay," he said over and over, squeezing her tight.

Zane watched the exchange, remembering the many times Scott had recounted the stories about Allison's cancer as a young girl and the havoc it had wreaked on their entire family. Scott had said many times that he'd never been through anything more difficult than that—life and death, wondering if his sweet and innocent sister would live or die. To hear Scott tell it, every day since then with Allison was regarded as a gift by their entire family.

"I'm fine," she said when he'd finally put her back down on the ground. "Really. Zane took care of me. He made sure nothing happened."

Scott clapped Zane on the shoulder, nodding in appreciation. "I owe you one for keeping her safe."

The guilt Zane had feared was slowly starting to crush him. He'd only done what a good friend would do. But then he'd also done what a good friend *wouldn't* do—he'd slept with his sister. "Honestly, I think she saved me more than the other way around. She would've been just fine on her own. She's too resourceful and smart to get herself into too much trouble." Zane shot her a sideways glance to let her know he had her back. He'd paid attention when they'd talked about this on the island. He understood that she was fighting for Scott to see her in a different light.

"You need to stop worrying so much," Allison said to her brother.

"Plenty of smart people die in natural disasters," Scott said. "Especially when there's flooding."

"She's an unbelievable swimmer. You should have seen her the day we snorkeled over to Mako Island. I could hardly keep up with her. And she wasn't tired at all."

"You two went to Makeout Island?" Scott asked.

Zane wasn't sure he'd heard that right. "Wait? What?"

Scott narrowed his sights on his sister and twisted his lips. "Didn't Allison tell you? That's where teenagers go if they want to hook up with someone and want privacy."

Zane would've laughed if it didn't make the two of them look incredibly guilty. "You told me it was called Mako Island," Zane said to Allison.

"It *is* called that. Scott's being childish." Just then, Allison's phone rang, and she answered it right away.

"Hello?" Her face lit up as she listened to what the caller was saying. "Ryan, you are so sweet," she said, distancing herself from her brother and Zane. "I'm totally fine. Just got back to the States. We're in Miami, safe and sound."

Allison's words reverberated in Zane's ears like a bass drum. *Ryan, you are so sweet.* No wonder she'd agreed that anything between them was to stay on the island. There were other men in her orbit, and she didn't want to mess with that. She'd given him an awfully hard time about his unwillingness to get serious with any woman, but she seemed to be playing the field just as hard.

"Hey. Can we talk?" Scott asked Zane.

Zane was not ready to fall under the purview of Scott's eagle eye, especially not when he was so distracted by Allison and her phone call with Ryan. She kept smiling and laughing, which was driving Zane nuts. He was back to not buying the story about working together. "Yeah. Of course."

The pair walked off to a corner of the gate area. Scott stuffed his hands in his pockets and looked down at the floor, seeming tormented. "Is there anything I need to know about? Anything with my sister?"

Zane's brain shifted into overdrive. He did not want to couch things with his best friend, so he was immensely thankful for the phrasing of the question. "There's nothing you need to know about." That much was true. What had happened between Allison and him was entirely private. Nobody's business. She was a grown woman, he was a grown man and they were two adults who had given their enthusiastic consent. End of story.

"You sure?"

"Well, it's been kind of a whirlwind, if that's what you're asking. Not quite the relaxing vacation I'd been hoping for."

"You know that's not what I'm wondering about. I know you. I love you, but there's a damn revolving door in your pants."

Funny, but last night, Zane had been thinking about that very thing, wondering if maybe it wasn't time to set aside his ridiculous bachelor ways. It wasn't making him happy, that was for sure. Those few days he'd spent with Allison were the closest he'd ever felt to having an actual relationship. They'd formed a partnership, they'd worked together and they'd done it well. Plus, being able to act on their incredible chemistry had been a transformative experience. But as Allison hung up her phone and fought a smile, Zane knew that they were back to being nothing more than friends.

"Sorry about that," Allison said, approaching Zane and her brother. The call had been from Ryan Hathaway, who was clearly a great guy. He'd heard about the storm on the news and wanted to make sure she was okay. How sweet was that? She was very excited about the prospect of him interviewing for Black Crescent. "I had to take a work call."

"Yeah. Right," Zane said, his voice clipped. "How's Ryan?"

Oh, hell no. Allison was not going to play this game with Zane, especially when he'd been the one to declare that things were "over" back on the island. "He's wonderful. Thanks for asking. He was really concerned about me and the storm. He wanted to make sure I was safe and sound."

"How nice. He sounds like a great guy." Everything in Zane's tone suggested he did not truly hold this opinion.

Scott looked back and forth between Zane and Allison, seeming perplexed by the conversation. "Uh, okay. I was able to snag the last three first-class seats on the next flight to New Jersey. We'd better get ourselves to the gate. It's boarding in less than an hour."

"What about Allison?" Zane asked, turning his attention to her. "Are you coming with us? I figured you were flying back to LA."

She'd been so nervous about accidentally revealing the Black Crescent information that she hadn't mentioned this detail to Zane. "Didn't I tell you? I'm actually coming back to Falling Brook for a week or so. I have some work I need to do."

"No, you didn't tell me. Do you have a client in town?" Again, his voice was nothing short of perturbed, but Allison was pretty determined to let him stew in his own juices.

"Yes."

"Who is it?"

"I can't say. It's confidential."

"How long is that supposed to last? Falling Brook is not a big place, and I have lived there my entire life. I'm going to find out sooner or later."

Allison's pulse raced. She felt queasy at the thought of Zane figuring this out. She knew exactly how he would react—badly. "If you were my client, I wouldn't talk about you to anyone else. It's just the right thing to do."

He rolled his damn eyes, not bothering to say that of
course it made sense for her to keep things to herself
for the sake of her business interests. She could hardly
believe how things between her and Zane had changed
in the last few hours. So much for fantasies brought to
life—she wondered now if it wouldn't have been better to keep Zane in her dreams, rather than begging
him to become a reality. *Careful what you wish for.* It
hurt too much to have him be such a jerk to her. And
to think that she'd been mulling over some ridiculous
confessions last night when she couldn't fall asleep.
She'd wanted to tell him that she wanted more of him.
So much more. And if he'd given her any indication
that he might feel the same way, she would have been
all in. She would have even called Kianna and told her
that they had to drop Black Crescent.

The Allison of last night was clearly an idiot. It
didn't matter that she and Zane had had an amazing
time on the island together, and not just in bed. It didn't
matter that he'd made her happy. Made her laugh. Made
her feel sexy and desired. Zane would always choose
his friendship with Scott over her, and she couldn't
entirely blame him. That relationship had longevity.
It had never faltered. He could count on it, and Allison understood how anyone would want to stick to the
things in life that were reliable, especially if you were
Zane, a man who'd been through the wringer.

That still didn't keep her from wanting him.

The three of them took a shuttle over to the com-
mercial terminal and waited to board, standing on the
concourse outside the busy gate area. Scott and Zane
had been knee-deep in conversation, leaving Allison

to feel like the third wheel until Zane wandered off to find a bathroom and Scott pulled Allison aside.

"You didn't tell him why you were coming back to Falling Brook?" Scott asked her pointedly.

"Wow. You really don't waste any time, don't you?"

"It's a valid question, and he's going to be back any minute now. You two just rode out the storm together and the topic of you coming back to Falling Brook never came up? Not once? It makes me wonder what in the heck you two did talk about."

"I don't want him to know about Black Crescent, okay? And I don't want you to tell him, either. You know how he feels about it. You know it hurts him to talk or hear about it, and you also know he has a blind spot when it comes to the Lowells. I don't want it to mess with our friendship."

"Since when have you two been close?"

If Allison could've shot laser beams from her eyes at her brother, she would have. Why did he have to think that only he could be close to Zane? "We've always been friends, Scott. You know that. I can't compete with your friendship, okay? So don't try to compare the two." She saw down the concourse that Zane was on his way back already. Even in rumpled clothes, with two days of scruff on his face and with an attitude that was decidedly cooler than the one she'd experienced during their last day on the island, he was irresistible. She was going to have to learn to resist. "He and I just went through a life-and-death situation, and I don't want to hurt his feelings unnecessarily. He's tired. I'm tired. Plus, there's a good chance that I won't get hired by BC long term. So if it's only a one-off, I really don't see the point in telling him and hurting his feelings for no good reason."

Scott nodded. "Okay. That's probably the right call then. Your intentions are good."

Zane smiled as he approached them. It still made Allison's heart melt. She was going to have to figure out a way to get over him. She had no idea how that would work. "You guys talking about me?" he asked.

"Always," Scott said.

"Never," Allison countered.

"Ladies and gentlemen," the gate agent announced over the intercom. "We're ready to begin the boarding process for Flight 1506 with nonstop service to Newark International Airport. We'll begin by inviting our first-class passengers to board."

"That's us," Scott said.

"Good. I can't wait to get home to a hot shower and a good night's sleep," Zane said.

Allison felt the same way. She also wished she could do those things with Zane. She was going to need to work up to this whole business of forgetting her attraction to him.

The three boarded the plane, but as soon as Allison figured out the seating arrangement, she realized just how much she would always be the odd man out when it came to her brother and Zane. The two guys were seated together, across the aisle from her. That had been Scott's decision, since he'd booked the flights, and Zane was obviously perfectly happy with it. Allison flagged the flight attendant and asked for a gin and tonic before takeoff. She needed something to soothe her ragged edges. Maybe she could catch some sleep after they were in the air.

But for now, since Zane and Scott were immersed in conversation, and the plane was still boarding, Allison took this chance to give Kianna a quick call.

"Tell me you're okay," she blurted without even saying hello.

"I'm fine. In one piece. On the plane to New Jersey."

"I can't believe that storm hit the island. It all happened so fast. I kept watching the forecast, hoping it would change for you. I can't help but feel responsible. It was my idea for you to go down there in the first place."

"No. No. It's not your fault. I wanted to go. And believe it or not, it was still a good trip. Despite the storm. Despite everything." She was trying to put the best possible spin on this, not merely for Kianna's sake, but also for her own. She didn't want to regret her time with Zane. She didn't want to believe that it might have been a big mistake. But what do you do when you get what you've always wanted and then it's snatched away by timing and circumstance? What do you do when the guy you've wanted for years tells you that it's over before it's had a chance to really start? Right now, it felt like nothing would ever sting as much as this rejection.

"Did you at least find a hot guy? Please say yes."

Allison couldn't suppress the smile that crossed her face. "I did. But I'll have to tell you about it later. We take off soon, and I have to turn off my phone."

"Okay, hon. Did you postpone your meeting with Black Crescent?"

"Nope. Still going in tomorrow. As planned."

"Did you talk to Joshua Lowell?"

"I texted his assistant. We're all good."

"You're a badass, you know that, right?"

Allison laughed. Her friendship and partnership with Kianna meant the world to her. She really hoped she wouldn't end up letting her down. This Black Crescent meeting had to go well. "I'm trying."

"Call me after the meeting tomorrow?"

"You know it. Talk to you then."

Allison hung up the phone, switched it to airplane mode and tucked it into the seat-back pocket. She swirled her gin and tonic, took a long sip and glanced over at Zane and Scott. Zane, who was sitting at the window, made eye contact with her. That instant seemed to speak volumes—there was a connection between them that hadn't been there before they got to the island. Zane knew it. She did, too. But he seemed resigned to setting it aside. Keeping it in the past. No matter how hot and passionate that connection was, it didn't seem to be enough for Zane.

He dropped his gaze and returned his attention to her brother. Allison's heart plummeted to her stomach, but she was used to the disappointment now. It was the story of her life with Zane. And exactly the reason why this visit to Falling Brook would be all about her role as businessperson supreme, not the woman who couldn't stop pining for a man she couldn't have.

Scott leaned across the aisle to talk to her. "Do you have plans tomorrow night?"

"Hanging out at your house. Not sure what else I would possibly be doing."

"I wasn't sure if you had work obligations."

Allison wanted to strangle her brother for bringing up Black Crescent while Zane was sitting right next to him. "Nope. I should be done by midafternoon. Why?"

Zane peered around Scott. "He invited me over for dinner."

"I wanted to thank him for taking such good care of my little sister," Scott added.

What in the world was her brother up to? "Okay. Sounds great."

Nine

Right on time, Allison pulled her rental car into the Black Crescent parking lot the following afternoon, shortly before two o'clock. She'd arrived back in Falling Brook in the nick of time—less than twenty-four hours before her scheduled meeting with Haley Shaw and Joshua Lowell. Anyone else might have used the fact that she'd been stranded on an island in the middle of a hurricane as an excuse to postpone the meeting, but that detail was a dramatic selling point. She could tell Josh Lowell that not even a natural disaster would keep her from doing her job, and doing it well. In the end, she and Kianna needed the Black Crescent contract. It was their best shot at keeping their company alive.

Of course, the only trouble with that was Zane. If she got the contract, she would have to tell him that she was working for the company that he considered the enemy. Even though there were no more remnants of romance between them, she couldn't keep the secret from him forever. As she walked up to the sleek and modern building that had always stuck out in the other- wise traditional Falling Brook landscape, she was well aware that if Zane knew what she was doing right now, he would tell her she was not only a terrible friend, she was foolish. The things he'd said while they were rid- ing out the storm in the Bahamas echoed in her head. *The Lowells destroy everything. Families most of all.* He'd been deeply hurt by the things the Lowell fam- ily had done to him and his parents, and it was clear that for Zane, it was about far more than the money. His entire world was turned upside down the day that Vernon Lowell made off with his family's fortune. As far as Zane was concerned, his old charmed life ended that day and his new, far less shiny life began.

Allison had a somewhat different perspective. Oddly enough, she felt a debt of gratitude to the Lowells. If Vernon hadn't disappeared with all that money, she might have never met Zane. That thinking might be employing some pretty messed-up logic, but that was truly the way she felt. Not having Zane in her life was an incredibly depressing thought, almost as sad as the other thought that had been winding through her head since the Bahamas—that Zane would ultimately be a thirst unquenched. She'd thought that making love with him would get him out of her system. But that had been a horrible miscalculation on her part.

The flight had given her entirely too much time to mull over Zane's latest rejection. She wanted to shrug it off and move ahead, but her heart just wouldn't let her go there. Her heart wanted to drag her down to the bottom of this murky sea in which she was adrift and remind her of the reasons why it was such a shattering disappointment to have him choose his friendship with her brother over a chance with her. She was in deep, and she had no idea how to swim her way out. Scott would never buy into the idea of her with Zane. He would always think of Allison as that little girl with cancer, even when she was strong and healthy and a grown woman. And if anyone knew Zane forward, backward and every other way imaginable, it was her brother. He was convinced that Zane wasn't capable of commitment. The allure of other women was too great, although Allison also suspected that there was more to it than that. Zane might have been unbelievably brave in the face of that storm, but he was afraid of commitment and was possibly even more terrified of love. That put Allison in the category of a good time, right where every other woman he'd ever met also resided. Allison didn't want to be just another girl, but it sure felt that way.

With the Black Crescent building looming before her, Allison couldn't afford to think about that. She had a job to do and a business to keep afloat. Her first allegiance had to be to herself and Kianna now. She straightened her designer jacket and shrugged her laptop bag up onto her shoulder, then marched into Black Crescent.

She approached the main-floor reception desk. "Allison Randall for Joshua Lowell. We have a two o'clock."

The receptionist picked up the phone. "One moment, please."

Before she could dial an extension number, another

woman emerged from a side door in the reception area. "Ms. Randall?" The woman was willowy with wavy blond hair. She offered her hand. "I'm Haley Shaw, Mr. Lowell's assistant. We're so glad you're here. Especially considering everything you've been through. I still can't believe you were able to keep this appointment."

Allison shook hands with Haley. "It would've taken more than some bad weather to keep me away from this opportunity."

"Come on. I'll give you the lay of the land and show you where we'll be conducting the interviews."

Haley led Allison upstairs to the second floor and a conference room right outside Joshua Lowell's office. The one thing that struck Allison about Black Crescent was that no expense had been spared. Every detail was of the finest quality. It did make Allison wonder if the rumors about Vernon Lowell were true, that he'd never actually left Falling Brook and had merely been in hiding this whole time. If that was ever proved to be the case, she could imagine Zane blowing his top. Another lie from Vernon Lowell would only reopen Zane's deep wounds. Plus, Zane was the sort of the man who wanted to get even. Knowing he could have hunted down Vernon all these years would at the very least eat at him.

"Please, make yourself at home," Haley said, gesturing to the gleaming mahogany meeting table. "Mr. Lowell should be here in a few minutes. He's just finishing up a phone call."

Allison set down her Louis Vuitton bag and pulled out her laptop. "Great. We're seeing three candidates today. Ryan Hathaway, Chase Hargrove and Matteo Velez."

Haley pursed her lips in a particularly odd way. "Chase Hargrove, huh?" Her voice was dripping with doubt, something Allison wanted to get to the bottom of before Joshua arrived.

"Yes. He's highly qualified for the position. And I was impressed with him when we spoke on the phone."

Haley nodded, but seemed unconvinced. "I'm sure he has the right credentials. I just don't know if he's a good fit for the office."

This was an interesting development. Allison had never had an assistant offer her opinion of a candidate, and especially not before the interview had even taken place. But in her experience assistants seemed to always know more about everyone and everything than the majority of their bosses. "Can you tell me why?"

Just then, a young man poked his head into the meeting room. "Ms. Shaw. Chase Hargrove is here for his interview."

"Can you let Mr. Lowell know? And can you ask Chase to hold on a minute?" Haley asked.

"Sure thing, Ms. Shaw." The man darted back into the hall.

"If there's something I need to know, now would be a great time to mention it," Allison said. She couldn't afford to mess up when it came to Black Crescent. She had to nail this job. On paper, Chase was a highly qualified candidate, and Allison had found him charming and affable during their one phone conversation.

Haley seemed deep in thought for a moment, as if she was calculating her response. "I'm afraid I don't have a specific reason for feeling that way about Chase. It's more of a hunch."

The meeting door opened again and in walked

Joshua Lowell. Allison had never met him in person, but she'd seen his pictures all over the papers and in business magazines, especially the last few years. "Mr. Lowell, I'm Allison Randall." She offered her hand.

"Please. Call me Joshua. It won't be long before I'm not the boss around here anymore."

"That's why I'm here, right?" Allison wondered if that aspect of her job might help her smooth things over with Zane whenever he discovered she was working for Black Crescent. So much of his hatred seemed aimed at Joshua, and she was in charge of finding his replacement. She tucked the idea away in her head. The idea of needing to explain herself to Zane, all in the name of making a case for them as a couple, was a stretch. She was sure he didn't see her as anything more than a fling.

"Absolutely," Joshua answered. "So, please, let's bring in these candidates."

Allison asked Haley to go ahead and bring Chase in for his interview. The instant he walked through the door, the energy in the room changed dramatically. Tall, handsome and completely self-assured, Chase was a formidable presence. With Joshua also in the room, it was no easy task to take center stage, but Chase seemed to do it at will. Was this the reason for Haley's hesitancy when it came to Chase? Was he simply too much to deal with?

Chase sat opposite the three of them at the conference table and Allison wasted no time conducting the interview. This was not about putting the candidate on the spot—she'd already gone over these exact questions with them over the phone. They'd also already been fully vetted by Allison and Kianna. This process was all for the client. This was Chase's chance to put his well-honed answers on full display for Joshua.

When Allison was finished, she was fairly certain Chase could not only land the job, but could perform the duties with aplomb. But she wasn't done with showing off the product of her hard work—Ryan Hathaway and Matteo Velez were up next.

"Thank you so much, Chase, for coming in today. We'll be in touch," Allison said.

All four of them stood and Chase began to round the table.

"I'll fetch Mr. Hathaway," Haley blurted, darting out the door before Chase had a chance to shake her hand and say goodbye.

Chase took notice, watching as she disappeared. "Ms. Shaw sure is on the case, isn't she?"

Joshua extended his hand to Chase. "She's the best. No matter who comes in as CEO, Haley needs to stay. She makes this office run."

"Believe me, if I get this job, Ms. Shaw is the last person I'd dream of replacing," Chase said. Allison couldn't ignore the glimmer in his eyes.

Just then, Haley walked in with Ryan Hathaway, who Allison recognized from his headshot. Typically, Allison did not want the candidates for a position to encounter each other in the interview room, but what was done was done. She made the introductions, and Ryan seemed immediately suspicious of Chase.

"I suppose this is my cue to make way for your interview," Chase said to Ryan before turning to Haley. "And, Ms. Shaw, I hope to see you again very soon."

Haley's face flushed with a brilliant shade of pink.

She was noticeably conflicted as they shook hands. "I wish you the best of luck."

Ryan seemed to take notice of the sparks between Haley and Chase, arching both eyebrows and pressing his lips together firmly as he witnessed their goodbye. He pulled Allison aside as Haley and Joshua talked privately.

"Is there something I need to know about that guy? Did he already get the job? I don't want to interview for a taken position," he said.

Allison shook her head, but she could tell that Ryan was seriously concerned. Given their earlier conversations, she was eager to put him at ease. "Everything's fine. I think he's just a little heavy-handed with the charm. If I had to place a bet on it, I'd say he has a bit of a crush on Ms. Shaw."

Ryan glanced over his shoulder. Joshua and Haley were still conferring. "Okay. Good."

Allison gently placed her hand on Ryan's shoulder. "You sure you're okay?"

He nodded enthusiastically. "Yes. Definitely. I'm just used to guys like that being rewarded for their bad behavior. You know what they say. Nice guys finish last."

Allison took a moment to consider Ryan's words. Had he been burned? Was that where that was coming from? If so, she felt his pain. She'd gone for what she wanted, and it had been a miserable fail. "Nice guys finish first with me. As long as they're qualified and nail the interview, of course."

Ryan grinned. "I'm glad you recruited me. I really enjoyed our conversation while you were on your trip.

I'm so relieved you weren't hurt in the storm. Everything I saw on the news looked terrifying."

"It wasn't fun, that's for sure." Except that it had been. It had been amazing. She'd never felt more alive when the sea seemed determined to carry them away, but Zane was resolute about keeping her safe. She'd let herself be vulnerable with him, something she rarely ever did, and in the moment, it had been so richly rewarding. Even with Zane behaving like an ass since then, and trying to discount everything that had happened between them, she knew in her heart that it had all been worth it. Kissing him, touching him, having his hands all over her body. She'd wanted him for so long. How could she have ever said no? Even if she'd known all along what would happen? She couldn't have.

Allison shook her head and brought herself back to the present. She couldn't daydream about Zane right now. Not with work on the line. "I have to ask if you're looking at other positions right now," she said to Ryan.

"I have a few more interviews over the next several weeks. But I'll be honest. This is the job I really want."

There was no greater satisfaction than finding the right candidate for the job, and Allison had a good feeling about Ryan. "Music to my ears. Now, let's see if Mr. Lowell and Ms. Shaw are ready to get this show on the road."

Ryan hit it out of the park during his interview, as did Matteo after him. When it was time to say goodbye to Josh and Haley, Allison knew she'd done an amazing job.

"Very impressive, Ms. Randall," Joshua said, sitting back in his chair. "Thank you for going the extra mile in making today happen."

"Literally," Haley added. "She just flew back from the Bahamas last night."

"I'll do whatever it takes to make my clients happy." Allison collected her papers into a neat stack. "Do you have a sense of the timeline for the hire?"

"I'm eager to get the new CEO in as soon as possible. What are your thoughts as far as the timing for second interviews?"

"It'll depend on the candidates' schedules and yours, of course, but Haley and I can coordinate. I do recommend you think about it for at least a week. Spend some time with the files and background info I provided. In my experience, it's best to not rush with a decision like this."

Joshua nodded, seeming to consider all she said. "I suppose you're right. I'm just ready to move forward."

Allison couldn't help but think of the subtext— he was eager to move on with his life. He had love and happiness ahead, and he didn't want to wait. "Of course. I understand."

"Will you be able to stay in Falling Brook for a few weeks? It would be great if I knew I could call on you to walk us through this process. The phone is one thing, but there's no substitute for having someone on hand."

Allison knew this was her opening for driving home the deal she wanted to make. "It depends on whether or not I'm on retainer. I have a partner out in Los Angeles and other clients who also expect my time."

"I'll pay triple your normal retainer for the next month." Joshua hadn't hesitated to up the ante. "That should give us enough time to make a hire for this position."

Allison swallowed hard. Three times her normal

rate was certainly a great starting point. "And beyond that?"

"The new CEO will ultimately make the call as to whether we put you on permanent retainer. But I will certainly have a say in it, and, as far as I'm concerned, you have the job."

Goose bumps raced over the surface of Allison's skin. Any sliver of victory in business felt good, and Kianna was going to flip out when she got the good news. Even so, there was a downside. A month in Falling Brook would make it impossible to stay away from Zane. And that meant she had to come clean with him about working with Black Crescent. "Fantastic. I'm staying with my brother here in Falling Brook, working out of his house. I can be on-site anytime you need me. Just call."

"You can expect to hear from me."

Allison strode out of the meeting, feeling as though she was walking on a cloud. She'd nailed it, in every sense of the term. She called Kianna and told her everything as soon as she got in the car.

"You are not only a badass, you're a rock star," Kianna said.

"It's only a month. It's not the long-term retainer we wanted."

"It'll come. I know you'll get it done."

"I'll do my best."

"So, can you tell me about the guy in the Bahamas?"

Allison hesitated, not sure she wanted to dive into the topic. This wasn't a quick conversation, and there was so much about this situation that she was still trying to mentally unpack. "His name is Zane. I've known him for fifteen years. He's a friend of my brother's, and we just happened to end up at Rose Cove at the same time." She decided to skip the heavier part of the story, the details about how she'd been longing for him all those years and that the idea of letting go was a miserable one.

"Did he at least rock your world?"

"Oh, yes. Several times."

"And now?"

"I don't know. I think we're back to just being friends."

"Are you happy with that arrangement?"

Allison sighed. She wasn't happy with it, but she also didn't see a way past it. Maybe it really was easier if she and Zane stayed friends. "I'm not sure, but I'll figure out at least some of it tonight. He's coming over to my brother's for dinner."

Ten

Zane's first day back at the office after the Bahamas trip was less than productive. Between a million phone calls from concerned friends and clients, and his pervasive thoughts of Allison, he got very little work done. For some ridiculous reason, he kept seeing flashes of Allison flitting around the island in her sarong. It was so bad that he'd referred to one of his marketing managers as Allison when her name was in fact Maria. He hadn't even been close. A mistake easily swept aside when he blamed it on the exhaustion from the storm, but it was a sign that he was going to have deal with this. It had been shortsighted to think that he and Allison could sleep together, shrug it off and return to their old dynamic. So where would they land? He had no idea.

By the time he'd hopped in his BMW to head to

Scott's house for dinner, he was still catching up. He'd left a voice mail for his mom, but she was just now calling him back. He pressed the button to put her on speaker.

"Hi, Mom. I take it you got my message?"

"I didn't even know you'd left the country. Shows you how out of the loop I am."

"Would it have been better if I'd told you I was down there? Wouldn't you have worried? I know you don't like to worry."

"Well, of course, I would've been concerned, but you're a survivor, Zane. I never doubt your ability to figure out how to find your way through a tough situation."

The undertone of her comment was that he'd managed just fine in his teenage years when everything had gone south. It was nice to get that stamp of approval, although he knew that it was just his mother being a mom. "Thanks."

"What took you down there? New marketing client in the Bahamas?"

"I went on vacation."

"No!" His mother gasped, which turned into her musical laugh. "My son? Went away for fun?"

Zane had to chuckle, too. "Believe it or not, yes. I've been stressed, and I needed to get out of Falling Brook to clear my head."

"Are things at work not going well?"

Zane took the turn onto Scott's street. Scott and his wife lived in one of the original Falling Brook neighborhoods, which was seeing a revival. Older, stately homes were being remodeled and updated, with young families moving in. Zane saw it as a move in the right direction. This town needed some freshening up. "Actually, things at work are amazing. We're too busy, but in a good way. We've reached the point where we're turning away potential clients. That's something I never even imagined six or seven years ago."

"Then what's bothering you?"

Zane pulled up in front of Scott's house, a recently restored five-bedroom Tudor with a pristine putting green of a front yard that was Scott's pride and joy. Zane put the car in Park and killed the engine, sitting back in the driver's seat and running his hand through his hair.

"You're being quiet," his mom said. "Just come out with it. You know you can tell me anything."

He knew that. It didn't make his embarrassment over what he was about to say any less real. "It's Joshua Lowell. I got sucked into some drama with him. Someone anonymously sent me a paternity test saying that he had a child he wasn't willing to claim responsibility for. I talked to a local reporter who was working on a piece about him."

"Have you lost your mind? Why would you get involved in that?"

"I don't know. Revenge? Or as close as I'll ever get to it? It doesn't really matter now. It all backfired. The story ran, without that bombshell, and Josh Lowell ended up smelling like a rose, he and the reporter fell in love and now he's getting married. He's even leaving Black Crescent."

She sighed heavily.

"I know," Zane said. "The guy is golden. Everything he does turns out perfectly, and it makes me nuts. I know it shouldn't, but it does. Just thinking about it is making my shoulders lock up." He cranked his head from side to side, hoping to loosen the tension.

"You realize that people think the same thing about you. That you're golden. That you can do no wrong."

"*You* might say that about me, but other people do not. Plus, that isn't the point."

"But it *is* the point. It's not just me who says it, either. Your father thinks the same thing. Your grandparents. Aunts and uncles. Your colleagues and employees. Remember when you invited me to your company Christmas party two years ago? All night long, all I heard about was how great you are and it's not just because you're the boss. I heard it from your clients, as well. I'm your mom, and even I got a little sick of it."

Zane laughed, but he was astonished to be hearing this from her. He'd never seen himself as anything more than the guy who was still striving to get back on top.

"Look at your life," she continued. "You have an immensely successful business. You own a beautiful home in one of the most exclusive towns in the country. You're handsome, and people love you. Whatever it is that you think the Lowells stole from us or from you, it doesn't matter. It hasn't kept you from having it all, and it never will keep you from it. You need to find a way to move forward."

"This isn't just about what they did to me. It's about what they did to our family. The Lowells are the reason you and dad split up."

"You know, your dad and I had a drink a few weeks ago. We talked about it."

"You did?" His parents' divorce had been as acrimonious as they came. To Zane's knowledge, his parents had only been in the same place twice since their split fourteen years ago, at Zane's high school and college graduations, and they'd barely spoken to each other. "You didn't tell me this."

"He came to Boston for work, and he called me. It was nice. We had a chance to say a lot of things that should've been said a long time ago. The truth is that your dad and I were never going to make it. Of course, losing everything put a massive strain on the marriage, but the underlying problems were already there. We weren't in love. I'm not sure we ever were. We would have split up eventually."

Zane was struggling to keep up, but he couldn't help but notice that it felt as if a weight was being lifted. A burden from his past was evaporating before his eyes. "Wow, Mom. You are kind of blowing my mind right now."

"Does that help you see that you need to let Joshua Lowell do his own thing and maybe get out there and keep looking for your own happiness? You know, I'd like to have a daughter-in-law, maybe become a grandmother at some point."

"Mom…"

"No pressure."

"Oh, right. No pressure." Zane glanced at the clock on his dashboard. It was seven o'clock and he didn't want to be late. "Mom, I need to run. Scott invited me over for dinner and I'm sitting outside his house. His sister, Allison, is in town."

"Oh, how nice. Say hi to them both for me. I've always adored those two, especially Allison. She's always been such a sweetheart to me."

And just like that, Zane felt like the universe might

be telling him to salvage the romance that had started at Rose Cove. It was at least worth trying. "Love you, Mom."

"Love you, too."

Zane grabbed the bottle of Chateau Musar he'd brought, which was Scott's favorite wine, and hopped out of the car. He strode up the long driveway and couldn't ignore the way his pulse picked up at the thought of seeing Allison again. Maybe this could actually work. Of course, there was a lot standing in his way. He'd have to find a way to sort things out with Scott. And he'd have to hope that there weren't other guys in the mix. He'd also have to smooth Allison's ruffled feathers. He'd been a jerk when they left the island. Allison deserved so much better than that. As to how difficult it would be to convince her to accept his apology, he wasn't sure. He was prepared to grovel. It was difficult for him to set aside his pride, but he'd overcome worse.

He rang the doorbell, and Scott quickly answered, waving him in. When Zane handed over the wine, Scott unleashed a mile-wide grin. "You're the best friend a guy can have. Let's get this decanted."

Zane followed him inside. He was looking forward to spending an evening with these people he cared about so deeply, but coming to dinner at Scott's house felt a bit like returning to the scene of the crime, given the kiss with Allison at his birthday party. He wished he could find a way to rewind the clock to that moment when her luscious lips first met his. If only he'd known then that she hadn't done it on a lark. She'd spent years building up to it.

They wound their way down the wide central entry

and into the newly remodeled gourmet kitchen. Scott's wife, Brittney, was cutting up vegetables at the center island. "Look who's here," she said, taking a kiss on the cheek from Zane. "I'm glad you could come over on such short notice. Scott was eager to express his thanks."

"He keeps saying that, but Allison would've been fine without me. Seriously. She's tough as nails."

She swept the contents of the cutting board into a large bowl. "I agree. But you know how he is. Super protective. Is there such a thing as a helicopter brother?"

"Hey. I'm standing right here." Scott sniffed the wine cork, then emptied the bottle into a decanter.

"Well, the kids and I are thankful if nothing else," Brittney said. "I swear the only thing that kept Scott from freaking out about Allison was knowing that you were down there with her."

"Did I hear my name?" Allison poked her head into the kitchen.

Zane's heart did a veritable flip when he saw her. There had been countless moments on the island when he'd been taken aback by her beauty, but right now, with her sun-kissed skin glowing and the stress of their life-and-death situation during the storm no longer showing its effects, she absolutely stole his breath away. "There she is."

Allison grabbed at the kitchen counter and dragged one leg into the kitchen, followed by the other. Zane peeked around the island and saw what was slowing her down—Scott's five-year-old daughter, Lily, had wrapped herself around Allison's ankle. "Sorry. I'm having some trouble walking today," Allison said. She gave her eyebrows a conspiratorial bounce.

"I noticed there's a large growth on your leg. I'd better take a look at it and make sure it's not anything contagious." He crouched down and looked Lily in the eye. The little girl was already giggling. "I might need to administer the tickle test."

"Noooo!" Lily unspooled herself from Allison's leg, rolled across the floor and scrambled off behind her mother.

"Miss Thing," Brittney said. "You and Franklin need to go get washed up for dinner."

"Can we eat in front of the TV?" Lily asked, warily peering at Zane.

"Yes. I think the grown-ups would enjoy some adult conversation anyway."

Scott scooped up Lily into his arms. "Come on. Let's go hunt down your brother."

Brittney nodded to two empty wineglasses on the kitchen counter. "Why don't you two grab a drink for yourselves? We'll be ready to eat in a little bit."

"You sure we can't help?" Allison asked.

"I'm sure. Cooking is one of the only things that relax me," Brittney said.

"Wine?" Zane glanced at Allison, wondering how she was feeling about being around him. She had every reason in the world to give him some steely attitude. And he was going to have to find a way to work through it. "We can go out on the balcony and catch up."

"About what? Not much has happened since yesterday."

He knew then that he was going to have to try a little harder. "You can tell me how your meeting with your client went."

* * *

Allison found it impossible to swallow and not much easier to breathe. Zane had picked the one topic of conversation she did not want to explore, especially not when he was looking good enough to eat. Damn him. It was one thing when he was wearing a pair of board shorts, but there was something about Zane in a pair of perfectly tailored flat-front trousers and a dress shirt, with the sleeves rolled up to the elbows, that absolutely slayed her. He would always have her number. Even when he'd been a jerk to her. Even when he was going around picking uncomfortable things to discuss. "Wine sounds great, but I'd rather skip work talk. It's been a long day."

"Whatever you want."

He poured them each a glass of wine, and she tried to ignore the pull he had on her. It came from the vicinity of her belly button, although just being around him made the more feminine parts of her body quake and yearn, as well. They stepped out onto the patio overlooking the back of Scott and Brittney's beautiful wooded lot. The early-evening air was warm and breezy, hearkening back to their time on the island. Part of her wanted to go back so badly and relive every unbelievable minute, but she knew that wasn't reality, and one thing she prided herself on, aside from her predilection for fantasies about Zane, was her ability to stay grounded.

"Did you sleep well last night?" He took a sip of his wine after he posed the question, regarding her with a look that took no effort from him and still felt like pure seduction.

"Like the proverbial rock."

"We didn't get much sleep during that last day or so on the island, did we?" He leaned against the balcony railing, inexplicably turning her on by leaving his firm forearms on display.

She smiled. Heat rushed to her face. "No, we did not. That damn storm kept us up."

A subtle blush colored his cheeks, and he hung his head, nodding. "Right. It was the storm that kept us awake. The weather was nothing if not distracting."

She sucked in a deep breath. She loved this glimmer of normalcy between them, their ability to fall into a fun back-and-forth, but it only made her crave more. Was there a way to get beyond the things standing between them? Even if Scott was ever able to get over himself, the Black Crescent problem was inescapable. Her meeting had gone exceptionally well today. She wasn't about to turn her back on hard-earned success, no matter how much she knew it would anger Zane. Yes, she would come clean, but everything else was on Zane. It was his choice. Not hers.

She glanced over her shoulder to make sure Scott or Brittney wasn't looking. "No matter what, I will never regret what happened, Zane. I need you to know that. It was amazing."

He straightened to his full height, leaving her in the shadow of his towering frame, and touched her arm gently. How could he bring her entire body to life with only an instant of caring contact? "Yes. Of course. I feel the same way."

Her heart began to gallop in her chest, beating an uneven rhythm.

"Dinner's ready." Scott was standing at the door to

the balcony. His vision noticeably landed on Zane's hand touching Allison's arm.

Allison reflexively pulled back from Zane, and he did the same. The instant it happened, a wave of guilt blanketed her. Resentment followed. These games were so stupid. And idiotic. She had to put an end to them. Part of that was finding the right time to tell Zane about Black Crescent. "On our way."

Allison and Zane joined Scott and Brittney in the dining room. On the front of the house, it had a splendid view of the front yard, and was appointed with all of the elegant trappings of a comfortable life. Allison didn't like to get too wrapped up in material things. There was plenty of that going on in LA. Still, she could admit that she wanted this for herself. She wanted a husband and a house and children. More to the point, she wanted love and a life partner. She wanted it all.

The spread Brittney put out was truly spectacular— filet mignon cooked to an ideal medium-rare, with rosemary roasted baby potatoes and green beans. The wine Zane had brought was a sublime complement to the meal, and Scott seemed nothing if not relaxed and content because of it. The conversation was fun and light, full of laughs and interesting stories. Zane and Scott told tales—a few from high school, but most from recent years, stories about pickup basketball, epic golf tournaments and even a few nights out drinking. All Allison could think as she watched Zane and Scott together was that she didn't merely appreciate that they had such a solid friendship, but that she also loved being witness to it. It was a real shame that Zane was a no-go because he was her brother's best friend. In a lot of ways, it was also what made him perfect.

There were a few moments when Zane delivered a knowing glance with his piercing gaze, leaving Allison to grapple with the resulting hum in her body. Did he know that he could affect her like that without so much as a brush of a finger against the back of her hand? Did he know how much it made her want him, and how frustrating it made the knowledge that she'd never likely experience his touch again?

At the end of the meal, the conversation continued in the kitchen as the four of them cleaned up. They were just about finished when Lily walked in, complaining of a stomachache.

"Come on, sweetheart," Brittney said. "It's probably time for you to go to bed anyway. Why don't you say good-night to Aunt Allison and Uncle Zane?"

Lily merely waved at them, curling into her mom's hip. "Good night."

Allison crouched down to give Lily a kiss on the forehead. "Sweet dreams, Lils."

"Good night."

"I'm going to help Brittney with bedtime. I'll be back in a few minutes," Scott said.

The quiet in the kitchen when her brother left was deafening. She and Zane had just been presented with the same scenario they'd been in last month. Except this time, the playing field had definitely changed. Gone were many of Allison's old reservations, replaced by newer and more intense ones. She didn't have to wonder how badly it hurt to be rejected by Zane. She'd experienced it firsthand.

"I forgot you were staying here." Zane took a step closer to her.

"Yes. I always do. The guest room is beautiful. Very

comfortable." She leaned back against the kitchen island, gripping the cool marble counter with both hands.

"Good bed?" he asked.

She laughed and shook her head. "Smooth, Zane. Real smooth."

He shrugged and inched even closer. "I had an opening, I had to take it." His hand was inches from hers. He reached out with his thumb and lightly caressed her fingers.

A zip of electricity wound its way down her spine. "Zane..."

"Yes? That is my name." He slipped his fingers under her hand and lifted it to his lips. It made her dizzy.

"My brother."

"His name is Scott. And he's in the other room. And we're here. And I've missed you." He kissed her hand again, except this time, he closed his eyes and seemed to savor it.

She nearly passed out, but she had to keep her head straight. "You're being so goofy. You missed me? I just saw you yesterday."

He opened his eyes. "I know. And I was an ass by the dock."

Hard to believe that had only been thirty-six hours ago. It felt like a lifetime. "Yes, you were. I get it, but it doesn't change the fact that I wasn't a fan."

Scott's voice came from the hall.

"Come on. Let's get out of here." Zane tugged on her hand.

"What? Now? Where?" Her vision darted to the kitchen entry, then back to Zane.

He rolled his eyes. "So many questions." He pulled

her back into the dining room, where they could buy a few more seconds of privacy. "Come to my place, Allison. I want to be alone with you. I need to be alone with you."

Her pulse went to thundering in her body the way it had during the storm. "What about what you said to me at the dock?"

"I was an idiot. I'm sorry."

"There's more to it, and you know that. What about Scott?"

"Now you sound like me." He again raised her hand to his lips and delivered a soul-bending kiss. "No more excuses. Let's get out of here, spend some time together and we'll deal with him later. I need to be alone with you, Allison."

How in the hell could she say no to that? She couldn't, even when there was a small part of her that wanted to press him for more. For an explanation. For clarification about everything. But the reality was that she'd been waiting forever to hear him saying something so desperate, especially unprompted. So she'd take Zane's offer. Even if it ended up being only sex. One more time. "What do we tell Scott?"

Zane pulled his phone out of his pocket and tapped away at the screen. He showed it to her. Taking your sister for a drive. Thanks for dinner.

"That's it?" she asked.

"That's it." He tapped at his screen one more time, took her hand and out the door they went.

Just like Allison had always wanted.

Eleven

This was crazy. Absolutely certifiable. But something about the impetuousness of stealing away from her brother's house with Zane, like a couple of brazen teenagers, made it so thrilling. Perhaps it was because at this time yesterday, when they'd been on the plane back to New Jersey, she'd been convinced this was never going to happen again. It might be foolish and stupid, but she had a glimmer of optimism. She hoped like hell Zane wouldn't end up quashing it again. If he did, the disappointment would be of her making. She'd said yes to this. She'd gone with him because her heart had convinced her to take another chance.

Zane was showing off with the car, taking turns a little too fast, changing lanes when he had a whisper-thin margin of error and generally acting as though he didn't care about repercussions. Allison sat back in the seat and allowed him his macho moment while she studied his grip on the steering wheel and counted the seconds until they would be at his place and those glorious hands of his could be all over her naked body.

The trip probably clocked in at under twenty minutes, but all of that anticipation made it feel as though it had been a cross-country trek. She'd never been to Zane's place before, which was in one of the newest and most exclusive neighborhoods in town. The street was lined with stately houses, but Allison found Zane's to be the most beautiful. Tucked away on top of a hill, a long stone driveway leading to it, the sprawling home was an oasis in this bustling town. She couldn't help but think about how it was so much like Zane—on its own, standing apart, quietly magnificent.

He opened one of three garage bays and pulled the car inside. Two other gleaming sports cars and a motorcycle were already parked there. Zane had done well for himself with his business. That much was clear. He turned off the ignition, and they were both noticeably rushing to get inside. He opened the door for her, shut off his security system via a keypad and took her hand, marching through the mostly dark house. They traveled through an unbelievable kitchen, nearly three times the size of Allison's back in LA, then down a central hall toward the back of the house. Allison was busy trying to look at everything—she wanted to soak up every bit of Zane's tastes. She wanted to scrutinize the artwork and try to speculate about what had drawn him to the pieces he'd chosen. She wanted to do the same with furniture and paint colors. She wanted to know him inside and out.

"A tour would be nice," she said when they'd reached a set of tall double doors at the end of the hall.

Zane pushed them open and flipped a light switch. "I know. Let's start here."

Allison stepped into the most stunning, jaw-dropping bedroom she'd ever seen, which was saying a lot since Zane was adjusting the dimmer to a level fit for seduction. The space was like something out of a magazine, with a soaring cathedral ceiling, a spacious seating area to one side with a modern charcoal-gray sectional sofa and a TV, and at the very center of the room, a gorgeously appointed bed. She took her chance to run her hand over the crisp white duvet, the threads silky beneath her touch. This room was nothing short of sheer perfection.

Zane came up behind her, gripping her shoulders and pressing his long frame against her back. He kissed her neck softly, bringing her body to a gentle boil. "Do you approve?"

Allison's eyes drifted shut, luxuriating in the action of his lips as he skimmed them over the delicate spot beneath her ear. "Which part? The room or your amazing mouth?"

He spun her around and wrapped her up in his arms, drawing her flat against his chest and kissing her deeply. His tongue wasn't playing—he was determined, consumed by a drive she could not see, but could certainly feel. "You were all I could think about last night. And this morning. And all day at work."

"Really?" she asked, grinning to herself in the dark.

"Yes, really."

"What were you thinking?" She'd shared her fantasy

with him…if he'd taken the time to think up one about her, she wanted to hear it. Every last word.

"About you and the sarong." He dug his fingers into her hair, gently tugging at her nape to encourage her to drop her head to one side.

"I'm listening. What else?"

His mouth, hot and wet, skated down the length of her neck, settling in the slope where it met her shoulder. One hand went to the zipper on her dress, slowly drawing it down while the other grabbed her backside. "I'm not as good at this as you are."

"Something tells me you could be great at this if you just applied yourself." She untucked his shirt and threaded her hands underneath it, exploring the landscape of his muscled back. "Don't think too much about it. Just tell me what happens with me and you and the sarong." To encourage him, she placed one hand flat on his crotch and rubbed his erection through his dress pants.

A raspy groan escaped his throat. "I untie it. I take it off."

She unhooked his belt, unbuttoned his trousers and unzipped them. Slipping her hand down the front of his boxer briefs, she caressed his solid length with her fingers. "Good. What else?"

"In my fantasy, you're already naked. No bathing suit." With a pop, he undid the clasp of her bra, then pulled the dress and the rest of the ensemble forward, leaving her chest bare to him. "I love your breasts. They're so perfect. Silky and velvety. I love the way they fit in my hands. So I do this." He lowered his head, cupped both breasts with his hands and swirled his tongue around her nipple. Teasing. Flicking. Then sucking.

Allison's eyes fluttered shut as white flames of lust seemed to envelop her thighs. She was so hot for him already. Having him tell her what he liked about her body was only heightening the experience. "That feels so good, Zane. You have no idea."

He dropped to his knees, pulling her dress down to the floor. She kicked her heels off, and he sat back on his haunches, gazing up at her like she was a goddess. "You didn't have these panties on in my fantasy, but I like them. They're sexy." He hooked his finger under the waistband of her lacy black undies, traveling from one hip to the other, just gently grazing her most delicate area at the center. "But they need to go." He tugged them past her hips, leaving her to step out of them. Then he stood back up. "In my fantasy, you're so wet for me."

Allison thought she might melt into a puddle. She also knew she couldn't take so little nakedness from him. Her fingers flew through the buttons of his shirt as he reached down between her legs, separating her delicate folds with his fingers.

"Yes. Exactly like this." He rubbed her apex firmly in a circle, kissing her neck again, using his tongue to drive her wild. With every rotation of his hand, he was sending her toward her peak. Pushing her closer to the edge.

"I want you. There's no hiding it." It took every ounce of strength she had to push his pants to the floor, but she had to have him in her hand. She needed to even the score between them. She stroked firmly, from base to tip, and kissed his chest. "What comes next?"

"Then I make love to you in several gravity-defying positions." He laughed against his lips. "I turned myself into quite the performer in this fantasy."

She smiled, but she wanted to explore this idea. She wanted to know his steamiest thoughts and act on them. "Show me."

"Really?" He ran his tongue along his lower lip, showing her his trepidation.

"Yes." She nodded and looked him right in the eye, wanting him to know how serious she was.

"Okay, then." He took her hand and led her over to the bedside table, where he opened a drawer and pulled out a box of condoms. He handed her the foil packet. "In my fantasy, you put it on for me."

"Accuracy is very important in a fantasy." She took her time, tearing it open, then carefully rolling it on, eliciting a groan of pleasure from Zane as she did it.

"Up against the wall." She stepped to the side of the table, where there was an expanse of open space. She placed her back to the wall, and he reached down for one of her legs and hitched it over his hip.

Allison wrapped her calf around him and watched as he took his erection in his hand and positioned himself at her entrance. He drove about halfway inside, taking her breath away, then pulled her other leg up around him. Her body weight rested against the wall, but his hands cradled her backside. This angle was incredibly gratifying from the start—it let her sink deep down onto him, centering the pressure in the ideal spot. She rocked her hips forward and back, her entire body buzzing with pleasure. She was close. So close.

"Was it like this?" She dug her fingers into his hair and kissed him, relishing the tension in his body right now—the flex of his biceps and forearms as he held her up and the tautness of his abs with every stroke.

"This is better," he said. "You're better in real life. The stuff that's in my head doesn't come close to the real you." The kiss he laid on her then was one for the ages, intense and raw. Honest and sincere. It sent her body over the edge, the peak rattling her to her very core, shaking her physically and mentally. Zane followed right after, pressing her harder against the wall as he rode out the waves of pleasure.

For a moment, neither said a thing, breaths coming fast and heavy as they coiled themselves around each other tighter. A thought flashed in her head, and she dared to utter it. "The fantasy just isn't enough anymore, Zane. I need this. So much more of this."

Zane's mind and body were reeling in the best possible way. It took every ounce of energy he had left to carry her over to the bed and set her down without dropping her. He was wonderfully spent.

He tossed aside the throw pillows littering the bed, then pulled back the duvet. Both a bit delirious, they found their way under the covers, immediately drawn to each other. Allison curled into his body and kissed his chest. He loved having her in his bed. As amazing as things had been on the island, this was different. The fantasy world had fallen away, but even framed by his everyday reality, being with Allison felt like a dream. Was he falling for her? The perpetual bachelor? His mom had certainly made a compelling case for his finally jettisoning those ways.

"You're so amazing," she muttered.

"You're the amazing one." The words came so fast.

He didn't even have to think about them. That was it—he really had fallen. He'd gone through life telling himself that he wouldn't let it happen. He'd seen what it did to his parents when love fell apart. There was no way that risking that much pain could ever be worth it. But being here with Allison and knowing that his heart wanted nothing else made him realize that there was no way to build up an immunity to love. It had taken the right woman to show him that. The perfect woman. Allison. He caressed her naked back with his hand. "No argument?" He'd half expected her to dispute his claim that she was the amazing one. Instead, she was being incredibly still and quiet. He must have really sent her to the moon and back. She'd certainly done that for him.

"I'm thinking."

"About what?"

"Everything."

He smiled in the dark. "Me, too." So many thoughts were swirling around in his head, all of them surprisingly good. When had things ever been like that? No time in recent history, that was for sure.

"I need to tell you something."

He'd been about to say the exact same thing, but she'd gotten to it first. "What is it?"

She drew in a breath so deep her entire body rose and fell in the cradle of his arm. "What I'm about to say... I just... I don't want you to get upset. But I would understand if you did." She rolled away from him and switched on the lamp on her side of the bed.

He squinted at the bright light. It got Zane's attention, and not just because he was enjoying the view of her naked backside while she was turned away. He sat up in bed. "Okay." Whatever she was about to say, he wanted to just get past it. He was tired of bad news and dire circumstances keeping him from happiness. Whatever it was, they would find a way around it. "Please. Just tell me. I can take it."

She grabbed a corner of the comforter and covered herself up. "First off, the job I'm working on here in Falling Brook is going really well. They've put me on retainer for the next month, and if things go the way I think they will, it will become permanent. They would be a big enough client for me to move back to Falling Brook. To stay here in town."

The relief Zane felt was immense. It was like someone had been standing on his chest and they'd finally stepped off. "That's amazing. I'm so happy for you." In truth, he was happy for *them*. Long distance would have been terrible and certainly no way for them to truly move forward together. Now he had one less thing to worry about.

"Thanks. I'm really happy about it, too. I've worked really hard for this."

Now that he'd had a minute for this news to sink in, his brain was starting to catch up. Falling Brook was a small town. Most businesspeople who lived here were CEOs or senior management for big corporations in the city, not local operations like Zane's. But who could it be? "And this company is based right here in town?"

"Yes, but hold on a minute. Before I get to that, I need to tell you that I realized tonight that I can't make the decision to stay here in Falling Brook until we have a discussion about us. And I don't want to hit you with some big heavy talk right now, especially after we just had totally mind-blowing sex, but I can't move back here and see you on the street or at the Java Hut and not be able to walk up to you and hug you. Kiss you and hold your hand. I've done that before and it nearly killed me."

Now he was starting to see where she was coming from, and he was totally on board. In fact, he couldn't ignore the happy feeling in his heart. She wanted him and he wanted her, for more than just sex. "So we need to come clean with Scott. I completely agree. We can either do it together or if you want, I can tell him on my own and then you guys can have your own talk. But no matter what, I think we need to make it clear that this isn't us asking him for permission. In the end, we're our own people. We make our own decisions. We have to do what's right for us."

She dropped her shoulders, seeming frustrated. "Yes. I completely agree. That is all true and that does need to happen. Right away. But first, there's one more thing I have to tell you."

An unsettling quiet filled the room. "Is this the thing that might upset me?"

"Yes."

His heart hammered. "Please tell me. Say it and get it over with."

"The client is Black Crescent."

The blood drained from Zane's face so fast that it made him sick. This couldn't possibly be happening. No. Absolutely not. How could what was starting to work out perfectly take such a nightmarish turn? "You're working for Black Crescent." He sat up a little straighter in bed. "You, quite possibly the most decent and upstanding person I know, are working for the most evil and vile company imaginable. You're working for the devil. Why would you do that?" With every word out of his mouth, his disgust grew. "Why would you even entertain the idea?"

"Zane, come on. Isn't that all a little overdramatic?"

Zane had been trying to keep himself in check, but that word pissed him off. He'd had it lobbed at him before, and he disliked it greatly. He threw back the covers and scrambled out of bed, plucking his underwear from the floor and putting them back on. He was so full of anger right now it felt like it might bubble up out the top of his head. He had to move to keep his mind straight. And he couldn't be naked in bed with Allison anymore. "Is that why you said all of that stuff to me on the island about letting it go? Is that why you were being so secretive about your work calls?" He ran his hand through his hair, pacing back and forth across his bedroom floor. "Does that Ryan guy work for BC? No wonder I had a bad feeling about him."

"Ryan is a candidate to take Joshua Lowell's place."

Zane's stomach turned. "So the guy you were talking to while we were on the island is going to be the new Josh Lowell? That's just awesome." He sincerely hoped the sarcasm was hitting home for her. He didn't want to be a jerk again, but he needed her to understand how hurt he was right now.

"Maybe. He's just interviewing right now. Actually, you should meet him. He's a really nice guy. I think you would like him. I think you would like all of the people who are interviewing for the job."

Zane made a point of looking at her as though she'd lost her mind. He didn't want to ask the question out loud, but he wasn't afraid to suggest it by other means. This entire line of thinking was so off base.

"Honestly," she continued. "I think you would really like Josh if you got to know him. In a lot of ways, he's just as much a victim of his dad as you are. None of what happened was your fault, but it wasn't his fault, either."

And to think, Zane had been so sure that Allison understood him. Now he knew that he was wrong. So very wrong. "That's okay. I think I'll skip the part of this scenario where you whip up some dream of Josh Lowell and me becoming best friends. I realize that it's your special talent to come up with fantasies."

"That's really mean. And completely uncalled for."

"It's the truth."

Allison grumbled under her breath. "You know what, Zane? Screw you. That's not what I was suggesting. All I'm saying is that I think you need to take a deep breath, try to take a step back and look at this from my perspective. You can't undo what happened, okay? You need to let it go. I'm sorry, but you do. At some point, you're going to have to get over this or you're just going to be stuck forever."

Zane disliked a lot of things, but he despised it when anyone told him to get over Black Crescent. His entire life had been ground into the dirt by the greed of the Lowell family. He and his parents had been treated like they were nothing, taken for their family fortune and cast aside, with absolutely zero repercussions for those who committed the crime. That injustice sat in the depths of his belly every day. He couldn't "just get over it." It was impossible. "I'm not talking about this anymore. You were there for the fallout. You know how badly I was hurt. You saw it firsthand. I not only shouldn't have to explain it to you, I won't."

"I'm sure you're going to say this is just a cliché, but every black cloud has a silver lining. If Vernon Lowell hadn't taken off with that money, you and I never would have met. You and Scott wouldn't have the friendship you have today. Black Crescent isn't all bad. I wish that you could see that."

"And I wish you could see why that is beside the point." He scanned her face, desperate for some sign of the Allison he so adored. Right now, it was hard to imagine he'd dared to think about the future with her. How could he have been so stupid? "I think you should go home."

"Seriously?"

"Seriously."

Allison whipped back the comforter and grabbed her dress from the floor where it had landed earlier. She threaded her arms through it, wrapped it around her body and zipped it. "You drove me here. I'm not using a ride app this time of night. I've heard too many scary stories about women ending up with creepy drivers."

Zane plucked his pants from the floor and fished his car keys out of the pocket. "Take my car. I'll get it back from you later." He tossed them to her.

She caught them, staring down at her hand for a moment. "Oh, right. Zane Patterson, the golden boy, the super successful entrepreneur, has an entire garage full of cars. He has them to spare."

"That's right. That's me. Mr. Perfect." Right now, he felt as far from that as he'd quite possibly ever felt. If that was what Allison truly thought, she'd lost it. So had his mom, for that matter.

"Goodbye, Zane. I'll let myself out." She pivoted on her heel and headed for the bedroom door.

"You *knew* this was going to happen, Allison. You knew this would be my reaction. Nothing about the conversation we just had should come as any surprise. And you knew it the whole time we were on the island, didn't you?"

She stopped in the doorway and turned back to him. "I'd foolishly hoped for a better outcome."

"You don't understand what this is like for me."

She shook her head with a pitying look in her eyes. "I do understand it, Zane. And I don't know what I have to do to convince you of that."

Twelve

Scott bellowed at the guest room door. "Zane Patterson, I know you're in there. Get out here. You have some explaining to do."

Allison pried open one eye and looked at the alarm clock on the bedside table. The numbers were a bit blurry, probably because she'd taken a sleeping pill last night after her big knock-down, drag-out fight with Zane. She was only half-awake.

Boom boom boom. Scott pounded on the door. "Up and at 'em, you two."

Allison scrambled out of bed. She wanted to shut her brother up before he woke up the entire house. She did *not* want her niece and nephew thinking the worst of her. She opened the door, leaving a space just wide enough to talk to him. "He's not here. Will you please be quiet? It's freaking six thirty in the morning."

"You know I get up early to work out."

"Good for you. I'm going back to bed." She left the door ajar and shuffled across the room, flopping down on the mattress. Her motivation was gone. In a lot of ways, it felt like her whole life was gone. She didn't want to work today. She didn't want to talk to anyone or go anywhere. She wanted to call in sick to life.

Unfortunately, Scott had followed her into the room and was standing at the foot of the bed. "Why is his car outside?"

"He gave it to me to drive home last night. He has several cars, you know. He gave me an extra." Last night was still a blur. It had started so amazingly and gone so incredibly wrong. She'd worried that Zane would take the Black Crescent news badly, but she'd underestimated the scope. She'd certainly never imagined he'd toss her out of his house.

"What in the world is going on, Alli?"

Allison sat up in bed and scooted back until she was leaning against the headboard. She blew out a breath of frustration and crossed her arms over her chest. Was she really ready to spill the beans to Scott? This was not going to be a fun conversation. But she had to take what had been handed to her, fun or not. She patted the mattress. "Come. Sit."

Scott joined her, but she sensed that he was deeply uncomfortable. He was sitting like he had a board strapped to his back. His shoulders were tight, as was his whole face. He had to know what was coming next.

"Zane and I slept together when we were in the Bahamas."

"I knew it." He practically pounced on her with his

words. "I knew that was going to happen. I warned you, and you just couldn't listen to me, could you? I'm just the lame older brother who's too heavy-handed with advice."

"I didn't listen because I didn't want to, okay? Scott, you need to know that I have had a thing for Zane since I was a teenager. We're talking fifteen years. I always hoped that it would go away, but it just didn't."

"What? No way. I would've seen it."

She pressed her lips together tightly. The years of longing for Zane would always bring a sting to her eyes, but they especially did now. "I'm serious. I'm just really good at hiding it. I can always put on a good face."

"So when you guys were acting so odd at my party, was that part of it?"

"We kissed that night."

"Ugh." His voice was rife with disgust. "Did you guys make a plan to meet up at Rose Cove? Has this been in the works the whole time?"

She shook her head. "No. It was just dumb luck, believe it or not." Now it felt like tragic luck. If it hadn't happened, her heart wouldn't be in tatters.

Scott got up from the bed and began pacing. "I love him, but I'm going to kill him. I told him you were off-limits, and he completely disrespected my wishes."

She pinched the bridge of her nose and made an inward plea for strength. "Will you stop jumping to conclusions and let me talk, please?"

He turned back to her with a distinct scowl on his face. "So talk."

"When I kissed him, he freaked out. He said he could never betray you. That's why he left that night.

And it was a big topic of conversation on the island. He refused to let it go. Believe me, Zane put your wishes first."

"Until he didn't."

"Until *we* didn't. It was both of us. We both wanted to do it, and we both knew exactly what we were doing."

Scott grimaced. "Please. Spare me the details."

Allison rolled her eyes. "I'm only saying that it was two adults doing what adults do. We were in a very intense situation with the storm and I guess that just made everything that much more heightened. As soon as we were rescued, he wanted things to go back to the way they were before."

"Really?"

"Really."

"So then what happened last night?"

She shrugged. "He had second thoughts, I guess. So we went back to his place."

Scott held up a hand to keep her from saying more. "Okay. I got it. But I don't understand. He made you drive yourself home?"

She shook her head. "Unfortunately, I had to tell him about Black Crescent. Things went really well there yesterday and I don't think it's going to be a onetime job. Joshua Lowell is putting in a good word for me, and he's put me on retainer for the next month. I was going to tell you yesterday, but I never had the chance."

Scott drew in a deep breath through his nose, the gears in his head clearly turning. "What did Zane say? Did he hit the roof?"

"He did. But then it snowballed from there and he

just sort of shut down. That's when he asked me to leave. That's why I have his car."

"So what now? Is it over?"

Allison froze as a single tear rolled down her cheek. As upset as she'd been last night, she hadn't cried. But something about those three words—*is it over?*—made the dam break. "I don't know. I don't want to think that last night was the end, but I just don't know. He has such a grudge when it comes to Black Crescent and the Lowells. It's so frustrating."

"Well, of course it is, but it's not like there isn't a good reason for it. The scars you get as a young person are always the ones that feel the deepest. It's just the way life is."

Allison had never thought of it that way. She'd never seen a parallel between her life and Zane's. Until now. Her brother was right. The pain she had from years of Zane being her unrequited love was very real. And there was something about it that had always felt especially raw. She hadn't been able to start exploring it until the kiss at Scott's party, but it hit her hardest at Rose Cove. A single "no" from Zane was far more devastating than any rejection she'd ever experienced. "Yeah. I suppose you're right."

"And as the person with a front-row seat when his family fell apart, I can tell you that it was incredibly difficult for him. The number of nights we sat up with him talking and me listening? I couldn't begin to count. I don't really know that I was equipped to help him through it. All I could do was listen and be his friend. I'm guessing the guy needs some therapy."

"You're probably right, but that doesn't help at the moment. I don't know what to do to make any of this better, and I hate feeling so helpless. I feel like scream-ing. Isn't love more important than any of this? Isn't it supposed to conquer all?"

Now it was Scott's turn to remain perfectly still. "Do you love him?"

She nodded, her sadness morphing into conviction to put it all out there with her brother. She had to make this declaration to somebody, even if nothing ever came of it. "I do. The big dumb jerk. I love him. And I don't know what to say or do to help him get past this."

Scott sat back down on the bed and took her hands. "This is why I didn't want you to get involved with him. I never want to see you get hurt."

Allison saw her chance to finally sort this out with brother, hopefully once and for all. "Scott, life hurts. Love hurts. I don't want to sit on the sidelines and be an observer. I can take care of myself, and if I get hurt, I'll be okay. Even now, with my heart in twenty pieces, I know that I'll be okay. I have a good career and great friends and an amazing family I love more than any-thing. I know you still look at me and see that sick lit-tle girl in the hospital bed, but that isn't me anymore, and it hasn't been me for a long time."

Scott's eyes misted. He was a tough-as-nails guy, but this got to him. "I realize that I was just a kid when it happened, but I've never been as scared as I was when you were sick. Never."

Allison felt like her heart was going to break every time she listened to Scott or one of her parents talk about this. She hated that it was still so raw for them, but they'd all understood that it was a matter of life and death. She'd been too young to understand, but she wanted to believe that she did now. "I know, honey. But I'm fine. I'm here. And you need to let it go."

He cleared his throat and collected himself. "Just like Zane needs to let Black Crescent go?"

Apparently they all had things they needed to let go of. "Yes. If you can figure out how to make him do that, I'd love to hear your suggestions." From the bedside table, her phone beeped with a text. Her brain flew to the thought that it might be Zane, but when she consulted the screen, her heart sank with disappointment. It wasn't him. "Speak of the devil. It's Joshua Lowell. He wants me to come in to the BC offices this morning."

"A little early for a work text, isn't it?"

"Apparently he's like you. He doesn't like to sleep in, either."

Zane hadn't slept at all. Not a damn minute. And he couldn't begin to process what he was feeling. Every time he followed one line of thought, he got distracted by another. He'd start to think about Black Crescent, familiar anger and pain welling up inside him. The fact that his feelings about BC were now tied to Allison made it even more difficult to sort any of it out. Her betrayal ran deep, registering in the center of his chest and causing him physical pain. Allison knew how he felt about Black Crescent. She'd not only witnessed the initial fallout all those years ago, he'd told her everything he was still feeling when they were in the Bahamas. And she hadn't said a thing. Not a peep. That hurt most of all. They'd made love, and she'd known that what she was doing would hurt him. She'd known it all along.

There was no telling how any of this would work out. When he tried to see his future—the days and weeks beyond now—he still saw Allison there. He'd seen her there last night before everything fell apart, and now in the light of day, she was still there. He didn't want to imagine tomorrow, the next day or the day after that without her. She'd opened something up in him on the island. She'd done it again last night. It didn't feel as though he could shut the door on that, even if he wanted to. So how was he going to get past this?

One thing Allison had said last night kept bubbling to the surface—how every black cloud had a silver lining. How BC had ruined one thing, but it had brought them together. It wasn't all bad, as much as he'd always seen it as such. And Allison in particular was easily the best thing that had happened to him ever. He couldn't fathom walking away from that. From her. It made no sense.

The realization made his end of the conversation from last night sting. He'd said some horrible things. He'd stupidly let his anger take control, as was so often the case with BC. If he was ever going to move forward in his life, he had to force himself to stop allowing what had happened with BC to define him. He was stronger than that. He knew that. He'd simply let his anger get the best of him.

He had to talk this out with Allison. He had to explain himself to Scott. He had to open himself up to the fact that he'd been wrong about more than a few things. His own mother had proved him wrong yesterday. Allison had done the same with everything she'd said about silver linings. And now he had to talk to her. To find a way through the mess he'd created from years of clinging to anger and resentment. This was about more than making amends. This was about making a future. He had to find Allison. Luckily, he knew exactly where to look.

He jumped in the shower, hoping a little hot water and soap might help to reset his head. He couldn't begin to figure out where to start with Allison. There was a part of him that wanted to confess his feelings and hope that would be enough to make her step away from Black Crescent. There was another part of him that wanted an apology. There was yet another piece of his soul that knew he should be the one to say he was sorry. He hated that his feelings were so jumbled out of control. He hated that he couldn't let everything go after all these years.

Freshly shaven and dressed for work, he drove his Porsche over to Scott's house. When he arrived, his BMW was parked out front, but Allison's zippy silver rental was noticeably absent from the driveway. Hopefully Scott had let her put it in the garage. He wasn't worried that she'd left town. Black Crescent was keeping her here for the foreseeable future. But he was concerned that she might not be home. He wasn't eager to chase her all over Falling Brook, but he would if that was his only option. He had to sort this out, and the only logical path started and ended with Allison.

He rang the doorbell, then stuffed his hands in his pockets. He'd never before been nervous to arrive at his best friend's house, and the feeling was unsettling.

Scott flung the door open, sweating profusely and wiping it from his forehead with a towel. "Looking for your car keys, I take it?" Scott's voice had a cutting edge. His best friend had never before taken that tone with him. He disliked it greatly.

"I'm actually looking for Allison. Is she here?" Zane peered around his best friend. "Can I come in?"

"I don't know, Zane. Right now, I'm trying to keep from punching you in the face."

At least Zane now knew that the cat was out of the bag. Clearly, Scott had been briefed on the state of his relationship with Allison. "You know I'll hit you right back, and then where will we be? Fighting in the middle of your front lawn for all of your fine and upstanding neighbors to see."

Scott stepped back and opened the front door wider. "Fine. Come in." He closed it as soon as Zane walked past him. "I could literally kill you for sleeping with Allison. How could you treat her like one of your hookups? She's my damn sister. You're my best friend, for God's sake."

Zane turned back to Scott. The guilt he bore from his own actions was eclipsed by his best friend's misguided characterization of what had happened. "I did *not* treat her like a hookup. I care about her. Deeply." He felt the wobble in his own voice before he heard it. As if he needed any more confirmation that he was in deep with Allison. "That's why I'm here. I need to talk to her."

"She left about ten minutes ago."

"It's not even eight o'clock. Where did she go?"

"I'm not sure I should tell you."

Zane swallowed the bile that rose in his throat. His best friend still felt the need to protect his sister from Zane. He had to put an end to that. "Look, man, you and I have got to get past this. I know I crossed a line, but you need to know that I did not do it without thinking about it hard, and for a very long time. I fought our attraction as long as I could, but in the end, Allison made a compelling case. I'm drawn to her, and she's drawn to me. We work well together, and we care a lot about each other." Zane directed his gaze down at his feet, knowing he wasn't 100 percent certain about her side of that assertion. "Well, I care deeply about her. I think she cares about me."

"Yeah?" Scott asked, seeming unimpressed.

"Yes, Scott. I care about her. I want to see where that can go."

"You. The guy with the revolving door in his pants."

"Hey. Am I not entitled to want more? Do I not get to change the direction of my life because I've found the right girl and I want to be with her? You found that with Brittney, and you're happy. In fact, you love to remind me of it. All the time." Zane again looked Scott square in the eye. "Please don't torpedo our friendship because I'm looking for the same thing that you have. It's not fair."

Scott drew a deep breath through his nose and leaned against the doorway into the dining room. "You have to swear to me that you will not intentionally hurt her."

"Of course."

"You promise?"

"Yes."

Scott clapped his hand on Zane's shoulder. "Okay then. You have my blessing."

"Now tell me where she is."

"She's at Black Crescent."

Just when Zane thought he couldn't take another

shock to the system, he got another. Black Crescent was the exact last place on the planet he wanted to visit. Was this the universe's way of forcing him to deal with every sticking point in his life all on one day? If that was the case, bring it on. He was done letting BC define him. He certainly wasn't going to let it stand in the way of what he really wanted—Allison. "Got it. Thanks." Zane reached for the doorknob.

"Don't make a fool of yourself, okay?"

Zane opened the door. "I won't embarrass Allison, if that's what you're trying to say. I would never put her job in jeopardy."

"Good."

"As for me, I've already made myself look like an idiot. Things can't get any worse." With that, Zane rushed down the driveway to his car. He knew that his conversation with Scott was as close as they would ever come to working things out in regard to Allison. If this next part went well, he and Scott would hopefully return to their affable, hypercompetitive dynamic. Another outcome to wish for.

"I can't believe I'm doing this," he muttered to himself when he pulled into the Black Crescent parking lot. He'd come here a few short weeks ago to come clean to Joshua Lowell about the anonymous DNA report he'd received and shared. Unfortunately, Josh had left the office. It took several hours, but Zane had been able to track him down in a bar in the neighboring town. Zane wished he could erase that entire chapter of his personal story with BC. He never should have gotten involved. He never should have let Josh get under his skin.

He pulled into a space with a decent view of the

entrance, rolled down the windows and sent a text to his assistant letting her know that at best, he'd be late getting in the office. In truth, he hoped against hope that he and Allison could work everything out and he wouldn't feel driven to go to work at all.

An hour passed. Then another. He knew better than to waltz into that office and ask for her, but damn he was tempted. He didn't want to wait. Impatience was gnawing at him. But he stayed put, running through the words he wanted to say, praying that somehow it all worked out. Even with all that preparation, he wasn't truly ready when Allison walked out of the BC building, looking like a million bucks in a sleek black skirt, white blouse and heels. She was smiling. A big, wide grin. And it stole more than a breath. It knocked the wind out of him.

The Zane of old would've allowed her facial expression to send him into a downward spiral. How could anyone walk out of that building and be happy? But he knew that his old thinking had gotten him nowhere. It had left him running in circles. Allison's business was important to her. It must have been a good meeting. He had to believe that whatever had happened in that building had made her happy. And that made *him* happy, which was yet another reason to see BC in a different light. Yes, his old life had been ended by forces within that company. But his new life, the one that left him with a sliver of a chance with Allison Randall, had started at the same time.

He jumped out of his car and called her name. "Allison!"

She startled, then swiped off her sunglasses. "Zane? You came to Black Crescent? Are you insane?"

"Maybe a little," he muttered to himself.

"What in the world are you doing here?" she asked, incredulous, marching toward him.

He rushed over to her and didn't wait another minute to just come out with it. "I'm sorry. So sorry about last night. I was wrong."

She shook her head. "No, Zane. I was wrong. I should've told you back on the island. Before anything happened. That was wrong of me, and I'm sorry that I did it."

Relief washed over him in a deluge. All was not lost. He took her hand, loving the feel of her silky skin against his. "It's okay. I forgive you."

"If anything, it should tell you how much I was worried about messing things up with you. I had to have my chance, and I couldn't bring myself to jeopardize it by coming clean."

He brought her hand to his lips and kissed it. He wanted to be able to do that every day. Forever and ever. "That's the sweetest thing anyone has ever said to me."

She turned for an instant and glanced back at the building. "I hope you know it's just a job. I mean, I will kick some serious butt for them, but it's what I do. It's not out of some grand allegiance to the company or the Lowell family. It's out of a commitment to being a professional, working hard and supporting myself and Kianna. That's all it is."

He nodded. "I know. And I get it. You weren't afraid to do the thing no one would've expected you to do. You're great at taking chances. It's something I need to get better at."

"I took a chance when I kissed you that first time."

"That's the perfect example. I need to stop playing it safe." He swallowed back the emotion of the moment, of how much she meant to him and how grateful he was that she'd stuck around and kept pushing when he'd been doing nothing but putting up walls. He was so lucky to have her in his life. "When you've lost everything, it's just easier to play it safe. Don't risk a thing. Don't put anything of importance on the line. Friendship. Your heart. But then you came along and took my heart from me. You have it, Alli."

She cocked her head to one side. "I do?"

"Yes. And I don't want it back." He took her hand and pressed it flat against the center of his chest. It had hurt so badly that morning, and now it was nothing but impossibly warm. A single touch from her and he was healed. "I want you to keep it forever. Promise me that you'll hold on to it. I love you, Allison Randall, and I don't want you to ever forget that."

Her eyes lit up, bright and brilliant. "Oh, God, Zane. I love you, too." She gripped his elbows and leaned into him. "I think I've loved you since the moment I met you."

His heart felt as though it had swelled to twice its normal size. He hadn't realized how little hope he had that she'd return the sentiment until the words crossed her lovely lips. They fell into the most memorable kiss yet—it was an unspoken promise, wrapped up in years of friendship, tied with a wish for forever.

They came up for air, and he rested his forehead against hers, holding her close, not wanting to let her go ever. "I want it all with you, Allison. I realize it hasn't even been a week since we first slept together, but I know that the foundation is there between us. I don't want to wait to build our life together. The two of us. Forever and ever. Husband and wife. Best friends. Platinum bands and wedding bells."

She bit down on her lower lip. "A Rose Cove honeymoon in a cottage up on the hill?"

"Will it make you say yes?"

"I don't need a trip to an island to know that I'll love you forever, Zane. Of course I'm saying yes. A million times yes."

Epilogue

One month later

Angelique and Allison's mom walked into Angelique's bedroom at the exact right moment—Kianna was putting the finishing touches on Allison's bridal hair.

"So beautiful," her mom said, smiling, then kissing Allison on the cheek.

"The most beautiful," Angelique added.

Allison's heart was already so full of love, she wasn't sure how she'd survive the wedding. She knew she'd better prepare. There was only a half hour until they'd walk from Angelique and Hubert's house for the dock at Rose Cove. From there, Marcus would be taking everyone via boat to Mako Island. Zane had decided it was only fitting that they get married there.

He liked the idea that no one else would ever be able to say that their wedding had taken place on that particular patch of sand in the Caribbean.

As for Allison, she was simply glad that they'd decided to have the ceremony be a small and informal affair. Only so many people could fit on Mako Island, so they'd kept the guest list small—Scott, Brittney and the kids, Zane's mom and dad, Allison's parents, Angelique and Hubert, and Kianna. The dress code was decidedly casual—bare feet and flip-flops, shorts and sundresses, hats and sunglasses. Allison had gone with a new white bathing suit—a simple one-piece for modesty since her parents were in attendance, but with a plunging back for Zane's required sexy factor. A white sarong embroidered with silver threads wrapped at her waist completed the look. Zane had once said that he loved her flair for fashion, and she was happy her bridal ensemble perfectly reflected her individual style. She could not have gotten away with this getup in Falling Brook. All the more reason to be glad to be far away from that.

"It's so amazing that you were able to get the guest cottages fixed up in time for the wedding," Kianna said to Angelique. "From everything Allison said, things were pretty messy."

"My husband was highly motivated. He had a crew out here as soon as Alli called to tell us the news. He didn't want her second visit this year to Rose Cove to be anything less than perfect," Angelique said. "It was mostly water damage. Luckily, all of the building structures rode out the storm just fine."

"I'm so glad," Allison said. "It could've been so much worse." Although that scary weather event had caused so much heartache, she was still oddly thankful for it. It forced her and Zane to get past their other issues. It brought them together. If it hadn't happened, she might have spent the rest of her vacation holed up in her cottage, mad at Zane. And the rest of her life feeling as though something big was missing.

"How is your husband doing?" Kianna asked Angelique.

"Hubert is a new man. The doctor gave him a clean bill of health, so it looks like we're in the clear, which is a huge relief."

A knock came at the door and Brittney poked her head inside. "I think they're ready for you. It's only forty-five minutes until sunset."

"Angelique, we'd better get the flowers," Allison's mom said. "We'll meet you on the boat, sweetheart." She cupped Allison's face. "I love you. Always."

Moments like that reminded Allison how precious her family's love was. It wasn't a burden as she'd sometimes felt. "I love you, too, Mom."

Angelique and her mom left, while Kianna made one final adjustment to the tropical flowers in Allison's hair.

"Thank you for being here for this," Allison said. "I know it's a pain to fly across the country to spend time in Falling Brook, then all the way down here."

She shook her head. "Do not thank me. I'm over the moon to be here. I couldn't feel more honored. Plus, I'd better get used to flying great distances to see you."

"You're sure you're okay with us running a bicoastal operation?"

"I don't want to do it forever, if that's what you're asking, but I'm cool with it for the next several years.

You got a one-month extension on the Black Crescent retainer, and we'll see how that plays out. Sounds like your future hubby wants us to do some recruiting for his company, and I figure it's just another selling point for potential clients that we can say we have offices in New Jersey and LA."

"Yes. I think so, too. We can cover the entire country. No problem."

"I will say, however, that if you decide to find a wealthy CEO in Falling Brook to set me up with, I could be very happy becoming an East Coast company, too."

"Really? You liked Falling Brook?"

Kianna shrugged. "I did. I can also admit to being a bit jealous. You have it all, girl. A beautiful place to live and the best man ever. Zane is a dream come true. If I can find a guy half that good, I'll be happy."

"You'll find him." She thought about it for a minute. "Although if it might get you to move to New Jersey, I might have to start looking for him myself. In earnest."

"Executive recruiter and matchmaker. I like it." Kianna unleashed her megawatt smile, her cheeks plumping up. "That could end up being your ultimate calling."

"I'm on it. As soon as I get married."

They walked down the crushed-shell path toward the dock, where the rest of the guests would be waiting on the boat. Zane and Scott had gone out to Mako Island an hour earlier so they could spend some time talking and Allison could still make her traditional bride's entrance. Scott and Zane's friendship had not only withstood the test of the romance between Allison and Zane, it had come out on the other side much stronger. Both Zane and Scott had admitted as much to Allison—not voluntarily; she'd had to drag it out of each of them separately. She was glad they had each other. She was relieved that hadn't gone away.

When Allison and Kianna approached the boat, the gathered family all stood and clapped. Allison felt a rush of pleasant warmth to her face. She didn't relish being the center of attention, but on this day, she lapped it up. They were soon on their way, the warm sea breezes brushing against her skin while the sky turned the most brilliant shades of pink and orange as the sun began to make its descent. Her heart picked up in anticipation when she caught sight of tiny Mako Island and could see those two tall figures standing on the beach—Scott and Zane. Her two favorite guys.

Marcus carefully motored the boat into the shallowest navigable water, then set anchor, instructed Allison's dad to roll up his pant legs and helped to guide everyone through the knee-high depths to shore. They all gathered under the shade of the largest palm with Scott standing at the center. He'd been ordained via the internet for the occasion, and was quite proud of his job as officiant, although Zane and Allison had designed the ceremony to be ultrashort and sweet. Zane was to his left, and even from this far away, with Allison still standing on the boat in the bobbing water, she could see how happy and relaxed he was. She hoped he could spend as many days of his life as possible looking and feeling that way. He deserved it. They both did.

Finally, it was Allison's turn to be helped off the boat. Her dad was standing only a few feet away, ready to walk her down the aisle, or, more specifically, across the sandy bottom. She kissed his cheek, then hooked her arm in his and snugged him closer.

"I love you, Alli," he said as they began their father-daughter ocean stroll.

"I love you, too, Dad. So much."

Ahead, all Allison could see was Zane, the man of her dreams. His heartbreaking smile seemed like a permanent fixture on his handsome face, which was exactly the way she liked him. Off in the distance, the sun was slowly sinking toward the horizon, coloring the sky with more deep and mesmerizing shades of summery pink, warm beachy orange and beautiful blue. At Allison's feet, tiny tropical fish darted through the water, and all felt right with the world. Everyone she loved was here. And she was ready to start her new life.

When she reached Zane, she gave her dad one more kiss before letting him join her mom. Then it was time to take the hand of the man who was her whole future.

"Hey there, beautiful," he whispered into her ear.

"You're not half-bad yourself." Dressed in a white shirt and pants, with the legs rolled up to midcalf, he was an absolute vision. She'd purposely asked him not to shave—she loved his late-day scruff. It was so sexy.

"Family and friends," Scott began. "We're gathered here today to witness the joining of Scott and Allison in matrimony. They will now share their vows."

Zane went first as they joined both hands and faced each other. She peered up at him, allowing herself to get lost in his eyes as he spoke. "Allison, you are my everything. You are my reason for getting up in the morning and the thing I am most thankful for when I lay my head down at night. I promise to always hold you in my heart, to support you in all your endeavors, and most of all, I promise to always love you."

"Allison, do you take this man to be your husband?" Scott asked.

"I do." She sucked in a deep breath and embarked on her own pledge. She'd practiced it one hundred times or more, but she'd wanted to get it just right. "Zane, you were once only a dream to me. And now you are my reality. When we're together, I feel nothing less than loved and cherished. When we're apart, I'm sad, but you're still there with me, in my head and in my heart. I promise to always keep you there, to support you in all your endeavors, and most of all, I promise to always love you."

"Zane, do you take this woman to be your wife?" Scott asked.

"Do I ever." Zane didn't wait for Scott to make the final proclamation. He gathered Allison in his arms, picked her up to her tiptoes and laid an incredibly hot kiss on her. It might not have been totally appropriate for a family gathering, but she was glad it was a taste of things to come. Their guests all clapped, hooted and hollered.

"Well, then," Scott said. "That makes you husband and wife."

After a few minutes of hugs and congratulations, everyone gathered to board the boat, with Zane and Allison last in line. They were actually hanging back a bit, taking their chance to wade through these warm waters, hand in hand, husband and wife. Zane pointed to the honeymoon cottage up on the hill. "I can't wait to spend the next few days with you up there."

"No storm this time."

"Not unless I manage to brew one up on my own."

Allison laughed and swatted Zane on the arm. "It's going to be perfect."

"It's where we fell in love," he said, pressing another soft kiss to her lips.

Allison knew then that all those years she'd lusted after Zane, it hadn't been love. Now it was nothing less. In fact, it was everything she'd ever wanted. "It absolutely is."

* * * * *

COMING SOON!

We really hope you enjoyed reading this book.
If you're looking for more romance, be sure to
head to the shops when new books are
available on

Thursday 11th June

To see which titles are coming soon, please visit
millsandboon.co.uk/nextmonth

MILLS & BOON

LET'S TALK
Romance

For exclusive extracts, competitions
and special offers, find us online:

 facebook.com/millsandboon

🐦 @MillsandBoon

📷 @MillsandBoonUK

Get in touch on 01413 063232

For all the latest titles coming soon, visit
millsandboon.co.uk/nextmonth

MILLS & BOON

THE HEART OF ROMANCE

A ROMANCE FOR EVERY KIND OF READER

MODERN

Prepare to be swept off your feet by sophisticated, sexy and seductive heroes, in some of the world's most glamourous and romantic locations, where power and passion collide.
8 stories per month.

HISTORICAL

Escape with historical heroes from time gone by. Whether you passion is for wicked Regency Rakes, muscled Vikings or rugge Highlanders, awaken the romance of the past.
6 stories per month.

MEDICAL

Set your pulse racing with dedicated, delectable doctors in the high-pressure world of medicine, where emotions run high ar passion, comfort and love are the best medicine.
6 stories per month.

True Love

Celebrate true love with tender stories of heartfelt romance, f the rush of falling in love to the joy a new baby can bring, and focus on the emotional heart of a relationship.
8 stories per month.

Desire

Indulge in secrets and scandal, intense drama and plenty of si hot action with powerful and passionate heroes who have it al wealth, status, good looks…everything but the right woman.
6 stories per month.

HEROES

Experience all the excitement of a gripping thriller, with an in romance at its heart. Resourceful, true-to-life women and stro fearless men face danger and desire - a killer combination!
8 stories per month.

DARE

Sensual love stories featuring smart, sassy heroines you'd want best friend, and compelling intense heroes who are worthy of
4 stories per month.

To see which titles are coming soon, please visit

millsandboon.co.uk/nextmonth

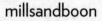
t might just be true love...